The Ringnonian Saga

PALMETTO
P U B L I S H I N G
Charleston, SC
www.PalmettoPublishing.com

Hardcover ISBN: 979-8-8229-3255-5
Paperback ISBN: 979-8-8229-3256-2
eBook ISBN: 979-8-8229-3257-9

The Ringnonian
Saga

C.E. LOOP

Dedication

The Ringnonian Saga is dedicated to the two sons I love so dearly. Jason has gone from us much too early. And David, who continues to be my strength and comfort in my old age.

Profound thanks to Oreita Daley, Professor of Master's Degree, York College English Department, and Brendan D. Jones, Editor in Chief, for their invaluable guidance in helping me to flesh out each character in the narrative fully. Also, thanks to Jesse Hernandez and Lauren Osborn for their great editing.

Ringnon Pronunciation	
Ankwot-(Ank-What)	Kotkye-(Kot-Keye)
Ascon-(As-Con)	Quanyo-(Kwan-Yo)
Claban-(Clay-Ban)	Quikat-(Qwi-Cat)
Colette-(Coal-Let)	Quill-(Kwill)
Cooloo-(Coo-Lou)	Revel-(Rev-L)
Dunwol-(Done-Wall)	Slawoo-(Slaw-Woo)
Flotoon-(Flow-Toon)	Torlack-(Tor-Lack)
Gribec-(Grib-Beck)	Twonay-(Twah-Nay)
Guanton-(Gwan-Ton)	Wajee-(Wat-Gee)
Gutlap-(Gut-Lap)	Wotkye-(What-Keye)
Kitaw-(Kit-Ah)	

Prologue

Charles woke to the sounds of the birds chirping in the still-dark morning. Pain is what jostled him to begin his daily routine. Pain everywhere, but especially in his lower back.

Cancer.

He looked at his Katherine, sleeping peacefully.

I'm going to miss you so much.

He went downstairs to the kitchen so that he would not disturb her.

He looked out at the garden as he put water into a teapot. He thought about the visit of his grandchildren, and he began to smile. What a joy it was whenever they came over. But they were all teenagers now, and their problems worried Charles.

The two girls were getting attention from boys at school.

Men are such dogs! They only want one thing from them. How can I help them to see the need to wait?

He thought about turning on the news but changed his mind.

The news is so depressing! War, deforestation, the environment, and sickness. Who can forget sickness?

His attention went back to his grandchildren. Two of the boys, Brian and Jonathan, were facing bullying at school.

The oldest, Aaron, was being teased because he looked so much like his mother. Her Asian background could be seen in him.

Kids are ruthless.

The teapot began to whistle, and he cut off the stove as he poured water into his mug labeled Grandpa.

He thought about his prognosis.

A year! That's not very long.

He turned and heard Katherine's familiar footsteps as she descended the stairs.

"Did I wake you?"

"No," Katherine said, "I was tossing and turning anyway. Why are you up so early? Are you hurting?"

"No more than usual. I was just thinking about the grandbabies," Charles said as he turned back to look out the window.

"They're not babies anymore. They are all teenagers," Katherine said.

"I just wish they didn't have to grow up in this rotten world without me in it."

Katherine came behind him and hugged him tightly. "You have been the greatest husband, father, and grandfather anyone could have asked for."

He held her hand as his eyes moistened. "I'm going to talk to them all today after they settle in."

"One of your wonderful stories, I assume," she said, smiling.

"Remember the one I told the boys when they were teenagers and facing some tough things in school?

"You mean about the Ring-Men?"

"Yes, the Ringnonian Saga! I think they are old enough to get the story's finer points. What do you think?"

"Sweetie, your stories always have finer points. Tell it to them."

The Ringnonian

Saga

Book One

Ring-Men

Chapter 1

(2073)

President Wilton Wiley leaned back in his chair as he looked at an editorial cartoon in *The Washington Post*. The caricature depicted him pinning an award on a large Ring-Man. It exaggerated his bushy eyebrows and small stature, showing the creature kneeling to allow the fastening of the medal.

Wiley put the paper down and stared at the portrait of his father on the wall. Reaching for his keypad, he hit an icon that revealed an album of photos. Moving quickly through the first set, he stopped at a picture of him and his father laughing as they fished on Lake Michigan. He smiled as he recalled the trip, puffed on his cigar, and ran his hand across his balding head.

"I've lost a lot of hair since then."

He traced his finger across the image as if he could feel his father's face.

"I won't let them forget what you did or why you did it, Pop."

Ben Tinsler, the Chief of Staff, entered the Oval Office. A short, wormy-looking man, Tinsler, wore thick black framed glasses and spoke with a high squeaky voice.

"Mr. President, I thought the speech should be less apologetic and concentrate on our gratitude for the help the Ringnonians have given us over the past half-century."

Wiley felt like a hypocrite, especially in light of his feelings about the Ring-Men. *What purpose would be served by giving awards to them now?*

"Listen, Ben, I'm giving the awards to those freaks, but as far as I'm concerned, they should have been wiped out with their fathers."

"I know how you feel, Mr. President," said Tinsler, "but this speech needs to be given."

"I'll make the speech, but pinning medals is out of the question. Did you see Orwell's editorial in the *Post*? Did you see how I'm pictured? He's been a thorn in my side for forty years."

Tinsler stood silent. He knew the president's moods and how vindictive he could be.

"Mr. President, this presentation needs to go forward," Tinsler said.

"All right," the president grumbled, biting on his cigar. "Show me the draft."

As Wiley read the speech, his mind drifted back to his memories of the Ringnonians.

The Ringnonians arrived forty years ago when their oblong-shaped ship crash landed in the marshes of New Jersey. The president was fourteen years old. The ship was quickly surrounded by hundreds of emergency vehicles, including police units from all the nearby counties.

All eyes watched in shock and amazement as the crew exited. Soon after the evacuation, the ship exploded with a release of energy so great that the shock waves could be felt as far as Washington, D.C.

Wiley recalled watching on television in his Minnesota home as their leader, Ascon, addressed the United Nations.

He remembered saying to his brother, Keith, "They look so human."

All their features—nose, eyes, and hair—were human-like. The obvious difference was their size. They were enormous, averaging over nine feet tall. They were magnificent specimens, with bronze skin and long black hair flowing past their shoulders.

At the time, Keith, eight years old, said to Wiley, "I thought aliens were supposed to be mean and ugly with two heads."

Wiley didn't answer him but watched in disbelief. What amazed him was that the creatures looked so friendly.

He remembered the first words from the giant. "We are from Ringnon, a planet in another solar system that has been destroyed. Earth was identified by our computer as a suitable planet for habitation and a former colony. A malfunction caused our ship to crash, and here we are."

Ascon then offered to lend Earth the services of the Ringnonians. He said, "With our help and advanced technology, your Earth could be a paradise."

Gwen Wiley, Wilton's mother was a petite blonde with a perky nose and a pleasant personality. "He's so handsome," she mused.

Many observers were suspicious, including his father, Senator Ben Wiley. The senator was a short, stout man with large ears and a less-than-attractive face. He made up for his small frame with a powerful voice and a bullying, mean-spirited personality.

"Shut up and get back in the kitchen," he snapped.

Young Wilton also heard his father warn, "Boys, don't trust those smiles."

Senator Wiley continued for years to gush derogatory statements about the strangers. Young Wilton, who adored his father, hung on his every word. His father's jealousy and hatred of the strangers poisoned his mind.

Twenty years after their arrival, Senator Wiley's hatred—combined with that of many other like-minded citizens—led to action.

The powerful senator from Minnesota became the most vocal opponent of the visitors. Among the inner circles of Washington, he sponsored and supported efforts to destroy the Ringnonians. Wiley cited the prolific breeding ability and tremendous power of the Ringnonians as the main reasons for his concerns.

But there were other reasons Senator Wiley hated the Ringnonians. He lost a fortune because of the inventions produced by the visitors. For instance, the value of his shares in two oil companies plummeted because of the anti-gravity cars that everyone could afford.

Almost overnight, he went from being a millionaire to living on "just" his generous senatorial salary.

Senator Wiley's powerful ally was an influential televangelist, Dr. Walter Kean. A tall, gawky, hooked-nosed man with a booming voice, Kean often sermonized about the giants. When the Ringnonians and human women produced children, Kean called it an abomination. He began to ignite his sermons with firey hate and preached extermination. Many agreed with his violent approach, and he developed quite a following.

The offspring from the union of a Ringnonian male and a human woman produced a hybrid with unusual characteristics. Always male and extremely large, they were known as Ring-Men. At two years of age, a Ring-Man was the size of a full-grown human. They grew to adulthood in seven years, at which time they became sexually active. The crossbreed could not reproduce, though. In this way, they differed from their fathers, who were quite prolific.

But they were very similar to their fathers in many ways. They were intelligent and quick, with the power of ten men. They also inherited their fathers' excellent eyesight and sensitive hearing. Skin color was the only characteristic received from their mothers. Everything else about them, their features, stature, and long flowing hair, was utterly Ringnonian.

The communication skills of both the Ringnonians and the Ring-Men were excellent. They were able to speak and understand any tongue or dialect they heard. It was also rumored that they could communicate nonverbally, though this was never confirmed.

Though mortal, they were tough to kill. Dozens of bullets were required to bring one down, as established when a Ring-Man fell in with a criminal element in Texas. Tearing through the state on a robbing and killing spree, he left the bodies of one hundred and twenty people in his wake. Included among the victims were ten police officers and four Texas Rangers. Finally cornered in a Texas bar, he was felled by twenty-eight bullets.

Senator Wiley used that incident to prove to onlookers that the Ringnonians and Ring-Men were dangerous. Editorials and news reports began to sway public opinion against the giants.

For the most part, both the Ringnonians and Ring-Men were law-abiding citizens. At times, they were bad-tempered and fought, mostly over women.

It was relatively easy for the Ringnonians to find human mates. After all, they were handsome, powerful, and extraordinary lovers, or so it was rumored.

Women flocked to them, lining up to be their next conquest. The drawback was that the women almost always became pregnant. The five-month pregnancies were very difficult. In one month, the mother looked full-term with a human baby.

Averaging twenty-five pounds, the newborns were always delivered by C-section. The mother could never have any other children, and many died during or soon after childbirth. The survival rate was about thirty percent, but many women willingly took that risk.

The Ringnonians were loving and caring fathers. However, Ringnonian family structure differed from human family life. Like the breeding habits of the walrus or seal populations of the Arctic, Ringnonians took many females and isolated, protected, and sheltered the children they produced. Taking exception to the presence of other Ringnonians, unrelated Ring- Men or human males, they jealously guarded their space.

The Ring-Men were even more attractive to women since they could not impregnate. They also collected numerous mates and were quite protective.

Dr. Kean preached in one of his fiery sermons, "The degenerate actions of these sinners are infiltrating our entire society. This affront to the human race must be dispatched with all haste. As God destroyed the Canaanites, so, too, these wicked creatures must be destroyed. As David slew Goliath, these giants must be slain."

The criminal acts of a few, combined with the deaths of so many women, added fuel to the movement instigated by Senator Wiley and Reverend Kean. Hatred and resentment toward the strangers grew to a fever pitch.

The Ringnonians and Ring-Men, sensing the abhorrence humans felt for them, moved further away from populated areas.

Over ninety Ringnonians took up residence in various parts of the United States. Most chose colder, higher elevations as locations to live in, some of America's most isolated areas. Taking jobs that allowed them to use their enormous power, such as logging, building roads, and even mining, they tried to lead quiet lives where they felt safer.

Four Ringnonians moved to China at the invitation of the Chinese government.

The Ringnonians lived up to their promise to help humankind through endeavors like the technology for anti-gravity cars, instant food growth, and cures for diseases such as cancer and AIDS.

One particular Ringnonian inventor and scientist, Guanton, showed the world powers how to repair the ozone layer. He also designed a more efficient system to desalinate water.

His greatest invention was a sophisticated satellite defense system to detect and destroy nuclear missiles and bombs. It was an effective deterrent to nuclear war. The result was the dismantling of nuclear arsenals and missiles.

Twenty-one developed countries owned a Satellite Defense System, or SDS. Each of those countries controlled twenty satellites for their defense. The locations of the satellite control stations were well-guarded secrets maintained by those nations.

Despite a fine record of helping humankind and leading quiet lives, many humans still felt that the Ringnonians needed to go. They were too different and simply bred too fast.

Of the one hundred Ringnonians (none were female), almost all mated with human women. In just twenty years, they produced over ten thousand offspring. "If allowed to continue to reproduce, they will outbreed humankind," Dr. Kean cautioned in another of his many tirades.

A decision was made to eliminate them and their offspring.

The Ringnonians exhibited one weakness: they required a rest period of about a month every calendar year, a hibernation of sorts. This need for sleep began in early January.

On January 12th of 2053, the U.S. military began the uneasy destruction of the Ringnonians and their offspring, the Ring-Men. Thousands of soldiers died trying to eradicate their huge opponents. Most of the human mates were also killed by the executioners.

The government, pointing to the many dead soldiers, tried to justify its actions, but there was no getting past the many photos and news reports depicting the dead strangers.

The Washington Post and a young reporter named Tyler Orwell were particularly critical of the government's actions. Orwell compared the killings to the destruction of the Native Americans and other genocides of the twentieth century. Many Americans agreed with him.

Especially disturbing was one image of a young Ring-Man holding his mother in his arms as she died. The photo, first seen in the Post, got national and worldwide attention.

The eradication program became a publicity nightmare.

A liberal group, the SPRD (the Society for the Prevention of Ringnonian Destruction), and mass protests and demonstrations forced a compromise in the government's position.

There were forty-five pregnant human mothers at the time. They were allowed to have their children, and if the mothers lived, raise them until adulthood. Weekly visits were permitted, but the Ring-Men were isolated from each other. Separated and housed in high-security developments, they could live out their lives. Some schooling was provided, but they were forever under the watchful eye of the government.

President Wiley was a lawyer at that time working in his father's senatorial office. He recalled the protests and complaints the office received after the eradication program began.

The senator held to his beliefs that the destruction of the Ringnonians was not only moral but was the only way to save humankind. He lost his reelection the next year and soon began to drink heavily.

The president remembered his father defensively slurring, "Don't ever feel sorry for them, Willie."

He died of a heart attack two years later.

The president always blamed the visitors for what he considered was the premature death of his father.

Twenty years later, the whole episode was buried or forgotten in the consciences of most Americans.

"I still think my dad was right," Wiley said to Tinsler.

"Be that as it may, Mr. President," said Tinsler, "we need the support of the SPRD, and we are going to need the Ring-Men if this war continues."

"Okay," conceded Wiley, "let's get this thing over with."

Chapter 2

China

"China has become a threat to world peace," Tyler Orwell stated in his television editorial. "Why have they attacked Russia?

"There is no reason for war. Food is plentiful all over the globe due to the instant food growth program initiated by the Ringnonians.

"The ozone layer has been repaired," Orwell said as he pointed skyward.

"Using anti-gravity cars and eliminating most combustible engines has slowed global warming and reversed it.

"Global desalinization has made clean water available, and solar energy runs ninety percent of electricity in cities worldwide. It is a good time for planet Earth.

"So, what's the problem?

"The problem from a Chinese perspective is overpopulation. Every city in China has too many people. China has reduced births again, but it hasn't worked.

"Overpopulation is a problem in India as well. But to the north of China is Russia, which has plenty of space, a weakened army, and no Ring-Men.

"That's right, I said Ring-Men. The same creatures that were cruelly murdered twenty years ago in this country are being used by the Chinese army.

"Remember the four Ringnonians that went to China? Well, according to my sources, they have produced thousands of offspring. Add them to the Chinese army, the largest in the world, and you see the problem.

"And so they have attacked Russia. The United Nations is helpless since China withdrew from that body twenty years ago in protest of the genocide of the Ringnonians and their offspring.

"And what does this administration do? It summons the forty-five Ring-Men still alive and offers them medals. But what can you expect from the son of the man responsible for their demise?

"That's just one man's opinion. I am Tyler Orwell, keeping you informed and aware of what's happening."

~~~~~~~~~~

Jonathan King picked up the phone on the third ring. "Jon, did you see Orwell's commentary?"

"Yes, I just finished looking at it."

"You know him, right?"

"Believe it or not, my mom dated him when she was in college."

"Meet with him and try to find out what he knows."

~~~~~~~~~~

Jonathan King had never seen anyone eat so much in one sitting. Tyler Orwell polished off two appetizers, soup, a huge salad, and a large end cut of prime rib. He washed it all down with four scotches and a bottle of wine. He also managed to consume two baskets of bread and two pieces of cake.

Orwell was seventy-two, six foot two, and weighed three hundred and fifty pounds. But his physical weight paled in comparison to the weight he carried in Washington, D.C. He was the most powerful columnist and newsman on the East Coast, probably in the United States.

On the other hand, King was short at five-six. His black toupee was immediately apparent. With a pinched nose and large ears, he looked unimposing despite the deep voice that was unmatched by his small frame.

As the Undersecretary of Defense, it was his job to manage the unpleasant meetings the Secretary of Defense wished to avoid. Meeting with Orwell was just such an occasion.

Orwell belched. "So, Jon, how is your mother?"

This pig could have been my father, thought King. "She is very well, thank you."

"By the way, look at this picture of my grandson. He's six months old today." Orwell showed King the photo on his cell phone.

If you keep eating like this, you will never see him grow up. "Looks just like you."

"So, Bill decided to send you instead of meeting with me himself," Orwell noted.

"He is tied up preparing for a meeting with the Senate appropriations committee."

"He is probably tied up with that new young secretary of his," Orwell said sarcastically.

King pretended to ignore the comment. *How is Orwell so well-informed?*

"Well, let's get down to business, Mr. King. I understand there are plans to release the Ring-Men and form them into a military unit," Orwell said as he picked his teeth.

They were seated in a private alcove, but Orwell's voice was loud enough to make King uncomfortable, and he worried they might be overheard.

He leaned forward. "I saw your column this morning, Mr. Orwell, and it mentions the president awarding the Ring-Men in appreciation, that's all," King said in a low voice.

"Cut the baloney, King! I know all about it," Orwell said with a smile.

King may have looked harmless, but beneath his silly toupee sat one of the shrewdest minds in Washington.

"Mr. Orwell, why not tell me what you know, and I will tell you what I can."

"Fair enough," Orwell said as he moved his large frame closer to King.

"Since the satellite defense system became operational, any nation or corporation seeking to deploy a satellite in space has to receive permission. That is quite a lengthy and costly undertaking," Orwell commented as he sipped from another scotch.

"Diplomacy and bribes are usually required to get all twenty-one participating nations to agree to a launch. As a result, the deployment of surveillance and communication satellites has slowed to a crawl."

King could not mask his surprise. *How does Orwell know these details?*

"Two months ago, India attempted to launch a satellite after receiving permission from all the nations. Of course, we know it blew up, supposedly a defect in the fuel system."

Orwell motioned to a passing waiter for another drink.

"We both know that it was a flash of destructive light from a Chinese satellite that was responsible for the destruction of that billion-dollar equipment."

Orwell received his refill and stirred the ice with his finger. "Am I right so far?"

"Please continue," King said as he leaned back in the booth. "India has protested to the United Nations, but since China withdrew from that body, the protest is meaningless.

"China has begun a no-fly-over policy. Commercial jets flying into their airspace are now at risk of being shot down by Chinese satellite controllers. For a while, no one could figure out why they had become so secretive and hostile.

"But then, in April, the Chinese attacked Russia. The offensive was launched from five points on the Russian and Chinese border." Orwell finished off the drink and wiped his mouth. "Russia has watched her armies suffer defeat after defeat. Finally, they have appealed to the U.N. for help.

"North Korea was the first to take action. They see China as a threat to their security. They allied with Russia and attacked China from the east.

"A force of seven thousand Ring-Men and four hundred thousand Chinese, with thousands of tanks, counterattacked with a fury. In two weeks of fighting, the North Koreans were retreating over their borders with over two hundred thousand casualties."

King now realized Orwell's source of information. He was a correspondent in China and North Korea many years ago. It was rumored that he fathered several children while on assignment in those countries. He remained close to many high-level people in both the Chinese and North Korean governments.

"You are quite well-informed, Mr. Orwell," King said as he motioned for the check.

"What I want to know, Mr. King, is when the U.S. plans to take action."

"At present, I don't know of any plans to intervene," King said as he examined the check.

King stood up and prepared to leave.

"Will Guanton be released also?" Orwell asked matter-of-factly.

King looked shocked, but he quickly recovered. "Guanton, he's dead, isn't he?"

"Oh, that's right," Orwell said as he looked at his empty iced-filled glass. "Did I ever tell you that I interviewed him once?"

King left the restaurant impressed by Orwell's knowledge. No more than twenty people knew what Orwell was hinting at.

Orwell called for another scotch as he pulled out his cell phone. "Dexter Orwell, please," he said and waited.

"Dex, I want you to get into North Korea and hook up with the North Korean army. I think this is going to be a great story. I'll send you the details right away." Orwell hung up, swallowed the last of his scotch, and left the restaurant quite satisfied.

~~~~~~~~~~~

General Daniel Watson sat in his office, looking out the window and drinking his coffee. The first Black Chairman of the Joint Chiefs of Staff since Colin Powell, he was apprehensive. The balding General ran his hand over his head and thought about his new grandson as he looked at his picture. *I thought I would leave a nice, peaceful world for you, Buddy. Now I don't know.*

At fifty-five, six foot one, and a little overweight, General Watson was considering retirement. So far, his friend, Secretary of Defense Bill Welch, convinced him to stay on.

"Colonel Weaver is waiting for you, sir," the intercom announced.

Brendan Weaver was a West Point graduate and the foremost statistician and weapons expert in the military. General Watson was so impressed by the twenty-eight-year-old that he promoted him from Captain to Colonel in two years and appointed him as his adjutant.

At six foot three, blond and blue-eyed, Weaver looked like the poster boy for a military ad.

"Good morning, General," Weaver said as he opened his portfolio.

"Have a seat, Colonel."

"Sir, I have the statistics you requested and the latest update on the Chinese movement.

Weaver handed satellite pictures to Watson.

"These are the four Ringnonians in China. They have become quite influential there. They are treated almost like gods.

"When the U.N issued the order to destroy the Ringnonians, the four in China went underground and were nowhere to be found. Everyone knew the Chinese government was hiding them, but no country, including the United States, wanted China as an adversary. China's population exceeded two billion, and its army was the largest in the world. It is now more powerful than it was twenty years ago."

Weaver handed Watson a breakdown of Chinese military units. "Besides numerical superiority, the Chinese have a technological

advantage over the Russians. The Russians, as you know, have

neglected their military for years. They have not remodeled or upgraded their tanks, and many lack the needed parts to run."

Weaver handed Watson another group of pictures.

"On the other hand, the Chinese have been gearing up for war. They have upgraded the T-96 and T-99 models, giving them greater armor and firing capabilities. Chinese engineers have also developed the monstrous T-101, the largest tank ever commissioned."

Watson fingered the picture. "That's a big boy."

"Yes, it is, sir. Holding a six-man crew and firing both missiles and armor-piercing rounds, it is one of the most sophisticated tanks in the world. Many are equipped with pulse cannon capability. The only tanks that can match them on the battlefield are the new British Thatchers and our new pulse cannon Powells."

Watson was handed another photo.

"The Chinese helicopter force is smaller than the Russian's. But the Chinese have developed a version of the heli-jet."

"Is it as sophisticated as ours?" Watson asked.

"Not quite, sir. Both are fast-moving aircraft with rotor and jet propulsion. Each also can hover, take off, and land like a helicopter. Both can switch to jet power and fly as fast as anything in the air. But we don't think the Chinese have mastered the camouflage aspect of our heli-jets."

"Here are the first reports on the Chinese Ring-Men," Weaver said as he handed the last pages to Watson.

"Good job, Colonel," Watson said. "I want you at my briefing with Secretary Welch this morning."

"Yes, sir, my summary is on the last page," Weaver said as he saluted and left.

Watson put the pictures down and looked out of the window. The sun broke through the clouds, revealing a beautiful rainbow. He turned back toward the report on his desk.

Watson read Weaver's summary:

War looks imminent, and it's going to be bloody. Without nuclear devices, the armies with the most men and best tanks will have the advantage. The effectiveness of our air power is reduced because of the satellites that everyone has. Any enemy can blast one of our billion-dollar jets from the sky with the touch of a button. With our air force's limited use, the heli-jets will become crucial to any battle plan.

Propeller planes are also an option on the battlefield. Unfortunately, the props must reduce their speed to fewer than two hundred miles per hour. That is as slow as the aircraft flown in WWII.

Over seventy percent of the landmass of the globe is under the watchful eye of the SDS. The unprotected areas are around the Arctic and Antarctica.

He looked again at the picture of the Chinese heli-jet. The real advantage of the aircraft was its ability to change direction quickly. It was still susceptible to satellite attack when flying above one thousand feet. Still, a good pilot could make targeting a heli-jet extremely difficult, similar to trying to swat a gnat.

"Man will always find a way to use something good for bad," the General thought as he shook his head.

"I sure miss the good old days when everyone knew who the top dog was. Well, at least we still have the best navy.

He looked at the report on the abilities of the Chinese Ring-Men. "Ms. Beagle," said Watson, "please get the Secretary of Defense on the phone." He waited, thinking to himself.

Twenty years ago, he was on a liquidation team that eradicated the Ring-Men. A captain then, he remembered how hard it was to kill just one of those powerful creatures.

His team broke in on what they thought was a sleeping Ring-Man in a South Dakota cabin. With a butcher knife, the half-asleep Ring-Man took out six Rangers before falling under a hail of machine-gun fire. Half dead, he threw his knife so hard that the squad leader was nearly decapitated.

My goodness, imagine an army of them on the attack.

"Your call, sir," Ms. Beagle announced through the intercom.

"Bill, did you see the report on the capability of those soldiers?" he asked, not wanting to use the word Ring-Men. "One of those soldiers, carrying their powerful weapons, can take out a company of Russians single-handed."

Bill Welch and Daniel Watson had been friends since boot camp. They were inseparable when they served together. When Bill received the Medal of Honor for heroism in a battle during the Second Afghan War, Watson was beside him, awarded the bronze star. After he was appointed Secretary of Defense, he maneuvered the promotion of Daniel Watson to Chairman of the Joint Chiefs.

Bill Welch was fifty-seven years old and in great physical shape. Though his blond hair was now mixed with gray, his energy level was that of a much younger man. Taking to politics after a brilliant military career, he never allowed his damaged hand to limit him in any way.

Welch lifted the report with a hand that was missing three fingers. "Yes, it's at the top of our agenda at our meeting this morning."

"We have got to take action right away; we're already behind," said Watson.

"We have some ideas. I'll tell you at the meeting," Welch said.

"Okay, see you at eleven." Watson hung up and thought about his friend.

Daniel trusted Bill and always admired the man's calmness under fire. His mind raced back to battle as he recalled Bill firing his machine gun until it ran out of bullets. Then they fought with small arms and finally hand-to-hand, covering the retreat of their unit. He would have retreated if Bill hadn't been so cool under pressure.

Bill's words echoed in his mind: "Calm down, Danny, I've got this under control."

And he did. When the bodies were counted, a hundred Afghans lay dead, and Bill's left hand was mangled. But he saved the lives of his entire platoon, including Watson's.

"Oh well, I sure hope we have plenty of bullets this time."

Chapter 3

Ascon

Ascon pushed himself ever harder as he neared the completion of the first part of his daily exercise routine. Perspiration glistened on his copper-toned brow as he finished running fifty miles on his specially-designed treadmill.

His muscles rippled as he began the first of one thousand push-ups—next, the weight exercises included bench-pressing nine hundred pounds.

Long ebony hair cascaded past the shoulders of his nine-foot, five-inch frame. He grabbed a towel and began mopping the sweat from his handsome face.

Imagine giving us an award now after trying to wipe us out.

He reread the letter.

"You are cordially invited to a ceremony acknowledging the contributions made by the Ringnonians for the benefit of humanity."

The letter from the Office of the President indicated that all of the Ring-Men were to be assembled to receive awards.

He thought about his mother. *I wish she were here to see this.*

He picked up her picture and kissed it. He remembered the last time he was with her, how weak and tired she was.

His mother, Megan, was allowed to live with him in his secluded apartment jail until he was seven. Weekly visits were then granted, and Megan saw him religiously.

She told him about the Ringnonians and his father, also named Ascon and how she met and fell in love with the large stranger from another world.

"He was so intelligent, so tall, and so handsome," she said. "I was in school at the time, a senior at Columbia University, and he was there lecturing about something. Who can remember…all I know is that when he spoke, it sent shivers down my spine.

"I was a twenty-one-year-old campus reporter, and I interviewed him. All the girls were so jealous of me. It wasn't long before I fell in love with him and agreed to become one of his mates."

Ascon smiled at how excited she became whenever she spoke about his father.

The one thing she would never talk about in detail was how his father died.

She spoke of it once as they walked outside in his caged exercise yard. That day, she also told him of the secret power he possessed, which she discovered quite by accident.

"I noticed when your father played with your brothers that he would do so without saying a word. Yet the children reacted as though they understood him. He could make them laugh or stop crying simply by looking at them.

"I didn't say anything about it then, but later, I mentioned it to Deana, a tall, beautiful black woman and one of Ascon's other mates.

"Deana was always charming. I told her what I saw, and she warned me not to mention the matter to Ascon or anyone else.

"I was two months pregnant with you at the time and very large," she said as she held his face with both hands. Ascon thought about her soft hands and her tender touch massaging his cheeks. Tears began to run down his face.

"Your father would comfort me by holding me close as he rubbed my large stomach. The soothing massage helped me sleep. Curiosity finally got the best of me, and I asked him about the non-verbal communication. He froze suddenly and stared at me. I saw anger in his eyes. It was the only time I was ever afraid of your father."

"You must never talk about this again," he said, grabbing my shoulders.

"I began to cry, and as my tears fell on his chest, Ascon released his grip. He was always so gentle with me and the other women. We lived as a close family unit high in the mountains without hinting jealousy or anger. Ascon could make all of us feel loved, satisfied, and content."

"This matter is something only discussed by Ringnonians," he said.

"I grabbed his large hand and laid it on my stomach. My son will be half Ringnonian, and I want to be able to tell him everything about you."

He looked into my eyes and smiled. "All right, my princess, I'll tell you. But you are to tell no one but him."

"I promise, my love."

"Ringnonians can talk non-verbally as long as the one speaking is in visual contact with the listener. Communication through electronic devices or binoculars is also possible. If you can see the Ringnonian, you can talk to him.

"I have experimented with the children, and they have the same power. Guanton and I have discussed this matter, and we are quite concerned."

"Why?" Megan asked.

"It is a powerful tool and weapon used for our protection. The more Ring-Men produced, the greater the chance our secret will be revealed. This knowledge about the communication power of the Ringnonians must remain hidden. Do you understand?"

"Yes, my love."

"He began to rub my belly again after gently kissing my forehead. Then he paused and got up from the bed. He sensed danger. Lifting me in his arms, he carried me to the basement and gently put me down in a closet. He pulled out a hidden pulse shotgun from a side cabinet."

"What's wrong?"

"Be quiet, my love; someone is outside the house."

"He covered me with a blanket and headed upstairs to rescue the others. Then I heard frightening sounds coming from upstairs. Gun blasts and screams from the other women and the children terrified me. I wanted to go upstairs, but I was so big that I could not get up.

"I lay in that dark basement as the racket gradually turned to silence. I crawled toward the stairs, and then the house exploded. The next thing I remember, I woke up in a hospital."

Ascon wiped the tears from his eyes as he kissed Megan's picture again. "I miss you so very much."

Megan died when he was ten. Now twenty, he was all alone. He put the picture down and lifted another frame from the desk—the picture of Samuel Isamov, his instructor, the only regular visitor he had received in ten years. He ran his finger over the picture as if he could feel the beard of the man in the frame.

Isamov was an old Jewish professor of German descent who taught a number of the Ring-Men at the facility where they were housed. Ascon was his favorite student. The professor conducted a three-hour session with his eager pupil twice a month. Isamov taught him everything from history to political science. Standing five feet six inches tall with bushy hair and an always unkempt gray beard, Isamov was a wonderful teacher. His earlier years saw him working as a scientist and inventor at Yale University. Even at 82, his desire and enthusiasm to teach was obvious.

Isamov also worked on the satellite defense system with the Ringnonian Guanton. He once told Ascon about the ingenious invention.

"Would you believe, my boy, the nations fought against installing the system? Imagine not wanting something that could end the threat of nuclear war," Isamov said with his thick German accent.

"Why did they fight against it?"

"Because governments are greedy and asinine," Isamov said.

"Finally, Guanton convinced one nation, Israel, to agree to install the satellites, and then the other nuclear powers soon followed."

"How does it work?"

"Think of an upside-down umbrella," Isamov said as he drew a picture of an inverted umbrella on the blackboard. The SDS, as it is called, is designed to stop nuclear war and took five years to install worldwide.

"The system has three levels of protection against nuclear attack. The first is protection at thirty thousand feet or higher. Any missile or plane flying above that altitude can be targeted worldwide by any nation controlling satellites. Nations are forced to cooperate to avoid accidents.

"The second level of protection is between thirty thousand feet and one thousand feet," Isamov explained as he strolled toward the world map on the wall. The extent of that protection is two hundred miles beyond the border of the controlling nation. In that zone, the satellites hone in on the heat of the engines. They can also attack any craft or projectile moving faster than two hundred miles an hour, which is considered a threat. Again, cooperation between nations is needed."

"What about aircraft flying low to the ground?"

"That's the final level of protection, from one thousand feet to the surface. Protection at that level is based only on speed. Anything larger than two feet, flying faster than two hundred miles per hour, can be targeted and destroyed.

"The range of protection is the same two hundred miles of airspace past the borders. Protection overlaps at times because some countries share common borders. For instance, Russia controls two hundred miles of Chinese airspace, and China controls the same amount of Russian airspace." Isamov pointed to those nations on the map.

"Did the system eliminate war?"

"Unfortunately, not, but it's been a great deterrent to nuclear war, at least from the sky. Some crazy person might bring a handheld nuclear device and set it off. But the nations can't bomb or send missiles to blow the world to pieces," Isamov laughed out loud.

"The system was created by the greatest scientist this world has ever seen." Isamov grew emotional, pulled a handkerchief, and wiped his eyes.

Ascon also missed Isamov. The instruction periods ended three months ago when Ascon became twenty. His last meeting with Isamov was a tearful farewell. He hugged the old man and watched as he left his cell for the last time. Ascon learned from a guard that Isamov died soon after the classes ended. Now Ascon was all alone again. He did have a library, computer, and television, but these were no substitutes for contact with other beings. He talked to himself quite a bit.

Ascon was excited about seeing other Ring-Men in person. He last saw one while watching television four years ago. He wondered if he possessed the communication power of his father. Peering at the Ring-Man on the screen, he tried to communicate with him. Almost immediately, he saw a reaction on the face of the Ring-Man—or was it his imagination?

At 8 A.M., he was shackled in specially designed restraints and escorted from his cell by six marines. Four were armed with machine guns, and two carried sound guns. Sound guns produced a loud, explosive-like noise that could incapacitate a Ring-Man. It was discovered that the Ring-Men's sensitive hearing could be exploited. Thunderous sound waves, such as those created by a sonic boom or explosion, could throw them off balance and render them helpless for about ten seconds. A sound gun system was installed around the compound as a fail-safe in case they tried to escape or became unruly.

Ascon was ushered into a hangar-like structure with huge chairs. Once inside, the clamps were removed, and he was free to roam about in the spacious building. There was one Ring-Man already seated. Who is that, he thought. Before he could ask, a voice boomed, "Revel."

An ecstatic Ascon continued to use his newfound silent communication power: *Hello, Revel, be careful about speaking. I think we are being observed.*

They were being watched. "Did you see that?" asked Warren Anderson. "He communicated without speaking."

"I think you're right," replied John Gaynor, Test Director in charge of the Ringnonian project. "Record everything they do; we will analyze it later."

Do you know why we are here?

Yes, we're here to receive some kind of award for all our fathers did for their people, Ascon answered.

I know. I have seen some of our brothers on television, but it is good to see you in person.

Revel was about seven inches taller than Ascon, a bit broader, and black. He stood about ten feet tall. His short-cut hair made his ears look even larger than they were.

We can't let them know that we have this power. We will warn our brothers as they come in.

~~~~~~~

Ascon was amazed at the diversity of the Ring-Men. There was the huge Samoan Ring-Man, Therion, and the Indian, Kilton. There were all races of Ring-Men among the forty-five now seated and listening to the instructor. All were over nine feet tall, and a few almost as tall as Revel. Ascon and Revel communicated silently with each Ring-Man as they entered the room. Immediately, they looked to Ascon as the leader, just as their fathers looked to Ascon's father.

It saddened Ascon to see that all the Ring-Men wore short haircuts. He remembered his mother explaining as she combed his hair: "Ringnonians take great pride in their hair. They usually wear it long, except when going into battle or on formal occasions. At those times, the hair is braided in a ponytail or worn on top in what is known as a Ringnonian topknot.

"You look so much like your father," Megan said as she helped him prepare his topknot. That would make him feel so proud. Ascon was the only Ring-Man with a top-knot that morning. *That will have to change*, he thought as he inspected the others.

It was evident that Captain John Roberson felt intimidated by the sheer size of his audience. He was six feet four inches himself, but he looked as small as a child as he made his presentation.

His voice cracked, "Gentlemen…please…could I have your attention." Ninety suspicious eyes watched his every move.

"The ceremony will begin in about an hour; please follow these instructions. You must remain seated at all times. We will not be restraining you, but as you see, guards surround the stage, podium, and doors. Please cooperate with us."

As he left the stage, he thought, I *hope we can convince them to fight for us*.

~~~~~~~~~

"The ceremony was short, and the human audience sparse. Many soldiers were present, and though their guns weren't visible, there were plenty of them trained in the direction of the seated Ring-Men.

Wiley made a conciliatory speech, praising the Ringnonians for all their contributions to human society.

He was glad he decided to forgo the pinning of medals on them. He would have difficulty reaching their chests if he stood on a ladder.

The newspapers constantly made him the target of jokes because of his small, five-foot-seven-inch frame. Speaking from a high platform, it still looked like he was eye to eye with his audience.

The stage was fifty feet away, with a not-so-subtle barrier between it and the chairs of the seated Ring-Men, so he was safe. But seeing creatures so big that looked so human still unnerved him. He didn't like anything about this situation, and he did not like the Ring-Men. To him, the giants were freaks of nature.

After his speech, he shook hands with the few human dignitaries on the stage, the last of which was Bill Welch.

The Ring-Men did not move or make a sound since they were seated.

"Tough crowd," Wiley whispered into Bill Welch's ear.

"Well, you gave them the sugar; now it's my turn to sell them on the idea," said Welch.

"I hope you can," said the president. Still waving to the small applauding crowd, the president was whisked away.

~~~~~~~

General Watson could not believe what he heard at the briefing. *How in the world can we control armed Ring-Men? What officer will they listen to?* Bill assured him at the meeting that it was going to work. "I've got an ace in the hole."

Well, Bill has always been a good poker player.

Chapter 4

Guanton

"More coffee, Mr. King?" asked the flight attendant.

"No, thank you." King watched her walk away, and then he looked out of the window. The words of Bill Welch rang in his ear.

"John, I think this thing with the Chinese will get very serious. Do your best to convince Guanton." He could not remember seeing Welch as worried as he was at that briefing.

King pulled a folder from his briefcase. He looked around before opening the dossier marked "Top Secret." The name Guanton was written in red.

The first page described the Ringnonian. Height listed just short of nine feet, two inches, three hundred and fifty pounds, intelligence marked at the highest rating possible.

~~~~~~~~

King was excited about talking with the Ringnonian again. His first meeting with Guanton had gone well. King was instantly impressed with the large alien. Guanton agreed to think about the offer from the government. Since then, the situation had become more critical. So, when word moved around that Guanton wanted to talk, King flew from Washington immediately.

King walked the hallway to the second checkpoint. He scanned his eye on the identification pad, and the door opened. Entering a huge lobby area, he nodded to the guard seated by a double door.

Guanton was housed at the most secretive complex in the United States, in the mountains of North Dakota. King approached Guanton's chamber and the guard stationed at the door. Sergeant Ben Williams stood up and saluted.

"How is he, Sergeant?" King asked as he signed in. Sergeant Williams was a forty-five-year-old, six-foot-three-inch black man with gray in his temples and a pleasant smile. He towered over the much smaller King. "He was a bit moody yesterday, but I think he's looking forward to talking to you again."

Guanton's chamber, a five thousand square-foot apartment, was protected by a high-tech security system and a division of marines. But Guanton accepted his imprisonment well. The solitude didn't seem to bother him. He didn't ask much, but what he did ask for was granted to him. He asked for a computer, giving him access to world news online. He also requested books, having read more than fifteen thousand during his twenty-year imprisonment. Although not lavish, he found his accommodations very comfortable. King pushed the bell, and Williams pushed a button that released the door lock.

"Mr. Guanton," King said as he entered.

"Just call me Guanton," a voice boomed.

Guanton, seated at a computer, stood and approached King.

Something about his eyes struck King immediately. One look at those black, steely orbs let one know that he was a serious person. He was not as broad as the other Ringnonians, though quite muscular. Guanton, when talking, paced constantly.

"Have you thought about our offer?" King asked, hardly able to control his excitement.

"Yes, but with a few conditions," said Guanton. "Please have a seat."

Guanton handed a sheet of paper to King. King put his glasses on as he read. Guanton repeated the words from memory as he paced.

"Number one: after I help, I want access to the technology and the materials that will allow me to build a ship to leave Earth."

Without waiting for a reply, "Number two: I want to talk to all the Ring-Men under my command alone, without any listening devices.

"Number three: I will need access to weaponry design because if Quanyo is leading the Chinese, as I suspect, we will need to design weapons to stop him."

"Quanyo?"

"Yes, he's probably the leader of the Ringnonians, and he is ruthless. Only Ascon could keep him in check. Quanyo wanted to conquer your world instead of helping it. He was voted down by most of us. Three Ringnonians sided with him. Guess where they are now?" Guanton asked as he walked toward his computer.

King already knew.

"I'm afraid I have more bad news," King said. Guanton turned around.

"Besides the Chinese, about seven thousand Ring-Men are under his command."

"What?" Guanton shook his head and sighed. "If that's the case, we have no time to lose. There is one more thing, Mr. King. The longer we can keep my involvement a secret, the better our chance of defeating Quanyo. He is quite shrewd and a lethal adversary."

King agreed to all of Guanton's conditions. They shook hands before King left. Guanton heard the door lock as he turned and looked into a nearby mirror. At two hundred and fifty years in Earth time, signs of aging appeared evident. Gray hair sprouted around his temples.

The planet Ringnon orbited its huge sun once every five years. Ringnon time is measured in sections, one section of Ringnon time equaling five years of Earth time. At fifty sections, Guanton was in the prime of life on Ringnon, but on Earth, he and the other Ringnonians, like humans, were victims of accelerated aging. Guanton blamed the radiation from the Earth's sun as the main reason for the aging process. Working on a solution to the problem was impossible while imprisoned.

If I don't get off this planet soon, I will die of old age.

Guanton sat down in a large chair and reminisced back to happier days.

Treated as celebrities when they first arrived, many offers and opportunities availed themselves. Anything and everything they wanted was given to them. Some were even offered jobs in professional sports.

"What a disaster that was," he laughed aloud. Sergeant Williams spoke through the intercom. "Are you all right in there, Guanton?"

"Yes, Willie," he said. "I was just thinking out loud."

"I'll cut off the listening device," said the sergeant. Williams knew how much it annoyed Guanton to be under constant surveillance.

Guanton thought about the kindly sergeant who saved his life. Williams, the commander of the unit sent to kill him twenty years ago, refused to follow through on his liquidation. Even the hardened marines under Williams' command felt Guanton's "aura" and followed their young captain in refusing to kill him. Court marshaled and jailed for not following orders, Williams' career was over. But then the order to execute Guanton was rescinded, and a decision was made to secretly jail him instead. Even the U.N. didn't know of his existence.

Guanton then made an unusual request. He asked that Williams be allowed to be his primary guard. The government felt that Williams' brilliant mind might be useful. They wanted to keep Guanton happy, so they granted that request. Released from prison, given the rank of sergeant, Williams became Guanton's jailer. Grateful to each other, they also became friends.

Guanton went back to his thoughts. He recalled when a Ringnonian named Fontoo had attempted to play baseball. It was no contest. Fontoo hit for an 850 average with forty home runs in just twenty-three games. The experiment ended when a pitch thrown at ninety-six miles per hour was hit back through the mound at three hundred miles per hour. The ball struck the pitcher, killing him, before ending up in centerfield. A Ringnonian who tried basketball had a similar situation. A nine-foot center was as tall as the basket and did not have to jump to score.

The Ringnonians also tried various occupations, but what they enjoyed most was making love to beautiful Earth women, of which there was a constant supply. Guanton did not take a mate from the Earth women. It's not that he didn't find some attractive, but he did not wish such companionship. Science and the memory of his mate on Ringnon and the problems on Earth kept him occupied in those days. The planet needed help. The ecosystems, polluted water, the ozone layer, food shortage, and disease all needed correction.

He thought about his mate, Winyee. How lovely she was. Compared to human women, she was tall, yet at six foot eight inches, she was shorter than most Ringnonian women. Her long black hair accentuated her beautiful green eyes. She was an extraordinary beauty. Though allowed three mates according to Ringnon law, Guanton chose to have only one. They were blessed with one child whom he truly missed. His son Guilton was now nine sections old.

"I hope they are still alive." He wiped a tear from his eye and got up. "To the task at hand."

~~~~~~~~~

The Ring-Men were not at all enthusiastic about Bill Welch's invitation.

"We will train you and make you into a fighting unit. After you serve this country, we will release you from prison, and you can lead normal lives."

Silence answered the offer. Then, slowly, anger and resentment began to build. Welch could see it in the eyes of the Ring-Men. He remained calm and looked over the audience.

The soldiers guarding the assemblage also felt the tension, and many removed the safeties on their weapons, anticipating trouble.

Ascon spoke up first. "Do you expect us to fight for you after you killed our fathers? Who will lead us—you?"

"No," Welch said, coolly. "We have someone else in mind." The big door to the right of the audience opened, and Guanton stepped in.

Guanton walked to the center of the room as the stunned audience stood. He didn't need to stand on the platform because everyone could see and hear him. As he requested, all the soldiers left the main auditorium and took guard positions outside the doors.

"All listening devices are turned off as you requested, Mr. Guanton," Welch said as he left.

Looking over the faces of the astonished Ring-Men, he spoke. "Hello, my sons. Please be seated."

All of them took their seats except Ascon, who remained standing. "I am Ascon, who are you?"

Guanton laughed aloud; his joy was obvious. "Was your father named Ascon also?"

"Yes," Ascon said.

Guanton's tone softened. "Your father was one of the greatest Ringnonians and my best friend. I am Guanton."

Chapter 5

Quanyo

Quanyo pointed to two waiting soldiers, motioning them to remove the headless torso of the former commander of the 16th division. The officer took responsibility for a minor setback at Sangdong that cost the lives of twenty Ring-Men. The penalty for that mistake? Execution.

Quanyo beheaded the man in front of the entire division, stating to the assembly, "I will not tolerate failure."

Having the body dragged from view emphasized Quanyo's lack of respect and total disdain for humans. He turned and began looking through his telescopic binoculars at the next target for attack. The new obstacle impeding his march south was the fortified city of Kanggye.

A large figure approached him from behind.

"Kitwan, I'm ordering you north into Russia," Quanyo said without turning around. "Our intelligence has located the Russian satellite station. The reports indicate that our troops are overrunning Russian positions everywhere. You should have no problem taking it."

"Yes, Commander."

Kitwan was much younger than Quanyo and the Ringnonian brothers Wotkye and Kotkye. Though not as intelligent as the others, he was as tall and powerful. He was also quite impressionable and followed Quanyo's every command without question.

"I am sending a thousand Ring-Men with you," Quanyo directed as he turned to face Kitwan.

"Yes, sir," Kitwan saluted, "and thank you." Kitwan went away. Quanyo assessed the younger Ringnonian. *Good warrior; too bad he's not smarter.*

Everything was going according to plan, and Quanyo hoped to be at the 38th parallel in a month. But Kanggye must be taken first.

Quanyo, the military commander for all of China, allowed the government to continue functioning. Having no desire to be an administrator, he could concentrate on his true passion, war. Originally, the Chinese general, Wong Sin-Chu, had overall command of the Ringnonians and Ring-Men. His authority ended during an awards ceremony. After the commanding general pinned Quanyo's chest, the big giant unsheathed his sword and cut the general in half. Quanyo's authority was never rechallenged.

His army of over three million men was divided into fifteen major groups of two hundred thousand each. One million each were stationed in Russia and North Korea, and the other million were kept in reserve in China. The seven thousand Chinese Ring-Men were divided into units of one thousand each, with Kitwan leading one group to Russia and Kotkye commanding the rest.

Wotkye led the armored units. One night—over tankards of ale—Quanyo convinced the three Ringnonians to take an offer made by the Chinese representatives.

"You all voted with me to take over this planet. We can free ourselves of Ascon's control and rule for ourselves. These humans don't want us here, but the Chinese do."

"What can the four of us do?" Wotkye asked.

"It won't be just the four of us. From what I've been told, women are lining up to breed with us. That should appeal to you, Kotkye." Quanyo poured ale into Kotkye's mug.

"It will take a few years, but once our brood is an army, we will be unstoppable. In the meantime, we just have fun," Quanyo suggested with a sinister smile.

Kotkye looked at his brother Wotkye, laughed, and asked, "When can we leave?"

"Ascon will want us to clear this with him," said Kitwan. Standing orders commanded the Ringnonians to remain in the United States. When human women began dying after the birth of the Ring-Men, Ascon ordered each Ringnonian to limit himself to three mates. That order corresponded with a law on Ringnon that allowed each male to have a maximum of three female mates. He also ordered his shipmates to lead less conspicuous lives. Ascon counseled them when they all met together.

"We want to be very careful now. These humans have become increasingly suspicious. Despite the things we have given them, they may turn on us at any time. I want all of you to move to isolated areas. Take your families and live quietly, but stay in this country."

"I am working on a way off this planet. But we must gain their confidence to get to the technology we need," Guanton added.

Kitwan reminded the three conspirators, "Ascon said to stay in this country."

"Let's get one thing clear. We are finished taking orders from Ascon or Guanton. When we get to China, remember that I am in charge. Agreed?"

The three Ringnonians toasted, "You are the commander!"

Quanyo relished the role of leader and commander. But, he was no behind-the-lines commander; he led from the front.

He stood nine feet six inches tall with long, flowing black hair that he wore in a ponytail when in battle. The constant scowl etched on his face obscured his good looks. He loved instilling fear in everyone around him, both friend and foe. Dressed in his full body armor and wielding a pulse machine gun or a sulfur flamethrower, he made an imposing figure on the battlefield. Strapped to his back was a Saracen five-foot curved sword. Quanyo loved battle, and nothing gave him greater pleasure than to use that sword.

Quanyo initially only thought a little of the Ring-Men since they were only half Ringnonian. But the Ring-Men proved themselves to be splendid warriors. Quick as Ringnonians and just as brave, once on the move, they were unstoppable.

The speed in which they moved, combined with their sheer power as they rushed forward, would frequently make the opposing force flee in terror. But artillery barrages slowed the charging of the Ring-Men. Loud blasts affected their hearing and equilibrium and temporarily disoriented them. That problem needed to be solved.

In the meantime, he planned to neutralize the enemy artillery with his armored units and heli-jets. Next, the Chinese would attack. Finally, his Ring-Men warriors would be unleashed and wipe out everything in their path. He readied for the attack.

Under Guanton's command, the Ring-Men took to the grueling training regimen with true dedication. Guanton felt the Chinese and enemy Ring-Men would reach the 38th parallel, the buffer zone between North and South Korea, in six weeks. His force needed to be fully trained by then to take on the formidable enemy.

He looked at Ascon, so much like his father, a natural leader. The other Ring-Men respected Ascon, and he was appointed platoon captain. Ascon convinced all of the Ring-Men to grow out their hair, and they were doing that as a sign of unity.

The 101st and 82nd Airborne and the 80th Ranger Regiment trained with the Ring-Men. The new elite unit was renamed the 1st

Ring-Men Division. The 7th Calvary helicopter, Heli-jet Battalions, and the 2nd Armored also deployed to support the group. The entire force numbered about thirteen thousand men and forty-five Ring-Men.

"Ascon," called Guanton. The Ring-Men agreed to speak vocally because of the humans training beside them.

"Yes, Commander?" Ascon replied as he walked toward Guanton. "How are things, my son?" Guanton asked.

"Very well, sir, if possible, I would like to talk to you about my father."

"What about this evening? Tomorrow, I must fly back to the weapon designers to check their progress."

"This evening would be fine, sir," said Ascon, delighted that Guanton took an interest.

That evening, they shared dinner at Guanton's quarters. After a fine meal prepared by a cook, they settled down to talk. Ascon was nervous about having dinner with the older Ringnonian. He recalled everything his mother and Isamov told him about Guanton. Each nursed his third tankard of ale, the favorite drink of the Ringnonians and the Ring-Men.

"Ale is the best thing about this planet," Guanton said as he filled his mug. "It was the first drink we were given at the welcome celebration the humans gave us when we arrived. We've loved it ever since.

"Your father and I would drink ourselves under the table with this stuff," Guanton recalled, smiling at the thought.

Half slurring, Ascon asked, "Tell me about my father."

Guanton paused. "He was one of the greatest of all Ringnonians, a warrior, a leader, and my dearest friend. I wish he were alive to help us in this situation."

"How did he die?" Ascon asked, saddened again by the thought. "He wasn't asleep; I'll tell you that," Guanton said. He took another deep gulp and continued. "He was in the mountains of Montana when they came to kill him. He possessed the ability to sense when any of us were in danger. A squad of their best-trained rangers came at him. He killed them all. But he was wounded and couldn't move.

"Finally, they brought in helicopters and blew up his cabin, killing him, two of his mates, and your two Ring-Men brothers.

"Your mother was wounded but was spared because she was pregnant with you," he continued, a tear welling up in his eye.

"One day, I'll get even," Ascon vowed, getting angry at the thought.

"Revenge is for fools," Guanton warned. "The best thing we can do is help these humans and get off this rock. I still believe that somewhere out there, some of our kind survived. Our job right now is to stop Quanyo."

"Why? It seems like he has the right idea about these humans, and he's like us," Ascon said.

"He's nothing like us," bellowed Guanton, spilling some of his ale.

"Quanyo is pure evil. I've seen him kill beings just for the fun of it. He's sadistic and cruel and wants to rule or kill everything. He must be stopped.

"I'll tell you what, though," said Guanton, smiling again. "Old Quanyo sure wouldn't want to face your father again. Ascon was the only one who could control him. I remember a mind contest that your father won against Quanyo."

"A mind contest?" Ascon asked. "What's that?"

"It is a test of wills, sort of like what humans do when they arm wrestle. Only with us, the one with the strongest mind usually leads. Want to try it?" Guanton wanted to test Ascon, and this was the perfect opportunity.

"Okay. What do I do?"

"Focus your mind on trying to make me submit or yield." Guanton turned to face Ascon eye to eye.

Each felt the other's mind pushing. They began to increase the pressure, and Ascon felt as though his head might explode. Things in the room began to shake, and light bulbs blew. Ascon tried to hold out but finally toppled off his chair.

"Ha! Good job, young lad. I haven't battled like that in years," Guanton mused as he took a gulp of ale and rubbed his ears.

"Now picture that contest between two of the most powerful Ringnonians, and you get the idea. Your father and Quanyo battled over the fate of this planet when we first got here. Instruments blew out over the entire ship and was probably the reason we crashed." Guanton reached to help Ascon to his feet.

"That wasn't the first time your father bested Quanyo. But that's a story for another day. Right now, I'm drunk, and my head is killing me."

"Thanks for talking to me," Ascon said.

"We'll do it again soon," said Guanton, holding Ascon's shoulder. "You just get our unit trained and ready for combat."

"Captain," Guanton called out. Ben Williams entered. Restored to his former rank, he now acted as Guanton's adjutant.

"Captain, please help Captain Ascon back to his quarters. I'm afraid he is a bit inebriated."

"Yes, sir."

Guanton found out what he wanted to know. Ascon's mind was strong. With a little more training, he might have a chance against Quanyo.

Oh, my head, he thought as he stumbled off to bed.

Chapter 6

Weapons

"The president wants you to keep a careful eye on Guanton," said Ben Tinsler. "He doesn't trust him."

Bill Welch remained silent. He didn't like Tinsler and was not afraid to show his contempt. Daniel Watson noticed the awkward silence and spoke. "Guanton feels that special weapons will be needed to stop the Chinese advance."

"The president realizes that, but he is afraid that Guanton could get his hands on technology that could endanger us."

"Listen, Tinsler, most Chinese regulars have new AK-87 rifles. Do you know what that means?"

Tinsler answered with a blank stare.

"It means that they can fire a clip containing eighty-seven high-velocity bullets. On the other hand, the Chinese Ring-Men are armed with state-of-the-art pulse rifles and larger pulse machine guns.

"Pulse guns fire electrical charges more powerful than any bullet. Those weapons are so devastating that they could sever your head or make a hole in your chest as big as a grapefruit."

"I was just saying—" Tinsler said, trying to interrupt. Watson ignored him and continued.

"The Ring-Men also have body armor that conventional rifle bullets cannot penetrate. High-velocity Gatling or machine guns firing armor-piercing rounds or a direct pulse rifle blast are the only effective ways to penetrate such armor. A Ring-Man charge is practically unstoppable unless those weapons are deployed."

"In summary, Tinsler, we need all the help we can get," Welch said. "Is there anything else I can do for you?"

"No, the president just wanted you to know his concerns," Tinsler said as he stood and prepared to leave.

"Thank the president for me, and tell him that we will keep a watchful eye."

Tinsler nodded to both men and left the office. "That little jerk," Watson said.

"Which one, Tinsler or the president?" Welch asked. "Where is Guanton now, Danny?"

"He is at our weapons testing facility in North Carolina. From what I have heard, he has already made substantial progress. Do you want me to check it out?"

"No, I am going to fly down there and see for myself," Welch said.

~~~~~~~~~~

"Welcome to Fort Green, Secretary Welch," said Major Joshua Lindsey.

"Thank you, Major. Where is Guanton?" Welch asked impatiently.

"He is testing his new command vehicle. He will join us shortly. May I begin your tour of the weapons testing facility?"

Lindsey, a six-foot-three-inch redhead with thick, black-framed glasses, looked like a nerdy college professor. He moved forward, followed by Welch and his entourage, which included Colonel Weaver. He stopped at a large tank-like vehicle.

"Guanton's reputation as an inventor and scientist has already been proven, both on Earth and on his planet. But Guanton is also a genius when designing weapons of war," Lindsey said.

"Guanton knows that the enemy Ring-Men outnumber our giants one hundred and fifty to one. Therefore, he has designed weapons to even the odds."

"I see you are quite impressed with his efforts," Welch said. "I'm sorry, sir, if I seem excited. He has done more in thirty days than we could have accomplished in fifty years."

"Go on with the tour, Major," Welch said.

"Yes, Mr. Secretary." He pointed to the tank. "This is the new anti-gravity tank. As you are aware, we have had the technology for anti-gravity craft for some time now, a gift to humanity from the Ringnonians. Anti-gravity vehicles are easy to construct, cheap, lightweight, and used for transportation by eighty percent of the world's population.

"Using the Earth's magnetic field as a springboard, anti-gravity craft can hover three feet above the Earth's surface. The maximum weight limit is fifteen hundred pounds with a top speed of about seventy miles per hour." Lindsey placed his hand on the tank admiringly.

"Guanton's newly designed tank can hover up to fifteen feet above the surface, carrying seventy-five hundred pounds of equipment and crew. The tank's maximum speed of ninety miles an hour makes it faster than any ground tank.

"The armament consists of two rotating Gatling guns that fire armor-piercing rounds, one on top and the other beneath. The bottom gun can rotate to the vehicle's top if the tank is on the ground. It is also equipped with pulse cannons front and rear, side grenade launchers, and mortars, making each tank a floating fortress.

"Mr. Secretary, would you care to look inside?" Lindsey pulled a lever, and the front hatch opened, exposing the vehicle's inside.

"It seats a crew of three, consisting of a pilot and two gunners. The pilot and gunners are equipped with helmets containing a mental targeting system.

Lindsey handed a helmet to Welch. "This specially designed system allows the wearer to sight and fire at a target by just looking at and concentrating on it. The weapons can be fired manually as well." Welch gave the helmet to Lindsey.

"To complement the tank, Guanton has designed an anti-gravity assault vehicle. It is armed with a pulse cannon and Gatling machine guns and capable of carrying a squad of twelve soldiers and two pilot gunners."

A humming noise alerted the group to the arrival of Guanton's anti-gravity command vehicle. It lowered to the ground, and the front hatch opened. Welch looked up to see Guanton step from the craft and remove his helmet.

"Mr. Secretary," his voice boomed through the entire hangar. Welch showed no fear as he moved forward and shook the giant's hand. "I am glad to see you again."

"I see Major Lindsey has shown you the anti-gravity tank. Allow me to show you some of the other surprises we have." The group moved through a secured door, and four armed guards allowed access.

Guanton lifted a metallic ball that was the size of a grapefruit. "These are nano grenades, Mr. Secretary," Guanton said as he handed one of the objects to Welch.

"Major Lindsey informs me that your people have been working on this technology for some time now.

"These nano grenades and mortar shells are ready for testing but very dangerous."

"Why is that?" Welch asked.

"Nanos are microscopic, fabricated creatures that eat through everything. Armor, leather, and skin will be eaten in seconds of contact with these hungry little attackers. Normally, they burn up in the atmosphere soon after dissolving their victim, but they are sometimes difficult to control. They can become an unruly fireball and devour everything on a battlefield.

"We used them in battle on Twuonay, a planet in the Ringnonian system. Their inhabitants, the Wannee, are large bug-like creatures with hard shells that prefer attacking in hordes. We launched nano mortar shells at the charging Wannee, and the horde was wiped out in minutes. But the momentum of the surging Wannee brought the nanos too close to our lines, and two hundred Ringnonians were also consumed. I think we should hold these as a last resort."

Guanton pointed to charts identifying other weapons. "The Gitan-Ray and acid bombs are not even close to testing. If only we had more time."

"But the floating napalm mines are ready." Guanton lifted a large metallic cylinder the size and shape of a football.

"I have seen the effects of napalm on a battlefield," Welch said. "Not like this, Mr. Secretary. We have added a feature. Napalm is a jelly-like, oxygen-fed explosive that attaches to and burns its victims on contact. But floating napalm seeks out victims and is fueled by carbon dioxide.

"Once a floating napalm mine is tripped or ignited, an explosive charge fires the napalm into the air, where it hovers and waits for a victim. A running, panicked soldier exhales more carbon dioxide and thus increases his chances of being attacked. The more excited the soldier becomes, the quicker the napalm will chase him down. The results are hideous to behold.

"I think the fields between the buffer zone at the 38th parallel should be covered with these mines," Guanton asserted as he replaced the explosive.

Welch left the meeting admiring the large alien but was also fearful.

"I would hate to have Guanton as an enemy," he said to Colonel Weaver.

~~~~~~~~~~

"The Japanese defense minister, Mr. Osokoo, is here for his meeting with you."

"Osokoo, I thought I was meeting Tashakaka," Wiley remarked as he looked up from his practice putting tee.

"You mean Mr. Tanashaka, Mr. President. No, sir, Mr. Tanashaka is ill and sent Mr. Osokoo instead."

"Well, Mr. Tinsler," Wiley said deliberately, "I'm not meeting with Mr. Osokoo. You handle it."

"Yes, Mr. President. Would you at least like a briefing on the current situation?"

"Go ahead, but make it brief," said Wiley as he lined up another putt.

"The Chinese have taken the Russian satellite station at Neryungri and now control Russian air space as well as theirs. The Chinese attack to the west has stalled at Chelyabinsk, a city north of Kazakhstan.

"The Germans have entered the war in support of the Russians. They have massed their artillery units and are using them quite effectively. The constant artillery salvos have kept the Ring-Men from charging. But our intelligence reports that the Chinese are working on something to solve the problem. Some sort of ear muffler.

"In the meantime, wave after wave of Chinese hit the lines of the Russians and Germans. They cannot hold out for long."

"I never liked the Russians, anyway," Wiley said as he hit another putt.

Tinsler ignored the comment and continued. "The Japanese minister is here to ask for U.S. support. They are about to join the fight and support the North Koreans. They see themselves as the next target of the Chinese."

"I don't know if we are ready to commit our troops," Wiley said. "But talk to him and get back to me."

Tinsler left the Oval Office, knowing why the president would not meet with Mr. Osokoo. Osokoo was three inches taller than Wiley, while Tanashaka was two inches shorter. Wiley would not meet with any head of state or minister from another country taller than him. So far, in the three years of his presidency, he had met with just one prime minister from some small African nation, whom he towered over. *How anyone as petty as Wilton Wiley ever became president is beyond me,* Tinsler thought as he entered his office.

"Japan is asking for our support against the Chinese," Bill Welch said. "The president is asking for our assessment; he wants to know when we will be ready."

Watson looked at Colonel Weaver, who sat sipping scotch and looking out the window in deep thought. "What do you think, Colonel?"

"Well, sir, the Chinese, having broken through at Kanggye, are now attacking Hamhung. But they are meeting fierce resistance from the North Koreans and two hundred thousand Japanese troops that have joined the fight." Weaver reached for his portfolio and pulled out photos. Weaver handed them to Welch.

"The first photo shows the new Japanese surface-to-air missile. It is small, less than two feet long. When it detonates, it fires like a shotgun, spreading shrapnel the size of golf balls. It is very effective against the heli-jets. We are working on a similar version that should be ready in a few months.

"The second photo is the new Chinese torpedo, the Skval 300. The number in that name indicates the knot speed it travels when fired. It is the fastest torpedo ever invented.

"That is why the Chinese have been able to sink most of the Russian and North Korean navies. While the Chinese subs are smaller and older than our submarines, intelligence has estimated that the Chinese have two hundred submarines patrolling the Pacific Ocean. On the other hand, we have a total of seventy-eight in our entire fleet.

"We have ordered most of our subs to the Pacific area and massed troops at the fortified 38th parallel. We can't move until we get superiority over the seas.

"Overeager Chinese controllers are shooting down civilian jets. Guanton thinks that Quanyo has given orders to shoot down anything that flies. Any aircraft flying within two hundred miles of Chinese or Russian airspace from any direction is subject to attack," Weaver said.

"We have also moved our carriers out of the range of Chinese airspace and formed new battle groups around the cruisers and destroyers. The closest that we dare fly to the Ring-Men division is Okinawa. From there, we must ship the unit to Japan and then South Korea."

"Then we are looking at…what?" Welch asked.

"At least a month, sir," Weaver replied.

"I hope we have that much time."

~~~~~~~~~

After reading reports about the Chinese Ring-Men's problem with explosions, Guanton designed a special helmet for his Ring-Men. His helmet not only muted loud noise but increased hearing ability as well.

"You are amazing," Ascon said after testing the helmet. "Maybe I'm not as bright as you think," Guanton said humbly.

"The satellite defense system was designed to eliminate global nuclear war. It is now being used offensively, not my intent at all.

"Flying by propeller-driven aircraft is not safe either. A tailwind or sudden air draft can increase the aircraft's speed by over two hundred miles an hour and make it subject to attack," Guanton said as he took the helmet from Ascon.

"If only I could have salvaged some of the crystals on our ship before it was destroyed."

"What crystals?" Ascon asked.

"Magnetic crystals were the energy source that powered the ship we arrived in. Those crystals were mined from the very center of our planet. The complex mixture of the charged crystals produces cold energy and makes satellite tracking impossible.

"Thousands of years ago, our ancestors did a geological study of Earth. The survey showed definite crystal deposits deep in the mountains of what is now Nepal and India. But getting to them now will require technology not yet available on Earth. I will have to design and manufacture a system to drill deep into the Earth's core to find the needed crystals. I was working on a design when the humans attacked us. Now I need a little more time and the available resources to begin the project."

"Perhaps after Quanyo is contained and this war is over," Ascon said.

Chapter 7

The Ringnonian Knife

Guanton read a report written by Major Robinson, one of the training officers. It read:

The Ring-Men are agile, quick-thinking in the field, and remarkable marksmen. Their ability to carry and fire heavy weaponry makes them a one-person army, but they also work well with each other and their human comrades. A Ring-Man leading a ten-man squad of rangers or paratroopers makes that unit equal to a company of regular soldiers. The Ring-Men possess an acute sense for trouble, ambushes, or traps. They are the finest troops that I have ever trained.

Guanton ordered the Ring-Men to assemble. In the gym, he observed them eagerly at attention. He stood before Ascon, saluted, and began the inspection of their ranks. He smiled as he noticed the length of their hair. After inspection, Guanton presented each Ring-Man with a package. Before they opened them, he addressed the group.

"I've noticed you growing your hair in an attempt, no doubt, to wear a top-knot. Good! It is traditional. What I have given you is also a Ringnonian tradition. Please open your packages."

Each of the Ring-Men opened his package and exposed a three-foot-long sword.

"What you have in your hand is a Ringnonian knife. Let me share some of this weapon's history.

"The Ringnonian, your ancestor, proudly wore his knife. He never went into battle without it. He was as skilled with his knife as with any other weapon. Once on the planet of Kittan, we faced a formidable enemy. The Kittans are lizard-like creatures that stand upright. Many are over ten feet tall with large hands. Their favorite weapon—the gonyo—is a triton-like spear." He paused, turned, and walked in the other direction.

"While battling the Kittans, their leader challenged us to a duel: 'Pit your one thousand warriors, using your knives, against our one thousand Kittans, using our gonyos,' he said. We took the challenge. It was a matter of honor.

"We split our forces into four groups. I led two hundred and fifty." He pointed to Ascon, "So did his father. Quanyo and Quill led the other two groups. We charged, and they charged, and we met in the middle. It was fierce fighting, hand to hand, knife against gonyo. In the end, only seven Ringnonians were left alive. All the Kittans, including their leader, were dead. The rest of the Kittans fled before us. This is just part of the history of the Ringnonian knife. Today begins your training in its use."

A remarkable weapon, the Ringnonian knife was three feet long with a six-inch wide, razor-sharp double-edge blade that narrowed toward the handle with a magnetic, armor-piercing tip. However hurled, the point always ended up in the direction of the intended victim. When not in use, it was strapped to its owner's back or attached at the side during ceremonies.

For the next ten days, the Ring-Men devoted themselves to training in using the deadly weapon. Guanton, an expert with the knife, personally trained the Ring-Men.

The human troops were envious and also requested to use the sword. Guanton designed a two-foot-long version for them. Thus, the entire Ring-Men division took the Ringnonian knife as a weapon and an emblem of their unit.

~~~~~~~

Quanyo and his army were on the move again. They crushed the North Korean and Japanese armies at Hamhung and were killing everything and everyone in their path. Newly designed ear covers worked considerably well for the Ring-Men.

Sixty thousand Japanese and eighty thousand North Koreans were killed defending Hamhung. His forces lost forty-eight thousand Chinese and sixteen Ring-Men. He did not care about the Chinese; they were expendable. But he needed to minimize the loss of the Ring-Men; they were not as easy to replace, and he did not have the time to make any more.

The Chinese, realizing the potential of an army of giants, officially encouraged the Ringnonians to produce as many as possible.

The government made young women "volunteer" to be consorts for him and the other Ringnonians. Night after night, the four lusty giants received these women.

The results were sons, seven thousand fighting already, with one thousand more due within the next two to three months. Another three thousand were spread out over China growing to adulthood.

The Chinese experimented with artificial insemination, but Ringnonian sperm would not live outside their host; it took time and actual mating to reproduce. Quanyo felt good being at war again; it was less work.

June and two weeks behind schedule, Quanyo wanted Russia destroyed by August. The army under Kitwan would then be free to turn east toward India and Pakistan. His army would crush Korea, turn south to attack Vietnam, Laos, and then Thailand. If all went according to plan, the mainland of Asia would be conquered by December. Japan would be targeted for invasion after his rest period in January.

Securing all the satellite control stations was crucial to his plan, which would broaden his protection from air attacks.

The North Korean station was next, with the Russian station taken and under Chinese control. According to Quanyo's intelligence, the North Korean control station was in Kangwon-Do province. It must be found and taken to advance south.

In the wake of the Chinese onslaught, millions of North Koreans fled south. The refugees, welcomed through the defensive lines at the 38th parallel, told tales of rape and slaughter.

The advancing Ring-Men and Chinese Army took no prisoners; they killed all. Women were often raped before being mutilated. The worst offenders, the Ring-Men seemed to be completely out of control.

Quanyo stepped in to restore discipline.

When he got to the front lines, he assembled the troops. Quanyo dealt with the Chinese first. He selected ten men from their ranks and, without ceremony, cut off their heads.

"If there is *any* repeat of this conduct or *any* lack of discipline, I will cut off a hundred of your heads." The Chinese were no problem after that.

The Ring-Men were a bit more difficult. Some challenged their officers. He needed to show them his other power.

He assembled a unit of Ring-Men and, in the presence of about one thousand of the giants, selected one. Tongee was his name, and he stood ten feet tall. Several reports showed him to be strong-willed and insubordinate but brave with great fighting ability. Escorted by two Ring-Men, he was brought before Quanyo. Tongee expected the worst and was relieved to see that Quanyo was minus his sword as he approached.

"So, I've heard that you are a fine warrior," Quanyo said, smiling as he moved closer to Tongee. "But you cannot follow orders."

Quanyo stood facing the taller Ring-Man. "Let us see how strong you are." Quanyo began focusing his mind on Tongee. Tongee felt the pressure and instinctively began to push back.

The mind battle lasted about a minute before the big Ring-Man tumbled to the ground, unconscious. Quanyo then turned to the stunned troops.

"We are superior to these humans, but remember, you are half-human. That means that I am superior to you. I will rule this world, and all of you will have a place in it.

But you must always remember your place." He looked down at the recovering Tongee.

"You must follow my orders and those of your officers. If I hear of any disobedience in the future, it will be dealt with more severely."

He motioned to the Ring-Men, who escorted Tongee to help him up. "Remember, I am the most powerful creature on this planet. Do not make me prove it again. You may kill all our enemies, but rape shows a lack of discipline and honor. It will not be tolerated. Am I clear?" he asked.

All in attendance shouted, "Yes, Commander!"

Quanyo pointed to Tongee and directed, "Bring that one to me."

Quanyo returned to his quarters. He sat in his huge chair and put his sword on the desk beside him. Tongee was escorted outside, where he waited. Quanyo called him in.

Tongee came inside expecting further discipline. "Yes, Commander."

"How would you like to be my aide?" Quanyo asked. "I'd rather fight, sir," admitted Tongee, surprised by the offer.

"Good! Then you will fight to protect my back. You are now my personal bodyguard."

"Yes, sir," said the big Ring-Man.

"You have a strong mind, and I will train you to make it stronger. That is all."

Quanyo watched Tongee leave. He saw something he liked in the Ring-Man. Kitwan was not bright enough and he did not completely trust the brothers Wotkye and Kotkye. But with proper training, Tongee could eventually become the second-in-command he needed.

Chapter 8

Deployment

Guanton flew to Washington, D.C., to meet with the Joint Chiefs of Staff. Comparatively few people knew Guanton's true identity. The Joint Chiefs thought he was a Ring-Man. Welch and Watson decided to inform them about the recently appointed Brigadier General Guanton at the meeting. General Watson wished to talk to him first.

Watson sat looking out of his office window, sipping coffee. He was a bit apprehensive about the meeting with Guanton. His part in destroying the Ringnonians and the Ring-Men troubled his conscience.

"General, your guest is here. He has been taken to the conference room, sir."

"Thank you, Ms. Beagle, I will be there momentarily."

Watson entered the conference room, and Guanton, standing with his back to the door, turned. A look of recognition crossed Guanton's face.

"General Guanton, how are you?" Watson asked as he extended his hand.

"I am fine, General Watson," Guanton said as he shook the smaller man's hand.

"Please have a seat so we can talk a bit." Guanton sat in a huge chair that was obviously meant for the Ringnonian. "I would personally like to thank you for all of the help you are providing, General."

Guanton wasted no time broaching a painful subject burned into Watson's memory. "You were involved in destroying my people," he said bluntly.

Watson looked into Guanton's eyes.

"Yes," Watson said, "I was a Captain, commanding a company that fought in the South Dakota area."

Guanton remained silent but continued looking directly at Watson.

"I was just following orders, Guanton," Watson said.

"That has been the cry of many soldiers in your history on Earth. I think the Nazis said the same thing at the Nuremberg trials."

Watson looked down and remained silent. He felt guilty for months after the destruction of the Ring-Men. He experienced nightmares and went to counseling, as did a number of the soldiers who took part in the slaughter.

"We were wrong for what we did, Guanton," Watson said finally. He looked up at Guanton, still staring at him. But Guanton was in deep thought.

"Our race has also been guilty of acts we regret. I, too, have followed orders my conscience told me were wrong."

The two warriors looked at each other and felt a sense of camaraderie. Guanton's admission, soldier to soldier, eased the pain of guilt that Watson had felt for years.

⌇⌇⌇⌇⌇⌇⌇⌇

Brigadier General Guanton was introduced to the room's six other Generals and Admirals. Seated around a large table looking at Guanton were General Wilber Scott of the Air Force and Admiral Chester

Whim of the Navy. General Aubrey Taylor represented the Army and the cigar-chewing General Flint Asbury, the Marine Corps.

The Vice Chairman, seated next to General Watson was Admiral Barry Skinner. They sat at another table in front of a huge screen showing China and the Korean peninsula. A number of adjutants sat behind the officers, including Colonel Weaver, Watson's aide. Guanton, however, remained standing and began pacing.

"I've analyzed Quanyo's plan of attack so far and determined that he is going after all the satellite system control stations. If he can control the satellites, he will control the airspace of Asia and most of Europe. He already has Russia's," Guanton said as he pointed to the screen. "If he's able to secure the North Korean station, your airbases in the Philippines and Okinawa will be useless. He will then sweep across the rest of Asia and Europe with his massive armies."

"What are the chances of the Koreans blowing up their station?" General Scott asked.

"They would never do that," General Watson said. "That would leave them vulnerable to attack in the future. Do we know where the station is?"

"We know that the station is somewhere in the Kangwon-do province, but we don't know the exact location," Admiral Whim said.

"I know exactly where all of them are. Remember, I installed them," Guanton said. He pointed back to the screen.

"The North Korean station is at Hoeyang-up, about fifty miles north of the 38th parallel."

"We can't let it fall into the hands of the Chinese even if we have to destroy it ourselves," General Taylor said.

"What's the latest report on the position of the Chinese in the north?" Watson asked Colonel Weaver.

"The Russians and Germans are holding the line at Tambov about four hundred miles southeast of Moscow," Weaver said. "The British have finally committed with two hundred thousand men and five hundred Thatcher tanks. The French are promising one hundred thousand men very soon."

"The French!" General Asbury said. "The French won't act until the Chinese are in Paris."

General Watson ignored that comment. "Go on, Colonel." Weaver motioned to the screen. "The South is the real concern.

The Chinese are north of the port city of Wonson." He punched a control, and the distance from Wonson to the satellite station appeared. "They are about a hundred miles from the station."

"We've got to move immediately," General Watson said, turning to the others. He addressed Guanton: "What's your plan?"

~~~~~~~~~

Watson called Major General Bradley Nelson, the commander of the Ring-Men division. Also on the line was Bill Welch.

"Brad, I know you are senior to Guanton," Watson said, "but I would defer to him on most of the combat decisions if I were you."

"Why not put him in command?" Nelson asked.

"Brad, Bill here. I selected you to command this unit. So, you know that I have the utmost confidence in your abilities," Welch said. "Guanton has experience fighting with the commander of the Ring-Men. He knows this Quanyo fellow. He knows how he thinks. Will you trust me on this?"

There was a pause. Finally, Nelson said, "You know I will, Bill.

Sorry, Danny, I didn't mean to get snippy with you."

"No offense taken, Brad, if I were in your shoes, I would probably feel the same way."

"What is the situation with your unit?" Welch asked.

"Seven thousand of our thirteen thousand troops have been flown by C-240's to Okinawa. The rest of the command will arrive by next week.

"From there, the unit will be transported by ship to the South Korean port city of Goseong, just south of the 38th parallel. The troops will then be moved to the border to link up with the 7th helicopter battalion. The 2nd Armored Division with its two hundred Powell pulse cannon tanks will join us there," Nelson said.

"What about the anti-gravity tanks and assault vehicles?" Welch asked.

"Thirty-two anti-gravity tanks and thirty-two assault vehicles are equipped for action. We should be ready before the Chinese reach the parallel, Bill," Nelson said.

"Thanks, Brad, all of America will be watching," Watson said.

Nelson concluded the call and sat back in his chair. He was fifty-eight and had been in the service longer than Watson and Welch. *I should have been in Watson's seat long ago. Now I have to take orders from an alien freak.*

Guanton was as amazing a tactician and strategist as he was an inventor. He designed the battle plan to take full advantage of his armor and anti-gravity tanks while minimizing the loss of his troops. Three hundred helicopters and one hundred heli-jets were also at his disposal.

The American Army was still the finest equipped in the world. The Ring-Men not in the gunship tanks were assigned to platoons of rangers or paratroopers. Each thirty-man platoon had one non-com Ring-Man. Each Ring-Man was equipped with a 210-pulse cannon (210 was the number of shots that could be fired before reloading), a thirty-five-pulse revolver, and his Ringnonian knife. He also carried a host of grenades and explosive devices.

The Ring-Men's body armor was lightweight but designed to withstand small caliber bullets and glancing pulse rifle hits. The helmet could mute the sound of explosions and increase hearing ability. The built-in high-powered targeting system enhanced the already excellent eyesight of the Ring-Man wearer. Altogether, the Ring-Men's gear weighed one hundred and fifty pounds, but the weight did not bother the eager soldiers.

Ascon commanded his own company, a special weapons unit with three Ring-Men sergeants and one hundred rangers. Ring-Men piloted fifteen of the thirty-two anti–gravity tanks with two human gunners; seventeen had full human crews.

The Americans were ready for action.

"We are ready to attack General. Everything is in place. All we need is the order to proceed," Guanton said.

Nelson reviewed the battle plan, looking for flaws, but could find none. On the contrary, he thought the plan was brilliant, but he would not admit that to Guanton.

"There is such a thing as diplomacy here on Earth," Nelson said. "The problem is the North Koreans. They will not grant permission for our troops to cross the 38th parallel. They are still defending their side of the buffer zone with about fifty thousand soldiers."

"I am aware of the diplomatic problems," Guanton said, remaining calm, "but the longer we wait, the greater the chance of the station falling into Chinese hands."

"The North Koreans are retreating south and fortifying a position five miles north of their station at Hoeyang-up. They have also asked the Japanese to stay away. The Japanese commander has taken what's left of his sixty thousand soldiers and retreated to Kosong-up to the east," Nelson said.

"The North Koreans don't want anyone near their satellite station, including anyone who can help them," Guanton said.

Guanton left Nelson's office thinking, *what a planet! Same fight, same species, and no trust. I can't wait to leave here.*

Quanyo looked over the reports of his casualties and troop disposition. Twenty-seven tanks were destroyed taking Hamhung. Thirty-eight thousand Chinese and sixty Ring-Men were also dead. *Too many,* he thought.

He would have to call for more Chinese troops before he could attack the 38th parallel. He anticipated the United States would enter the war when he attacked South Korea. According to his intelligence, the U.S. equipment was quite advanced, and there were sketchy reports of larger-than-normal soldiers. He wondered if they were Ring-Men. *Could some of them be alive?* He would know soon enough.

Wotkye knocked on the door, and Tongee let him in. The huge bodyguard then took his position behind Quanyo, seated at his desk.

Wotkye acknowledged Quanyo with a half salute. "Commander, all the units are ready for the final assault." Wotkye was the older of the two Ringnonian brothers. Though he respected Quanyo, he did not fear him as much as his brother. He was as tall and broad as Quanyo. A deep scar, made by a Kittan gonyo many years ago, marked his face on the right side.

"Your losses were extremely high at Hamhung," Quanyo said, half sneering.

"You are the one who ordered the frontal attack against those Japanese missile positions. If you remember, I asked for the infantry to attack first. The losses were your fault, not mine."

"Remember your place!" Quanyo said. Tongee moved from behind Quanyo as if to attack. Quanyo held up his hand, and Tongee returned to his place.

With his eyes glaring at the Ringnonian standing before him, he said calmly, "We attack at first light, and half of your armor will be kept in reserve. When ordered, you will attack and keep attacking until you reach the satellite station. Is that understood?"

"Yes, Commander," Wotkye said, regaining his composure. "Is that all, sir?"

"Yes. You are dismissed," said Quanyo without changing his expression. "Send in your brother."

Wotkye left the command hut and met his brother outside.

"He wants you." He leaned close to Kotkye and whispered, "One day, I'll kill that fool."

"Quiet," said Kotkye. "Don't say everything you think." Kotkye was a few inches shorter than his brother and was the opposite in demeanor. He did not like Quanyo either, but he did not hate him as much as his brother. Kotkye wanted to get the war over so he could return to making love and drinking ale.

"Relax, my brother. I've got a keg of ale in my tent. Go get some." He watched as his brother stormed away, and then he knocked on the door of Quanyo's hut.

Ushered in, Kotkye gave a full salute as he stood before Quanyo. "Yes, Commander," he said, almost shouting.

"Are the Ring-Men ready for the attack?"

"Yes, they are, sir," said Kotkye. "Two regiments will attack after the armor and the Chinese have made the initial charge."

"Your main target is the satellite station. It will be heavily defended but must be taken at all costs. Is that understood?" Quanyo said as he stood up.

"Yes, Commander," repeated Kotkye with a full salute. As he left the hut, Kotkye thought, *Wotkye will kill him after this war is over, and I'm going to help him.*

Quanyo watched the younger Ringnonian leave. *I'm going to kill both of them when this war is over.*

Chapter 9

Hoeyang-up

"The North Koreans are pulling out all the stops," Dexter Orwell announced.

The son of the famous reporter and columnist was determined to make a name for himself. His father pulled strings and helped him get a cushy assignment with CNN's Asian branch. But Dexter wanted action, so he persuaded his father to get him to where the action was.

Using his connections in their government, Tyler Orwell got Dexter attached as a correspondent to the North Korean army.

Dexter's wife, Eileen, adamantly opposed his going. "Why, Dex, why are you leaving us? We are doing okay; we're making enough money."

"This is our chance, sweetheart," he declared as he tried to comfort her. "My dad has set it up. I'll be at the front but at a safe distance. I can win a Pulitzer. Don't you see? This is my chance to be famous."

"Fame, is that all you Orwells ever think about? Tell that to our baby. Please don't go, please." Her pleading did no good.

"Fifteen hundred aircraft, including prop planes, have been assembled at Pyonggang-up and Kosong-up. The North Koreans know that most will be lost to satellite strikes, but there is little reason to be cautious now. If the Chinese take Hoeyang-up, the war is lost. This is Dexter Orwell reporting to you from the front lines, keeping you informed and aware of what's going on."

The North Korean army drew a defensive line five miles north of Hoeyang-up. The line was twenty miles long, with every tank, helicopter, and artillery piece remaining. Even the buffer zone at the 38th parallel was stripped of soldiers, and a token force of five thousand men was left to defend it. A second position was set up around the satellite station. The Koreans placed forty thousand crack troops and two hundred of their heaviest tanks there. The Air Force would be called in if the Chinese got that far. In all, two hundred and seventy thousand soldiers were dug in, ready to defend the last strongholds.

~~~~~~~~

Quanyo observed the quiet stretch that would soon become a battlefield. At 6 A.M., the shells from two hundred powerful 125mm cannons would unleash a deadly barrage followed by a tank assault over the two-mile dead man's land. Next, the bugles would signal four hundred thousand Chinese to begin a wave after wave attack. On the left flank, two regiments, two thousand Ring-Men led by Kotkye, would attack. They would work their way toward the satellite station and take it. His Chinese air force was ready to fly if the North Korean air force attacked as he anticipated they would. *Of course, some of our jets will be destroyed by friendly fire from the satellites, but so what? That's a chance I'll take.*

The whirring sound of artillery shells passing over his head excited Quanyo. He would lead a regiment of one thousand Ring-Men on the right flank. Wotkye was ordered to stay in reserve with four hundred tanks and three thousand Ring-Men at the center. Camera radios allowed Quanyo to keep in communication with the other Ringnonian officers.

Dexter Orwell reported on the action on the Korean side of the battlefield as he looked through his telescopic binoculars.

"Artillery is pounding the lines of the North Koreans. The Chinese tanks' roar and clinking can be heard as they move forward. First, the fast T-96s, followed by the larger T-99s. Above, heli-jets have gone into action and are firing pulse cannons at the Korean lines. Fireballs and explosions light the battlefield." Dexter adjusted his position. "I see T-101 pulse tanks coming up, the two-second whine of their cannons signaling when they are about to fire. Bugles are blowing, and the Chinese are leaving their trenches yelling and screaming. They look like locusts swarming across the field as they approach the Korean lines.

"General Kwaunon, the North Korean commander, has ordered his tanks forward. These are older versions of the T-96s purchased from China years ago. About two hundred and fifty have moved to meet the oncoming Chinese.

"One by one, they are being destroyed by the heavier armored opponents. North Korean helicopters have moved in to strike at the tanks, but the Chinese heli-jets blast them from the sky. The Korean soldiers are bracing for the ground assault."

~~~~~~~~~

Twenty-five T-101 pulse tanks remained behind on the left flank, and as they moved forward, the Ring-Men led by Kotkye moved in behind them. Quanyo looked at his handheld camera radio and asked Wotkye, "How far before our troops engage their front lines?"

"About five hundred yards," Wotkye said.

Quanyo contacted Kotkye. "What's your position?"

"About five hundred yards on the left flank and about five miles from the satellite station," he said.

"Let's go," Quanyo said, turning to Tongee.

~~~~~~~~~

General Nelson handed the satellite images to Guanton. "It's not good," he observed as he snuffed his cigar.

"We have got to move now," Guanton urged.

"North Korea won't budge on letting us help them," Nelson said. "In another two hours, there won't be a North Korea," Guanton said as he pushed the satellite images onto Nelson's desk.

Nelson paused, "Get your troops moving."

Guanton gave orders to his aide, Ben Williams: "Get the helicopters and heli-jets airborne, fire up the tanks, and get the men ready to move. We've got orders to cross the parallel."

"What are our orders if the North Koreans fire?" Williams asked. "If they fire on us," Guanton said, "We'll take them out."

Dexter Orwell opened his eyes but could not see through the thick smoke. He tried to get to his feet, but the pain in his leg prevented his movement. The command bunker he reported from suffered a direct hit from a pulse cannon blast fired from a Chinese heli-jet. Dead bodies covered the floor. Among the dead was Chin-Wang, his American-born Korean translator and assistant. Two medics came to his aid and helped him to a truck preparing to leave.

General Kwaunon ordered his remaining troops back to the second defensive position around the satellite station and commanded the air force to attack. Dexter saw the Koreans making the hasty withdrawal from his vantage in the truck. He also witnessed the destruction of the North Korean air force.

Dexter winced in pain as he reported using an undamaged laptop. "The Korean troops are retreating on all sides, the wounded being helped as they stagger back to the rear. General Kwaunon has ordered in the Air Force. Bright flashes of light from the heavens illuminate the morning sky, obviously the Chinese satellites in action. The Koreans are being massacred."

The North Korean pilots broke the formation and tried to reach the target area independently. They were easily picked off and destroyed. Some of the Korean propeller aircraft reached the battlefield and began bombing and strafing runs. But the slow-moving relics were no match for the pulse cannons and heli-jets that easily shot them down. It took about twenty minutes to shoot down all fifteen hundred of the aircraft.

Guanton was some kind of weapons designer. Quanyo thought as he observed the destruction. He did not have to order his air force into action. The satellite system proved so effective that the Air Force was not needed.

Quanyo contacted Kotkye: "ETA to the satellite station?"

"About two miles," Kotkye said. "But we are meeting strong resistance."

"I'll get you some support," said Quanyo, signaling to a Ring-Man commander of a Chinese regiment. "You there, what's your name?"

"Talwot, Commander," replied the eager Ring-Man.

"Take as many men as possible and support the left flank." He looked into the radio, "Wotkye, move your units forward and support the left flank."

He gave the radio to Tongee. "We must take the station as soon as possible."

Chapter 10

The 38th Parallel

The buffer zone between North and South Korea is a two-and-a-half-mile wide area extending across the country's middle from east to west. It is the most heavily defended area in the world. It was established as a neutral zone and part of the treaty ending the Korean War in 1954. At any one time, about one hundred thousand soldiers on each side patrol the lines, ever watchful of the other side's activity. But now, the North Korean side was stripped of soldiers due to the battle in the north.

Guanton decided to cross just north of Ihyeon-ri, a lightly defended area. The satellite station was a straight shot of about forty miles from that point. Satellite surveillance indicated that only five thousand North Koreans defended the buffer zone. Only two hundred soldiers patrolled the line at Ihyeon-ri. Forty-five heli-jets were the first to cross. They flew low using rotor power to go undetected by the Chinese controllers. The North Koreans, however, picked them up on radar and began firing.

Colonel Arnold "Wing" Miller called to control: "They are firing. What should we do?"

"Take them out," the command center answered.

The heli-jets swung into action. Half began firing pulse cannons, and the others opened up with Gatling guns. In a matter of moments, the guns of the North Koreans fell silent.

"All resistance is neutralized," Miller said.

Roger," said command. "Continue forward, scout the terrain, and head to checkpoint one, over."

"That's affirmative," Miller said. To his other units, he said, "B team, go left, C, go right. Stay in contact with my group."

The fifteen heli-jets from B team moved one thousand yards to the left, and fifteen from C team did the same to the right.

One hundred Apache 250 helicopters crept behind, supporting the tanks beneath them. Mine detector tanks led the way, clearing and exploding any mines in the buffer zone left by the North Koreans.

Thirty anti-gravity tanks led by Revel flew ten feet above the ground. Ascon and his one-hundred-man special weapons assault team, and Major Robinson leading the other three companies of the Ring-Men Recon battalion, rode behind them in the anti-gravity assault vehicles.

Guanton's anti-gravity command vehicle came equipped with an intelligence system that allowed him to see everything around him. The unit could send out tiny drone camera robots to give reconnaissance up to thirty miles. The entire system was also connected to surveillance satellites, giving an instant aerial view of the battlefield. The communication officer, a human named Jack Walker, was personally trained by Guanton. Dunwol, a Ring-Man, was the pilot-gunner.

"Revel, scout ahead," Guanton said. "We need to get Ascon's team in as close as possible before they are detected."

"Yes, sir," said Revel, his deep voice easily recognizable on the radio.

"Be careful, big guy," Ascon radioed to his friend.

"You too," said Revel.

Quanyo stepped from his vehicle to assess the carnage at the satellite station. The losses sustained made Kotkye nervous. Taking the station resulted in the deaths of eighty Ring-Men and the destruction of eighteen tanks. Dead Chinese and Koreans littered the field. Many were locked in positions indicating they fought hand to hand before dying. Quanyo seemed elated.

"Good job," he said, slapping Kotkye on the shoulder.

"Our losses are very high. They put up a good fight," Kotkye said. "Their commander was wounded, but he has been taken alive. He's over there."

Quanyo looked at the bleeding General Kwaunon. "Your men fought well. You may die with honor. Who is that?" Quanyo asked as he pointed to Dexter Orwell.

"He says he is a reporter. He also says that his father is famous."

Quanyo pointed to a Chinese soldier, motioned for his pistol, and walked toward the captives.

Dexter held a picture of his wife and young son. His hand shook as he lifted the picture for Quanyo to see. "This is a picture of my boy," he said nervously.

Quanyo ignored the photo. "It's a shame you won't see him grow up."

He pulled out his sword and unceremoniously cut off Dexter Orwell's head. He turned toward the General, seated upright despite his shoulder wound. "I'm sure you would prefer this to my sword."

He handed him the pistol.

As Quanyo walked away, General Kwaunon took his own life.

"Is the station intact?" Quanyo asked.

"Yes, sir," Kotkye said as he looked at the two corpses.

～～～～～～

Colonel Miller's heli-jets penetrated about ten miles, and he observed the retreating North Korean soldiers. Still operating on rotor power, he moved his unit over a tree-covered area, away from any roads, and radioed command.

"Eagle One to Eagle Two."

"Go ahead, Eagle One."

"We found the staging area and are ten miles from you and about twenty-eight miles from the target," said Miller, adjusting his headset. "The trees are low enough for the assault team to come in."

Guanton mapped out a plan to destroy the North Korean satellite station. The strike force would attack just east of the station, coming in low over the trees. The heli-jets would lead, followed by the assault team in anti-gravity tanks and assault vehicles.

The route to the station was perfect for an anti-gravity approach. Low tree cover meant the tanks and vehicles did not have to go higher than their fifteen-foot maximum elevation. Also beneficial was a ten-mile stretch of valley leading directly in front of the station.

Guanton and his reserves would wait for the assault team at the staging area marked by Miller and prepare for a counterattack. With the team recovered, they would beat a hasty retreat back to the 38th parallel.

Retreating North Korean soldiers were allowed to cross the buffer zone into South Korea as the defeated North Korean government pleaded for help. With no interference from the North Koreans, Guanton ordered the mining of the buffer zone with the new floating napalm charges. The Japanese at Kosong-up pushed to the west and linked up with other retreating North Korean units. That total combined force numbered about eighty thousand men.

"Quanyo will want to deal with that army before advancing further south," Guanton said to General Nelson. "He will smell another battle and redirect much of his force away from the station. That's when we will have a chance."

~~~~~~~~~~~

"They just won't give up," Quanyo told Tongee as he looked at a report.

"The Japanese and remnants of the North Korean army are moving toward us," Tongee said.

"I want Wotkye and his armor to move to meet this new threat. Mobilize the Chinese, also. I will join him with the Ring-Men, and we will crush the North Koreans and Japanese once and for all."

"What about the prisoners we've captured?" Tongee asked. "There are over twenty-five thousand of them."

"March them back to China," Quanyo said. "We will execute them later. Our losses are quite high. About forty-five thousand Chinese have been killed. I can't leave many soldiers behind to defend the station. Tell Kotkye to come in."

The big Ring-Man went to the door of the command hut and ushered Kotkye in.

"I'm leaving you here to secure this area. The Chinese technicians and reinforcements are on the way. I want this area fortified, and these bodies buried,"

"How many troops are you leaving?" Kotkye asked.

"I'm leaving ten thousand Chinese and eight hundred Ring-Men. I'm taking most of the armor with me," Quanyo said without looking up from his reports.

"Quanyo, do you think that is enough men? I have a ten-square-mile area to defend, and many of my troops are wounded."

"That should be enough for a good leader. You should not have lost so many taking this place."

"Yes, commander," Kotkye said as he looked down. He knew that further protesting would only invite more berating.

Quanyo looked up at the Ringnonian. "You're dismissed."

Kotkye left, his hatred of Quanyo growing almost to the level of his brother's.

Chapter 11

The Station

Guanton deployed four camera drones. The little observers were under six inches long and equipped with infra-red telescopic lenses. They hovered above the tree tops about three hundred feet from the station, sending a steady stream of information to Guanton and the advance team.

Guanton viewed the area around the station and assessed the enemy troop strength.

Surveillance satellite imagery showed the bulk of the Chinese army moving eastward to meet the Japanese.

"Eagle One," radioed Guanton, "it looks like they're busy burying bodies. I can see what looks like three tanks to the station's right and two to the left, over."

"That's a copy," said Miller. "We're running silent rotor and are about three miles away. But when we go to attack speed, they're going to hear us."

The heli-jets could lower their rotor speed to be barely audible. The craft could also blend in by changing to the color of the tree it was hovering over. This chameleon-like feature made the craft almost invisible, especially at night. It also allowed the heli-jet to lie in wait and ambush approaching enemy aircraft.

"Affirmative," said Guanton. "Attack at top rotor speed, remove the tanks and do as much damage as possible. Don't switch to jet power unless their heli-jets show up, copy?"

"Copy that."

"Revel, wait until our heli-jets engage, and then come in with your tanks just in front of the assault team," directed Guanton.

"Affirmative."

"Ascon, you have to be quick. Set those charges and get out of there," Guanton warned. "We move in five minutes."

───〜〜〜───

Quanyo couldn't put a finger on it, but something troubled him.

He grabbed his radio and called Wotkye. "What's your position?"

"About ten miles from the reported enemy position," said Wotkye. "Our heli-jets have engaged the enemy, but the Japanese missiles have taken out a number of them already."

"Order them to the rear. We can't afford to lose any more. Send in the Chinese," Quanyo said.

He switched to Kotkye and asked, "What's the situation there?"

"All's quiet. Burial details are working, and the Chinese technicians have arrived."

"I'm sending the heli-jets back to your position. Have your men cut out a landing zone for about fifty of them," Quanyo said.

"But my men need rest. Many have been up for twenty-four hours," Kotkye protested.

"I don't care. Just do as I say. I want a place for those jets to land, and I want those satellites operational. Do I make myself clear?"

"Yes, Commander," Kotkye said.

───〜〜〜───

The Chinese technician manning the ground-level radar remarked to his commander, "sir, I've got what looks like heli-jets coming in from the west."

"Yes, we are expecting a flight of our heli-jets at any time now," the captain said nonchalantly.

At 5:30 A.M., the American heli-jets moved forward. They increased their rotor speed but stayed below two hundred miles an hour. Miller was surprised that no one fired. Dividing his units into three groups, he took the center. B group came in from the east and C from the west.

Miller's group flew over the front security fence and opened fire on the tanks to the left of the satellite station. Firing pulse cannons and Gatling guns, they quickly disposed of the tanks and the soldiers at the front of the entrance. B group came in behind the station, took out three tanks stationed at the back gate, and mowed down the Chinese defenders to the rear. C group wiped out the defenders to the right and hovered at tree top level at the main roads leading to the facility. The battle was over in a matter of minutes.

"Eagle One leader to Eagle Two assault...all clear and ready for your team," Miller reported. Revel's lead tanks floated in seconds later, followed by the assault vehicles.

Major Robinson deployed his units around the station, creating a defensive barrier. The satellite complex was huge and built in a triangular shape. Robinson covered the three sides and extended the perimeter to the outside to await a counterattack.

Ascon's team landed in front of the entrance. Revel used his cannon to blow a hole in the front door, and Ascon moved in with his team.

~~~~~~~~~~

Kotkye was two miles away in a small town that previously served as housing and recreation for former North Korean personnel. Almost all the Ring-Men drank and took advantage of the few women who did not escape.

"After all," Kotkye told one of the Ring-Men, "the digging of graves and cutting of trees was beneath them and could be left to the exhausted Chinese." He was drinking a mug of ale when he heard the explosions. Kotkye got up from the table and went outside. Many of the Ring-Men were also outside, trying to zero in on the direction of the explosions.

"Get to the station," he said. Kotkye ran to his vehicle and tried to radio the satellite station but received static. Then, he reluctantly called Quanyo.

Quanyo was furious. He immediately halted his column and ordered it back toward the satellite station. He knew this would take time since they were about twenty-five miles away. He radioed Wotkye. "The station is under attack. Keep moving forward. I'm returning to the station with half the units."

"Who's attacking?" Wotkye asked.

"I don't know, but I suspect the Americans have crossed the 38th parallel." Turning to the radio operator in his truck, he asked, "Where are the heli-jets? Tell them to get to the station and attack immediately."

Ascon's team met minimal resistance as they entered the station. Most of the defenders were already dead, killed by the blast from the anti-tank. The assault team disposed of the rest. One Chinese Ring-Man was on duty, but Sergeant Kilton quickly dispatched him. The Indian Ring-Man threw his knife and hit the Chinese Ring-Man in the torso, pinning him to the wall.

Special high explosive charges were set in the station control and satellite direction rooms. Guanton showed the team what needed to be destroyed so that nothing from the system could be salvaged. Then, the rest of the complex was mined with explosives and primed for electronic detonation.

Ascon's unit prepared to move out when he heard Miller say, "Incoming heli-jets moving in from the west. There's a lot of them."

"How far away?" Ascon asked.

"About one minute. They're using jet power, so we'll get into position to jump them when they start their descent. The tanks will have to cover your retreat," Miller said. He knew that the Chinese satellite operators would be unable to distinguish between the American and the Chinese heli-jets. They would be reluctant to fire and hit their own. The best strategy would be to mix with the Chinese and try to bring down as many as possible.

"Roger that. We'll be out of here in twenty seconds," Ascon said.

Then he told Robinson, "We're ready to move."

"That's affirmative," Robinson said. "My men are already loading."

Robinson's men were retreating to their assault vehicles, and the tanks covered the withdrawal. The Chinese fire increased as more troops joined the fight. Pulse blasts fired from a distance indicated that the Chinese Ring-Men were getting closer.

Three anti-gravity tanks covered the main road leading to the station. Lowering to a height of three feet, they blasted away at everything moving up the road. Two Chinese T-101 pulse tanks were knocked out and lay smoldering at the side of the road.

It was 6 A.M., and a faint hint of sunrise lit up the night sky. A terrific blast completely engulfed one of the anti-gravity tanks, killing everyone on board—all human occupants.

Sergeant Gunter, the Ring-Man squad leader, blasted the remnants of the tank to pieces. Orders were to leave no evidence of weaponry or any trace of a Ring-Man presence. Guanton knew that eventually, Quanyo would figure out that the Americans received Ringnonian help, but he wanted to conceal that fact as long as possible. Gunter received orders to pull out, and he signaled the remaining tank. Both tanks reversed and retreated at full throttle over the tree line. Ten seconds later, the satellite station and much of the surrounding area were blown to bits.

Chapter 12

The Retreat

The American heli-jets waited in ambush for the incoming Chinese flying in on jet power. If not stopped or at least slowed, the heli-jets could catch and wreak havoc on the retreating assault forces. Miller figured that the Chinese would slow to rotor power to assess the damage at the station. His group hovered above a section of forest about two thousand yards from where the station previously stood. The sun was rising, and his group risked detection at any time.

Soldiers overran the area surrounding the demolished satellite station. Many of them stood watching the remnants of the station burn. The fifty Chinese heli-jets slowed as Miller had anticipated.

Chinese surveillance satellites did not pick up anything that looked like the retreating attack force on any road heading south. *Where are they?* Kotkye wondered.

An instant later, the sky was illuminated by explosions as a number of the Chinese heli-jets became balls of fire. The first salvo from Miller's team destroyed sixteen enemy craft. The remainder reverted to jet power and flew in different directions. The American heli-jets did the same as they engaged the Chinese.

What followed was a fast-moving dogfight of heli-jet against heli-jet. The swift aircraft resembled bees as they darted back and forth in the early morning sky. Twenty ships were brought down before the melee ended. The Chinese commander signaled his unit, and they unexpectedly retreated westward. That almost led to disaster for the remaining Americans.

As the Chinese veered off, the American heli-jets faced the deadly Chinese satellite fire. Lasers shot three American aircraft from the sky. Miller quickly ordered his ships to revert to rotor power, but they grew susceptible to pulse cannon fire from the ground in daylight. Six more ships were shot down before the rest of the group could flee.

Miller's heli-jet was hit, and his right leg severed. He had one more trick up his sleeve. Though half dead, he aimed his damaged jet at a group of soldiers and crashed into their midst, killing fifty, including ten Ring-Men. Twenty-eight of the forty-five American heli-jets escaped. They destroyed thirty enemy heli-jets and covered the withdrawal of the assault team at the same time.

~~~~~~~~~~

By the time Quanyo reached the destroyed satellite station, he was incensed. Kotkye fearfully approached him from behind. Without speaking, Quanyo turned and struck Kotkye with such force that it sent him crashing to the ground, unconscious.

Quanyo thought about beheading him, but he reconsidered. If he killed Kotkye, he would have to kill his brother, also. Instead, he told two nearby Ring-Men, "Get him out of my sight."

There were no reliable reports to indicate where the attackers came from or where they went.

No answers, just a destroyed station. Something is very strange about this. I've got to find out what's going on and who I'm up against.

~~~~~~~~~~

Guanton's units stayed beneath the forest cover for the rest of the afternoon. He would have moved them if pursued, but his drone and satellite surveillance indicated that Quanyo and his troops were not heading south.

The Japanese successfully broke off their feint attack and were headed south to join the American and the combined Korean troops at the 38th parallel. Guanton's plan worked perfectly. His own losses numbered twenty-eight human soldiers and two anti-gravity tanks. Also missing were the seventeen heli-jets and their heroic crews.

Not bad, but Quanyo will be ready for us next time.

~~~~~~~~~~

"Both ours and the Japanese navies have gone on the offensive," General Nelson said. "We have identified and destroyed over one hundred and eighty Chinese submarines and most of their surface craft. The rest are damaged or blockaded in their ports.

"Guanton's plan worked to perfection," General Nelson admitted. "What about our losses?" Watson asked.

"Twenty-two subs, four missile cruisers, and eight destroyers have been damaged or sunk. Japan has also sustained heavy casualties, losing eighteen submarines, numerous surface vessels, and over five thousand sailors. But to get their submarines, I believe it was worth it."

"Good job, Brad. What about the Ring-Men unit?"

"Guanton has told me that we should prepare for an all-out attack and that the Ring-Men unit will return by nightfall."

But no attack came. Instead, Quanyo fortified the area around the ruins of the satellite station and ordered Wotkye to do the same at Kosong-up. After the failed attempt to take the North Korean satellite station intact, many observers felt that the war in Russia would heat up. Instead, the Chinese halted their advance and also dug in.

What's Quanyo up to? Guanton thought.

Chapter 13
Arika

Because of their fine training record and the success of their first mission, most of the Ring-Men division was given leave in Japan. The forty-five Ring-Men roamed about Tokyo and enjoyed the freedom denied for so long.

Despite their physical differences, all the soldiers considered themselves brothers. The experienced human soldiers of the Ring-Men division were more than willing to show the Ring-Men the seedier side of Tokyo.

Ascon's first experience with a woman other than his mother was at a gentleman's club in Tokyo. He met a petite, black-haired Japanese woman named Arika, who worked there as a hostess.

Ascon was mesmerized by her large almond-shaped eyes that matched her ebony hair. Her perfect features were only excelled by a riveting personality and a gentle, intoxicating laugh. He had never seen anyone as beautiful, and he fell in love on the spot. She sat at his table and introduced herself in broken English, "My name Arika. Your name, what?"

"I am Ascon," he responded in perfect Japanese.

Revel, seated with the couple, recognized their mutual attraction and went to the bar.

"What do you do here?" Ascon asked.

Arika blushed, "Among other things, I serve as a hostess. My brother owns this club. You speak Japanese!"

"Yes, I do."

"You have never been to a gentleman's club before?"

"No, this is my first time," he said as he embarrassingly looked down at his mug of ale.

"You are very different," she said with a smile. "I think I like you, Ascon." The mention of his name on her lips sent shivers down his spine.

He spent that first night at her apartment and did not leave it for two weeks. He knew now what was missing and never wanted to return to solitude and loneliness again. Arika also felt that she finally met someone wonderful. This huge Ring-Man was gentle and kind but powerful simultaneously. Though inexperienced, he turned out to be a wonderful lover. No man ever made her feel like this gentle giant. She felt so safe in his arms.

At 32, she felt the urge to settle down and get out of the life she was in. Having more than enough money and even owning the apartment building she lived in, she was financially set. She laid her head in his arms and felt his heartbeat as he breathed.

He will belong to me forever, she thought.

The South Korean freighter entered the harbor at Tsunuga, Japan. The manifest indicated that it contained iron ore and salt from Russia. But there was something else loaded in the hold. Hiding in secret compartments below deck were three hundred Ring-Men.

After the defeat of the Chinese navy, a blockade imposed a stranglehold on Chinese shipping.

One night in September in the Sea of Japan, a launch flashing emergency lights and seemingly in distress received aid from a South Korean freighter. As the ship came alongside, ten Ring-Men boarded and killed all but the captain and a few of the officers. The vessel was then steered to the Russian port of Slovyansk. Captured earlier, the port town had communications cut, and hundreds of its residents massacred.

The captain and the remainder of the crew were also killed and replaced with Korean-speaking Chinese. Refitted and loaded with the Ring-Men, the ship was steered to its original destination of Tsunuga.

The Chinese captain handed control to the Japanese harbor pilot, who navigated the ship and docked it at the port. The papers were presented, and everything appeared to be in order. The cargo would be unloaded the next day.

Quanyo found out through Chinese intelligence that the Japanese satellite station was at Ogaki, about thirty miles south of the port. Twenty trucks procured by Chinese agents were on hand, supposedly for unloading the cargo the next day. Instead, the Ring-Men loaded onto the trucks and headed toward Ogaki.

They came armed with pulse cannons and machine guns. Included among their weapons was an assortment of explosives, including a small nuclear device. Besides the Ring-Men on the assault team were twenty Chinese technicians, specialists in satellite technology. They also drove the trucks so the Ring-Men could remain inconspicuously hidden in the rear.

"The mission has several possible outcomes," Kotkye told Quanyo.

"One, the station can be taken and controlled. Thus, with Japanese airspace under our control, American warships can be attacked by our massive air force. Two, we can destroy the station, making Japan vulnerable to attack from the air. A third result will be the shock value created

by three hundred Ring-Men on the loose, killing everyone in our sight."
Kotkye devised the plan trying to curry the favor of the bitterly angry
Quanyo. It was approved with the provision that Kotkye lead the mis-
sion and that it dare not fail.

"Why do you have to go?" Wotkye asked. "You know that it's a suicide mission."

"I have to get away from him, my brother. Besides, I think it is a
good plan and has a chance to work. I tried to get you assigned to go
with me, but Quanyo was having none of it."

"You're crazy! Let's kill him and be done with it," Wotkye suggested.

"That won't be as easy as you think. Be patient, Wotkye, and besides,
I don't plan on dying. If we take the station intact, we have a bargaining
chip."

Ascon was not ready to go back on duty. He and Arika enjoyed
their two weeks together. They made love and talked constantly. He told
her everything about himself, his mother, his confinement, even what
he knew of his father. Arika listened and cared. She would put her tiny
hands into his when he talked to her. He loved everything about her—
the smell of her skin, her cute little nose, and how she threw her hair
back when she laughed. But most of all, he loved how she lay in his arms,
so petite and fragile. He cherished her.

"I love you, Ascon," she declared in his arms. A sensation he never
felt flowed through his entire body.

"I love you, Arika."

"I never thought I could love a man after what my father did to me,"
she said as she cried.

"What did he do?" Ascon became angry at the thought.

"He...took advantage of me...when I was young," she sobbed.
Ascon didn't know what to say, so he remained silent.

"He was always drunk, and he beat me often. I have not forgiven him. To this day, I say very little to him." As he listened to her, Ascon stroked her long, lovely hair.

"No one will ever hurt you again, I promise you."

Ascon was happier than he had ever been in his life. He could have stayed in that apartment forever, but eventually, orders came. Revel came to the apartment and informed him they were moving the next day. He held Arika in his arms for the last evening before leaving and promised her he would return.

~~~~~~~~~~

The trucks approached the first checkpoint leading to the satellite station. Barricades were visible, and a thick, electrified barbed wire fence surrounded the entire complex.

Intelligence reports indicated that the famed 15th Samurai Division was stationed in and around the base. Only one regiment of the unit, about one thousand men, was at the station; the rest of the unit was still in Korea guarding the parallel.

The guard left his alcove and approached the first truck. The Chinese driver pulled out a pistol and shot him in the head. To the rear of the canvas-covered truck, fifteen Ring-Men dismounted and charged the gate, firing their pulse cannons in every direction. They killed all the guards on duty and began blowing holes in the fencing.

A squad of Japanese marines, their leader brandishing a sword, was mowed down as they rushed toward the gate. The other trucks sped through the gaping holes created by the pulse blasts. Three squads, about fifty Ring-Men, set up a defensive perimeter at the front gate. The other Ring-Men grouped into squad teams, went through the entire complex and killed everyone in their path.

The Japanese marines were overmatched. Their small caliber bullets proved ineffective against the body armor of the giant soldiers. The last defense was in front of the satellite station itself. One hundred marines, some firing machine guns with armor-piercing rounds, took down a few Ring-Men. Soon, superior firepower and Ring-Men strength overwhelmed them.

With all the marines dead, the occupants on the inside surrendered. The Japanese technicians were herded outside and shot. The Chinese technicians were then ushered in to begin their work inside. The entire attack took just thirty minutes.

Kotkye radioed Quanyo, "The station is ours."

Chapter 14

Oğaki

Guanton was in his quarters putting the final touch on the design for his core drill. The lull in the fighting allowed him to join his unit in Japan. Though some of the Ring-Men unit was to return to South Korea, he would remain in Japan for at least two more weeks. He thought about *Quanyo. It's not like him to give up fighting. He loves it too much. He's up to something, but what?*

At 5 A.M., the phone rang. Guanton never answered the phone when he was working. A knock on the door preceded Ben Williams bursting into the room. "The Chinese just attacked the satellite station at Oğaki," he announced.

~~~~~~~~~

The Ring-Men unit, at quarter strength, assembled and prepared to move. The bulk of the armor, heli-jets, and helicopters were in Korea. Ten anti-gravity tanks were available, but Guanton chose not to use them for this assault.

All of the Ring-Men and three thousand soldiers of the division flew the two hundred miles to Gifu, the nearest airfield, and then traveled the final five miles by truck. The Japanese marshaled about ten thousand men from surrounding bases and established a perimeter around the station complex. All was quiet since the takeover three hours earlier.

When Ascon's company arrived, sentries ushered them to the front lines where Guanton waited. Ascon met Revel, and both reported to Guanton and awaited orders. Guanton was looking through his binoculars at the defenses. A faint hint of sunlight appeared as a morning mist evaporated from the still-moist ground.

"Looks like they are dug in pretty good," Guanton said as he paced, still looking through his glasses.

"Sir," Revel said, "Our anti-tanks could blast them right out of there." He wondered why the tanks were left behind.

Guanton ignored the remark and continued to look through his field glasses. Then he froze and focused on one spot. Guanton was in eye contact with one of the Chinese Ring-Men.

The soldier crouched and, after a few seconds, ran to the door of the station. Inside, he found his commander, Kotkye, and informed him that someone was trying to contact him.

"Who is it?" Kotkye asked.

"I don't know, sir; he just asked to talk to the officer in command," said the Ring-Man.

Kotkye followed him to his position. The Chinese Ring-Men were using the overturned trucks as barricades. Kotkye looked through his binoculars but could not see anyone in particular. Then he heard it.

You are in a hopeless position. Your forces should surrender.

There was something very familiar about that thought. He looked harder, trying to locate the source of the communication.

Over here!

Kotkye turned and focused on Guanton peering at him.

Guanton, I thought you were dead.

Kotkye, as I remember, you were always a better lover than a fighter.

I still prefer that, but Quanyo wants this station destroyed.

Quanyo! Why did you throw in your lot with that evil Ringnonian?

That's a good question, but it's a moot point now. I've got a nuclear device that will blow you and half of this island to bits.

That's a shame; there will be no more lovemaking for you ever again.

Kotkye put his glasses down and thought for a moment. He picked them up and looked at Guanton again. *Unless…*

Guanton paused and then turned to his officers. "They have a nuclear device. We must attack. Bring up the Powells."

Five huge Powell tanks appeared over the hilltop. The big engines roared as they halted in front of the station.

Kotkye ordered all of the Ring-Men and Chinese technicians outside of the station. Before they left, he demanded the handheld nuclear device.

"If they get through you, I will detonate the bomb myself." He bolted the door and was alone in the station.

The tanks moved forward and fired with pulverizing accuracy. The large pulse cannons on the Powells blew holes in the barrier and killed many of the Ring-Men. Armor-piercing Gatling guns killed many others. About one hundred Ring-Men, seeing their position indefensible, charged. But the Rangers of the Ring-Men division cut them down. All but seven died, and they were severely wounded.

Inside the station, Kotkye spoke to his commander by radio. "sir, they have surrounded us, but we are fighting well. I'm afraid the station must be destroyed."

"Very well," Quanyo said. "You will always be remembered as a good soldier."

Kotkye turned off the handheld radio. *That's not how I want to be remembered.*

~~~~~~~~~~~~~

"Sir, you need to get out of here. He'll certainly blow the station at any moment," Ascon said as he lowered his smoking pulse gun.

Guanton just smiled.

Chapter 15

Detonation

"The shock waves were felt as far as Tokyo. The blast killed ten thousand people and destroyed a ten-square-mile area, including the small cities of Ogaki and Gifu. The fallout of nuclear material is minimal because the device used was so small, and the prevailing winds carried it out to sea," observed the reporter. That was the broadcast on the Japanese and world news.

Non-nuclear high explosives made an enormous blast. Even the massive mushroom cloud that appeared over the bombsight was fabricated. The crater created by the explosion was centered between the cities of Ogaki and Gifu. The only damage to those cities was the many broken windows.

The people in both cities were evacuated, supposedly for their safety, and a twenty square mile perimeter was cordoned off and guarded by the military. Reporters received satellite photos of the blast site. The area became a no-fly zone, and no other photos were allowed except those given out to the press.

Guanton brainstormed this elaborate ruse, suggesting it almost immediately. An area close to the real station was selected as ground zero. High explosives, truckloads of camphor, and other smoke-making chemicals were combined. The mixture, once detonated, created an enormous explosion with a large smoke billow.

The real satellite complex was located against the side of a mountain, easily camouflaged to look as if an actual blast had destroyed it. The news report said nothing about the satellite station's destruction.

But, to Quanyo, that would make sense. What country would tell the world that it was again defenseless against air attacks?

Put on alert, the U.S. Navy was ready for action. The Japanese station suffered significant damage, but they were repairing it. The South Korean defense satellites could cover some of southern Japan, but northern Japan, including Tokyo, was vulnerable without the Japanese system operational. It was hoped that it would be ready for the anticipated attack.

Guanton wanted Quanyo to believe that the suicide mission succeeded, and he hoped for that attack. He told Ascon, "All we can do is wait to see if they take the bait."

~~~~~~~~~~

Quanyo looked at the satellite reports and felt a sense of joy. Kotkye was dead, and the Japanese satellite system was destroyed. His air force would now attack northern Japan and also strike at the U.S. Navy. Then, he could turn his full attention to Russia and crush it.

"Tongee, tell the generals I will meet with them in one hour to give them my orders." He thought of Kotkye. Just three of us left. That is until this war is over. He laughed as he got up from his desk.

Kotkye, far from dead, was having the time of his life. He decided to trade sides long before the mission took place. His real hope was to bargain with the Japanese once he controlled the station. But Guanton's appearance made the switch of sides even more appealing. Kotkye revered the older Ringnonian and regretted his decision to side with Quanyo. His only concern now was for his brother Wotkye.

He was awarded a cozy jail-like accommodation, complete with a lager ale tap and a swimming pool for trading sides. Four beautiful Japanese ladies volunteered to keep him company. Precautions were taken to prevent their pregnancy. The ladies received permission to leave the facility anytime to get Kotkye anything he requested.

Kotkye supplied Guanton, the Japanese, and the Americans with all the information they asked for about Quanyo and the Chinese.

He told them about troop placements, positions, and strengths. The only thing he would not talk about was his brother, Wotkye. So Guanton never pressed him on that.

One day, Guanton asked him, "Would you like to leave this planet with me when I go?"

Kotkye, who was lying down, sat up. "Where would we go?"

"We would go to the area where our planet was. We would search for any evidence of life or at least try to find out what happened," Guanton said as he paced the floor.

"I know there was the threat of the plague on Dalmate reaching Ringnon, but I can't figure out how the whole planet just vanished." Guanton sighed and walked the other way. "And that's what I have to know."

Kotkye laughed. "Well, I'm with you as long as we can bring a couple of women along."

"You and your women," Guanton said before he gulped down the last of the ale in his mug.

~~~~~~~~~~

"Remnants of the Chinese air force are spread over the Sea of Japan for miles," Tyler Orwell concluded his commentary. It was his first appearance since finding out about the death of his son. His eyes were red and puffy, but his voice was as strong as ever.

"Relying on the information that the Japanese satellite system was destroyed, the Chinese ordered over fifteen hundred aircraft to attack the U.S. fleet and the Japanese mainland.

"They thought we were sitting ducks to bomb out of existence. With the fleet destroyed, launching an invasion of Japan would then be open.

"But the U.S. fleet and the Japanese were waiting for the dastardly cowards, and so was the satellite system. The Chinese flew north into Russian air space and then south toward Japan. As the Chinese reached Japanese airspace, they were ambushed and massacred by our boys." Orwell choked but managed to hold back a sob before continuing.

"Japanese satellites destroyed about half of the aircraft. Realizing their danger, the rest of the attack force scattered and went north and south. Many veered into South Korean airspace and were likewise shot from the sky. The anti-aircraft batteries of the U.S. Navy and Japanese missiles took out the rest. About twelve hundred aircraft of various sorts were demolished. The Chinese air force is no longer a threat.

"Hopefully, we will soon rid ourselves of the other threat to world peace—the Ring-Men. This is Tyler Orwell, keeping you informed and aware of what is going on."

He left the broadcast in tears. His overwhelming grief, coupled with his enormous weight and unhealthy diet, proved to be fatal. He died from a heart attack two days later.

~~~~~~~~~~

Quanyo seethed. He stared straight ahead and tried to figure out what happened. *There's no way these humans can outmaneuver me. They're definitely getting help from someone?*

"Tongee," he said. "Get in touch with someone in our government who can get a diplomatic message to the Americans."

~~~~~~~~~~

General Watson flew to Japan to meet with Guanton. The Chinese sent messages indicating that they were interested in a truce. While unwilling to meet with Guanton, President Wiley nonetheless wanted the Ringnonian general's opinion. General Watson watched Guanton as he read the message.

Guanton turned to Watson. "Quanyo is trying to figure out who is responsible for his defeats. So far, he's underestimated us, considering humans inferior. His pride has always been one of his weaknesses."

General Watson got up from his seat and walked over to a screen that showed troop disposition. He pointed, "Right now, we have him bottled up to the north and the south. Maybe he's ready to count his losses and leave the table."

"Quanyo doesn't care about losses," Guanton said, "and he doesn't want peace. He's a warrior class Ringnonian. Even when he sleeps, he dreams of killing,"

Guanton stopped pacing and stared at the map.

"Quanyo is stalling for something. It says here that he wants to meet somewhere near the 38th parallel."

"Will you meet him as our representative?" Watson asked.

Guanton paused. "Yes," he said. A smile was on his face. "It may be time to talk with my old friend Quanyo again."

Chapter 16

The Meeting

Quanyo waited at the agreed site, the North Korean side of the 38th parallel, for the truce talks. Standing beneath a large tent erected to protect the attendees from the heat of the October sun, he was becoming impatient and angry.

"How dare they make me wait!" He was about to signal to Tongee that he was leaving when he saw the vehicles approaching. According to Ringnonian protocol, the side most desirous of peace was the earliest at any peace conference. Quanyo thought that he was arriving late and was elated when he saw what he thought were the American representatives. But then Major John Robinson told him that the negotiating team was delayed and would arrive shortly.

Guanton did many things to irritate Quanyo. Being late to the conference was one. He also traveled to the meeting in an anti-gravity vehicle and came in at its maximum elevation.

Showing Quanyo the quality of the technology he was facing and the pomp of his enemy being lowered to the ground would also annoy the waiting Ringnonian.

Each side agreed to bring an entourage of ten individuals. Quanyo selected Tongee, Wotkye, and eight other smartly attired Chinese Ring-Men. Among Guanton's selections were Robinson and two human captains of the Ring-Men Division. Dressed in their finest parade uniforms, they proudly wore the red berets of their unit.

As the vehicles lowered, Ascon and six Ring-Men stepped from the rear. They undraped two flags and moved toward the waiting party. Revel, the large black Ring-Man, carried the American battle flag, followed by the equally tall Therion displaying the unit flag.

A representation of a Ringnonian knife on the unit flag caught Quanyo's attention as it flapped in the morning breeze. Quanyo also noticed the same weapon at the sides of the American delegates. Then he saw the topknots worn by the Ring-Men.

Ascon led his team to the tent, and they fanned out into single file, facing Quanyo. Ascon then barked, "Parade, halt!" The team stopped on cue.

"Parade, atten-hut!" was the next command as the American unit stood at attention. Quanyo saw something familiar about the leader of the honor guard.

As Quanyo tried to recognize the face, someone he thought dead stepped into his view. Standing before him was Guanton, looking magnificent in a full-dress uniform.

The shock on the faces of Quanyo and Wotkye was evident as the Ringnonian stepped forward. Quanyo quickly regained his composure and acted cavalier about Guanton's sudden appearance. Wotkye, on the other hand, moved forward as if to hug his long-lost comrade. Quanyo shot him a glance, and he went back to his position.

"Guanton, it is good to see you," Quanyo said, acknowledging him with a partial bow of his head. Guanton always outranked Quanyo when they served together, and Quanyo still respected his rank.

"Quanyo," he said as he bowed back, but not quite as low.

"I would like to say it's good to see you if it were not for the circumstances."

Guanton then acknowledged Wotkye. "Hello, Wonta," he said looking at Wotkye. A Wonta was a student.

That familiar address brought tears to Wotkye's eyes. For a moment, Wotkye thought of all the lessons he and his brother learned from their teacher and guardian. Wotkye bowed low.

"Hello, my Qualla. It is good to see you." The term Qualla meant more than just teacher. It also meant wise counselor and mentor.

Quanyo, recognizing the respect that the title implied, said, "But you are no longer our teacher."

"You are right about that because I never taught you to kill and destroy without purpose," Guanton said, reacting to Quanyo's barb.

"But I do have a purpose." Quanyo motioned Guanton to the seats provided. Guanton took his seat and motioned to Ascon to take the position as his second. According to Ringnonian protocol, the trusted aide of the leader stood directly behind him. It was a position of honor.

Quanyo also took his seat and called for Tongee to take the place as his second.

Wotkye expected to be called forward for that privilege. Visibly upset, he asked to be excused. Quanyo was delighted that the big Ringnonian took offense and agreed to his request. Wotkye stormed away from the tent, hoping to get even for another insult.

"You requested this meeting, did you not?" Guanton said, getting down to business.

"This meeting would be further south if you were not helping your betrayers," Quanyo said. "What I want to know is why."

"Because we don't belong here," Guanton said. "I don't blame the humans for what they did. In a hundred years, our lusty shipmates would have bred the human race out of existence, and you know it."

"So, it was acceptable for them to kill us?" Quanyo asked sarcastically.

"No," Guanton said, "but we would have done the same thing. Don't you remember Dalmate?"

The Dalmaten society was dying. A strange plague ravaged the planet and killed thousands. The Dalmatens asked for help and then asylum. Ringnonian scientists were dispatched to Dalmate, but many of them also became sick and died. It was determined that the disease was incurable. The planet was quarantined, and no one was allowed to leave. Many left anyway, and most came to Ringnon. To protect the Ringnonian society, they were killed. Thousands more were executed when the Ringnonians invaded and then destroyed Dalmate.

"You make my point for me," Quanyo said. "We are a warrior breed. Let's take this planet by force and rule it as we want."

"No, you've missed my point. These humans did what they did to survive. It was wrong, but we were wrong on Dalmate. I won't let what happened on Dalmate happen here."

"You have always been too soft for a true Ringnonian. I told my sister that when she became your mate," Quanyo said.

"Yes, you're right about being too soft," Guanton said, remaining calm. "I should have let Ascon kill you instead of saving your life."

"I take it, then, that you will continue to help the humans?" Quanyo asked, already knowing the answer.

"Yes, unless you wish to surrender now and save me time," Guanton said.

"So then, there can be no peace?"

Guanton stood, signaling the end of the negotiations. "No, there will be peace, just not your kind of peace."

"That is too bad. What about you?" Quanyo asked, looking at Ascon. "You look more like me than these humans. They can't be trusted, and you should know that by now."

Ascon looked at Guanton as if he were asking if he could respond.

Guanton nodded approval.

"Humans killed my father. That's true. We could conquer them, which is also true. But there is good in some of them, and good must always be found and nurtured."

"You sound like another Ringnonian I once knew," Quanyo said.

"Ascon was his father," Guanton said proudly.

"I might have known." A half-smile crossed Quanyo's face. "Your father was a powerful Ringnonian, but he always thought like Guanton and sided with the weak. Obviously, you must think that way also?"

"My father trusted Guanton's judgment, and so do I."

Quanyo pointed to the knife at Ascon's side. "Are you as skilled with your mind and knife as your father was?"

"A master is teaching me to use both."

"One day, we will see," Quanyo said as he walked away.

~~~~~~~

As they left the meeting and headed back through the buffer zone, Ascon asked Guanton, "What do you think he will do?"

"He will continue to attack, even if it means the death of millions," Guanton said. "By the way, you spoke well. You would make your father proud."

About a mile from the meeting site, the anti-gravity vehicle stopped, and Kotkye came aboard. He handed a pair of telescopic binoculars to Guanton.

"Well, did you contact him?" Guanton asked. "Yes, and he's with us," said Kotkye, smiling.

Chapter 17

All Out

Before the meeting with Guanton, Quanyo alerted his reserve forces in China. He also called for Kitwan and his one thousand Ring-Men to join him in the south. It was now November, and with no resolution to the war in sight, he ordered the reserve troops south toward the 38th parallel. More than two million Chinese and seven thousand Ring-Men headed toward a showdown to crush the American forces and their allies.

The time for rest approached, so Quanyo wanted the Americans in the South destroyed as quickly as possible. "We will use our numerical superiority and overwhelm them," Quanyo told Tongee.

The American force numbered two hundred fifty thousand soldiers, the South Koreans added another sixty thousand, and the remaining North Korean Army numbered forty thousand men. The fifty thousand Japanese troops made the combined force about four hundred thousand men. The Americans and their allies were outnumbered five to one.

General Watson sat with Bill Welch, drinking coffee as they discussed the present dilemma.

"Bill, the other generals think we should abandon the 38th and move south about twenty miles," Watson said.

"What do you think, Danny?" Welch asked.

"Well, we'd be under the protection of our air power. On the other hand, it would mean either destroying the South Korean station or risking its capture by the Chinese."

"Leaving it for possible capture is out of the question," Welch said. "What does Guanton think?"

Watson paused. "Guanton thinks we should stay at the 38th. He assures me that we can defend the line."

Welch looked at Watson, who was staring into space. "You think a lot of Guanton, don't you, Danny?"

Watson turned toward Welch. "He's the most remarkable person I have ever met."

"Well, then, trust his judgment," Welch said.

The decision was made to fortify the line further and wait for the attack. Most of the buffer zone was mined with floating napalm and a host of other explosive devices. The pulse cannon firing Powell tanks and M-2 Abrams were strategically positioned to give their support. Three hundred attack helicopters and the remainder of the heli-jets were poised to defend the vulnerable points of the defensive line.

The problem was not if Quanyo would attack, but where? The troops needed to defend an area two and a half miles wide and one hundred and sixty miles long. With as many men as Quanyo commanded, he could mount targeted attacks along that line. Guanton decided to keep the Ring-Men mobile. In that way, they could move to help any area under severe attack or overrun.

Quanyo looked through his binoculars at his moving units from a hill overlooking the road. In the fading sunlight, he watched the columns of men and equipment; he smiled. He thought of Guanton. *I can't remember any defeats you've ever suffered; this will be your first.*

Wotkye and Kitwan stood behind him, along with the ever-present Tongee. They remained silent as Quanyo assessed his troops.

"Kitwan," he said without turning around. "I want you to take command of all the Ring-Men and keep them in reserve at a location that I will choose."

He turned and addressed Wotkye. "Your armor will lead. When you have blasted through their defenses, the Chinese will follow. They will probe and find the weakest spot. Then, the Ring-Men will rush and crush the enemy with the force of that charge.

"Once our hordes have engaged, they will spread south of the satellite system and continue about fifteen miles.

"Hopefully, you can take the station intact and hold it. Perhaps you are a better commander than your brother," Quanyo suggested sarcastically.

Wotkye seethed inside but refused to take the bait and show it outwardly. "I will do my best, Commander." He turned and walked to his vehicle, already knowing what he would do.

Quanyo, surprised by Wotkye's composure, thought. *Perhaps, with his brother dead, he will be easier to control.*

"We attack tonight," he decided as he handed his binoculars to Tongee.

~~~~~~~~~~~~

As Guanton's command vehicle moved across the front line, he got word that the 38th parallel was under attack.

Chinese heli-jets using pulse cannons blew a path through the mine-laden buffer zone. The efficient Japanese missiles destroyed some of the heli-jets but were being targeted and destroyed. Guanton decided to hold back his helicopters and heli-jets for the moment. He sent out his camera drones to reconnoiter.

"What do the satellites show, Jack?" Guanton asked. Almost immediately, Guanton's screen came alive with the positions of enemy troop movement. It looked like the entire Chinese army was attacking simultaneously. The center of the attack appeared to be at Ihyeon-ri.

"Ascon, get your units on the move," Guanton ordered.

"Yes, sir."

"General Nelson, I suggest you get our armor to section 2-A43 to prevent a breakthrough," said Guanton. "Hold the Apaches close to the rear, and we'll use the heli-jets to protect the station."

"That's affirmative," Nelson answered.

Where are Quanyo's Ring-Men? Guanton asked himself.

"You better look at screen four, sir," Walker warned. The drones showed thousands of Chinese charging across the buffer zone.

"Prepare to detonate the napalm," Guanton said.

The napalm mines were placed deep beneath the surface to prevent premature detonation by mine-clearing tactics.

Guanton ordered his forces to pull back slowly to simulate a retreat.

The buffer zone was loaded with waves of charging Chinese, many trying to climb the barriers and fortifications.

Guanton looked at his screen and turned to Jack Walker. "Are our troops in the safety zones?" Walker hesitated and then answered, "Yes, sir."

"Detonate the charges."

The ground in the buffer zone began to shake, and pressure from below pushed cone-like protrusions through the soil. Thousands of what looked like little volcanoes spewed a fiery liquid about ten feet into the air.

Many of the soldiers froze as they watched the molten gases catapult skyward. The mixture swirled and formed into fiery clouds.

Fear was in their eyes as some slowly retraced their steps. One by one, they retreated. The retreat soon turned to panic as the soldiers ran toward their side of the buffer zone.

The napalm then began its assault as if it fed on their fear. Fear, however, did not feed the flames; the carbon dioxide the men exhaled stoked the attack.

Like swarms of angry bees, the napalm swooped down on the running men. The fireballs engulfed them, one after another. Men shrieked and screamed as the jelly-like fire attached.

The napalm consumed in seconds, latched onto the next victim, and repeated the sequence.

Guanton watched as the Chinese ran through the buffer zone, making a complete withdrawal.

He purposely designed the mixture to delay midair to create panic. That effect caused the enemy to run toward their lines and minimized any chance of his men being attacked. It worked to perfection, but it saddened Guanton to see men die that way.

This war must end, he thought.

Quanyo could not believe his eyes. Thousands of his men ran toward him like human torches.

"What in the world? Give orders to open fire on our retreating soldiers immediately," he yelled to Tongee. "Kitwan, take your Ring-Men and start shooting down those men, or what they are running from will kill us."

Chinese pulse cannons and machine guns began tearing into their men. Chased by the napalm from their rear and being fired on from the front, the bodies started to mass, creating a wall of dead. The dead bodies blocked the retreat as thousands were overtaken by the fireballs and devoured.

The napalm eventually burned itself out, but in its wake, it left the charred, gruesome remains of over five hundred thousand Chinese soldiers.

"Guanton and his weapons," Quanyo cursed angrily as he pointed to Tongee. "Where are Wotkye and his armor? I've been trying to contact him, but there has been no answer. Send someone to find out where he is."

But Wotkye was gone. Giving orders to his second-in-command not to break radio silence, he moved his tank out of the advancing column, maneuvered it to the rear, and was not seen again.

Chapter 18

Hibernation

The Chinese were in full retreat. Quanyo looked over the reports and shook his head. The losses were staggering: five hundred and fifty thousand Chinese dead and another two hundred thousand wounded. Almost all the heli-jets and most of the armored units were destroyed. Included among the dead was Wotkye, his charred uniform found next to the remnants of his tank.

The British and Russians were attacking and advancing on the northern front and were very close to retaking the Russian satellite station. At the same time, North Korean and Japanese forces harassed the retreating Chinese as they headed back to China.

Quanyo thought about sending Kitwan and the Ring-Men to Russia again but changed his mind. He decided to keep them close in case there was trouble from within. After the defeat at the 38th parallel, the Chinese government made peace overtures toward the Americans and the United Nations.

Quanyo sent six thousand Ring-Men to Jinan, the location of the Chinese satellite station. He concluded that the Chinese would turn on him. But with the satellites under his control, no attack could succeed from the air.

He and his Ring-Men could handle any attack on the ground. He would rest at Mt. Tai, fifty miles east of the station and one hundred miles south of Beijing.

After his rest, he would march on Beijing and deal with the government.

One troubling problem was how to keep his soldiers awake and alert. Both the Ringnonians and the Ring-Men felt the need to sleep in early January. The days might fluctuate a day or two, but all would feel a desperate need to sleep by the second week. The Ring-Men's rest lasted about two weeks. The Ringnonian sleep lasted a full thirty days.

~~~~~~~~~~

Late in December, the Chinese sued for peace. The army was in disarray and deserted Quanyo completely.

Six thousand of Quanyo's loyal Ring-Men warriors surrounded the Chinese satellite station. Quanyo was dug in high on Mount Tai with seven hundred Ring-Men, but Quanyo and the Ring-Men were very tired.

~~~~~~~~~~

"The Chinese in the north are retreating to China after suffering defeat at the hands of the Russians and British," Tinsler said. "The Russian satellite station is back in Russian hands."

"Then the crisis is over, I assume," President Wiley said as he leaned back in his chair and puffed on a cigar.

"Not quite, sir. The Ring-Men are still a serious threat," Tinsler said.

"The British have withdrawn, but the Russians, ever eager to take advantage, have continued to attack. What's left of the Chinese army is defending against their onslaught.

"China is asking us and the United Nations for help to end the hostilities. They have also requested assistance getting rid of the Ring-Men," Tinsler said.

"Well, well, well, imagine China pleading for our help. If they listened twenty years ago, those freaks would all be dead."

"There's more, Mr. President," Tinsler said. "The Russians have offered to stop at their border. Their one condition is that all the Ring-Men in China must be eliminated. I believe the Russians have run out of steam, anyway.

"The North Koreans, having taken back most of their demolished country, are in no position to seek revenge. They are holding what's left of their army at their border. With their satellite defense system destroyed, they are seriously talking to the South Koreans about unification. North Korea is also seeking reparations from the Chinese, insisting on justice for the atrocities committed by Quanyo."

"It seems like we have all of our enemies exactly where we want them," Wiley said.

~~~~~~~~~~~~

General Watson arrived at the Oval Office for a meeting with President Wiley. Directed in by a secretary, he saluted the Commander in Chief as he signed papers. The president didn't return the salute but continued working on the papers before him.

Watson had never liked the president. He felt that he was two-faced and could not be trusted. He released the salute and stood waiting. Wiley looked up from his desk and gave Watson a cursory nod. He gathered all the papers and gave them to Ben Tinsler.

"Please leave us, Mr. Tinsler." Tinsler left the office.

"General, how are you?" Wiley asked as he invited Watson to have a seat.

"Very well, sir."

"I understand you have some objections to the plan," Wiley said as he lit a cigar.

"No, sir, it's not the plan. I know the Chinese Ring-Men are a problem that must be dealt with. We don't feel we can give the Chinese this kind of weapon to deal with it. It's not safe in their hands." Watson handed the president a report. "I've spoken to Guanton about the nano bomb; he feels it's much too dangerous to use right now."

"Guanton again!" shouted Wiley as he got up from his chair, waving his cigar-free hand in the air. "To hear you guys talk, this guy is as wise as Solomon. Listen, I want those freaks dead, and we will use anything we need to get the job done."

Watson left the president knowing what he wanted. It was not just the Chinese Ring-Men that Wiley wanted dead; it was all of the Ring-Men and Ringnonians on Earth, especially Guanton.

~~~~~~

What was left of the Chinese army tried to take back their satellite station. Attack after attack failed with the loss of thousands.

The six thousand Ring-Men under Kitwan's command did an excellent job of defending the station. The Ring-Men inside the station controlled the satellites so that no air attack could be launched.

The few remaining Chinese helicopters and heli-jets attacked but with little success. The biggest challenge the Ring-Men faced was staying awake.

Kitwan radioed Quanyo. "We are holding, but the Ring-Men are very tired." It was the 2nd of January, and he was so exhausted that he could barely think straight.

"Stagger the sleep of your troops. If you can hold out two weeks, we'll be fine," Quanyo said, almost pleading.

"We will try, Quanyo," Kitwan said.

Quanyo thought about Wotkye.

Wotkye's sleeping pattern was unusual. His rest typically started a week after the other Ringnonians, and he still woke up a day or two earlier. He was also a light sleeper, waking to any sudden noise or disturbance.

Too bad Wotkye is dead, he thought.

But Wotkye was not dead.

Wotkye was alerted to Kotkye's presence at the truce meeting. Angered by what he felt was a deliberate insult, he walked away from the tent. Hidden in the grass about a half mile away, Kotkye watched with high-powered field glasses, hoping to spot him. When Wotkye left the tent, he got his chance.

Wotkye, it's me, Kotkye. You are not dreaming, and I'm not dead.

Stay calm and don't show any reaction or try to locate me, just listen. As you already know, we have chosen the wrong side. We need to help Guanton to end this war. Go to the water coolers and have a drink. Under the second stack of cups, you will find a small radio transmitter and receiver.

Wotkye walked to the coolers that were set up earlier in the day. He took a drink and picked up a small receiver the size of a coin. Quickly palming the device, he put it in his pocket and returned to where he first heard Kotkye.

I will contact you tonight. If you agree to join us, remove your scarf and wipe the sweat from your brow.

Wotkye removed the scarf from his neck and wiped his perspiration.

Good, I will talk to you later, my brother.

The rescue occurred during the battle at the 38th parallel.

Leading the armored units, Wotkye ordered the bulk of his units to continue forward. He also requested radio silence. He pulled his platoon of tanks out of the advance column and moved them to a predetermined position.

Wotkye waited as the napalm did its damage. As the Chinese troops retreated, he ordered his remaining tanks to the rear. Pretending to stay behind to cover the retreat, he dismissed his five-man crew and signaled Kotkye.

Ten minutes later, as the napalm-laden field smoldered, three anti-gravity tanks and one anti-gravity vehicle honed in on that signal.

Wotkye took off his uniform shirt and left it half exposed in the tank hatch. The anti-gravity vehicle landed, and Wotkye greeted his brother, who grabbed his hand and pulled him in. The tanks pulverized the T-101 and were then piloted back to their lines.

Chapter 19

Nano Attack

Three American helicopters flew low as they approached the Chinese station from the west. The Chinese asked for the weapons to deal with the Ring-Men but were instead offered American military assistance. Rejected at first, the Chinese reconsidered after their fifth attack on the station failed.

U.S. forces assured the Chinese that the weapons used would destroy the Ring-Men but not damage the satellite station. They were also told that their troops should move back to a safe distance of three miles. The Chinese did not trust the Americans, however, and kept a division of soldiers, about sixteen thousand men in the trenches around the station.

The helicopters spread out in attack formation, five hundred feet from each other. Moving to firing range, they unleashed six nano rocket bombs. Two were aimed at the station, and the other four at the defensive lines of the Ring-Men.

Each bomb blast left a twenty-five-foot-high mushroom cloud. The six separate clouds became funnels, much like small tornadoes. Nano creatures began firing out of the funnels in all directions and attaching themselves to everything around.

The steel door to the satellite station was no challenge for the nanos. They ate through it and proceeded to devour everything and everyone inside. One by one, the Ring-Men were eaten alive by the hungry microscopic creatures.

Kitwan, asleep in his command tent, felt an intense pain in his leg. He turned his lamp on. Horrified, he watched his feet being eaten. There was no time to scream because, seconds later, the rest of his body was consumed.

The nanos, having devoured the Ring-Men, would have evaporated if the Chinese were further away. But they were too close, and soon the nanos attacked and ate them. In just one hour, they consumed everything in the valley. The nanos then disappeared.

From the air, the helicopter crews watched the nano attack in amazement. Captain Will Johnson described the spread of the nanos in his report: "Like milk clouding a cup of coffee."

When more Chinese troops arrived, they found nothing remaining. No wire, leather, steel, or plastic, not even the outside structure of the station. It was all gone, as though it never existed. The Chinese, suspicious and angry, protested again, but again, the protest fell upon deaf ears.

The U.S. military decided not to use the nanos again. Keeping the existence of the devastating weapon a secret would secure its possible use in the future. Instead, they used conventional air power to blast Quanyo and the remaining Ring-Men from their last stronghold.

Mount Tai's strong defenses were no match for an attack by the U.S. Air Force. On the 10th of January, the rest of the Chinese Ring-Men were bombed out of existence.

A five-hundred-man battalion of North Korean commandos, expert mountain climbers, were sent in to locate Quanyo.

Finding his isolated cabin in a quiet valley, they attacked in the early morning hours.

~~~~~~~~~

A blast blew the door apart as five North Koreans burst through firing machine guns. Tongee took wounds to the shoulder and abdomen as he reached for his pulse shotgun. Swinging the deadly weapon into action, he pumped blast after blast, sending the men reeling backward. He kept firing until his weapon was empty.

Explosions rocked the cabin, knocking him to the floor.

Quanyo, in the other room, tried to wake himself from his sleepy stupor when he heard Tongee yell, "Master, behind you!"

Having blown a hole in the wall, two Koreans entered and aimed their weapons. Quanyo readied his flamethrower and fired into the opening. The Koreans, engulfed in flames, died screaming. Another blast took out a section of wall, sending Quanyo to the ground.

Tongee swung a table leg at the soldiers coming through the opening. "Get out, Master!" he yelled as he clubbed a soldier.

Quanyo threw his pulse cannon to Tongee and grabbed his sword with his free hand. They fought back-to-back, firing at any target that entered. Grenades thrown through the openings exploded and blew both giants off their feet.

Tongee was severely wounded and bleeding profusely. Quanyo leaned over the dying Ring-Man. "I could not have picked anyone better to watch my back."

Tongee smiled as he choked on blood. "Thank you, Quanyo," he said before he died.

A fire raged through the cabin, making it hard to see the doorway. Grabbing his sword, Quanyo jumped through the opening, fully expecting to die. The cabin exploded behind him as he cleared the doorway. Wounded and bleeding, he fell to the ground, unconscious.

Quanyo was bound, dragged, and airlifted back to North Korea.

He was spirited to a secret holding chamber.

The Chinese government protested again. They felt that Quanyo should be tried for the crimes he committed in China.

China also officially declared that Quanyo and the Ring-Men forced them to go to war in the first place. Like the other protests, that one also went unanswered. The Chinese then started an eradication program. They executed all the young Ring-Men and all the mothers who were pregnant.

That ended the era of the Ring-Men in China.

~~~~~~~~~~

The American Ring-Men fared much better. The entire unit was sent back to Japan and welcomed as heroes. Of the forty-five Ring-Men in the unit, all survived.

Many employment opportunities opened up for returning warriors in Japan and worldwide. None of them wanted to return to the United States.

Ascon knew what he was going to do. He was going to live with his lovely Arika.

She waited patiently for him as the transport carrying his unit flew from Korea. When he saw her, his heart almost stopped. She ran to him. He lifted her into his arms and gently kissed her. When he put her down, she put her tiny lovely hand into his and led him home.

Guanton flew home earlier with Wotkye and Kotkye. They worked earnestly on the drilling equipment necessary to mine the crystals to power the ship that would take them away from Earth.

There were, however, elements in the U.S. government that wanted a different fate for the Ringnonians and the Ring-Men.

Chapter 20

Betrayal

Watson met with Bill Welch soon after the hostilities ended. "The president wants the Ring-Men unit disbanded and the Ring-Men sent back here," Welch told Watson.

"Bill, you know what the president wants with the Ring-Men. How can we do that to those soldiers?" Watson asked.

"Well, he has to find them first, right?" Welch asked, looking directly at Watson.

"I understand," Watson said.

~~~~~~

President Wiley was incensed. *How dare the Ring-Men refuse the direct order to return?*

"Ben, where is Watson?" Wiley asked.

"He should be here at any moment, sir. The traffic coming from the Pentagon is very heavy," Tinsler said.

Since the end of the war six months ago, Guanton had resigned from his commission and was working with the Ringnonian brothers on a special project in India. The forty-five Ring-Men stationed in Japan refused to return to the United States. The officers among them also threatened to resign if forced to go back.

A call on his intercom alerted the president to Watson's arrival.

The secretary showed in General Watson.

He saluted and got no return. *This little non-military jerk.*

"Watson, why is the Ring-Men unit still in Japan instead of here as they were ordered?" Wiley asked.

"Most of the unit has returned, Mr. President," Watson said, pretending not to know what Wiley was talking about.

"I mean the big ones, the forty-five freaks," said Wiley excitedly.

"Oh, you mean the forty-five non-coms and officers who fought for this country at the 38th parallel," Watson said.

"Don't get smart with me, General," Wiley sneered.

"I'm not sir. I'm simply relating the facts."

"Well, here is a fact," Wiley said, trying not to show emotion. "I want those things here in the U.S. in one week. Is that clear?"

"I will do my best, sir, but remember, fifteen are officers, and they can resign. Nine are sick in a hospital in Tokyo. The rest are with Guanton on an expedition in India and Nepal."

"Who gave them permission for that?" Wiley asked.

"I believe it was requested and approved through channels weeks ago. They are somewhere in the mountains, and we're unable to contact them," said Watson, laughing to himself.

Watson tried to protect the Ring-Men when he heard rumors of the president's treachery.

First, he pushed through promotions for fifteen of them so that they could resign if forced to go. Then, he ordered twenty to join Guanton on his expedition to look for his crystals. The nine who were sick were purposely given fever-inducing drugs so that they could be hospitalized.

As Watson left, he knew his stall tactics would not last long. Wiley's intentions were clear. The president wanted to follow through on his father's original plan to eliminate the Ring-Men.

~~~~~~~~~~~~~

Guanton found what he was looking for, a mother lode of crystals located deep in the mountains of Nepal.

The drill he invented bore through the rock mass, and the cache was enough to power twenty ships into space. The Ring-Men and the Ringnonian brothers, Wotkye and Kotkye, could mine in days what would have taken months for men of smaller dimensions.

Five trucks loaded with crystals headed down the mountain on the treacherous road leading to base camp. One lane and unpaved, the road wound around the mountain at a steep angle. As the trucks moved slowly downhill, single file, a rocket tore into the first one.

The truck exploded and plummeted down the rocky mountain cliff, killing the Ring-Men driver and passenger. Another rocket exploded near the second truck, killing a Ring-Man who got out.

Pulse cannon fire opened up to the rear of the column, and the last truck in the column exploded, killing five Ring-Men in the process. Therion came from the last truck wounded in the shoulder.

"About a hundred men are coming down the hill behind us," he warned.

The third truck carried the weapons. The remaining Ring-Men and the Ringnonians scrambled to get at them.

Another rocket hit beyond that truck, and the explosion rocked the ground. Guanton grabbed a pulse cannon, aimed at the rocks above the road where the men charged, and fired three blasts. The mountain rocked, and an avalanche of rocks and boulders crashed down on the attacking soldiers.

But there were still about one hundred soldiers in front of the convoy. Guanton could not cause a rock slide there because it would wipe out the road and prevent their escape.

That is when Therion, the wounded Ring-Man, took charge. He charged down the road with a pulse cannon in each hand, blasting away. Two other Ring-Men, Revel and Kilton, followed him down the winding mountain road, firing.

The speed and accuracy of the attack were so effective that the enemy company was soon eliminated. But the cost was high. Kilton was dead, with two holes in his chest and his right arm severed.

Therion was barely alive when the trucks reached him.

You are a true Ringnonian," Guanton said as he held his hand.

Therion looked up at Guanton, smiled, and died.

Revel, severely wounded, was loaded onto one of the two remaining trucks. Before leaving, Guanton examined one of the bodies of the attackers. There was no dog tag or identification, but he looked American. Guanton jumped onto one of the trucks as they returned to base camp.

~~~~~~~~~~

Ascon was with Arika when he got a call. She was asleep in his arms, and he tried to pick up the phone without waking her.

On the other end, someone said, "Get out of there. They are coming to kill you." Then the phone went dead.

"Hello, hello," Ascon said as he tried deciphering the message. He got up from the bed, and Arika woke up.

"Who was that?" she asked in a sleepy voice.

"No one. Go back to sleep," he said as he slipped on his pants.

Arika lived on the top floor of a five-story building with a walk-out balcony. He walked onto the balcony and looked over the rail. Two American military trucks pulled up and began unloading two squads of soldiers. They were armed with pulse rifles.

Ascon went back in immediately and grabbed his pulse pistol and knife. Arika was dressed and met him as he came through the balcony door.

"What's wrong?"

"Soldiers are coming to kill me."

He went to the front door as if to defend it.

Arika calmly grabbed his hand and said, "Come with me. There is a back staircase."

She opened a rear closet door that hid a back stairwell. As they closed the closet door, they heard the blast of a pulse gun shatter the front door. Going quietly down the stairs, they quickly reached the ground floor. The back stairwell led to an alleyway entrance that was rarely used. Ascon opened the door slowly. He listened very carefully and heard someone cough. Looking into the dark alley, he focused on two shapes holding guns. Ascon closed the door and turned to Arika. He held her in his arms. He did not want her hurt, no matter what happened to him.

The building janitor, Mr. Amorou, opened the door to his apartment and came out. He beckoned them to follow him, and he led them to the boiler room of the apartment building. A smaller, more efficient unit had recently replaced the large old boiler in the building. But the older unit had not been removed. It was empty and large enough to hide both Arika and Ascon.

With a finger to his mouth, he motioned them inside and signaled them to remain quiet. He returned to his apartment, but before entering it, he pushed the rear door open as hard as possible. As he went inside, soldiers came down the stairs. The two stationed outside also hurried to the rear door.

"Did he come out this way?"

"I don't think so."

"You know, they are very quick."

"Not that fast," said an officer. "Search the building."

Ascon held Arika tightly with one arm and gripped his pistol with the other. Perspiration poured from his face as they waited in the hot boiler. The soldiers searched the building.

He heard them as they entered the boiler room. A small crack in the boiler allowed light from a flashlight to filter against the inner wall. Ascon prepared to fire as he drew Arika closer.

"There's nothing here, he must have gotten away," said the officer as they left.

Ascon stayed frozen in the boiler until the old janitor came to open the door. He told them that the soldiers were gone. Arika hugged the old man, who smiled and blushed. He gave Ascon the keys to his truck that was parked just outside.

He also gave him a slip of paper with an address. "Go there. You will be safe there."

"Thank you, Father," Arika said.

"That is the least I can do for my daughter," he said as he wiped a tear from his eye. "Now go."

They opened the rear door slowly, rushed to the old truck, and got in. A few seconds later, they drove away into the night.

Chapter 21

Aftermath

The base camp—destroyed; the cabins, the lab and the supply huts—all demolished. Two Ring-Men lay dead, but there was no sign of the enemy.

Guanton approached the lab cautiously. He saw Ben Williams lying face down on the floor. Guanton rushed to his friend, turned him over, and cradled him in his arms. Life barely flickered in him.

"Willie, what happened?" he asked, wiping blood from his face.

"Guanton," Williams whispered. "They were after you." He coughed and choked on blood but continued, "They were American." He squeezed Guanton's hand and died.

Guanton carried him to one of the trucks. Tears welled in his eyes as he put him down gently. "Rest, my dear friend," he whispered.

Kotkye ran toward Guanton. "The ship is okay; it appears that they could not find her. But they destroyed just about everything else."

Guanton and his team transported sections of the spacecraft from Japan to India. Cutting a hangar into the mountains, they assembled the ship. With the crystals needed for powering the anti-gravity craft secured, testing on the ship could have begun in a few weeks. Now, they would have to test her on the run.

"How soon can the crystals be ready for charging?" Guanton asked Kotkye.

"I can have them ready in twelve hours."

"Good. Then we will test the ship tonight, but first, I need to find out what's going on."

"Wotkye," Guanton said.

"Yes, my Qualla?"

"Help me bury our friends." Guanton lifted the body of Ben Williams.

~~~~~~~~

Ascon hid on Arika's uncle's farm near Saitama outside of Tokyo. They would be safe there for the time being. Arika purchased a non-traceable phone, and Ascon tried to contact Major John Robinson back in the States. Robinson, now working at the Pentagon, could not be reached initially.

Ascon would not leave a return phone number, just a message saying that Eagle Two would call at 3 P.M. Washington time. Robinson would know who was calling.

Ascon called at the specific time and was put on hold. About thirty seconds later, a familiar voice came on the line.

"Major Robinson here."

"This is Eagle Two, Major Robinson."

"Yes, Eagle Two, those reports were sent on July 3rd to 723 Wilber Avenue, room 1421." Robinson hung up.

Ascon waited two minutes and then called 703-723-1421, Robinson's secure cell number. Robinson answered on the second ring.

"Ascon."

"John, what's going on?"

"Where are you?" Robinson asked. "Are you alright?"

"Yes, I'm fine. I'm outside Tokyo. Why are they trying to kill me?"

"I can't tell you everything now, but stay out of Tokyo. They have already killed all the Ring-Men in the hospital. They said it was a virus.

"Listen, I tried to warn you as quickly as possible, but I only found out the night of the operation. I sure am glad you got out."

"Where's Guanton?" Ascon asked.

"Nobody knows. The last time we contacted him, he was in Nepal or India doing some drilling. They found his camp destroyed, but there were no signs of him or the Ring-Men with him.

"I'm headed to Tokyo. I'll be there in a day or two. Lay low and be safe, and call me in two days."

Robinson hung up. He paused and turned to the man seated in his office.

"He's somewhere outside of Tokyo."

"Why did you call to warn him?" Tinsler asked.

"You want Guanton, don't you? Guanton will try to contact Ascon, and then we will get them all."

~~~~~~

The American satellite defense system controller noticed something strange on his screen. Turning to his commander, he reported, "sir, something is wrong. Two of our satellites have disappeared."

The officer, Major Michael Johns, looked at the screen. "Get Command on the line."

~~~~~~

Guanton moved the location of his base camp miles from the previous one. There, hidden in a cave, was the vessel that Guanton named the *Winyee*.

The craft, circular with a circumference of two hundred feet, could comfortably hold a crew of twenty-five. The stealth technology made it practically invisible to radar or any tracking device.

Propelled by anti-gravity, it could negotiate into space without fear of satellite attack. Having the same capabilities as the heli-jets, it could hover or fly as fast as any jet on Earth. The hyperdrive propulsion, when engaged, allowed it to fly faster than the speed of light when in space. The complex navigation system could chart a course to all the known galaxies.

The communication system masked transmissions, allowing Guanton to talk with anyone on Earth without being traced.

The vessel was armed with two machine gun lasers, two pulse blasters, and a Gitan-Ray.

The Gitan, named after its Ringnonian inventor, was a powerful weapon with the ability to discharge in any environment or atmosphere. Storing energy from the sun, the Gitan could fire multiple times and dissolve matter. The Gitan could also remove or displace earth, rock, or any other material in seconds. This powerful instrument cut the cave, serving as a hangar, from solid rock.

The first test mission proved successful. Flying undetected into space, the *Winyee* destroyed two American satellites and returned to base.

~~~~~~~~~~

Guanton called the Pentagon and asked for General Watson. The operator connected him to the office of the Chairman of the Joint Chiefs of Staff. When asked who he was, he simply stated, "Guanton."

A brief pause was followed by the deep voice of the General, "Watson here."

"Well, General, surprised to hear my voice, or were you just following orders again?" Guanton asked.

"No," said Watson. "Not surprised, but I am delighted to hear it.

I assure you, Guanton, I knew nothing about the attack."

"Be that as it may, we are now prepared to leave this treacherous planet. We want all the Ring-Men who are still alive to leave with us. Are any of them still alive?" Guanton asked.

"I'm not sure, but I will find out," Watson said. "Guanton, I had nothing to do with it. I hope you believe me."

Guanton paused. "You are a good man, General, but your leader, like his father before him, lacks honor. Let him know that if the rest of the Ring-Men are not delivered to me, we will destroy the remainder of your satellites as we leave. You should be missing two about now."

"I understand," said Watson.

"One more thing," Guanton said. "If they are alive, I want them taken to an area where I can see them on a local Japanese television station."

Watson hung up and called Bill Welch. He waited until he was announced.

When Welch picked up, Watson said, "Bill, I just had an interesting call."

Chapter 22

Escape

Bill Welch met with the president in the Oval Office.

"We simply have no choice. To lose the defense satellites because you have a personal vendetta is ridiculous."

"Must I remind you who you are talking to, Welch?" Wiley asked.

"I know who I am talking to, Mr. President. The person who, because of his vindictiveness, will leave this country defenseless," Welch said, not backing down.

~~~~~~~~~~~~~~~~

Welch received permission to deliver the remaining Ring-Men to Guanton. There were only four still alive in Japan. Three were held in Tokyo, and there was Ascon, still in hiding. John Robinson flew to Tokyo to try to meet with him.

The Japanese people were in an uproar, protesting the actions of the Americans and the violence committed against the Ring-Men. But the

Japanese government was secretly sympathetic to the Americans. They, too, wanted to be rid of the Ring-Men.

Ascon called Robinson and informed him of his location. He convinced Arika to stay on the farm. Before leaving, he held her in his arms, kissed her gently, and said, "I will be back for you."

Robinson led a convoy of three trucks to the farm. Ascon, seeing soldiers, thought he'd been betrayed until he saw the reassuring smile on Robinson's face. He climbed into the second truck and saw the familiar faces of three Ring-Men.

"Where are we going?" Witloon asked.

"Is this all of us?" Ascon said.

"Yes, the rest were killed."

"All of them dead and that rotten Quanyo still alive in North Korea," said Cravarn.

"Where did you hear that?" Ascon asked.

"Remember, I was assigned to intelligence before they tried to kill us," Cravarn said.

They were taken to a large hangar set up as a studio. Two television cameras watched their every move. The four Ring-Men stood before the cameras and waited. The camera feed was then broadcast on a local station.

Guanton watched the station on the *Winyee* and was elated to see Ascon among the survivors. He focused on Ascon.

A smile crossed Ascon's face.

~~~~~~~~~

Guanton contacted Watson again and gave him the coordinates for the delivery of the Ring-Men. They were flown by helicopter outside the city of Hitachi, and then transported by truck to the designated area. The *Winyee* was already there.

Flying her to Japan the night before the pickup, Guanton used the Gitan-Ray to cut out a section of earth in the pattern of the *Winyee*.

When the ship landed, it was buried in the ground. Later, rocks and shrubs were added to make the camouflage complete.

The area selected for the landing was a large open pasture with a marsh to the right and trees behind it. Guanton knew the rescue was going to be very risky. He was not concerned about attack from the satellite system, but he was apprehensive about the heli-jets. The maneuverability of the heli-jets could pose a threat to the *Winyee's* escape.

The truck carrying the Ring-Men stopped, and the four jumped off the rear. Ascon shook hands with Robinson, and the truck rolled away.

A drone hidden in the trees focused on Ascon.

Guanton looked at the screen on the *Winyee's* monitor. *Ascon...turn to your left and start walking toward the trees.* The four Ring-Men began walking. *Now just a little to your left...good...now straight ahead.*

They were directed to the *Winyee*, and with the top hatch open, they came aboard.

It looked like the ground swallowed the Ring-Men to Major Robinson and the other observers.

"What happened?" Robinson asked. "Where are they? Close in now."

"I think they escaped into the marsh," said a voice from his radio.

Spotlights and headlights lit up the area. Heli-jets appeared over the scene, searching with their lights. Men came from the tree line, scouring the ground in front of them. Robinson was furious, "Don't tell me they just disappeared!"

They hadn't disappeared. Robinson and many of the soldiers were standing on the *Winyee*. Robinson ordered a search of the whole area, particularly the marsh and the trees. Guanton's little camera allowed him to observe and hear everything going on. In the ship beneath the surface, he and his crew waited.

"I need to get Arika," Ascon said.

"We can't take her with us," Guanton said.

"Guanton, I love her. You know what that's like. If she can't come... then neither can I."

Guanton thought of his own lovely Winyee. He was about to travel millions of miles hoping to find her.

"Where is she?" he asked.

"Can I bring someone along that I love?" Kotkye asked.

"You've never loved anybody in your life," Wotkye said as they all laughed.

Guanton waited two hours. The drone showed all the heli-jets and soldiers clear of the area. The anti-gravity engine engaged and the *Winyee* floated quietly into the night sky.

The farm was easy to find, and Arika did not hesitate about leaving with Ascon. When he asked her to come, she simply replied, "I will go with you anywhere."

As the *Winyee* prepared to leave the atmosphere, another complication arose. Cravarn told Wotkye about Quanyo's imprisonment in North Korea.

"It could not have happened to a nicer person," Wotkye said.

The crew became silent. The thought of one of their own jailed and tortured saddened them. "Do you know where he is?" Kotkye asked.

"The last information we received confirmed that he was on the army base at Pyonggan-up," said Cravarn.

Guanton looked around at the faces of the crew. "I take it that you want to bring him along, too?"

"He is Winyee's brother," Kotkye said.

"Don't remind me," Guanton said as he steered the ship toward North Korea.

~~~~~~~~~~

Pyonggan-up was not the fortified base it once was. The base was severely damaged when the Chinese moved south through the region, with very few repairs made in the interim. Guanton deployed two drones to assess troop strength and locate the prison.

There were two possibilities. One was a two-story brick building guarded by a squad of soldiers. The other was a one-story building surrounded by barbed wire. Air vents extended from the back of that building, indicating an underground chamber.

"That looks like a jail," Guanton said as he motioned to the screen. "What's the plan?" Ascon asked.

~~~~~~~~~~

The *Winyee* landed in front of the jail and unloaded Ascon and ten Ring-Men armed with pulse cannons and their knives. It was dark and hushed. Guanton floated the *Winyee* silently over the jail and used the Gitan-Ray to remove the front wall. Ascon and six Ring-Men went into the prison while four stood guard.

The light from the gun attracted the sentries, and they opened fire. The four Ring-Men returned fire, killing the sentries as they set up a defensive perimeter outside the jail.

A squad of North Koreans moved toward the Ring-Men, shooting as they came. Slawoo intercepted them, taking fire to his armor before he shot five soldiers. A grenade knocked him to the ground. Wotkye fired a laser machine gun from the *Winyee* and killed the rest of the Korean squad.

As they moved him to safety, Wajee and Dunwol came to Slawoo's aid.

Ascon's team shot two guards at the front desk and moved down the corridor toward the dungeon. The steel doors blocking their way were blasted.

The hallway led to a giant holding pen. There, chained to a wall, beaten and naked, was Quanyo. His head was shaved, and he was bleeding. The cell smelled of urine and feces.

A North Korean officer burst through the door, firing. Cravarn unsheathed his knife and cut off the soldier's head.

Ascon blew the chains loose. He radioed Guanton, "We have found Quanyo."

Guanton zeroed in on the signal and used the Gitan-Ray to remove the ceiling. The *Winyee* descended, almost landing on the building. Wotkye opened the bottom hatch, lowered a ladder, and jumped down from the ship to help with the loading. The team loaded Quanyo as they boarded the *Winyee*.

A tank advancing up the road fired on the ship. Kotkye turned the guns on the *Winyee* loose and blew it apart.

The *Winyee* moved to the front of the building. Slawoo was dragged aboard, followed by the remaining Ring-Men.

The *Winyee* then accelerated into the air.

Quanyo and Slawoo were moved to sickbay, joining Revel.

Arika helped clean and bandage Quanyo's wounds. As she wiped blood from his forehead, his eyes suddenly opened. He looked up at Arika.

"Who are you?"

"I am Arika, and you are safely aboard a ship taking you home."

Quanyo smiled at her, "You are a beautiful sight to awaken to." Then he fell asleep, the result of a sedative.

Ascon took note of the remark and looked at the wounded Quanyo jealously.

Guanton asked, "Is there anyone else we have forgotten?" Everyone laughed.

"Then let's go home."

The *Winyee* slid silently into space with its cargo of four Ringnonians, twelve Ring-Men, and one human.

The Ringnonian

Saga

Book Two

Return to Ringnon

Chapter One

In Space

Wotkye stared at the instrument panel as he sipped hot molaka from a large mug. He put the mug down as he ran his hands through his hair, trying to clear his head. A wave of energy coursed through his body. Molaka, a staple on all Ringnonian war vessels, was ale made from fermented honey. The brew helped to counteract the malaise that occurred after deep space sleep. The effect was immediate.

Kotkye, you are a master brewer.

Looking at the gauges, Wotkye computed the *Winyee's* location and distance of travel. The ship, having slowed, was no longer in hyper-drive.

Now what? He asked himself as he picked up the mug and swallowed more of the strong elixir.

He thought about all that had occurred over the last ten sections. Fifty years was a long time to be away from home. Then he remembered that his home was gone. So was most of his family.

His father, Wotvan, was killed in the war with the Wannee years ago, while his mother and sisters were victims of a merciless disease.

Kotkye was all that remained of his family. Guanton had stepped in and filled the void of guardian, insisting on taking them aboard each vessel he served. This ship was the fifth.

He took another gulp and smiled as he thought of his fun-loving brother. Two things were clear. One—Kotkye was the best engineer in the Ringnonian fleet. Second, he was the greatest distiller in the universe. Of course, he could never tell his brother or give him credit for either fact. Nor would he tell him of the sorrow he felt when he thought that Kotkye was dead.

A noise caught his attention, and he turned to see Guanton stumbling toward the bridge.

"Are you alright, my Qualla?" Wotkye asked as he helped his commander into the co-pilot seat.

Guanton nodded as he motioned for a sip of Wotkye's ale. Guanton took a deep gulp, wiped his mouth, and shook his head,

"Molaka?"

"Yes," Wotkye answered. "Kotkye brewed it before we went to sleep."

Guanton looked at the mug in disbelief.

"It brings back memories of home."

"Yes, it does."

"Did you rest well, Wotkye?" Guanton asked.

"As well as I expected, my Qualla. Hyperdrive makes my head ache."

"How is the ship handling?" Guanton asked as he tried to hand the mug to Wotkye.

"Like a Ringnon cloud," Wotkye said, refusing the mug. "You could not have designed her better. The only problem I can see is a slight leak in the air compressor of the life support system."

"Is that what took us out of hyperdrive?"

"Yes, I think so. Kotkye might be able to do something about it."

"Have you estimated the distance to our system?" Guanton asked as he looked at the gauges.

"About another two weeks of hyperdrive if my calculations are correct."

"Go wake up, Kotkye," Guanton said. "I want that leak repaired. We may have to set down someplace. Where are we?"

"We are close to the Nebula system. Do you remember the last time we were there?" Wotkye asked as he left the bridge.

Guanton didn't answer. He sipped the ale as he ran his fingers through his hair and thought about his home.

~~~~~~~

Arika was awake and milling about sickbay looking after her patients. She tried to convince herself that she was equally concerned about them, but her attention kept focusing on Quanyo.

"The *Winyee* is not designed for female passengers," Guanton explained soon after they left Earth.

"I know Ascon is in love with you, but I must ask you to refrain from any displays of affection while we return to Ringnon. Females are never allowed on Ringnon war vessels, and I am asking you to sleep here in sickbay and help our wounded. I hope you understand. I will also talk to Ascon."

Arika agreed. She kept her contact with Ascon to long stares and the occasional touch of his hand. Two weeks into the journey, the *Winyee* accelerated into hyperdrive, and the entire crew went to sleep, making the separation easier. But now awake, she longed for Ascon's touch.

"But why am I thinking about Quanyo?" she asked herself as she looked at the sleeping giant.

~~~~~~~

Kotkye approached Guanton on the bridge with a disturbed look. "What's wrong?"

"The air compressor is leaking and must be repaired immediately. We must land somewhere. If we go into hyper-drive as it is now, the pressure on the hull will cause it to rupture, and our life support will fail."

"The nearest planet is Nebula," Guanton shared as he walked toward the charting computer.

Wotkye shook his head. "Nebula is a dangerous place to do anything, let alone repair a ship."

"We have no choice," Guanton stated, looking at the charts. "The next system is light years away. We have no chance of reaching it without the hyperdrive."

"One more thing," Kotkye uttered as he wiped his hands on a towel. "The magnetic crystals are breaking down faster than I anticipated. We will need more crystals to complete our journey."

"Why is that?" Wotkye asked.

"First, the Earth crystals are not as hearty as our Ringnon variety. Second, we lost half the load when we were ambushed, if you remember. And third, we did not have as much time as I would have liked to charge the crystals due to our hurried exit. Does that answer your question, Wotkye, my brother?"

Wotkye knew any question that challenged Kotkye's expertise would irritate his younger brother. He smiled as he noticed Kotkye's annoyance.

"Nebula has no mountains," Guanton said to the two brothers. "We must search elsewhere to find the crystals to get home. Wotkye, go assemble the crew so that we can discuss our options."

~~~~~~~~~

"How do you feel?" Ascon questioned Revel. While he cared for his friend, his real reason for visiting the sickbay was to see Arika.

Revel noticed Ascon's attention diverted. "I feel better than I did before I went to sleep. That is, of course, if you are genuinely concerned."

"I am, my friend," Ascon assured him, smiling.

He kept his eyes on Arika as she re-dressed the bandage on Slawoo's arm. Ascon spoke to her as he entered sickbay and received a smile and greeting in return. But he was disappointed, especially after the long separation of hyper-sleep. Despite Guanton's order, he felt that a warmer reaction was warranted. *Does she still love me?*

Ringnonian and Ring-Men possessed tremendous recuperative power. Revel's severe wounds were almost completely healed. His leg still ached, so Ascon gave him a hand, and Revel stood for the first time in months.

Slawoo thanked Arika as he began stretching exercises. Quanyo showered, singing a Ringnonian war song.

"I would feel even better if I could silence that terrible noise coming from over there," Revel said, pointing to the shower.

Quanyo emerged, a towel covering his lower torso. He looked fit except for the striped scars on his chest, the obvious result of the beatings he received at the hands of the North Koreans.

"I see we have visitors," he said, his booming voice filling the room. His hair had grown back. Still wet, it hung to his shoulders as he dried his chest. "Come to see me, young Ascon."

The word "young" attached to his name angered Ascon. The thought of Arika in close contact with Quanyo infuriated him.

Ascon stepped forward, but Revel grabbed his arm. "Help me to the shower, Ascon."

Arika tried to avert her eyes from the half-naked Quanyo, but she found herself staring at the Ringnonian.

Quanyo saw Ascon's reaction and laughed. "Arika, can you help me dress?"

"You are healthy enough to do that for yourself," Arika said calmly as she left sickbay.

Ascon started to reply to Quanyo, but he was interrupted by Wotkye as he entered.

"Guanton wants to see the entire crew on the bridge."

"Well, look who's here," Quanyo said. "Traitors abound on this ship."

"Be careful, Quanyo, you don't have your bodyguard with you," Wotkye warned.

"I don't need one," Quanyo said, stepping toward Wotkye.

Wotkye moved to square off, but the sickbay door slid open.

"What's going on here?" Guanton asked as he walked to the center of the room. "Wotkye, go and round up the rest of the crew. Ascon, you and Slawoo help Revel to the bridge."

The door closed behind them as they left.

Quanyo began dressing with his back turned to Guanton.

"Quanyo, we need to talk," Guanton said, pacing.

"Before you call anyone a traitor, you should know that it was the decision of the entire crew, including Wotkye and Kotkye, to save your life. You owe a life debt to everyone on board."

A life debt was a serious obligation in Ringnon culture. It meant that Quanyo was beholden to the entire crew.

Quanyo's jaw tightened, but he remained silent. "Turn and face me!" Guanton ordered. Quanyo turned and looked at Guanton. He could see the anger in his eyes.

"You also disobeyed a standing order by going to China. Even now, according to our law, you could be severely sanctioned or put to death. Wotkye and Kotkye showed remorse for their error. I have not seen any from you. I don't want to hear the word traitor again, or I will apply it to you. Is that understood?"

Quanyo nodded in agreement.

"Say it!"

"I understand, my Qualla," Quanyo replied humbly.

Guanton's tone softened. "Quanyo, we need your experience and courage to make it home and find our people. This is a young crew, and we will face many challenges, the first of which is landing on Nebula."

"Nebula," Quanyo said.

"Yes, and you know the dangers waiting for us there."

"I will do my best, my Qualla," Quanyo said.

"The female is Ascon's chosen mate," Guanton said.

"She is off limits to you or any of the crew.

One more thing—you are to befriend Ascon and train him in all the ways of our people. He is a born leader, much like his father. You are to protect his life at all costs. Is that understood?"

Again, Quanyo affirmed.

"Now finish dressing and come to the bridge," Guanton insisted as he left sickbay.

Quanyo was angry, but then he thought about his imprisonment and torture.

The North Koreans were extremely cruel. They tried to make him mate, but he refused, so they whipped him. The beatings were severe and regular. They drew pints of blood and experimented on him. At one point, Quanyo wished for death.

He was happy to be alive.

As he finished dressing, he recalled his last visit to Nebula.

If we go there, some of us are going to die...but it is better to die fighting.

Chapter Two

Nebula

The crew gathered on the bridge. It was the largest area where they could all assemble. Guanton addressed them.

"The *Winyee* was built hastily, and we could not put her through the rigorous tests we would have liked. We also improvised, using materials inferior to those found on Ringnon. Now, we have developed some problems."

"Tell us what they are," Guanton said, pointing to Kotkye.

"The major problem is a leak on the ship's underbelly. It is affecting the air compressor and the life support. If not fixed and we attempt to go to hyper-drive, the strain will increase the pressure on the ship's hull, and we could be blown apart. Or we could run out of oxygen and die in our sleep."

"What is needed to repair the problem? And how long will it take?" Guanton asked.

"We must reseal the hull beneath the vessel. I estimate five to six hours of repair," Kotkye said, pointing to the ship's chart.

"We cannot use the Gitan-Ray to cut an area into the ground and camouflage our landing since we will be working beneath the ship. We must land so that we will be in the open," Wotkye added.

Guanton pushed a button on the instrument panel, and a hologram image of Nebula appeared.

Guanton explained, "Nebula is a strange planet, made up of either desert plain or dense jungle. Both are very dangerous. The best place to land is on the plain close to the jungle. The planet rotates around two suns; the safest time to land is when both suns shine brightly. That period lasts about four hours. After that, the suns set and leave the planet in a hazy half-lit state."

"And that's when the lions come out," Wotkye said, staring straight ahead as if he were looking into the past.

"What kind of lions?" Revel asked.

"Large, ravenous beasts, with huge spiked manes, fifteen to twenty feet long. Some prides number as large as a hundred. They attack in packs, and if they get close enough, they use their poisonous claws to tear you to pieces."

"The only antidote to that poison is a brew made from the bark of the Acala tree found in the jungle," Kotkye said.

"Why the plain? Witawn asked. "Why not land in the jungle?"

"Both are just as deadly, but the jungle is full of creatures you can't even imagine. The snakes are so large they can smother a Ringnonian in seconds. There are also vines that attack and strangle and ants as big as my fist that spray acid. Believe me, you don't want to be anywhere near that jungle," Wotkye said. "On the plain, all you have to fight are the lions. Just don't let them get too close."

"Quanyo will be in charge once we are on the ground," Guanton said, pointing at Quanyo. "What will be our best defense?"

Quanyo couldn't hide the surprise on his face at this apparent honor, especially after his recent rebuke.

Ascon was shocked and looked at Guanton as if to protest, but he remained silent.

Guanton ignored the looks and stares of bewilderment and watched Quanyo step forward. Guanton calculated the move and knew what was best for the entire crew. Feelings aside, Quanyo was the best commander on the field. Despite his faults, he was fearless, and now he would lead the Ring-Men with a renewed vigor to prove his worth.

Quanyo cleared his throat. "How much support can the guns on the *Winyee* give us?" he asked Wotkye.

"Three sides will be protected. The pulse machine guns can cover two sides, and the Gitan-Ray can command the front," Wotkye said.

Quanyo, gaining the confidence of command as he spoke, said, "That leaves the rear to defend. Kotkye, how many will you need to repair the ship?"

"Guanton on the inside with one Ring-Man and three helping me on the outside," Kotkye said.

"Wotkye, you and two others must handle the guns inside." Quanyo did some quick calculations. "That leaves six of you with me to cover the rear. Ascon, I want you on that team. You too, big one," he said, pointing to Revel.

"If Kotkye's calculations are correct, and he is usually very accurate about such things, then there is going to be a window of one or two hours of very fierce fighting."

Kotkye took note of the praise and said, "I will do my best to shorten the time of repairs."

"I think a Ringnonian pinwheel is the best formation for our defense, my Qualla."

Guanton smiled and thought, *Nothing like a battle to unify foes.*

"Very well," he said. "Train your team in the formation."

~~~~~~~~~

The landing went very smoothly. The *Winyee* set down just as the two suns reached their zenith. They felt the heat immediately. With the life support system shut down, it was too hot to stay inside. Those not working with Kotkye or Guanton took refuge beneath the *Winyee* for protection from the sun's scorching rays.

Tension began to mount as sunset approached. The crew took guard stations, watching the plain for any sign of the lions.

Arika kept the crew irrigated as she supplied water. When she came to Ascon, she delicately wiped the sweat from his brow.

A warm sensation filled his heart. "I've missed you," he said. "I love you more than ever."

"I, too, my love," Arika said as she gave him a second cup of water. "We will be together soon." She squeezed his hand and moved to the next Ring-Man, about ten feet under the ship. Ascon watched her as she left. Revel reminded him to keep his eyes focused.

She came to Quanyo next. A landing strut blocked Ascon's view.

Quanyo looked down on her delicate frame and took a cup of water offered by her tiny hand. "I never thanked you for all you did helping me to recover."

"I helped all of the injured. I treated you the same as the others," she said as she tossed back her long black hair.

"Is that so?" he said with a knowing smile. "I understand you are Ascon's mate."

"That is true," she said without looking up at him.

"Do you love him?"

"Why does that concern you?" she asked as she looked into his eyes.

"Just wondering," he said as he handed her the cup.

She took the cup and walked away. The jug was empty, and she climbed the ladder to retrieve more. She glanced in Quanyo's direction. He was still looking at her.

~~~~~~~~~~~~~

"How long before the repairs are complete?" Wotkye asked as he climbed down the ladder beneath the ship.

"At least another two hours," Kotkye said.

"We have a problem," Wotkye said.

Guanton had been working inside the *Winyee* and was completely drenched with sweat. He was drinking water. He turned to face Wotkye. "What is it?"

"One of the Gitan-Ray's absorption units is burned out; it just got too much sun. I have to replace it, but it is too hot to remove now. I have to wait until the sun goes down."

"How long?" Quanyo asked as he walked toward Wotkye, overhearing the conversation.

"Fifteen minutes for the glass to cool and another thirty to replace it," Wotkye said.

Guanton looked at Quanyo. "That's why I put you in charge. Figure out a defense; you have about fifteen minutes before sunset."

Guanton climbed the ladder and said, "I'll send Wajee down; I don't need him anymore."

"I can spare one," Kotkye said, motioning Dunwol to go with Quanyo.

"All of you come here. We have to devise a new plan."

~~~~~~

As the suns began to set, the roars of lions were heard across the plain. It was quite unnerving.

Quanyo stationed four Ring-Men forward of the *Winyee* with Ascon in command. Revel commanded the three Ring-Men to the rear of the ship. Quanyo would move back and forth between the two units, lending support to the side needing the most help.

The rear unit would also protect Kotkye and the two Ring-Men who worked on repairing the *Winyee*.

When the Gitan–Ray was repaired, it would cover the forward area. Ascon's group could then join Revel's group at the rear and keep the lions as far away as possible.

If the lions got too close, Quanyo would call for forming the Ringnonian pinwheel.

The pinwheel formation maximized firepower in all directions. Five Ring-Men would kneel and spread out like the spokes of a wheel, covering seventy-two degrees of a three-sixty-degree circle. Four others, standing behind them, would fire patterns at ninety degrees. The overlapping fire would stop and demolish any charge. If any team member were disabled, the wheel would shrink, still protecting in all directions.

The first lion appeared on the horizon in front of the ship. It was male with a full mane, about twenty feet long. It looked toward the *Winyee* and paused as if trying to recognize the creature it was looking at. It roared and began to approach very slowly at first. It was followed by a second lion, then a third.

Slawoo noticed a large pride meandering toward the ship from his vantage on the port side. He counted at least forty of the large beasts. He armed his weapon. The lions were about two hundred yards away.

Cravarn, on the right side, saw nothing. He viewed the two hundred yards to the jungle but soon lost interest because no lions appeared to be coming from that direction. He focused on the front of the *Winyee*, aiming his guns that way. His gun could cover about fifty percent of the front of the *Winyee*.

Revel saw lions appear to the rear. Over twenty of the huge beasts were moving excitedly as though alerted to something. The lions saw Kotkye and his repair crew and were hurrying to their meal for the day. They began to charge, kicking up dust and obscuring Revel's view of the lions behind them. He could not count the lions now heading toward the *Winyee*. "Quanyo, here they come!"

"Open fire when they get in range," Quanyo commanded.

Revel and his team opened fire, felling ten lions, but ten more appeared after them. The pride to Revel's side was the largest, about a hundred lions. Ten more were shot down, but they seemed to be getting closer.

Slawoo opened up with his gun, taking down five lions. The lions to his side retreated.

Quanyo noticed that Slawoo's gun was quiet. "Slawoo, redirect your fire to the rear."

The lions forward of the *Winyee* began to pick up their pace.

Ascon's unit opened fire. Since Cravarn saw no lions on his side, he redirected his fire to the front of the *Winyee* and stopped the charge of the lions in that direction.

Quanyo asked Ascon, "Can you spare anyone?"

"Yes, Cravarn is giving support forward; I'll send you two. Gutlap, you and Ankwot go to the rear."

Wotkye was working feverishly to repair the Gitan-Ray. The parts were small and his fingers clumsy, so Arika stepped in to help.

"How much longer?" Guanton asked Kotkye. "Seven more seals, about an hour."

Two lions crawled secretly into the tall grass on the jungle side of the *Winyee*. Two more worked their way in that direction, laying low. Cravarn didn't notice.

The lions to the rear were stopped. At least a hundred lay dead in the grass, some as close as a hundred yards from the ship. As if signaled by the failure of the lions to the rear, the lions to Slawoo's side charged.

Slawoo fired, taking many of them down, but they kept coming. "Quanyo," he said, "port side."

"Revel," Quanyo said, "You and Gutlap stay here. You four come with me."

Quanyo hurried to the port side of the ship. That was the side that Kotkye and his crew were working. The five warriors set up a defensive position on that side and opened fire. Lions began crashing to the ground, felled by the accurate fire from the guns.

Wotkye shouted to Quanyo, "The Gitan-Ray is operational." The whine of the Gitan engine was followed by a light and then blast after blast as the ray gun blew holes in the field in front of it.

Cravarn laughed as he saw the destruction of the lions, and then he noticed movement to his side. He looked and saw hundreds of eyes about fifty yards from the *Winyee*. They were inching toward the ship.

"Starboard side, Quanyo," he said. The call almost came too late.

Revel and Gutlap came to the right side, firing as they ran. Quanyo ordered Slawoo to keep firing and took three Ring-Men to the starboard side, leaving Wajee to guard Kotkye and the workmen. Ascon and Dunwol moved in from the front.

"Ringnonian pinwheel!" Quanyo shouted.

The defense formed just in time. The lions were about ten yards away when the firepower from the formation began its destruction. In a matter of minutes, sixty lions lay dead.

A ghastly scream was heard from the port side. Two lions had pounced on Wajee and were dragging him away.

"Keep your eyes open, Cravarn. Come, Ring-Men!" he shouted as the team moved toward Kotkye and the repair crew.

Quanyo moved forward, away from the protection of the *Winyee*, firing as he attempted to rescue Wajee. But three more lions moved in, and a final scream signaled Wajee's death. Quanyo moved back to the safety of the ship.

Witawn turned his welding torch into a weapon to fend off two lions. A lion to his rear hurled itself at Witawn. Ascon saw the threat and threw his knife at the lunging lion, hitting it in the throat. It fell at the foot of the repairman. Two pulse shots killed the two lions as Witawn withdrew.

A lion charged and swung its claw, slashing Gutlap across his back. Quanyo severed the lion in half with an accurate blast to its midsection.

More lions moved in from the rear, hundreds of them.

"How much longer, Kotkye?" Quanyo asked.

"Last seal now," said Kotkye. "Jarwan, you and Witawn get inside." The Ring-Men helping Kotkye moved to the ladder.

"Pinwheel!" Quanyo ordered.

The Ring-Men formed up just as the lions from the rear made another charge. The lions were annihilated.

Quanyo ordered the Ring-Men into the *Winyee* one by one. They helped Gutlap board the *Winyee*. He was bleeding profusely from his wounds and foaming at the mouth.

Finally, only he and Ascon were left outside. "Into the ship, young one," Quanyo said.

"After you, Quanyo," Ascon said. Quanyo laughed and boarded the *Winyee*, followed by the Ring-Man.

Chapter Three

The Jungle

The **Winyee** flew low over the jungle, looking for an opening to land. Before leaving the plain, Guanton searched for Wajee's remains, finding them in a section of bloody grass. The three lions gnawing at his bones were killed, and the area torched. The crew was greatly saddened by the loss of one of their own.

Gutlap was comatose as his fever spiked at one hundred and six degrees.

"If we don't get him some of the bark brew, he's going to die," Wotkye said. "He's got about two hours to live."

The bark from the Acala vines boiled into a brew would act as anti-venom to the poison attacking Gutlap's body.

"There are no clearings in this thick stuff that I can see," said Ankwot, piloting the **Winyee**.

"We'll use the Gitan to cut an opening if we can't find one," Wotkye said.

Guanton briefed the team going for the bark. "This is a perilous mission and could cost lives if we are not careful."

Dunwol asked a question on the mind of some. "Guanton, is it worth the risk?

"If it were you lying there, would you want us to take the risk? You are only half Ringnonian, Dunwol, so I don't expect you to know everything you should about Ringnonian honor. We do everything in our power to save each other, even if it means dying."

Dunwol felt ashamed. He looked down and apologized, "Foolish question, my Qualla."

"Besides, the bark has tremendous healing power and works on various ailments. It will be useful for us beyond its benefit to Gutlap. We originally explored this planet to collect the bark. But the loss of so many Ringnonians made harvesting it too dangerous.

We will collect enough bark for personal use and keep some to barter with. Acala bark is one of the most valuable commodities in the universe. Remember, we need magnetic crystals, and if we can't mine them ourselves, we may be able to trade for them."

~~~~~~~~~~~~

"Look there!" Wotkye pointed.

An opening appeared beneath them. Flowers and green grass covered the small area. A running stream traversed the landscape, an idyllic scene.

"I think we have something. It looks peaceful enough," Wotkye said to Guanton.

Guanton looked for himself and thought of the past.

His previous visit to Nebula was a disaster. A mysterious clearing appeared then also. The setting was as beautiful as this one. The unsuspecting Ringnonians, many of whom were scientists and botanists, left the ship's safety and began exploring.

All was quiet and going well. The scientists gathered samples and specimens with orders not to venture into the forest. Some sat in the grass and played as if at a country fair. Lulled into a false sense of security, the guards relaxed.

Suddenly, the jungle attacked. Vines lunged and snatched victims before they could stand. Others, running to the safety of the ship, were caught and dragged screaming into the forest.

Unable to retreat, some began to fight the vines with knives and flamethrowers, only to be overwhelmed by hundreds of giant ants that boiled from the ground. Firing a thick acid, the ants blinded and disabled their victims before consuming them.

It appeared as though the jungle made the opening and set a trap.

Guanton and Wotkye escaped because they were aboard the vessel when the attack began. Quanyo and Kotkye were with a survey party and barely made it out alive. They entered the ship just before liftoff, as the jungle closed in around them. Only five out of a crew of one hundred lived to tell the story.

Guanton looked again at the tranquil setting. "It's too peaceful," he said. "Perhaps we can use that to our advantage."

~~~~~~~~~~

The *Winyee* landed fifty feet from the flowing stream and two-hundred feet from the trees.

Quanyo and his team established a perimeter and positioned motion and sensor mines around the *Winyee*. When tripped or ignited, a fiery border would protect the *Winyee*. If the forest enclosed suddenly, the *Winyee* would not be trapped.

The area beneath and around the *Winyee* was checked for ant nests. The nests were topped with a mesh covering made from the acid-like saliva of the ant and soil. Unsuspecting prey stepping into the five-foot-wide entry point would be inundated and overwhelmed by hundreds of the creatures. Stung or bitten and pumped full of formic acid, the victim would be paralyzed before being eaten alive.

An ant nest was found close to the ship and quickly torched.

Guanton knew the mission would be risky. He surmised that the jungle was a living, breathing animal setting a trap, much like some orchids set lures for insects. If they could turn the tables, they could gather all the vine bark they needed.

Quanyo and seven Ring-Men would fan out and act as bait. Guanton gave them instructions. "If you are snatched by a vine, use your knife to pin yourself to the ground until help arrives. Those of you with lasers will slice the captive free. Use the flamethrowers; the vines fear fire. Also, be aware of the ants. I believe they have a symbiotic relationship with the vines and protect them when attacked. We will gather as much bark as possible and get off this planet. Remember, the vines won't attack us until they feel we are relaxing or unaware."

"I don't want to be plant food, so everyone stay alert," Quanyo prompted.

Wotkye and Kotkye would man the guns aboard, and Ankwot would stay at flight control, ready to fire the engine for immediate lift-off.

Guanton permitted Arika to leave the ship with orders to stick very close to Ascon. He and two others would guard the *Winyee*.

~~~~~~~~~

"It is beautiful here, isn't it?" Arika said to Ascon as they walked close to the running stream.

"Not half as beautiful as you are," he said as he picked flowers and handed them to her.

She was lovely, dressed in a pattered kimono he had never seen. It matched the landscape with its purple and yellow flowers. Her black hair, loose and flowing, was swirled effortlessly by the light breeze.

"We have not been able to talk privately since we left Earth. I hope you still feel the same way about me," Ascon said.

"What makes you think anything has changed?" she asked, running a hand through her hair as she sniffed the flowers.

"What a beautiful aroma!" She pushed the flowers toward his nose.

Ascon pushed them away. "I am serious...do you still love me?"

"Of course, I love you, Ascon. I will...always...." She became faint and stumbled, almost falling.

Ascon caught her and easily lifted her into his arms.

"What's wrong?" he asked with panic in his voice.

Guanton, standing beneath the *Winyee*, looked through his field glasses at the surrounding terrain. He observed Quanyo and his team as they spread across the field trying to look nonchalant. The warriors, trained to be alert, had difficulty looking unconcerned.

Guanton turned to see Ascon carrying Arika toward the ship. He also noticed movement a hundred yards behind the running Ring-Man. Branches of vine moved toward them

"We've got movement behind the stream," Guanton reported.

Quanyo's team froze. "The jungle is moving," he said.

Large vines were inching across the surface of the ground in all directions. Seven different strands were moving from the jungle. Four more closed in on the *Winyee* behind Ascon.

Quanyo motioned his team to move back toward the *Winyee*.

The vines seemed to notice the team retreating and began to speed up.

Ants boiled from a nest, and Cravarn nearly fell into the mass. He fired his flamethrower, roasting the insects as they attacked. Popping sounds were heard as the ants exploded under the intense heat.

Quanyo, fifty feet from Cravarn, saw his dilemma. "Cravarn, behind you!" he shouted.

A vine caught the Ring-Man, wrapped around his right leg, and pulled him to the ground. Revel fired his laser, cutting the vine. The vine recoiled, but ten feet of the plant was still attached to Cravarn's leg. He was in obvious pain and bleeding as the vine continued to squeeze. But

Cravarn was more concerned about the approaching ants spraying acid in his direction. He leveled his flamethrower and burned as many as he could.

Quanyo moved to the aid of the wounded Ring-Man. The rest of the team followed, establishing a defensive perimeter around Cravarn. Witloon flamed the remainder of the ants and destroyed the opening they came from.

The vines surrounded the group and cut off their escape route, clawing and searching for a chance to seize a victim. The team, using flamethrowers, kept the vines at bay, but their fuel was running low.

Ascon lifted Arika into the *Winyee* and tried to revive her. He felt relief when she stirred.

Kotkye, firing one of the *Winyee's* guns, turned to Ascon. "She will be alright. Leave her and go help Guanton. Take an extra flame tank."

Ascon, frozen with worry, leaped into action. He jumped down the ladder and back into the fight, taking two flamethrowers.

The vines reached the *Winyee*. Guanton and Slawoo were firing lasers and severing fingers from the vines. The vine quickly grew branches as they were cut and continued to strike at the crew under the ship.

Guanton hoped to get Quanyo's team into the perimeter before igniting the mines, but seeing them cut off and surrounded, he knew they could not get back to the *Winyee*.

"We're running low on fuel. Our flamethrowers are almost out," Quanyo said.

"Help is on the way," Guanton assured him.

"I'll go," Ascon said as he strapped a tank to his back. He slung the other unit under his left arm and prepared to leave. Guanton grabbed his arm.

"I'm going to ignite the charges and get the *Winyee* airborne," Guanton said, "We will get all of you out."

"I know you will," Ascon answered as he lit his flame and moved forward.

The area beneath *The Winyee* was thick with attacking vines almost blocking out the light. Guanton and three Ring-Men made a circle, using the landing struts and flamethrowers to ward off the vines. Guanton watched Ascon leave and then ordered Wotkye to ignite the mines.

They exploded with a tremendous *whoosh* as the perimeter around the *Winyee* turned into a ball of fire. The vines inside the perimeter retreated. Guanton could have sworn that he heard them scream as they pulled back.

Ascon moved slowly, firing flames from side to side, clearing the way as he headed toward the trapped crewmen. The vines appeared to make a path so that he easily moved a hundred feet to his comrades. He handed the extra tank to Dunwol and joined the team fighting off the vines. Four of the flamethrowers were empty, and the Ring-Men were using their knives to lop off vine sections.

Quanyo's flamethrower gave out. "I hope Guanton has a plan," he said as he turned to Ascon.

"Here, take this. Maybe you can hack our way to the ship," Ascon said as he handed Quanyo his knife.

Ants moved in, shooting acid as they crawled closer. Down to two flamethrowers, Ascon and Dunwol took turns firing at the ground and the vines. A vine grabbed Witloon around his waist. He severed the vine, but the grip tightened, and he fell to the ground.

The *Winyee* was airborne and tried to reach the cut-off group, but the vines reached skyward in an attempt to drag the ship from the sky.

"Fire up the Gitan," Guanton said. "Blast that area over there and keep firing."

The Gitan fired rapidly, blowing gaping holes in the jungle floor. After seven blasts, Guanton yelled, "Hold your fire!"

A strange *whine* filled the air. The jungle responded like an injured animal licking its wounds. The vines began to slowly recede.

"Three more blasts," Guanton said.

The Gitan roared. More explosions followed, and the vine re-treat quickened.

The *Winyee* set down next to the exhausted team, who were strewn about, resting on one another. Guanton appeared below the ship.

There were hundreds of cut-off vine pieces, some still writhing with life.

"Pick up the pieces and throw them into the ship. We have to lift off as soon as possible. You can't rest here all day," he said, smiling.

Chapter Four

Healing

"Arika!" Ascon called as he tried to revive her.

Guanton leaned over the semi-conscious woman. "Give her a small sip of this."

Ascon gently leaned her head forward and made her drink a little of the brew. He watched her as she swallowed.

A few seconds later, she opened her eyes. "What happened?"

"The flowers you sniffed were loaded with an intoxicating sedative," Guanton said. "Normally, the flowers emit the gas in small doses as the victim is lulled into a happy, relaxed state. Then they attack. You got a full dose. But you will feel better in a few moments."

"The drink is a brew made from the Acala bark," Kotkye said.

How is Gutlap?" Guanton asked.

"His fever is gone, and he is awake. All the wounded have been given brew, and they are already healing. This is marvelous stuff," Kotkye said as he tasted the brew.

"Be careful. Too much of it can make you as drunk as a Kittan hog," Guanton warned.

"I've got something else brewing for our enjoyment that's even better," Kotkye promised with a mischievous look.

"What, another one of your concoctions?"

"You'll see," the Ringnonian said as he left sickbay.

We've been fighting quite a bit—first, the Chinese, then the North Koreans, and now lions and vines. Perhaps we're due for some relaxation, Guanton thought.

He looked down at Ascon, still nursing Arika, and thought about his mate, Winyee.

I wonder if I will find her alive. He left sickbay, a tear welling in his eye.

~~~~~~~~

The bark, cut into small pieces and boiled, made a tea that could heal any ailment or injury in minutes. It was so potent that a two-inch cutting made a pot of brew sufficient for the entire crew. A piece of bark chewed into mulch and placed on a wound resulted in the same healing effect as a small piece swallowed. Guanton ordered the vines to be cut into small cube-like sections and then frozen.

"How much bark do we have?" Guanton asked Wotkye.

"Over 200 pounds," Wotkye answered.

Guanton thought of the trading market on Ringnon and the merchants selling coin-sized portions of the bark at exorbitant prices. With as much bark as they had, they could trade for magnetic crystals and still have enough for future use. But caution would be necessary; knowledge of their cargo could invite attack.

Guanton looked at the charting computer. "I don't want to go to hyper-drive with such a low crystal count. What do you think, Wotkye?"

"We can trade on the moon of Gabet. Hopefully, most miners will be on the planet plying their trade. If not, we have enough firepower to take what we want."

"I don't want to risk a fight," Guanton said. "We still have a long way to go, and I don't want the ship damaged. We will go in easy and try to trade. Set a course for Gabet and try the outpost on Krilla. I know the owner of that establishment. He's a thief and a liar but deals in crystals."

Arika was sitting up as Ascon tenderly fed her soup.

"The nurse is herself being nursed, I see," Quanyo said as he entered the sick bay. "How are you?"

"I am doing well, thanks to Ascon," she said.

"Yes, I must thank him, also."

Ascon looked up, surprised.

"Did he tell you that he saved our lives?" Quanyo asked. Arika looked at Ascon. "No, he didn't."

"Well, he did. If he had not gotten to us when he did, we would be digested by now."

Ascon stood up, uneasy and embarrassed by the attention.

"You are now my Kitaw. It means you are my brother and son, my blood and my protectorate. I owe you for my life. Twice." Quanyo embraced Ascon. "I will train you and fight side by side with you. I will see no harm to you, even if it means my life."

Quanyo released his grip and left sickbay.

Ascon was shocked by what happened. "What was that all about?"

Kotkye, who was dispensing brew, answered. "That was a great honor. It means that Quanyo has adopted you."

"What if I don't want to be adopted?"

"It doesn't matter," Kotkye added. "He will protect your life at all costs, even if it means giving up his own. I have never seen Quanyo react that way before. You should be honored he feels that way about you."

165

Kotkye left, deeply touched by the emotional display he saw.

Ascon sat down next to Arika, who remained silent through the exchange.

She ran her hand through his hair and hugged him. "I am so proud of you, my love."

Ascon sat stunned by the recent development.

~~~~~~~~~~

Quanyo sat on the bridge gazing at the stars as the *Winyee* sped through space. Most of the crew was sleeping, helped by Kotkye's distilled creation. He somehow had combined molaka and the Acala brew into a liquor that boggled the mind. A celebration worthy of Ringnonians ensued. The crew laughed, sang, and drank.

Quanyo watched Ascon approach and sit in the co-pilot seat.

"I'm still amazed by the beauty of space," he said as he offered Ascon some of his drink.

"No more for me. My head is still buzzing," Ascon said as he rubbed the back of his neck.

"Kotkye outdid himself this time," Quanyo said as he emptied his mug.

"I think you may have overreacted with all this adoption talk," Ascon said, still wondering why Quanyo made him his Kitaw.

"That is because you don't know the history between your father and me."

"I thought you and my father hated each other."

"It was not always that way. We were the best of friends at one time."

Quanyo circled his finger around the top of his mug and thought of the past.

"Your father and I were both warrior-class Ringnonians."

"Warrior class?"

"Yes. There are two classes of Ringnonians: intellectuals and warriors. Sometimes, they overlap, as in the case of Guanton, an intellectual trained to be a warrior. From birth, your father and I were trained to fight. We were classmates instructed by Guanton's brother, Quill. Quill was one of the greatest warriors in Ringnonian history. He saw something in your father, and your father worshiped him. I guess I was always a bit jealous of their relationship.

"But Quill was right. Your father was a born leader. He was courageous, and he always sensed when trouble was amiss. He also beat me at everything," Quanyo said with a big smile. "All except in one thing."

"What was that?" Ascon asked.

"There was a female that he adored. Her name was Seneca, and she was beautiful. He would fall on his face whenever she was around." Quanyo refilled his mug from a pitcher. He paused, looking into the swirling brew as if he could see her face.

Ascon waited, then asked, "Well, what happened?"

Quanyo leaned forward and looked at Ascon, a tear in his eye. "She did not love Ascon. She loved me. I don't know why." Quanyo took a big gulp and sat back.

"I took her as a mate, but I did not love her. I guess I did it to prove I could beat your father at something." Quanyo looked out at space again.

"But I treated her badly. Eventually, she mated with someone else and became pregnant. I was infuriated. Under Ringnon law, I had the right to put her and the child to death."

Quanyo drained his mug. "Guanton and Quill asked me to be merciful, but I would not listen, and I killed them both."

He put his mug down and looked at Ascon again. "The child was male, and the father was Ascon. He tried to kill me, but Guanton stopped him. He hated me, and I got the reputation of being ruthless and evil. I have tried to live up to that label ever since."

Ascon remained silent, letting what he heard sink in. "So, by making me Kitaw, you think it makes up for that."

"Nothing will make up for what I did," Quanyo said as he stood. "That memory haunts me to this day." He left the bridge.

Guanton was listening, unnoticed. Quanyo staggered past him on his way to his quarters.

Guanton took the seat vacated by Quanyo. Ascon remained silent in deep thought.

"He left out a few things," Guanton said as he looked over the instrument panel.

"He loved your father like a brother. He was also unaware of who the father of the child was. He found that out later.

"Your father broke our law when he mated with Seneca. If he had taken Quanyo's life, he would have compounded that error, and he would have been put to death. I could not let that happen, so I stopped him from killing Quanyo."

"But Quanyo killed my brother."

"Men on Earth killed your father and your brothers, yet you love Arika. This is his way of making amends. Accept and become his Kitaw. That is my advice to you as well as my order."

Ascon nodded his head in agreement.

Chapter Five

Moons of Gabet

The huge planet of Gabet was a floating mine. Multiple veins of ores and a mother lode of magnetic crystals made it one of the richest mineral sources in the universe. It was also one of the deadliest.

With no sun to warm it, Gabet was always cold. Fires and explosions were a constant threat due to the noxious sulfuric gases floating in the atmosphere.

Clabans worked the mines on the planet. They were the only creatures brave or foolish enough to risk working on the deathtrap.

Huge creatures with four arms, Clabans were not war-like by nature but quite dangerous when angered or aroused. Green skin covered their large bulbous heads and ten-foot-long bodies. The large, sharp claws on those four arms made digging easy, but they were also lethal weapons.

Two moons just as deadly, Latbee and Krilla, orbited the planet. Large, overworked oxygen-converting stations produced an artificial atmosphere on the moons, making breathing barely tolerable.

A trading post existed on each moon. There, bartering for everything from liquor to weapons took place. Prices were always marked up due to the lack of competition.

Guanton decided to land on Krilla, also the proprietor's name. Krilla's family built the outpost over a century ago. Guanton had dealt with him before and didn't trust him. But landing on Krilla was better than the alternative of Latbee, known as a haven for pirates.

Shuttles arrived once a week with hundreds of overworked miners to the outposts. They boiled out of the shuttles, ready to drink themselves into stupors. Desirous of females of any species, they often fought to the death for what was always in short supply.

"Be careful of the Clabans," Wotkye warned. "Most of the time, they are peaceful and just want to drink and gamble. But at times, they like to fight, especially with strangers."

"Quanyo, you, Ascon, and Dunwol will come with me to bargain. Revel, I want you and a strike team to shadow us with heavy weapons in case of trouble," Guanton pointed to the Ring-Man.

"Wotkye, I want you and Ankwot prepared to move the ship if there is trouble. I don't want her damaged."

"I would love to taste some Krillan ale," Kotkye added.

"That's just why you are not going," Guanton stated. "We must be very cautious. If anyone finds out how much bark we have, we will have a deadly fight on our hands."

"Communicators are unreliable in this atmosphere, so stay in line of sight so we can communicate. I want the ship ready to go into hyper-drive as soon as we take off," Guanton said to Kotkye.

"We won't bring our heavy weapons, just our handguns and knives. We will try to look as peaceful as possible," he said to Ascon and Quanyo.

~~~~~~~~~

The **Winyee** landed on the outskirts of the outpost. A dusty haze obscured their arrival, and Guanton and his team eased off the ship and headed toward the trading post.

Revel took his team of six Ring-Men and stationed each at strategic points between the **Winyee** and the trading post. He made sure each could see the next.

On board the **Winyee**, Wotkye manned the Gitan while Kotkye and Gutlap the other guns. Ankwot remained ready at the pilot controls.

~~~~~~~~~~

Guanton entered a large warehouse, one of three buildings on the outpost. Carefully scanning the room, he walked to an area that served as a canteen. Quanyo and Ascon followed, each looking for threats. Dunwol, last through the door, watched the rear as he closed it.

"Welcome," greeted Krilla, getting up from a stool and moving behind the bar. Krilla was a Kleeten and stood about five feet tall. His large ears were pointed, and he was hairy from head to paw. Large whiskers protruded from the brown and black fur covering his cat-like face.

Guanton removed his helmet, and a look of recognition crossed Krilla's face.

"It's been a long time, Guanton," Krilla said, adding a smile.

"Yes, it has. But I see this place hasn't changed much, still as dirty as ever."

Ignoring the insult, Krilla asked, "What brings you to this part of the galaxy?"

Guanton surveyed the half-lit room. A massive Claban enforcer sat on a stool in one corner, holding a laser shotgun in two of his claws. Four customers sat in a far corner, drinking from mugs of ale.

Quanyo took a seat facing the door. Ascon sat on a stool, facing the seated patrons with his back to the bar. Dunwol remained standing, his back to the door.

Quanyo looked closely at the seated creatures. They were large. He guessed ten or eleven feet tall. Draped in dark cloaks, they made loud slurping sounds as they drank from their mugs, but he realized they were not drinking. They were sucking up ale with their mouths. Green eyes beneath their headgear barely illuminated their faces. The only thing worse than their noise was the smell from their direction.

"I'm here to do some trading," Guanton answered, removing his gloves.

"Then you are talking to the wrong person," said a voice from among the seated creatures.

"He's a Kagan," Krilla whispered.

"Yes, I'm Kagan and the owner of this establishment. He's just the bartender," the voice said.

Guanton looked at Krilla, who looked down at the bar, embarrassed.

Kagans were half-humanoid, half-insect with two claw-like hands and long whiskers. They were also the scourge of the universe and a menace to any society. Ruthless murderers and pirates, they never traded but took what they wanted by force.

Guanton turned and looked at Quanyo and Ascon, giving them non-verbal instructions.

"Then perhaps I can deal with you," Guanton suggested as he unwrapped the small package in his hand.

"What have you got there?" the Kagan asked as he stood—enormous—over eleven feet tall. He moved slowly toward Guanton, and his three companions stood.

"Look for yourself," Guanton said as he moved closer to the Kagan.

"What is that, Acala bark?" the Kagan asked as he reached with his left claw. He quickly pulled a blaster with his right claw.

But Guanton was faster. In one motion, he pulled his knife and backhanded the blade across the Kagan's throat. The Kagan stood motionless. Green ooze spurted from the Kagan's neck as he fell dead to the ground.

The attack happened so fast that the other Kagans barely reacted. Seconds later, two of them felt the butts of Ringnonian knives deeply embedded in their torsos. The third was floored by a shotgun blast from the Claban's gun.

"I thought you were with them," Dunwol said as he lowered his blaster.

"My name is Cooloo, and I hate Kagans. Besides, they stink very badly," he said.

"You are getting quite good with your knife, young Ascon," Quanyo commended as he moved to check the bodies.

Ascon did not consider being called "*young*" an insult this time. Instead, he looked at Quanyo. "You were also very quick, my brother."

"Now what?" Quanyo wondered, looking at Guanton.

"Now, we get the crystals from Krilla and get out of here," Guanton said, pointing to the Kleeten.

"No, please, help us," Krilla begged. "These pirates came here months ago and have taken over. They robbed the miners and took all the females. Now the shuttles won't land."

"How many pirates?" Quanyo asked.

"Over one hundred, in three vessels," Krilla said. "They stay airborne most of the time, waiting for victims to land and watching for the shuttles from Gabet."

"It's not our concern. We are here for magnetic crystals, not to save your business," Guanton said. "Do you have crystals?"

"You would also be saving one of your own," Krilla said.

"What do you mean?" Ascon asked.

"They have taken the ten females that were here. One of them is a Ringnonian," Krilla said, first looking at Ascon, then Guanton.

"You're lying," Guanton said, looking at Cooloo for confirmation.

"No, he is being truthful," the Claban said. "Her name is Colette."

Chapter Six

Pirates

The third pirate ship followed the first two and landed close to the outpost. Ninety Kagans, thirty from each ship, cautiously debarked and spread around the three structures. Zoalart, their commander, was the last to unload.

He and four others entered the warehouse and discovered their comrades dead and Krilla bound and gagged.

"What happened?" Zoalart asked as he ripped the gag from Krilla's mouth.

"Clabans led by Cooloo killed your friends and headed south to a ship to escape."

Guanton's drones watched every move made by the pirates. The *Winyee* was partially buried just south of the outpost with its guns waiting to spring an ambush. Revel and a strike team of seven Ring-Men concealed themselves fifty yards to the right of the *Winyee*. Guanton hoped to even the odds with a deadly crossfire.

Cooloo identified the flagship as the likely holding pen for the females. Quanyo, Ascon, and three Ring-Men kept themselves hidden. They would try to disable the ship holding the prisoners and attempt their rescue.

Cooloo promised to bring help from Gabet. He would also act as the bait to lure the pirates into the trap.

Stepping from an alcove disguised in a Kagan cloak, he unloaded his shotgun into the nearest pirate. Then, he headed south, running as fast as he could, followed by the Kagans seeking revenge.

Cooloo's path led directly past the *Winyee*. The gunners on the *Winyee* waited until the Kagans were almost on top of the ship and then opened fire. Revel and his crew began firing seconds later.

Over sixty pirates were cut down in the first salvo. The remainder fell back toward the outpost.

Cooloo circled the outpost and then sprung his second surprise.

Two hundred Claban miners moved in from the north side of the outpost.

Most carried mining weapons, but some carried guns. They caught the unsuspecting pirates retreating and tore them to pieces.

The flagship tried to take off, but a blast from Ascon's cannon disabled the engine. The other ships took off and escaped.

Quanyo approached beneath the flagship and blew a hole in the hatch. Witawn threw a grenade through the opening, waited for the blast, and entered the ship. One Kagan was lying dead on the deck. He moved cautiously through the corridor, followed by Ascon and Quanyo.

"Look out!" Quanyo yelled as a Kagan fired a blast from a laser. Quanyo fired back, blowing a hole in the Kagan and sending him sprawling backward.

Witawn had taken a shot to his chest. He crumpled to the floor, his eyes wide and lips quivering. The wound, cauterized by the blast, left a gaping hole in his thorax.

"Give me a piece of bark!" Quanyo yelled to Witloon, who had yet to enter the spacecraft.

Witloon handed a piece of Acala bark to Quanyo. He broke it into a bite-sized chunk and pushed it into Witawn's mouth.

"Get him to the *Winyee*," Quanyo said as he lifted the wounded Ring-Man down the hatch hole.

Ascon continued to watch the corridor. "Okay, let's make sure there are no more of them on board," Quanyo said as he and Ascon moved forward.

The two dead Kagans were the only ones aboard. But the cargo hold held ten sick and dehydrated females; one was Ringnonian.

<hr />

Barricaded in the warehouse, Zoalart and two Kagans fired blasters to keep the Clabans out.

Krilla slipped behind the bar. He felt for a hidden shotgun. "Perhaps you should surrender," he urged the chief Kagan.

"Is there a back way out of the warehouse?" Zoalart asked.

"Yes, this way." Krilla lifted the shotgun and fired point-blank into Zoalart's midsection. The other Kagans turned and were similarly dispatched.

The Clabans outside heard the blasts and Krilla's voice reassuring them: "It's all over, boys."

Revel surveyed the battlefield, which was strewn with Kagan body parts and green ooze.

He looked up and saw two Ring-Men carrying Witawn toward the *Winyee*.

"Is he alive?" he asked.

"Yes, but barely," Witloon said.

They hurried him to the Winyee and sickbay.

<hr />

Sickbay was bustling as the wounded were bandaged and given Acala brew to help the healing process.

The amazing mixture saved Witawn's life. In just two days, the opening in his chest had closed. A day later, there was only slight discoloration, and he was talking.

The Claban miners also received the brew. Many were severely wounded; twenty died.

The female captives also recovered quickly. They were quite talkative and grateful for their release. Six were Clabans, and three were Mokot females. Mokots were tall and blue-skinned with black hair that stood straight up above their heads. Nine of the females wanted to remain on Krilla, peddling their trade at the canteen.

Colette, the Ringnonian female, was the exception. She kept to herself most of the time. She was young, four sections or twenty years old by Earth time. Kidnapped and abused, she was forced into a trade she hated. Guanton tried to get information from her, but she was unwilling to speak. She also shied away from all the males.

Arika tried talking to her as she brushed her matted hair. She also sang Japanese songs to Colette, but she would not say a word. She just sat staring, holding a small pouch in her hand.

~~~~~~~~~~~

"We need those crystals," Guanton demanded of Krilla.

"And you shall have them, my friend. With the pirates gone, the miners can now transport them to me again," Krilla said. "And because you helped me, I will discount the price. Let's say, oh, half of the Acala bark you have on your ship."

Guanton grabbed the Kleeten by the throat and lifted him into the air. "I want the crystals here in five hours, and for the four packets of Acala bark we agreed to. If not, there will be fur spread all over this floor."

Guanton left, heading back to the *Winyee*. Krilla watched him go. "We need to find a way to get the bark away from them, Cooloo."

"How is she?" Guanton asked Arika.

"About the same; she just sits there staring and playing with that pouch around her neck."

"Has she said anything?" "No," Arika said.

"Well, keep trying to talk to her. We have to find out how she was captured. It might give us some idea of where our people are," Guanton said as he left.

Ascon stepped behind Arika and wrapped his large arms around her. "Guess who?"

"I hope it is my love, Ascon," she said playfully. He gently kissed her neck, and she giggled.

He turned and noticed Colette's wide eyes staring at him. "Davar," she said as she handed him the pouch.

Guanton headed to the canteen with Quanyo and Ascon, fully determined to get the needed crystals. Entering the door, they noticed that Cooloo was tending to the bar.

"Where is Krilla?" Guanton asked.

"He's over there," Cooloo said, pointing to a bloody pile of fur on the floor. "The rest of him is being prepared for supper."

Guanton looked at Krilla's remains and then at Cooloo.

"I caught him trying to contact the pirates on Latbee to make another deal. A deal is how they got here in the first place. He wanted all of your Acala bark."

"Thank you, Cooloo. You have truly shown yourself to be a friend."

"Your crystals are waiting for you, Orloo. Go get them."

Orloo had taken Cooloo's place as the enforcer. The big Claban lumbered to the warehouse to retrieve the crystals.

"I have doubled the amount of Acala bark," Guanton said.

"You could make a fortune killing pirates," Cooloo said. "We would pay handsomely for your help in ridding ourselves of the Kagans."

"I am sorry, my friend. We must find our people."

"Perhaps you will come back when you find them. Your kind is always welcome here."

Orloo handed Ascon and Quanyo four large packages.

"Will you stay for supper? Boiled Kleeten stew is delicious," Cooloo said.

"No. We must be on our way. Perhaps another time."

"Have a safe journey," Cooloo said as they left the canteen.

Chapter Seven

Colette

"It's an information cube," Kotkye said as he examined the small three-dimensional object.

"I know that," Guanton snipped, "Can we read it?"

"I don't remember seeing this kind before, but let me work with it." Kotkye turned to Arika. "Did she have anything else in the pouch?"

"No, just that cube she handed to Ascon, and she called him Davar."

"Interesting. Look at this, Guanton." Kotkye placed the cube under a light. "See these two small holes? It looks like something fits into them, like a key. I think this box opens."

"What does Davar mean?" Ascon asked.

"It means father. What were you two doing when she gave you the cube?" Guanton asked.

"Well…" Ascon hesitated.

"Ascon was holding me," Arika said.

"You two must have reminded her of her parents. Arika, keep trying to talk to her," Guanton said.

"I have been trying. Perhaps she doesn't understand Japanese."

"Any language a Ringnonian hears is understood. She also can respond. Be patient. I believe you can help her," Guanton confidently smiled.

~~~~~~~~

Ringnonian and Ring-Men's ability to speak any language amazed Arika. They picked up even the small nuances and slang of a spoken tongue.

"You are very pretty," Arika told Colette as she brushed her hair.

Colette was small by Ringnonian standards, about five feet five inches. Black wavy hair fell past her shoulders. Her features were slight, and her eyes were green. She was quite beautiful.

"My name is Arika. What is yours?"

Arika was surprised when she answered, "Colette."

~~~~~~~~

"It's a journal," Kotkye said. "It tells us what happened to Colette's mother and what happened on Ringnon."

Kotkye inserted a small pin, and the box opened, becoming a square pad. Seconds later, a hologram of Colette's mother appeared above the pad.

"My name is Colette, lead scientist on Project K-2053—Plague Investigation."

Kotkye stopped the projection and demonstrated how the information pad worked.

"See, by tracing your finger across the bottom of the pad, you can move forward or backward in the journal entries. Some of the program has been compromised, but we can get a pretty good idea of what happened on Ringnon."

"Play it from the beginning," Guanton said.

"My name is Colette, lead scientist on Project K-2053—Plague Investigation. Entry 12. The plague is now on Ringnon, having slowly moved across space from Dalmate. It is a living, flesh-eating organism that is difficult to control and impossible to eliminate. The cities of Tooloon and Flotoon have been quarantined. We are trying a new serum in the hope of controlling its deadly effects."

"Entry 18. There is no stopping the spread of the disease. Tooloon and Flotoon are deserted cities. Thousands have already died. The disease is spreading faster than we anticipated. The mountain city of Quikat is now affected and under quarantine."

Kotkye stopped the transmission. He looked at Guanton, who remained silent. Quikat was his home. He was raised there. He and his mate Winyee made their home in that lovely mountain city.

"Go on with the recording," Guanton prompted somberly.

"Entry 22. The council has decided to evacuate the planet. We will use two habitation ships and then destroy Ringnon. Core detonation will occur two weeks after the ships have departed."

"Entry 25. The habitation ships have departed. Gorlon leads our vessel with Bouas as his second. I have been selected as lead scientist. Quill is leading the other vessel with Torlack as his second and Winyee as the lead scientist."

Kotkye turned and smiled at Guanton. "I thought you would like that part."

"I hope they are still alive," he said. "Go on with the message, please."

"Entry 26. Today, we cried as we watched our home blown apart. Hopefully, we can make Ringnon live again when we settle on other planets. Of the four exploration vessels sent sections ago, only two have returned. There is still no report from the Quillow commanded by Houvor or the Triveron commanded by Ascon."

Guanton thought about his original mission, to see if Earth was a possible place for the Ringnon civilization to settle. Instead, their vessel was destroyed and the crew was left stranded on Earth.

"Entry 30. *Ringnon One*, with Quill in command, is headed for our colony on Kittan. We on *Ringnon Two* are headed to Twuonay. We have developed some crystal deterioration, but our engineers assure us we will make our destination."

"Entry 40. We are floating in space, powerless. No way to communicate with *Ringnon One*. We're running out of food. We'll use our shuttles in an attempt to escape."

"Entry 45. Landed on the moon of Wotkoo. Four hundred colonists will try to make it our home. I have agreed to take Nomee as a mate. Our new home is a beautiful place, with plenty of food."

"Entry 62. I am with child. Our colony now numbers six hundred. The sounds of laughter fill the air. I cannot wait to hear the laughter of my own child."

"Entry 70. My lovely Colette is beautiful. Nomee is a wonderful mate. He insisted that I name her after myself."

"Entry 75. Kagan pirates struck our colony today. We fought them off, but we think they will be back. Nomee is wounded but able to walk."

"That's the last transmission, Guanton. If I work on it, I might be able to salvage more."

"You have done a fine job, Kotkye," Guanton praised. "At least we know what happened on Ringnon. Perhaps we may find out more from the girl."

~~~~~~~~~~

"Arika looked into Colette's eyes. She began talking softly, reassuring her that she was safe and loved. She told Colette of her own experience of being abused.

"I felt like dying. I felt worthless and used." Arika began to cry.

She did not want Colette to feel worse, so she got up and walked away. Colette came behind Arika and embraced her.

Colette began talking freely but only to Arika. She was still apprehensive about talking to the males, though she smiled at Ascon.

She also smiled when she told Arika about her happy years with her mother and father on Wotkoo. She grew sad again when she spoke of her father's death at the hands of the Kagan pirates.

"We were captured by the Kagans," she recalled, staring straight ahead. "I was young, about one section at the time. We were taken and traded to Gleeba on Latbee. He was a fat, smelly Claban who ran the trading post. He liked my mother, but she hated him.

"Mother began serving at the canteen. That smelly Claban would not let anyone touch my mother. He wanted her for himself. Finally, he threatened to hurt me if she didn't give in to him. She did, to save me." She broke down crying but continued telling her story.

"Things were alright for a while, and I began to grow. I would help my mother at the bar and in the warehouse. Then mother got sick and could no longer work at the canteen. Gleeba became very cruel."

She looked at Arika. "Then he began to bother me. First, it was just the way he looked at me. Then he tried to touch me." She looked down, obviously ashamed, and she began sobbing again.

Arika did not push her. She just listened and stroked her hair. "You did nothing wrong, Colette."

"I did…I told my mother and I should not have done that. She confronted Gleeba, and he beat her severely. He reminded her that she and I were his property, and he would do as he pleased." Colette paused in deep thought.

Arika's curiosity was aroused. "What happened?"

"Mother pulled a laser shotgun that Gleeba kept hidden, and she blew a hole in him," Colette said calmly. "The other Clabans killed her, and I was traded to Krilla. That was one section ago."

That last section had been one of horror. Colette went on to tell Arika about her enslavement and how she was traded and abused by several males of various species. Finally, she went into a sort of shock and did not speak.

"That seemed to help. Most Clabans are superstitious about someone who is mute. But it did not stop the Kagans."

Again, Arika waited. Colette wiped her nose and continued.

"Oh, if only I hadn't said anything. My mother would still be alive."

She placed her face into her hands and wept quietly this time.

Arika embraced her. "If you were my daughter, I would have wanted you to tell me. Your mother was very brave, and you did nothing wrong," Arika comforted. Arika thought about her mother, who refused to believe that her father abused her. Finally, Arika befriended a man who was Yakuza. He taught her karate and took it a step further by almost beating her father to death. Of course, his protection came at a price, and that led to another form of slavery and ties to the Japanese underworld. But the abuse stopped. Arika was so happy to be free from that life.

She held Colette in her arms, and they cried together.

~~~~~~~~~~

Chapter Eight

Kittan

"Beautiful, isn't it?" Ankwot said as he viewed the planet Kittan for the first time.

"Yes, it is, but only from a distance," Wotkye said.

"Guanton told us about the great battles fought there."

"They are still fighting. We have waged war with the Kittans off and on for over twenty sections. They will never allow us to settle peacefully, and we will never give up.

"We sent settlers to Kittan to try to colonize the planet. The colonists went missing, over two thousand. So, we sent in a small force to locate them. They, too, disappeared without a trace."

"What happened?" Ankwot asked.

"The next expedition found out. We found the bones of thousands. Most were tied down or staked to the ground. We knew then that we were up against savage opponents, the Kittans.

186

"I was on that team. So were Guanton, Quanyo, and my brother Kotkye. I was almost killed there. That's how I got this." Wotkye pointed to the scar on his face.

~~~~~~~~

Guanton pointed to a hologram visual of the planet.

"We control this small section on Kittan. Fortunately, it is the highest elevation on the planet. We have a string of four forts escalating up this mountain range, linked by underground tunnels. The most heavily defended position is the lower fort, Post One. Heavy guns guard the valley entrance." Guanton pointed to that defensive position.

"The next two posts are parallel to one another. Post Two and Three safeguard the west and east sides of the slope. A huge hangar cut into the mountain allows access from the air. It is protected by a magnetic shield and guns that prevent attack from above.

Guanton paused and pointed to another section. "This is post four, the nerve center and safest area in the complex. The high rock walls prevent attack from the ground and allow for observation across miles of the planet. Our people are housed in an underground complex built beneath the forts."

Guanton pointed to Quanyo. "Please tell us about the Kittans."

A three-dimensional hologram showed a Kittan warrior. "Our enemy is quite intelligent, so don't underestimate them just because they look like lizards. Their main weapon, the gonyo, is a triton-like spear. They use it to jab but also throw it with great accuracy. Kittans are also excellent bowmen and use arrows dipped in poison."

Quanyo pointed to the center prong of the triton. "This section of the gonyo fires an acid concentrate. If it comes in contact with your armor, it will dissolve it, seep into your skin, and poison your body.

"Kittans are over ten feet tall and very powerful. They have large black eyes and claws that look like hands. One of their favorite tactics is to use their long tails to knock you to the ground before attacking with razor-sharp teeth. Biting or slashing with those teeth enables them to secrete their saliva, which is a deadly poison that kills in minutes. Wotkye, please add your thoughts."

"Kittans always attack in large groups. They don't mind losing ten to kill just one of us. A female Kittan produces a litter of fifteen to twenty young, fully mature in two years. Their armies are continually replenished, which is why the war against them has lasted so long."

"Don't surrender or get captured by the Kittans either," Wotkye said. "They will stake you to the ground and let their young eat you alive."

"You have been fighting them for twenty sections. That's a hundred years," Slawoo said. "What makes that planet so valuable?"

It was a question that many of the Ring-Men wanted to ask.

"The planet is one of the natural food sources in the universe. Wheat grows wild in the fields, with stalks as high as fifteen feet. The huge wild boars that roam free are delicious when roasted. But most of all, it's the honey," Kotkye said.

"Honey?" Ascon asked.

"Kittan has giant bees that produce the best and most nutritious honey in the universe," Kotkye said, licking his lips at the thought. "You should taste the molaka fermented from that honey."

"How big are the bees?" Gutlap asked.

"Oh, about three feet long," Kotkye said, spreading his hands to show their size. "Their heads are a foot wide, with mandibles so powerful that they can sever your hand with one bite."

"They sound as dangerous as the Kittans," Gutlap said.

Kotkye laughed. "I haven't told you about their stingers yet. They are a foot long with a toxin that paralyzes instantly."

Ascon asked, "Is there any good news?"

"Well, the bees don't discriminate. They attack the Kittans, too."

"Enough!" Guanton shouted. "Survivors of Ringnon are down there. Remember, you have Ringnonian blood coursing through your veins."

He walked in front of the crew with a serious scowl. "We will either win this planet or help our race escape it."

～～～～～～

"We are getting a strange communication from a spacecraft just out of range of our guns, Commander. They are requesting you at the command center."

"Who is?" Quill asked as he sat at the edge of his cot.

"The watch commander, sir," said the nervous Ringnonian.

"This had better be important. Tell them I will be there momentarily. Wait outside."

"Yes, sir," said the obedient messenger.

Quill was tired. He got up and looked into a small mirror as he doused his face with water. The constant headache of command was taking its toll. He ran his hand through his thick gray and black hair and slipped on his tunic. At nine feet six inches tall, he was as imposing a figure as any of the younger Ringnonians. But he was feeling his age of fifty-two sections. Quill still presented the appearance of a person in full command of any situation. But his people's present dilemma had no discernable solution.

He looked again into the mirror and thought. *This constant fighting with the Kittans…overcrowded conditions…the lack of food…I wish we'd had more time to prepare before we left Ringnon. But I have to remain positive, no matter how hopeless the situation is.*

"But what are we going to do?" he said aloud.

"Did you say something, sir?" asked the eager Ringnonian.

Quill didn't answer. He stepped from his quarters. "Lead the way."

Chapter Nine

Quill

"Please identify your vessel," said the Ringnonian communicator.

"Has Quill been located?"

"Identify yourself, or we will fire upon you."

"We are out of range."

"What is it, Captain?" Quill asked as he entered the command post.

"They won't identify themselves, sir. They want to talk to you," explained the officer.

"Identify yourself," Quill ordered.

"Have I been away so long that you don't know who I am?"

"That voice...no, it can't be...Guanton, is that you?" Quill asked.

"In the flesh, as you will see if you open the magnetic barricade and allow us to land."

A wave of joy filled Quill's heart. Joy like he hadn't felt in a long time.

"Open the barricade."

A large wall opened on the west side of the mountain fortress. Lights lit the opening to a cavernous hangar, and the *Winyee* landed gently on Kittan.

~~~~~~~~~~~~~~~~

Guanton was the first off, the *Winyee*. He turned and saw his brother standing before a welcoming group of Ringnonians.

Tears were in Quill's eyes as he stepped forward, and the brothers embraced. They stood holding each other for what seemed like minutes. Quill kissed his brother's cheek and hugged him again.

"Enough," said Guanton, "I must save some for my mate."

Quill laughed and pulled back. "I had given up all hope of ever seeing you again," he said, still shaking his head in disbelief.

"I came back to see one person, and it's not you," Guanton said. "Is she well?"

"Yes, my brother, she is."

"What of my son?" Guanton asked.

Quill became sullen. "The plague took Guilton, along with my mate Sonia."

Guanton stood silent as he thought of his son. He controlled the desire to lament openly.

Ringnonians, while showing emotion at times, always held back public displays of grief.

"I'm sorry, Guanton," Quill said, noting Guanton's restraint.

"I am also sorry for your loss, my brother. I know how much you loved Sonia."

Guanton paused, and then he asked, "Where is Winyee?"

"She is at the lower fort. I have sent for her. It will take some time for her to come. Let us talk before she gets here."

"Of course, but first, I want you to meet the rest of my crew."

The ship's personnel stood quietly behind Guanton, not wanting to interrupt his reunion.

Quill inspected the assembled group. He recognized Quanyo immediately.

"Quanyo, still alive, I see." He laughed as he approached and hugged the Ringnonian.

"Yes, Quill, you know how hard it is to kill me." He turned and saw the two smiling brothers, Wotkye and Kotkye.

"Wotkye, fine warrior, how are you? You, Kotkye, are you still brewing those concoctions?"

"Yes sir," Kotkye said.

He noticed Ascon, but there was something different about him. "Is that you, Ascon? You look younger than ever."

"That is my name, Commander," Ascon replied.

"He is Ascon's son," Guanton said. "Ascon was killed on Earth."

Quill turned, "I'm sorry, but a son? How is that possible?"

"Earth women are quite beautiful, and we were there for quite a while. See for yourself." Guanton pointed to Arika.

Quill approached her. "I see what you mean. What is your name, my child?"

Arika looked at Guanton for an interpretation.

"He wants to know your name," Guanton said in Japanese.

"Arika."

"You are quite lovely, Arika. Welcome," Quill said in perfect Japanese.

"Thank you," Arika said.

"What a lovely language," Quill said, looking at Guanton.

"Just one of the thousands of dialects on Earth," Guanton said.

"And who is this?" Quill asked, watching Colette as she hid behind Arika.

"That is Colette, a survivor from *Ringnon Two* that we picked up," Guanton said.

A surprised look crossed Quill's face.

Guanton whispered, "I will explain later." He pointed to the remaining crewmembers standing at attention.

"These are the Ring-Men," Guanton said.

Quill looked at the Ring-Men. "No…they look like Ringnonians to me. Welcome, all of you."

~~~~~~~~~

Guanton walked with Quill as they inspected *Ringnon One*, the large habitation vessel that transported the Ringnonians to Kittan.

"I believe we can prepare her for travel to a more suitable planet. I just don't know where that should be," Quill said.

Guanton asked, "What about Twuonay?"

"*Ringnon Two* was headed there; so is the plague. That plague is a living animal that sucks the life out of everything that it touches. I am afraid that every planet in this solar system, including this one, will eventually experience an attack from that plague. What about Earth?" Quill asked.

"It is a wonderful planet but governed very poorly. Over two hundred different rulers have divided the planet into sections called countries. We did solve some of the major issues there, but suspicion led to them trying to kill all of us."

"Are they not one species?" Quill asked.

"Yes, but they fight constantly among themselves," Guanton said.

"There are two unclaimed areas that we might develop," Guanton said. "One is the North Polar area, and the other is in the south, called Antarctica. Radiation makes aging accelerate. We would have to find a solution for that."

"Will we be welcomed?" Quill asked.

"That is a good question. I'm not sure," Guanton admitted. "I helped them install a satellite defense system to keep them from using nuclear missiles to destroy the planet and each other. What they don't know is that I have the codes that control all the satellites."

"Are they using nuclear fission? That's not very smart. On the other hand, you, my brother, were always your mother's smartest son."

"Guanton!"

Guanton recognized the voice immediately. He turned and saw Winyee. She looked lovely standing there dressed in an orange work jumpsuit. Tears flowed from her eyes as she ran and jumped into his arms.

They kissed tenderly.

"Oh, my love, I never gave up hope of seeing you again." She laid her head on his chest.

"Nor I of you, my dearest love," Guanton said as he ran his hand across her head.

"I should have waited until I was more presentable. I look a mess."

"You are as beautiful as ever."

She squeezed him again and began to cry. "I'm afraid I have bad news about Guilton."

"I know, my sweet," Guanton said, caressing her back. "We will talk about it later."

"I will go and prepare our quarters," she said, pulling away from him as she dried her eyes.

~~~~~~~~~

"I know you haven't had any real Ringnonian rum in quite a while," Quill said as he poured from a large pitcher.

They were sitting in Quill's private quarters talking. Quill listened intently as Guanton described life on Earth and their journey to Kittan.

"We must leave this planet as soon as possible, but there are a few problems," Quill said. "The first is the shortage of food. This facility was designed to house about ten thousand, and we now have fifty thousand in these four forts."

"How goes the fighting?" Guanton asked.

"The Kittans have a new leader named Gribec. He won't talk or reason. He has ordered attacks at least once a day for the last eight months. They began attacking soon after our sleep period ended. We have been unable to gather what we need the most—food. In the meantime, our losses are mounting." Quill emptied his mug.

"What is the condition of *Ringnon One*?"

"She needs some minor repairs, but basically, she is good to go." Quill leaned forward. "To leave, we need food."

"Honey," Guanton stated. "We will fill storage tanks full of honey and eat that as a starter. Then, we will gather as much wheat as *Ringnon One* will carry. If we need more food on the journey, we will trade for it on Gabet. Remember, we have plenty of Acala bark.

"It is good to have you back, my brother. I've missed your clear thinking," Quill said as he poured rum into his mug. "More rum?"

"No, I don't want to be drunk when I see Winyee."

"Quanyo looks and acts differently," Quill said.

"Yes, he is different. We saved his life, and he appreciates that. He has also taken Ascon as his Kitaw."

"Really? I didn't think Quanyo cared about anyone but himself."

"As you said, he has changed." Guanton drank the last of his rum.

"Tell me about young Ascon," Quill said.

"He is just like his father—brave, intelligent, and a born leader. He is in love with the Earth woman."

"I can see why. She is quite lovely. Are they all so beautiful?" Quill asked.

"Not all, but many are just like her."

"I have been to Earth once. Have I ever told you the story?" Quill asked, obviously inebriated.

"Yes, you have...many times, my brother. I must go and see my mate." Guanton stood and put his hand on Quill's shoulder. "We will talk again tomorrow."

"Yes, tomorrow," Quill agreed as Guanton left.

~~~~~~~~~~

Arika was billeted with Colette, who would not leave her side. Colette adopted Arika as a second mother. Arika did not mind. The attention helped satisfy the maternal void she had felt for years.

Also sharing their quarters were two Ringnonian sisters; the plague on Ringnon had killed their parents. They were cordial, friendly, and curious about life on Earth.

"Your Ascon is very powerful, is he not?" asked Willow, the youngest.

"He is half-human, is he not?" Triess asked.

Arika was happy to answer any questions. She became fond of the friendly sisters, as did Colette.

Ascon and Arika could not spend any time together. The few precious moments they saw one another were interrupted by Colette, who stayed close to Arika, serving as an unwanted chaperone.

Chapter Ten

Winyee

Winyee lay in Guanton's arms, listening to the beating of his heart. She leaned on her elbows and looked into his eyes.

"The Earth woman," Winyee asked, "Is she Quanyo's mate?"

"No, Ascon's. Why did you ask that?"

"I don't know. It's just the way she looks at him. Are all of the Earth women as attractive as that one?"

He knew the question was coming. "Quite a few of them are." He laughed to himself, waiting.

"Well, did you?"

"Did I what?"

She hit him in the ribs.

He feigned pain. "Ouch! Are you trying to injure me?"

"Answer me," she said in a sweet tone that he found irresistible. He ran his hand through her hair and looked into her eyes.

"No, my love. I found no one, nor did I want to. Now tell me, my sweet, what happened to our son?"

He waited to broach the subject, not wanting to sadden their tender moment together. But now he wanted to know.

"Tell me, Winyee, please."

She rested her head on his chest.

"The plague looked like a slow-moving green cloud as it entered our atmosphere. Three weeks after the cloud was sighted, it landed and started down its destructive path."

Guanton felt tears warming his chest. He began to stroke her hair.

"The first city affected was Tooloon. Ringnonians died by the thousands. Medical teams were sent in, but we could do nothing. The city was quarantined and finally destroyed.

The surrounding areas were firebombed in the hopes of destroying the plague, but it just laughed at us and moved on.

"We called the plague K-2053 after Kono, the first scientist to die fighting it on Dalmate. We tried serums, cold, heat, and everything in between, but nothing stopped the plague. I thought we were safe in Quikat so high up in the mountains, but I was wrong." Winyee began to sob.

Guanton brought her closer and held her tightly.

"I was working late at the lab one night when I got a call. Our section of the city was attacked by the wind-driven virus. I got home, but I was too late." She broke down crying uncontrollably.

Guanton said nothing. He just held her and began to weep.

~~~~~~~~~~

Guanton woke up with Winyee still lying in his arms. He promised himself that he would never leave her again.

Winyee stirred and looked into his eyes. "You are awake, my love."

"Yes, I am, and I am so sorry I was not here with you."

"Nonsense, you were doing your duty. Guilton told everyone about his father, the great Guanton. He was so proud of you."

"I wish I could have seen him grow up." Guanton sat on the edge of the bed.

Winyee moved behind and embraced him. "He loved you as much as I do."

"Quanyo told me that you saved his life," she said in an attempt to change the subject.

"I was not alone," he said, facing her.

"I thank you for my brother's life. I know how you feel about him."

"He has changed," Guanton said as he got up and reached for a packet on a dresser.

His tone indicated to her that he did not want to talk about that subject any longer. She knew her mate well, his likes and his moods. "Is that a present for me?"

"Not exactly; it is a piece of Acala bark." She took the package and opened it.

"Have you kept any samples of the plague?"

"Yes, we have it in the lab. We feed it rodents to keep it alive."

"Examine that bark. It has great healing properties, and the plant we took it from was also a living, thinking organism."

~~~~~~~~~~

Guanton and Winyee breakfasted in one of the large dining rooms next to an older couple. Three such feeding facilities were spread across the complex, and a schedule was maintained to prevent overcrowding.

The male asked his mate, "What have we got today?"

"The same as usual, porridge and a little bread, "she said.

Winyee looked at Guanton with a knowing smile. "You have probably tasted better food over the last few sections."

"Boiled rocks would taste good as long as I could eat them next to you," he said, looking down at her.

A siren alerted the dining facility of an attack. The warning signal was followed by a voice ordering, "All warriors to your battle stations. There is an attack on Post Two."

Guanton kissed Winyee and hurried to the action. Post Two was the center fort on the west side, located halfway up the mountain.

Guanton met Quill as he moved toward the command center.

"Good, I'm glad you're here. Did you have an enjoyable night?" he asked, smiling as they walked together.

"Yes, quite nice. What is the situation?"

"The Kittans look like they are searching for a weakness. This is the second time they have attacked Post Two this week."

A captain met Quill as he entered the command post. "Looks like an all-out attack, sir."

"We need to get upstairs," Quill said as he and Guanton moved into an elevator.

The doors opened to the sound of machine gun lasers and cannons blasting away. The alleyway was crowded with Ringnonians moving to their battle stations.

"What's the situation?" Quill asked of a Ringnonian officer who approached him.

"Thousands of Kittans attacking the west face of Post Two," the officer said.

"Where are our gunships?" Quill asked as he looked through his field glasses at the charging Kittans.

"The three that are functional will be here momentarily," said the captain.

"Tell them to concentrate on the center and try to drive a wedge in their formation," Quill said.

Guanton remained silent, observing his older brother issue orders. "What do you think?" Quill asked.

"Why don't we have more air support?"

"The Kittans have become more sophisticated since you last fought them. They have a new strategy against our gunships. They are firing larger gonyos filled with that nasty acid of theirs that eats away at our armor." He handed Guanton his field glasses.

"See there," Quill pointed to a large gonyo as the Kittans prepared to fire.

"Looks like a giant catapult," Guanton said.

"Yes, primitive, but quite effective."

"Such numbers! There must be five thousand in this bunch," Guanton said as he looked over the battlefield. From his vantage, he saw Quanyo, Ascon, and several Ring-Men helping to repel the attack. He felt a sense of pride.

True Ringnonians, he thought.

Three gunships arrived and began pulverizing the center of the Kittan's line.

A giant gonyo nearly hit one of the ships as it dodged the large projectile.

"Do you have any Gitan firepower?" Guanton asked.

"Just the one on your ship," Quill said.

"Kotkye began a full overhaul of the *Winyee*'s engines this morning. I think she will be ready by tomorrow."

"We will be able to weather this attack. Look, they seem to be retreating anyway," Quill said, pointing to the Kittans, who were falling back.

"Besides, I have something far more important for you and your ship to do."

Chapter Eleven

Honey

The *Winyee* slid silently into the dark morning sky, followed by several other ships. The small armada comprised four harvest ships, two troop transports, and two gunships.

Two harvest ships had tanks large enough to hold thousands of gallons of honey. The other two would serve as silos, stuffed with as much grain as they could carry.

The troop transports carried one hundred soldiers each to protect the harvesters. Two hundred gleaners were also on board. They would use high-speed cutting and collection machines to gather the wheat.

Guanton created a large smoke dispenser and attached it to the *Winyee*. A smoky mixture made from Acala bark would be pumped into the nest. The sedative was designed to initially make the aggressive bees sluggish and lethargic, then eventually comatose.

Gatherers could then safely extract the honey from the hive using the large vacuums on the harvest ships.

"You must succeed," Quill told Guanton as they met on the flight platform.

"You get our people ready to leave, and I'll get the food they need," Guanton told his brother as they embraced. He turned to Winyee.

"I'll not be gone long, my love," Guanton told her.

"That is what you said the last time," she chided, trying to bring some levity to the situation.

Guanton kissed Winyee and left her crying.

~~~~~~~~~

"Did you hear that?" asked the sentry on duty on the lower level of Post One.

"Hear what?" another guard asked.

"I keep hearing a scratching noise, sounds like scraping."

"It's probably one of those big Kittan rats. You know we are at the lowest point of the fort. What do you expect?"

"I hate rats."

"Well, go then. You're relieved."

The relief guard sat and began to eat his meal, paying no attention to the activity behind the wall.

~~~~~~~~~

One troop transport and two harvest ships landed in the middle of a large wheat field.

The stalks measured over fifteen feet and hid the ships perfectly. Torcon, the group commander, ordered his one hundred soldiers to set up a wide defensive perimeter.

"Torcon, unload your reapers and begin loading the wheat. I will leave one of the gunships with you. Keep it hidden in the wheat unless you are attacked. If that happens, signal me and get out with whatever you have. Is that understood?"

"Yes, sir."

"We are heading to the hives," Guanton said.

One of the gunships broke free from the formation and landed in the wheat field.

Quanyo commanded the second troop transport. Ascon, eight Ring-Men, and ninety Ringnonians were also aboard.

Quanyo stood and addressed his troops. "Hopefully, the bees will be dormant, but if you are attacked, aim for their antennae. Those appendages are used to communicate, and they are helpless without them. When killed, the bees emit a pheromone that summons others. That will cause a swarm, and we don't want that."

The troop ship landed a hundred feet from a large mound with a thud. It was still early, and the bees were quietly at rest in the hive. The entry hole was a gaping opening over ten feet wide. Guanton ordered Wotkye to maneuver just above it. Seven huge sentry bees guarded the passageway. The *Winyee* lowered slowly. The bees did not move.

"Extend the smoke tube," Guanton ordered, almost whispering.

Thick smoke began to ooze from a long tube suspended from the *Winyee*.

There was no reaction from the bees. Suddenly, one of the large bees dropped to the ground.

"It's working," Wotkye sighed with relief.

~~~~~~~~~~

Ascon led a masked squad of eight Ring-Men into the entry hole. Bees lay everywhere, silently sleeping as the team moved slowly through the labyrinth. Thirty harvesters followed closely behind and moved cautiously, pulling the large hoses designed to suck the valuable honey from the hive.

A bee stirred momentarily and flew toward Ascon. Influenced by the intoxicant, it flew into a wall and fell buzzing to the ground.

Ascon, armed with a smoke gun loaded with the stupefying mixture, fired a small burst directly into the face of the bee and silenced it. They explored the rest of the hive and found the entire nest sedated.

"They are asleep, Guanton," Ascon said as he motioned the harvesters to begin their work.

"Tell them not to destroy any of the larvae," Guanton said. "The darker colored combs have young grubs in them, and tell them to hurry. The Kittans will be moving when the sun comes up."

Like all cold-blooded reptiles, Kittans became active as the sun warmed their bodies. Guanton knew that they would be moving soon.

"Come in, Torcon," Guanton called.

"Yes, sir."

"How's it going?"

"One ship is almost loaded with wheat."

"Once loaded, send it back to base," Guanton said, " It's warming up. Keep your soldiers alert. You can expect action at any time."

"Guanton, we have found the queen's chamber. There are six of them," Ascon said excitedly.

"Don't disturb or damage them. If hurt or killed, they will release a particularly strong pheromone, and bees will be summoned from all over the planet."

~~~~~~~~~~

Chapter Twelve

Wheat

It was very quiet. The hum of the reaping machines was the only noise disturbing the morning peace. The machine's engines were disguised to imitate buzzing bees to avoid detection by the Kittans.

"Wouldn't wild boar taste great for dinner?" Kueott asked the Ringnonian stationed to his left.

Kueott aimed his blaster and fired at a large pig grazing on wheat. The hog fell to the ground in a heap.

"Who fired that shot?" asked the commander.

"It was I, Kueott, sir."

"What were you firing at?"

"A large boar, sir."

"You idiot! Do you want to bring the Kittans down on us? Only fire at the enemy. That goes for all of you."

But it was too late. Stirred by the sun's warmth and alerted by the blaster, Kittans began to move in on the wheat-gathering team.

~~~~~~~~

"The tanks on the first ship are loaded with honey, Guanton," Wotkye said. "They are requesting permission to head back to base."

"Tell them to take off," Guanton said.

"We are under attack. They are everywhere," said the distress call. "Torcon…Torcon…. report," Guanton said.

"He's dead, sir. They are all around us!" said a panicked voice.

"Guanton to gunship two, come in." There was no answer.

"Quanyo," Guanton called.

"Yes, Guanton?"

"Load your Ringnonians; get to the wheat field and take charge. Wotkye, tell our gunship to support Quanyo's troopers. Ascon, hurry up; we've got trouble at the wheat field."

~~~~~~

"I keep hearing it, and it sounds like digging," said the guard as he put his ear to the thick stone wall. "Do you think I should report it?"

"Report what? Rats on the outside of the wall? Go ahead. Report it and look like a fool," said the second sentry.

"I don't care what kind of fool I look like. I'm reporting it."

~~~~~~

Arika, Colette, and the two sisters were making themselves useful. They were helping by making clothing in one of the two factories located on the lower level of Post One.

Arika always enjoyed sewing. As she worked, she listened to the beautiful singing of the Ringnonian women. She did not understand the words, so she hummed the melody as they sang.

It was morning, with no attack launched by the Kittans. The entire fort was a hubbub of activity as preparations for the rumored departure were underway. There was a feeling of happiness and optimism all around.

~~~~~~

Quanyo's troopship moved over the wheat field, which was now a battlefield. Isolated pockets of Ringnonians were trying to fight off hundreds of Kittans in the high grass.

"Gunship One," Quanyo said, "blow a hole in the wheat over to the right of the transport. We will land and set up a defensive position."

He looked at Gunship Two and saw her hopelessly disabled. "Smart, they took out the gunship first."

"Gunship One... continue firing as you circle the transport. We have got to get it into the air."

The troop transport landed, and Quanyo was the first off the ship. His troops made a defensive square in the area cleared by the gunship. "All troops fall back to the transport and this position," he commanded.

The scattered Ringnonian warriors and reapers, some wounded, fell back to the position.

Kittans charged; some hurled gonyos while others fired arrows at the defenders.

Ringnon firepower began to drive them back. Of the hundred Ringnonian warriors and two hundred reapers under Torcon's command, twenty escaped the high grass.

"How much wheat is loaded on the transport?" Quanyo asked one of the wounded reapers.

"It is about half full."

"It will have to do. We are getting out of here. Gunship one, blow a path from my position to the transport," Quanyo said.

The gunship moved obediently into position and burned out the high wheat, opening a fifty-yard path to the wheat transporter.

"A large group of Kittans are coming from the rear, Quanyo," said the gunship.

"Gunship one, cover the retreat to the transports. I'll take care of the Kittans."

"Go!" he said to the large group. "Get that transport in the air. I need ten of you with me." Ten Ringnonians remained as the others moved toward the ship.

"They will be all over us in a moment, form a pinwheel." The Ringnonians formed with Quanyo in the center.

Fifty Kittans burst from the tall grass, thirty feet from the small team. Another group moved in twenty yards on the right, and still another group to the left.

Quanyo gave the order, "Fire!"

Tremendous firepower blasted holes in the charging Kittans, but they continued forward. The fallen Kittans formed a barricade, but the Kittans climbed over them and kept coming. The bodies were so close that green blood spurted on the Ringnonian's armored suits.

"All are aboard! Quanyo, get out of there!" said the gunship operator.

Quanyo turned toward the ships and fired his cannon through the massed bodies. Lizard parts and green slime flew into the air, creating a path toward the transports.

They ran for the ship with Kittans following closely behind. The gunship fired, attempting to slow down the pursuing Kittans. A Ringnonian was hit in the back by a gonyo and fell to the ground.

"Quanyo, help me," he pleaded.

Quanyo saw the soldier fall. He reversed direction and began firing his cannon. He reached the wounded trooper just as a Kittan prepared to finish him with a thrust from a gonyo. The Kittan saw Quanyo approach and swung the gonyo at his head. Quanyo ducked the blow and, in the same motion, used his knife to gut the Kittan.

Two more Kittans faced him. One used his gonyo to jab at Quanyo's midsection. He grabbed the gonyo and pulled the Kittan forward as he used his knife to slash the Kittan across the back of its neck. It fell to the ground dead.

The second Kittan fired acid from his gonyo. Quanyo eluded the poison and returned fire with his cannon, hitting the Kittan in the chest. The blast at such close range blew the Kittan twenty feet away.

The retreating Ringnonians followed their captain's lead and returned to their wounded comrade. They began firing their blasters, killing one Kittan after another. The Kittans retreated.

Two Ringnonians picked up the wounded soldier and carried him to the waiting ship.

Quanyo was the last to board.

~~~~~~~~~~~

Chapter Thirteen

Breech

"Commander, this sentry has something I think you need to hear," the captain said as he ushered the guard in to see Quill.

"Well, what is it?" Quill asked impatiently.

"Commander…it may be nothing, but I thought…I thought I heard some digging behind the walls."

He didn't have time to say anything else because a tremor shook the fort.

"What was that?" Quill asked.

"Sir, explosion in the lower fort. Kittans are entering a breech in the wall."

———— ∿∿∿∿∿∿∿ ————

The females in the clothing factory felt the brunt of the explosion. Smoke and dust filled the room. Many were killed outright, and a number were wounded or stunned. Arika saw Colette knocked cold by the blast and ran to her aid.

Both Willow and Triess lay dead beneath the blast's rubble. Arika heard the Kittans' strange grunts as they entered through the opening made by the explosion.

The moaning of the wounded mixed with cries for help. A huge Kittan stood over Arika; a piece of red quartz hung from his neck. He pointed his gonyo in her direction.

~~~~~~~~~~~~~~~

"We have a breech in the wall of Post One. Kittans are pouring into the fort." The message was faint but clearly understood.

"Ascon, we've got to move," Guanton insisted.

"We're pulling out right now and just in time," Ascon said. "The bees are beginning to stir."

Then Guanton brainstormed, "Are you close to the queen's chamber?"

"Yes, I am passing it now," Ascon said.

"Drag one of the queens from the nest," Guanton said.

"What?"

"You heard me. Secure a queen and drag her from the nest."

Ascon and two Ring-Men did as commanded. The queen was twice as large as a worker bee, almost six feet long. The effects of the drug were wearing off, and she was moving. Ascon and the others managed to pull her from the nest.

"Now tie the other end of the rope to a strut on the *Winyee*."

The queen was awake and agitated.

"Everyone get aboard the vessels except you, Ascon."

The soldiers loaded onto the *Winyee*, and the harvesters boarded the transport. Guanton ordered the transport back to the base.

"Now, Ascon, cut her open and come aboard." Ascon was puzzled but followed Guanton's instructions.

The bee's entrails fell to the ground as the *Winyee* lifted her into the air. The ship paused in mid-air, waiting. Bees began to arrive from every direction…two…twenty…a hundred…a thousand, all swarming around the *Winyee*.

The *Winyee* began to move slowly toward the fort, the swarm in close pursuit.

"Guanton, get back here; we need air support," Quill said.

"I'm bringing you plenty of air support. Get all of our troops inside and seal the upper levels."

"What?"

"I've got bees coming to help us, but our troops must be protected."

"Get everyone inside and close all the outside shutters," Quill said to an officer. He smiled as he realized what Guanton had in mind. "Move our soldiers to the lower level before we are overrun. Try to hold the Kittans there."

The huge Kittan grunted and squeaked as it motioned to Arika. Arika could not understand his instructions, but Colette, though groggy, understood him.

"He's ordering us to go with them."

Of the one hundred Ringnonian females in the clothing factory, thirty survived the blast. Some were severely wounded. Arika, Colette, and ten others suffered minor cuts and bruises but could walk.

Colette interpreted more of the grunts and tweaks from the huge Kittan.

"He says if we can't move, they will kill us."

Arika helped Colette to her feet, and they moved toward the opening. Hundreds of Kittan warriors sped past them, headed for the upper levels. Arika and Colette were ushered through the breech. As they left, they heard the screams of the females who could not walk.

"We're holding on level two, but the fighting's fierce," Quill told Guanton. "Thousands of Kittans pushing through the breech trying to get in."

"Yes, I see them. I'm going to drop this carcass as close to the opening as I can."

The *Winyee* hovered above the swelling mass of Kittans and released the dead bee.

Thousands of bees followed her to the ground and began attacking the Kittans.

The Kittans fought back, killing hundreds of bees. The strong pheromone released by their deaths attracted even more bees. Bees moved in from all corners of the planet and joined in the assault on the Kittans.

Without the momentum of the Kittans pushing from the outside, the attack on the inside lost steam. Fighting downhill, the Ringnonians began to push the Kittans in the fort back through the breech. Kittan casualties mounted as they retreated.

Chapter Fourteen

Pursuit

Thousands of Kittans and bees lay dead outside the fort. A similar scene was replicated on the lower level with dead Kittans and Ringnonians everywhere.

Quill and Guanton surveyed the damage.

"We must prepare to leave as soon as possible," Quill said. "How much food did you bring in?"

"The honey transports are full, and plenty of wheat was collected. We can bargain for what we don't have on our journey."

Guanton shook his head as he saw the Ringnonian bodies, many of which were females and children. "What a waste."

"Yes, it is. We must leave before they attack again," Quill said.

~~~~~~~~

"I have not been able to find Arika," Ascon told Guanton.

"Colette is also missing," Guanton said. "They were captured by the Kittans."

Ascon seemed stunned but quickly recovered. "We must go after her."

"She has probably already been fed to their young," Kotkye said.

"She is alive, and we will find her," Quanyo said reassuringly.

"The habitation ship must leave. We cannot wait for the Kittans to attack again," Guanton said.

"We do everything in our power to save one another even if it means our death," Dunwol urged.

Guanton smiled as he recalled his words now being repeated by the Ring-Man.

"Take the *Winyee* and the last gunship. We will load *Ringnon One* and prepare to leave. Who is going with you?" Guanton asked.

All of the Ring-Men stepped forward. So did Quanyo.

"We will bring them back," Quanyo said.

~~~~~~~~~~

The Kittans moved quickly across the rocky terrain, headed for their home in the swamp. They waited for no one, not even their own wounded. Anyone who could not keep pace was put to death.

Arika was exhausted. "I cannot go any further," she said.

"You must," Colette said as she helped her to keep stride. "If you stop, they will kill you."

One of the other captives offered to help. Her name was Kimmee, and she was a large female well over seven feet tall. She was also bulky and quite strong. Ringnonian women were not trained to be warriors, but that did not mean they could not fight. Most were quite athletic and able to defend themselves.

"Put her on my back," she told Colette. Kimmee easily carried the smaller-framed female.

~~~~~~~~~~

"We must catch them before they enter the swamp," Quanyo communicated to Ascon.

Ascon and his crew of twenty Ringnonians and five Ring-Men

sped along in the gunship, scanning the landscape for the retreating Kittans.

The *Winyee*, piloted by Wotkye and commanded by Quanyo, did the same. The remaining Ring-Men and twenty Ringnonian volunteers were aboard, joining the rescue effort.

The Kittans retreated in two columns that veered off in different directions. Their trails were easy to follow. The gunship followed one, the *Winyee* the other. The unit finding the captives would attempt to slow the Kittans until the other came in support.

"Look over there," Ascon directed, pointing to a cloud of dust. The gunship moved in that direction.

"About five hundred Kittans…I see the females," Revel exclaimed as they flew over the fleeing Kittans.

"Quanyo, we have found the group with the females. They are a short distance from the swamp's edge," Ascon advised.

"You have to stop them before they enter the swamp. If they get in there, we will never find them. We are honing in on your signal," Quanyo said.

"We can't fire the guns on the ship; we might hit the females," Revel warned.

"Speed to the edge of the swamp," Ascon decided. "We will try to stop them on the ground."

He turned toward the anxious crew. "The odds are against us, but remember—we are Ringnonians."

~~~~~~~~~~

Guanton took in the view of the sunset from an alcove in the fort. His mind was fixed on the Ascon and Quanyo's desperate struggle. Winyee silently moved toward her mate, not wishing to disturb him.

"I wish I were with them," he said.

"They will be fine, my love. You are needed here. There is much yet to do," Winyee said as she held him. "By the way, I have tested the sample of Acala bark you gave me."

"What did you find?"

"The bark killed the plague," she said as she looked into his eyes.

Guanton said nothing. He continued staring at the darkening evening with a pensive expression.

~~~~~~~~~~

"Spread out," Ascon said. "Remember, we can't let them get to the swamp. Be careful when choosing your targets; we don't want to hit any females. Wait for my order to fire."

Ascon divided his force into groups of five. High grass partially hid the warriors as they took cover behind large rocks and fallen trees.

Each group was stationed twenty feet apart while waiting for the approaching Kittans. The gunship was hidden, out of sight. Ascon would call for it if it were needed.

The first Kittan appeared moments later. A large specimen, gonyo in hand moved quickly from the tall grass, fifty yards in front of a larger group.

Ascon waited until more than half of them were in range.

"Fire!" Ascon ordered.

Laser blasts lit the evening sky. The first salvo took down forty of the large lizards.

The Kittans massed and moved as one to attack. Cannon blasts accurately directed to their center stopped the charge, with sixty more falling dead to the ground.

The Kittans tried to flank Ascon's position by attacking the left.

Ascon ordered in the gunship.

Revel opened up with synchronized machine gun blasters and demolished that left flanking maneuver.

The Kittans headed in the opposite direction but were similarly frustrated by two teams of Ringnonians that Ascon repositioned, having anticipated that move.

The Kittans retreated. More than two hundred lay dead, killed by the ambush.

But there was no sign of the captives.

~~~~~~~~

Arika and the other prisoners lay motionless in a clearing as two Kittan warriors stood guard. Their feet and hands were bound to prevent escape. Arika was tied to Kimmee.

"Distract the guards. Make a noise and pretend you are sick," Kimmee whispered to Colette. She showed Colette a large sewing scissor that was hidden in her apron. She had freed her hands and Arika's also.

"Ooh… oh…my stomach," Colette screamed as she writhed on the ground.

A series of grunts and squeaks indicated the displeasure of one of the guards as he approached the young Ringnonian. He leaned over her, demanding that she stop screaming.

Kimmee sprung onto his back and drove the scissors deep into his skull with all her might. The Kittan fell dead to the ground. She fell with the dead Kittan, and one of her legs was pinned beneath his body.

The other guard reacted quickly, firing a full blast of acid from his gonyo at Kimmee. The acid hit her in the shoulder and splashed on her face. She screamed.

The Kittan moved in to finish her. Arika came to her rescue, using a skill she thought she had forgotten. She fired her body into the air and gave the Kittan a karate kick to his head that knocked him to the ground.

The Kittan, momentarily stunned, soon recovered. He moved toward Arika but was stopped by a hurled gonyo. It lodged deep in his chest, and he fell to the ground. Kimmee, having freed herself, had thrown the projectile that hit its mark.

She fell to the ground in excruciating pain as the acid ate through her body.

Arika tried to help her, but it was too late. Kimmee foamed at the mouth and died. "You are samurai," she said to the brave Ringnonian female.

Arika freed the other captives, and they escaped into the tall grass.

Chapter Fifteen

Rescue

An irate Gribec hit the Kittan closest to him with the butt of his gonyo. He grunted, ordering a search for the escapees.

As the Kittans began to disperse, Quanyo and his team arrived and opened fire on the group.

Twenty Kittans fell dead in the clearing. The others retreated, running in panic in all directions.

"They are coming your way, Ascon," Quanyo warned.

~~~~~~

Ascon's teams spread out and moved forward cautiously, searching for the captives.

Ascon's heart almost jumped from his body when he saw Arika emerge from the grass with Colette and the others. She ran to him and jumped into his arms.

"We have the females. All teams assemble on my signal. Quanyo, we have Arika and the others," he radioed.

There was no time for him to hear the response. Charging Kittans exploded through the bushes and were upon them. A hurled gonyo missed his head by inches. Ascon whirled and fired his blaster point-blank at a Kittan two feet away. The large lizard fell dead at his feet.

Another lunged with its gonyo and knocked the blaster from his hand. Ascon pulled his knife, and they squared off.

The Kittan wore a piece of red quartz around his neck that Arika instantly recognized.

The four others in Ascon's squad engaged in a bitter life-and-death struggle with eight Kittans.

Ascon reached for his blaster, but the agile Kittan got there first and kicked it away. He swung his gonyo, just missing Ascon's head. Ascon countered, swinging his knife at the midsection of his opponent. The big reptile was too quick and easily eluded the stroke.

The Kittan fired acid from his gonyo. Ascon moved left to avoid the deadly mixture. The Kittan anticipated the move and swung his huge tail, whipping it across the back of Ascon's leg.

Ascon heard his leg snap as he fell to the ground.

The Kittan turned toward Arika, who was frozen with fear. He pointed his gonyo and prepared to fire acid at the terrified woman.

"Run, Arika," Ascon yelled.

She hesitated, then backed away and disappeared into the brush.

The Kittan turned to Ascon. "I am Gribec. I wanted you to know who it was that killed you."

He raised his gonyo, preparing to pin Ascon to the ground. The gonyo shattered as it was blown apart up to the handle.

Gribec turned and saw Quanyo and his team.

Quanyo fired again, but Gribec nimbly avoided the blast. An instant later, he was gone, escaping into the high grass.

~~~~~~~~~

Nine Kittans and three Ringnonians lay dead.

Quanyo knelt beside Ascon, in great pain, his leg bone sticking through his armored suit. He broke off a piece of Acala bark and pushed it into Ascon's mouth. Two Ring-Men held Ascon as he set the leg.

"Where's Arika?" Ascon asked before he passed out.

Quanyo looked around. He assumed she was with the other females receiving food and water from their rescuers.

"Where's Arika?" He asked, looking at Colette.

"She was here just a moment ago," Colette observed, looking around. Then, they heard a chilling scream.

"I see a Kittan carrying someone into the swamp," Wotkye said from the airborne *Winyee*.

Everyone knew it was Arika.

~~~~~~~~~~

Chapter Sixteen

The Swamp

Ascon awoke, but he could not move.

"We had to keep you restrained to prevent you from doing further damage to your leg," Revel said as he watched his friend.

"Where am I?"

"You are in the infirmary at Post Two. You were really out of it," Revel said as he rang for the nurse.

"Where is Arika?" Ascon asked. Revel did not answer.

"I see you are awake," said the nurse as she entered Ascon's cubicle.

"Revel...tell me...what happened to Arika?"

The nurse watched Revel, knowing that the answer would upset her patient.

Revel sighed and told him.

"She is still in the swamp. Quanyo went in after her. He refused to let anyone else go along."

"How long have they been gone?" Ascon asked.

"Two days, and we have not heard a word from him. He has a rescue beacon, and he said he would signal when he found Arika…if he finds her."

"Let me out of here. I need to help him find her."

"You are not going anywhere," the nurse said. "If it were not for the Acala bark your friend gave you, we would have amputated your leg. It is mending nicely. If you want to walk again, you'll stay put."

"I don't care about walking. I want Arika."

That was the last thing he said before the nurse sedated him.

Quanyo stretched after awakening from a short rest. The morning light was beginning to shine through the thick tree cover. He only glimpsed the lizard once in the day and a half that he tracked it. He wondered if the Kittan would simply kill Arika and escape. Or was the Kittan drawing him deeper into the swamp to spring a trap?

Quanyo thought that he would be able to make up time by tracking the reptile at night. But travel at night was dangerous in this swamp. He had already killed two large snakes that tried to make him their meal. It was safer to rest when the sun went down.

As he took a drink from his canteen, he heard something behind him but pretended not to notice. Quanyo ducked as a gonyo whooshed past his head and embedded in a tree. Turning just as the Kittan sprang from ambush, Quanyo reached for but could not grab his blaster.

Quanyo rolled out of the Kittan's path and jumped to his feet. He pulled out his handgun and fired. The Kittan was too quick, veering to the right to elude the shot. The lizard whipped its tail and knocked the gun from Quanyo's hand.

The Kittan retrieved his gonyo from the tree as Quanyo pulled his blade.

The Kittan tried to fire acid, but the gonyo appeared empty. "Out of ammunition," Quanyo said.

"I can kill you without a weapon. Your people are the cowards who fight without honor, blowing up and destroying everything."

"That hole in the fort shows me that you've also learned how to blow things up."

"We have learned to adapt. It took months of digging and the lives of thousands to accomplish that. We will eventually find a way to rid our home of your kind."

The Kittan jabbed the gonyo at Quanyo's midsection. Quanyo easily deflected the thrust.

The lizard whipped its tail in an attempt to take out Quanyo's legs.

Quanyo leaped into the air and followed that with a roll that brought him beneath the Kittan. The Kittan swung its gonyo, but it was too late. Quanyo slashed the Kittan's left arm and severed it from its body.

The Kittan howled and dropped the gonyo. Quanyo grabbed the legs of the large creature and tossed it headlong into a boggy marsh.

The Kittan righted itself but could not pull itself from the mire. It began to sink slowly in the quicksand.

"Where is the female?" Quanyo asked.

"She will die in this swamp."

"So will you if you don't tell me where she is," Quanyo said.

"Help me out first," the Kittan said.

"Tell me where she is first. Hurry, you are slipping fast."

"Then, will you help me out?"

"I will. I give you my word."

"Look down that path. She is staked to the ground."

Quanyo was down the path in a flash. He heard the Kittan protesting as he left.

He found Arika bound and unconscious, but she was alive. He cut her ties and lifted her into his arms. He gave her water and also gently poured some on her forehead. She began to stir.

The Kittan was down to its neck, barely holding to a vine with its one claw. Quanyo thought of letting it die. But then the lizard said something that changed his mind.

"I guess your word is worthless."

Quanyo reluctantly cut a long vine, looped it beneath the Kittan, and pulled it from the mire. Both opponents fell to the ground, exhausted.

"Who are you?" Quanyo asked.

"I am Gribec," he said.

"Remember that I saved your life, Gribec," Quanyo said.

"It changes nothing. You are still my sworn enemy."

"Why? This is a big planet; why not share it?"

"Never!" Gribec growled as it got to its feet.

"Well, it doesn't matter. There is a plague coming that is going to kill every living thing on this planet."

"Is that another one of your lies?"

"No, it's not. We are leaving this planet for good very shortly."

"That is the only way that there will be peace."

"I am sorry about your arm."

"Don't worry, it will grow back." A moment later, Gribec was gone.

~~~~~~~~~~

Quanyo rested with Arika high above the jungle floor. Not wanting to risk traveling with her at night, he carried her into the trees. In the morning, he would activate the rescue beacon and wait for pickup.

He knew that Kittans rarely, if ever, moved about at night. *But why take a chance?* At least, that was the excuse he told himself.

Or was it that I would have her all alone … all to myself for the first time?

He looked at her as she slept. Her creamy skin glowed as it soaked in the moonlight. Her long black hair reflecting the light made her beautiful face appear angelic. Quanyo had never been in love before.

Why am I thinking like this? She is Ascon's; he is my Kitaw. Pay attention and stay alert. Danger may still be lurking beneath us.

"Where are we?" Arika asked quietly as she awoke.

"We are safe for now. We will signal for pickup in the morning. Are you hungry?"

"No, a bit thirsty, though."

He handed her a canteen. "Drink slowly. You're dehydrated."

"What happened to that beast?"

"He's gone. He was a great warrior."

"You defeated him. That makes you an even greater warrior, doesn't it?"

"It could have gone either way."

"Thank you for coming after me," she said as she handed him the canteen.

"Ascon would have come if his leg were not smashed."

"Is he okay?" Arika felt guilty. She had not thought about Ascon.

"He will be fine. He is also quite brave, and he loves you very much."

"I know," she said.

"You have not said you love him," Quanyo said, probing her feelings.

"I do love him," she said as she turned away.

"You don't sound very convincing."

"Let's change the subject."

"Why? I only want to know what is in your heart." He reached out and stroked her hair.

She turned and looked into his eyes. "You already know what is in my heart."

She reached out her hand and touched his.

~~~~~~~~~~

Chapter Seventeen

Truce

Morning sunlight filtered through the leaves and woke Quanyo. He looked at Arika as she lay in his arms. He always scoffed at the idea of being in love. Now, he was experiencing the sensation for the first time. He loved Arika, and he was not about to give her up. *But what am I going to tell Ascon?*

"Wake up, sleepy," he said, giving her a gentle nudge.

"Good morning," she said, smiling as she looked into his eyes.

"We need to signal for rescue and return to the fort."

"I have already been rescued," she said as she squeezed him tighter. "I'm afraid of what will happen when we get back."

"You have Ascon waiting for you, remember?" he teased.

"You must help me tell him."

"I am afraid it is not quite that simple. You see—" His words were interrupted by a noise he heard beneath them. "Quiet," he whispered.

He looked down. What he saw horrified him. At least twenty Kittans stared up at the tree.

"Kittans," he said as he reached for his guns.

"Come down. We know you are up there," grunted their leader. The voice was familiar. It was Gribec.

Quanyo remained quiet as he tried to figure out a way to escape.

"Come down, and you will not be harmed. You have my word," grunted the voice again.

Quanyo holstered his pistol and slung his blaster.

"You wait here," he said, climbing down from the perch.

"It's coming from over there," Wotkye announced as he watched the direction finder on the instrument panel of the *Winyee*.

Guanton was anxious as the *Winyee* approached the location of the signal.

"Do you see what I see?" Wotkye asked.

Below them, in a clearing near the jungle, stood Quanyo, Arika, and twenty Kittans waving excitedly as the ship approached.

The ship landed, and Guanton exited cautiously.

What is going on here? Guanton asked Quanyo using silent communication.

It is good news, I assure you, he replied.

"Guanton, may I introduce you to Gribec, the war leader of the Kittans?"

Guanton nodded his head, as did the Kittan.

"He wishes to speak to the Council," Quanyo said, smiling.

"Ascon, how are you?" Arika asked.

Ascon was exercising his leg, which had improved to the point that he could put weight on it.

"Arika!" he said excitedly. He forgot his injury for a moment and stepped heavily on the still-healing limb. After stumbling, he reached for a crutch and moved toward her.

She came to him, and they hugged. He sensed that something was wrong.

"What is wrong, my love?"

"We must talk," Arika said.

From her tone, he knew that there was a very serious problem.

~~~~~~

Five well-respected Ringnonians sat on the Council of Ringnon. All major issues and judicial decisions were made by that body, with no appeal beyond them.

The oldest member of the Council was Gortook, an intellectual known for his mercy and wisdom. His expertise was in science, and he supervised that department. His responsibilities included overseeing such things as space exploration and new instrument and weapon development.

Quintan was the most knowledgeable. His specialty was law. He wrote, interpreted, and studied law and judicial decisions made for Ringnon and throughout the universe. He was also an intellectual who thought long and hard before asking pertinent questions.

Treena was the lone female on the body. One female was always required to voice the feminine concerns of the Ringnonians. Those concerns could include anything about being a female in a male-dominated society. Both beautiful and wise, she supervised the health of her people, ranging from nutrition to childbirth. Her vote on the Council was equal to the others.

Torlack was a warrior and the most suspicious and cynical of the group. His war record and battle scars spoke for his bravery, and he had the final word on all military issues. Quill was filling that role while

Torlack recovered from a wound. Still weak, Quill felt he was fit enough to resume his duties on the Council.

Finally, there was Quill. Warrior, ambassador, hero, and legend, he was the chairman of the Council. Especially known for his wisdom and patience, he always listened carefully before voicing an opinion.

There were no jails on Ringnon because there was no need. If a Ringnonian committed what was considered a crime, he was brought before a leader or officer and charged. Witnesses testified to his act. Then, the accused was allowed to admit guilt. If the matter was not settled, the Ringnonian was brought before the Council for final judgment.

If he was innocent, he was freed. If guilty, he was put to death. Even young ones were subject to the Council's decisions, but parents could plead for mercy in their case. There was little if any, juvenile delinquency on Ringnon.

Gribec spoke before this group.

"We appreciate your desire to speak to us," Quill said as an introduction. "Please proceed."

"As long as I can remember, we have fought you on my planet. You came here uninvited, destroyed our swamp land—our home— and killed a great many of my people.

"I carry this red rock." Gribec held the quartz stone for all to see. "It indicates that I decide all matters involving warfare. If it were my decision, we would fight you until the last drop of our green blood was spilled on the soil.

"But the Elder, the oldest living Kittan, has ordered me to talk to you. What your warrior Quanyo said, is it true? Will our planet suffer death at the hands of something unknown?"

Quill spoke up. "Bring in the specimen, please."

Two Ringnonians rolled in a cart carrying a huge glass tank. A cloudy-green, oozing mass was visible at the bottom of the glass cage.

"This is our enemy," Quill said. "It has killed three worlds in our system already. It is heading here unless we can stop it. Gortook, please conduct your demonstration."

The old Ringnonian got up and walked slowly toward the tank. He was shorter than most of the other Ringnonians. Old age and a bad back made him stoop, but as a scientist, he was a giant. He ran his hand through his gray hair as he spoke.

"The plague is a living, breathing, thinking organism. It hides when it moves through space and reveals itself when it appears in the atmosphere. By then, it is too late to do anything about it, and it kills all living tissue. Drop in the rodent."

A large Kittan rat, over two feet long, was placed over the casing. A vacuum sucked the rat into the glass tank. The rodent stood motionless and then curled in the corner, shivering with fear. The green ooze began to move toward the rodent.

The rat tried to run from the moving mass, but the green cloud spread out and enveloped the rodent. The rat squeaked and squealed as its flesh was slowly absorbed. A minute later, there was nothing but bone. A few seconds later, there was only dust.

The ooze then moved to one corner and sat immobile.

"That will happen to every living thing on this planet unless we can find a way to stop it," Gortook said.

"Now, light a piece of bark and put that in the tank," he said.

A small piece of Acala bark was set afire, placed on the tank and sucked in. The tank began to fill with smoke. The green ooze tried to move up the side of the tank like a slithering snake looking to escape. The mass turned red and finally disappeared completely.

"This bark has properties that kill all dangerous bacteria and make healing possible. The problem is that we need access to the entire planet to protect it." Gortook walked back to his seat.

Gribec seemed shocked by what he saw. "What can we do?"

"We must declare a truce," Quill said. "Our scientists have been working on a solution, and we think we may have one, but we must stop this constant fighting. We must build a string of stations and towers over the planet's entire surface. They will evenly dispense vapor as a mist into the atmosphere. We hope we will be able to stop the spread of the plague."

Quill stood and walked toward Gribec. "We must also send an expedition to Nebula to retrieve some of the bark to grow on Kittan. It will be a very dangerous mission."

"We will end hostilities and help you in any way you suggest. You have my word," Gribec said.

Chapter Eighteen

Confrontation

Arika was worried. For a third morning in a row, she felt sick. On Earth, she had been told that pregnancy for her was not possible. But now, she exhibited the telltale signs of a woman expecting a child.

Arika dressed quietly, trying not to wake Colette. "Where are you going?" Colette asked in a sleepy voice.

"Go back to sleep. I have to see someone. I'll be back soon."

She left their quarters, hurried down a corridor, and stopped in front of Guanton's compartment. She paused, thinking of what she would say and hoping Winyee would answer the door. Arika nervously pushed the button on the intercom and was relieved when Winyee answered.

"Who is it?"

"It's Arika. Winyee, may I talk to you?"

A buzzer released a lock, and the door slid open. Winyee smiled when she saw Arika.

"My child, how are you?" Winyee asked as she embraced the smaller female.

Winyee noticed the worried look on Arika's face immediately. "What's wrong, little one?"

Guanton heard the conversation and stepped from his sleeping area dressed in his work tunic.

"What is the matter?"

Arika hesitated, "Oh…nothing. I would just like to talk to Winyee for a moment."

Winyee sensed Arika's need to talk privately and interrupted. "Female talk, my dear. I will meet you later for our morning meal."

"I know when I am not wanted," he joked. He kissed Winyee on the forehead and left.

"Come, have a seat," she said, directing Arika to a small seating area. "I have just made some honey brew. Have a cup."

"I'm afraid I cannot hold it on my stomach right now."

Winyee knew immediately what the problem was. She looked at Arika's face. It exhibited the Ringnonian glow. Expecting Ringnonian women flushed the first few weeks of the pregnancy. Their cheeks glowed red in the morning and sometimes in the evening. She also noticed Arika's slight weight gain.

"Now, what's wrong?" she asked reassuringly.

"I am afraid… I might be pregnant," she said as she fell into the arms of the taller female.

"I thought so," Winyee said as she hugged her and stroked her hair.

"Not to worry…you are mated already. We will set up a chamber for you and Ascon and…"

She paused and thought. *Guanton told me that the Ring-Men can't reproduce.*

She pushed Arika back slowly as she held her shoulders and looked into her eyes.

Winyee knew without asking, but she asked anyway. "Quanyo is the father, isn't he?"

Ascon sat with Revel, drinking ale. Two weeks had passed since Arika told him she could not be with him. He remembered the conversation like it was yesterday.

"I do still love you… just not the way you want me to love you."

"What do you mean?" he asked.

"I mean that it cannot be the way it was on Earth."

She left in tears, leaving him with questions he could not answer.

He reached for his mug.

"She has mated with you, so you do hold a claim on her," Revel said. "But you mated on Earth and not within Ringnonian jurisdiction, so I don't know if the law applies in this case."

"I don't want her if she does not want me," Ascon said, slamming his mug on the table.

"Then what is the problem? Forget her and move on. Besides, the way Colette looks at you, I'd say you could replace her anyway."

Ascon ignored Revel's well-intentioned advice. He still loved Arika, and he still wanted her.

"This could turn into a disaster. They deserve whatever happens," Guanton said after Winyee informed him of Arika's predicament.

"Will you help them?" Winyee asked as she held Guanton's hand and looked into his eyes.

Guanton was powerless when Winyee talked to him like that. She had a way of bending him to her will. Always kind, always loving and caring, she knew how to make him yield to her.

"I will not get involved," Guanton said as he turned his back on her.

She came behind him and hugged him tenderly. "Please, my love, he is my brother, and she is like the daughter that I never had."

The words softened his heart. "I will see what I can do, but no promises. This is a very complicated situation. I must tell Ascon; he will not take this information well."

~~~~~~~~

Ascon bellowed when Guanton broke the news to him. "He stole her from me! I will kill him!"

Guanton took the precaution of bringing Revel and Wotkye along. The two warriors were barely able to control the irate Ascon.

"You must control yourself," Guanton said calmly.

"How can you say that to me after his actions?"

"My suggestion to you is to move on with your life, my son. Nothing good can come from seeking revenge. You must let it go," Guanton said, trying to reason with him.

"That is easy for you to say. You have Winyee. He has taken the one I love; I cannot let that go. He must die!" Ascon roared, breaking free from the grasp of his two restrainers.

They started after the fleeing Ring-Man, but Guanton stopped them. "Let him go."

"But he will kill Quanyo," Revel said.

"No, he will not."

~~~~~~~~

Quanyo was instructing a class of young Ringnonians in the use of the Ringnonian knife. Thirty trainees watched as he demonstrated footwork and defensive maneuvers. Three-foot-long sticks called wetkas replaced the deadly cutting blades.

"When will we get our knives?" asked one student.

"When you have earned them," Torlack said as he walked toward the group. He was observing the class and was impressed by their eagerness.

Torlack was short at seven and a half feet and quite thin. He lost an eye a section ago in a battle with the Wannee and recently an arm fighting the Kittans. Bitten by a Kittan, he cut off his limb at the elbow to keep the saliva from poisoning his body. A prosthetic replaced that limb, and he had become adept at using it.

The class bowed their heads after the rebuke, and Torlack smiled as he looked at Quanyo.

"Master the wetka first; one day, you may be worthy of a knife. Continue with the class, Quanyo."

Ascon burst through the door as he entered the exercise yard. "Quanyo!"

Everyone turned as the enraged Ring-Man approached the instructor, knife in hand. Quanyo stood motionless, aware of the reason for Ascon's rage.

"Arm yourself. I am going to kill you."

Quanyo remained silent but moved his wetka to his right hand.

"What is this?" Torlack shouted.

"It is a private matter," Ascon said as he approached Quanyo.

"There are no arms allowed on this level," Torlack said. "Put that weapon down."

Ascon ignored the older Ringnonian and moved to attack mode. Quanyo positioned himself to defend, using his wetka.

"Did you hear what I said? Torlack insisted.

Ascon swung his blade. Quanyo parried and moved to the right. Torlack closed his eyes and focused on Ascon.

A sharp pain to the head crumpled Ascon to his knees. It was pain like he never felt in his life. He knelt on the ground, unable to move.

Torlack opened his eyes but kept concentrating on Ascon's brain. He walked toward the immobile Ring-Man, knelt beside him, and quietly whispered in his ear.

"How dare you interrupt my class with such rude behavior? Your conduct is disgraceful and will not be tolerated. When I release you from my grip, consider yourself in my custody."

Torlack released his control, and Ascon collapsed, unconscious.

Revel and Wotkye entered the yard, having searched the complex for Ascon.

"What is this all about?" Torlack asked Wotkye.

"Ask him," Wotkye said, pointing to Quanyo as he and Revel helped Ascon to his feet.

"I have wronged him," Quanyo said. "It is a matter for the Council."

Chapter Nineteen

Trial

"These three stand before us accused," Quill announced.

Standing before the Council, Quill read the charges against Quanyo, Ascon, and Arika.

Hundreds of interested observers crowded into the hearing chamber. Thousands of others viewed the proceedings on the many screens located throughout the complex.

Trials were normally held almost immediately after the accusation. But in this case, the Council wanted to wait until Arika gave birth to her child. Despite a difficult delivery, she gave birth to a healthy baby boy.

Eight months had passed since Ascon's assault on Quanyo. Kept under house arrest, he was allowed daily exercise as his only privilege. His meals were taken in seclusion, but he was allowed visits from any who chose to see him.

Guanton came to see him several times, and so did all the Ring-Men.

On Guanton's last visit, he pleaded with Ascon as he tried numerous times before.

"I wish you would change your position, my son," he told Ascon. "If you renounce your claim to Arika, we could make this whole episode disappear. She's given birth to the baby, and she is in love with Quanyo. So many other females can make you happy."

It didn't do any good. Ascon remained obstinate and refused to talk to Guanton about the matter.

Quanyo was given free rein in the complex but not allowed to see Arika. He saw her just once in that period, at the birth of their son.

Though he fathered thousands of Ring-Men on Earth, the birth of this boy by Arika was special to him. He felt tremendous pride as he held the baby in his large hands. It was the only thing he ever produced that he cared about.

"I will protect him with my life," Quanyo told Arika. Winyee and Guanton overheard his pledge and smiled. They also viewed the child with special affection.

"I hope the Council does not rule against you, Quanyo," Guanton said. "The way Ascon feels at present, he could demand the baby's death."

"I would die first before I let anything happen to him," Arika vowed.

"Do you think it would do any good for me to talk to him?" Quanyo asked.

"I think that would make the situation worse," Guanton said.

"But perhaps Arika could reach his heart," Winyee suggested.

But she could not. Ascon refused to talk to her. His heart had become stone.

Ringnonian law was quite strict in the case of infidelity and was hardest on the guilty female. The innocent mate, if male, had the right to kill the female. If a child was produced, the child was also subject to that severe penalty.

The guilty male could be sanctioned or beaten for his first offense and put to death if the action was ever repeated.

The law also punished any innocent mate who took matters into their own hands. Any male acting in revenge was subject to judgment by the Council.

Ascon was charged with violating that law. If he renounced his claim to Arika, there would be a minor sanction, but Quanyo and Arika would be freed.

"Ascon is charged with an attempted attack on a citizen within the community," Quill stated.

"Quanyo is charged with mating with a female claimed by another."

"Arika is charged with mating with a male who was not her mate. What do you say to these charges?"

Quill looked at Ascon first.

"I am guilty," he grunted angrily.

"I, too, am guilty," Quanyo admitted, looking at the judges.

Arika, dressed in her best kimono, stood. "I and my child are innocent."

"Innocent!" Torlack shouted. "How is that possible? Do you admit to mating with both males?"

"Yes, but I did not know that I broke any law by doing so."

"Do you think you can mate with any male who comes along?" Torlack asked sarcastically.

Treena rescued Arika from Torlack's badgering. "Please, tell us, my child, is it normal to mate with more than one male on Earth?"

"Well, it has become custom to mate with whomever you wish without any formal attachments. Many years ago, women waited until a male committed to them and then mated. But that is now considered old-fashioned by many on my planet."

"Does that mean that your people mate as recreation?" Gortook asked.

"Yes, that is the case much of the time, my lord," Arika explained.

Treena asked, "Can you see why such action is foolish, my dear?"

Treena spoke not only to Arika but also to all listening observers.

"The female body is precious. To give in to the wanton lust of the male without commitment allows the male to use and discard us without any regard for our feelings. If that were allowed here, children would not know their fathers and the family unit would fall apart."

"I am afraid that has happened to a great extent on Earth, your honor," Arika said.

Kotkye squirmed in his seat and looked at his brother Wotkye. They were guilty of breaking that law on numerous occasions on Earth. Wotkye spoke to Kotkye non-verbally, *I told you so*, before turning his attention back to the trial.

Quintan spoke. "Did you feel any moral wrong in mating with Quanyo when you knew Ascon felt you were his?"

Arika hesitated and began to sob. "Yes, my lord, I did feel guilty. I knew it was wrong. But please punish me, not my baby."

Ascon turned and looked at her for the first time.

"Are there any other questions?" Quill asked as he looked at the members of the Council.

"Then we shall deliberate in private to judge this matter."

~~~~~~~~~~

"She is guilty," Torlack stated simply as he sat in his chair in the judgment chamber. "She admitted it. You all heard her."

"She was unaware of our law, Torlack," Gortook said as he paced the room.

"She is also a stranger here," Treena offered. "I have talked to Colette about her. Did you know that her father abused her? That could have influenced her and led to promiscuity on her part."

"I thought you would come out with some of your feminist thinking and take her side in this affair," Torlack sneered.

"It is not a matter of feminist thinking; it is a matter of doing what is fair and just," Treena replied, ignoring the insult directed at her and all females.

"What is the law in this matter, Quintan?" Quill asked.

"She did know the moral law," Quintan explained. "But I don't know if we can condemn her for violating that law. Besides, she mated with Ascon on Earth. Guanton has informed me that they never mated on the ship coming here or since arriving."

"Then you feel that no punishment is in order?" Torlack asked.

"I don't think that we can allow Ascon to put her to death under our law," Quintan said.

"We must teach a lesson, though," Gortook said. "What about the baby?"

"We must not allow that innocent one to die," Treena said.

"I don't think Ascon would put the baby to death," Quill said as he poured water from a pitcher on the table. "Did you see the look in his eyes when she mentioned the child?"

Chapter Twenty

Judgment

"We have made our judgment on this matter," Quill said to the waiting audience.

The three defendants stood facing the Council. Quill looked first at Arika.

"Arika is no longer under any charge of wrongdoing. She was unaware of our law and is now mated to Quanyo by her own choice." He turned toward Quanyo.

"Quanyo is also free. He is now mated to Arika and must provide for and protect her."

Quanyo glanced at Arika, who was looking down without expression.

Ascon was seething, his anger evident as he glared at Quanyo.

"Ascon, too, is free from any further restraint or punishment. We hope he has learned a lesson about going beyond our law and taking matters into his own hands."

Ascon turned back toward the panel. His eyes betrayed that he was unrepentant.

"Regarding the baby, we have decided that the decision as to its life or death rests with Ascon. He is the offended party, and it is his right to decide."

"What is your decision, Ascon?" Quill asked.

Ascon looked first at the Council and then looked down. "Let the child die."

"No!" Arika screamed. "Ascon, you cannot be that cruel. I know you are kinder than that, please."

Ascon, seemingly unmoved, continued to stare at his feet.

"You will address the Council and not the other defendant," Quill said.

Arika broke down in tears. Her hands covered her face as she wept.

Quanyo moved forward, as did the four large Ringnonian guards stationed by his table. "I will forfeit my life to replace that of my son," he said.

Regaining her composure, Arika asked, "May I say something?"

"Yes, you may," Treena said sympathetically.

All eyes turned toward the Earth woman, including Ascon's.

"I cannot live with the shame of my son's death. I am Japanese and a samurai, and we live by our honor also. When my son dies, I will commit seppuku a moment later."

Silence filled the court as all the onlookers soaked in the meaning of what Arika had just said.

Quill broke the tension. "Our decision is final. The execution will take place a week from today."

~~~~~~~~~~

Quanyo rang the buzzer to Ascon's quarters. The door slid open. Ascon stood before Quanyo, his eyes glaring with hatred toward the Ringnonian.

"I have been commanded not to kill you, and I must obey. But I will do the next best thing. I will kill your son as you killed my father's son." Ascon turned his back and walked away.

"If you do that, you will kill a part of yourself. You will regret it for the rest of your life; believe me, I know. You will never forgive yourself."

Ascon said nothing.

"You do realize that you will be killing Arika. Let the boy live. I will leave the planet, and you can take Arika as your mate. Just let the boy live. I beg you."

Ascon remained silent with his back to Quanyo.

"By the way, we have named the boy Ascon," Quanyo said as he walked away.

~~~~~~~~~~

"The construction of the towers is going quite well," Guanton told Quill.

Quill knew why he was there, but he went along with Guanton as he updated him on things he already knew.

"Now, if we can secure enough Acala bark and keep the plague from attacking before we are ready, we may be safe." Guanton paused. "Quill, I must ask."

"Guanton, a decision made by the Council is final, you know that," Quill said, cutting Guanton off.

"We cannot let Ascon take the life of that child. I have tried to talk to him, but jealousy and hatred have blinded his heart to mercy and compassion."

"That is his decision; we cannot interfere. I'm sorry."

"I am sorry, too," Guanton said as he left Quill's quarters.

~~~~~~~~~~

The ceremony room was filled with spectators. Quanyo was forced to attend and was again guarded by four huge Ringnonians. Arika was dressed in a white kimono and knelt close to the platform where the execution would occur. She was amazingly calm for a woman who was about to see her child cut in half.

She was prepared to join her baby in death moments later. She would lift the knife lying at her knee and thrust it into her throat, committing ritual suicide. Suicide was illegal on Ringnon, but the Council decided not to interfere with her drastic decision.

The Council entered and took their seats above the ceremonial platform. They were dressed in long white gowns with green sashes.

Guanton stood on the sideline close to the platform.

A constant murmur could be heard coming from the crowd.

Ascon entered, and the entire room became eerily quiet. All eyes focused on the vengeful Ring-Man as he moved toward the platform dressed in a white robe with a red sash.

His hair was worn in a Ringnonian topknot, and he wore his knife in a scabbard to his left side.

He heard hundreds of voices silently talking to him, pleading for clemency. He ignored them all.

He looked at Arika. He felt a twinge of guilt as he looked down at her pitiful form kneeling on the floor. He saw the knife lying at her side. She would not look up.

Ascon walked to his assigned station and waited for instructions.

The baby squealed as Winyee wheeled in a covered bassinet from Ascon's opposite side. She was weeping as she moved the portable carriage into position. She tried to make eye contact with Ascon, but he would not look at her.

Voices from the crowd cried out, "Be merciful, Ascon." Ascon remained unmoved.

Quintan stood and read from a scroll.

"A wrong has been committed against this Ringnonian. He has not been able to show mercy and forgive the transgression. He asks for the transgressor's blood. In this case, the child is the result of the wrong."

"Can you show mercy, Ascon, and forgive?" Quintan asked.

Ascon shook his head.

"You must answer verbally," Quintan said.

"I cannot forgive," Ascon said.

Guanton spoke silently to Ascon. *Remember the kind of person your father was. Do you think he would ever kill something as innocent as this young child?*

It was a question Ascon had been asking himself for a week. He stared at Guanton and then looked away.

"The offended has stated that he cannot forgive," Quintan said somberly. "Proceed with your revenge, Ascon."

Ascon drew his knife and moved forward amid cries from the sympathetic crowd.

The baby cried as he neared. Ascon raised his knife and stood over the bassinet. He watched Arika reach for her knife as she prepared to kill herself.

Ascon paused, stumbled backward, and dropped his knife. With tears in his eyes, he looked again at the tiny woman he loved. He turned toward the Council.

"I grant mercy, my lords."

A rousing ovation broke the tension of the moment, and the entire complex shouted in appreciation of the compassionate Ring-Man.

Ascon was mobbed as Ringnonians ran from all directions to hug and congratulate him for his merciful action.

Arika wept openly as Quanyo reached out and lifted her into his arms.

Winyee quickly whisked the bassinet away. She shuttled the infant down the hallway and headed toward the nursery. As she moved it down a passageway, she was met by Treena. The two females embraced.

Quill walked from a doorway. "Well, let's have a look at the fine fellow."

Winyee and Treena looked up, startled by his presence.

"Perhaps in a few moments, he needs a change at present," Winyee said as she tried to move past him.

"Oh, come on, let me look," he insisted.

He uncovered the netting and discovered a doll draped in a blanket. A small recording device making the sounds of a crying baby was also lodged in the crib.

"Oh my, it looks just like Quanyo," he said. He allowed Winyee her escape as he enjoyed a hearty laugh.

"You knew I could not allow that baby to die," Treena said. Treena had devised the plan as a safeguard against the other outcome.

She tenderly caressed Quill's face. "You know I have a soft spot for little ones. And for the one I love."

He watched her as she slowly walked away, and he smiled.

Chapter Twenty-One

Restoration

Ascon watched Arika as she sat on a hillside. She laughed at the antics of her young son as he played with his father at the bottom of the hill. She wore a floral kimono, and her hair was woven into a braid that trailed down her back. She seemed blissful.

He thought the two years of separation would make him feel differently, but it didn't. His feelings remained; he still loved her.

"Arika, how are you?"

She turned and saw him. "Ascon, you're back!" She jumped up and ran into his arms.

He embraced her, and for a moment, his mind raced back as he remembered the time that she was his.

"You look as beautiful as ever," he said as he pushed her away and looked down into her eyes.

"I never got a chance to thank you for my son's life," she said as she embraced him again.

"I regret the cruel way I dealt with that. Jealousy made me a bit unhinged."

"You were right to be jealous. I wronged you. Can you ever forgive me?"

"I already have. Are you happy?" Ascon looked at the young boy playing with his father.

"Yes, I am extremely happy. Would you like to meet young Ascon?"

"No, not now, perhaps another time. By the way, why did you name him Ascon?"

"It was Quanyo's idea, and I agreed. He said something about giving your father back the son he took. Why not talk to him?"

"I have to report to the Council," he said without answering her request. "I will see you again before I leave."

"You are leaving again?"

"Yes, very soon. I have another important assignment." He kissed her forehead and left.

Quanyo watched the Ring-Man leave. He wondered if he and Ascon would ever reconcile.

~~~~~~~~

"You have done well, Ascon," Quill commended as the members of the Council banged the table in approval.

"The Kagans—will they be difficult to defeat?" Torlack asked.

"We were able to eliminate them from Krilla and the surrounding area. But they are well-established on Latbee, and they possess over fifty ships. I will need a larger force to end the Kagan threat forever."

"This Claban called Cooloo, can he be trusted?" Gortook asked.

"I believe so, my lord. He urged the other Clabans to join, and they fought alongside us. He also assures us that once the Kagan threat is removed, he will supply all the crystals we need."

Quintan leaned forward. "We want you to return to Nebula and bring a live bark specimen here. We know this will be a dangerous mission. If we can grow the bark on Kittan and control it, we will have an inexhaustible supply."

"Try to bring back some ants, if possible. We would like to know more about their relationship with the bark," Treena requested.

~~~~~~~~~~~

"So, Ascon, I understand that you are off on another adventure," Guanton said as he passed a mug of molaka to the Ring-Man.

"Yes, I am taking the *Winyee* to Nebula to bring back a section of bark to plant here on Kittan."

"That hardly seems fair. You have just returned," Winyee said. "Someone I know is very anxious to spend time with you."

Guanton looked annoyed. He and Winyee had discussed this matter, and she agreed not to bring up Colette.

"The *Winyee* is being refitted. She looks wonderful," Guanton said, trying to change the subject.

"Yes, it will take about a month. Who is anxious to see me?" Ascon asked as he turned toward Winyee.

"Colette, silly," she said as she cleared the plates from the table.

Guanton threw his hands into the air and waved a linen napkin, trying to signal Winyee.

"Colette is a child," Ascon said as he thought about the pretty Ringnonian female.

"Ascon, she is just one section younger than you are," Winyee said as she playfully pulled the napkin from Guanton's grasp. "I have invited her here for desserts."

Guanton could not hide his surprise.

The buzzer rang.

"Close your mouth, Dear, and please answer the door," Winyee said, smiling.

Guanton got up, still in shock, and released the lock. The door slid open, revealing Colette.

She was beautiful, dressed in a long green Ringnonian gown. Her braided hair was threaded with emerald green ribbons that matched her eyes. Her endearing smile had the desired effect on those present. Guanton was stunned. Ascon was mesmerized.

They mated two weeks later.

~~~~~~~~~~

The next section was one of unprecedented peace on Kittan. The Ringnonians and Kittans worked together in every endeavor of life.

Bark-dispensing towers were erected planet-wide. The towers were designed to release the plague-killing vapor slowly into the air, acting as a planetary immunization shot. If the green death clouds were sighted, rockets launched from the base of the towers would burst into the atmosphere, distributing the antidote to the pestilence.

Though the Kittans were not farmers, they were excellent herders of the large swine that roamed the planet. They also loved the honey produced by the giant bees but always found it difficult to extract the delicious elixir.

A tradeoff proved beneficial for both Ringnonian and Kittan. Ringnonian technology made extracting honey quite efficient and caused no risk to the bees. The instant growth of wheat and other farmed products produced the pollen necessary for a bumper crop of honey.

The Acala bark shootings thrived in the swamps on Kittan. A section of the swamp was cordoned off to grow the precious plant, and measures were taken to restrict the aggressive plant so it would not overwhelm the environment.

Winyee tested the retrieved ants. What benefit did they receive in the symbiotic relationship with the Acala plant? Was there a way to work alongside this living organism?

~~~~~~~~~~

"There it is," Quanyo said as he chased his quarry through the Kittan swamp.

Quanyo and Gribec had become close friends and hunted together often. Gribec helped Quanyo master the use of the gonyo and the Kittan bow. They often took their children on their hunts.

Gribec moved ahead of Quanyo and pushed a tree branch in a slingshot fashion that barely missed Quanyo's head.

"Hey! Watch out!"

"Stay on your toes," Gribec warned. "This one's mine."

Gribec stopped and, in one motion, pulled back his bow and fired. A large Kittan rat toppled head over heel.

"Good shot," Quanyo said.

They rested by a small lake, catching their breath and listening for their sons.

Young Ascon was close behind them, followed by two of Gribec's young.

"Your son is strong," Gribec observed. "I see him as a great warrior."

"Your sons are like you, my friend. They, too, have a bright future."

"I hope so. I worry about that plague killing my people."

"Davar, may we go for a swim?" Ascon asked.

Quanyo nodded approval, and the three were soon diving into the lake.

"The plague may have passed us already. Besides, the atmosphere…" Quanyo's words trailed off as he saw the tentacles.

He drew his knife and was in the water before Ascon screamed. Gribec followed him, gonyo in hand.

Two of the creature's four tentacles were wrapped around Ascon and one of Gribec's sons. A third reached for the other.

The murky water partly hid the creature's mass, but Quanyo found the head.

He plunged his knife into the large beast, but it refused to release its victims. Quanyo cut the tentacle holding one of Gribec's sons, and the young Kittan swam ashore.

Gribec swam beneath the animal and drove his gonyo deep into its body.

The creature released Ascon and escaped into the depths of the lake. Moments later, Gribec emerged holding his other son.

Ascon choked on water and gasped for air as Quanyo dragged him to the safety of the shore. The boy grabbed his father's neck and held him tightly. Quanyo felt relief and a satisfaction he never experienced.

He looked into Ascon's eyes. "We must keep this from your mother, agreed?"

"Agreed," the boy said, looking up at his father with adoring eyes.

Chapter Twenty-Two

Departure

It arrived on an early spring morning as a faint hint of green in the eastern sky. Fear gripped the populace as the towers fired burst after burst of rockets, carrying the bark into the air.

"The plague seems to be holding in the atmosphere, but it also seems to be spreading across the sky," Gortook said to the Council.

"Is the bark killing it?" Treena asked.

Gortook hesitated and motioned Winyee to speak.

"My Lords, I am afraid that the vapor from the bark holds the plague at bay, but it is not killing it. The cloud seems to be trying to find a weakness in the barrier. I am most concerned with the speed with which the cloud encircles the planet."

"At the rate the cloud moves, I believe the planet will be completely covered in two months. We will then be in total darkness," Gortook said.

"In other words, that plague is forcing us to let it in," Quintan said.

"Yes, it appears so," Winyee said.

"What can we do?" Torlack asked.

"There is nothing we can do…except to leave this planet," Quill said.

"But if we leave, what happens to the Kittans?" Treena asked.

"We can't take them; we don't have room in *Ringnon One* for all of our own people," Torlack said.

"What do you think, Guanton?" Quill asked.

Guanton was sitting, quietly observing. Since neither he nor Winyee were members of the Council, they had to be asked for an opinion before they offered one.

"We owe the Kittans," Guanton said as he began to pace. "Honor demands that we help them. But we must also save as much of our race as we can. I think I have a solution that will save our honor and our people at the same time."

"First, we must encourage the growth of the Acala bark across the planet."

"That plant is almost as dangerous as the plague," Torlack said.

"Yes, it is dangerous. But we have found some interesting things while experimenting with the plant. I will let Winyee explain," Guanton said as he motioned to his mate.

"We have tested the Nebulan ant and found the reason for their relationship with the Acala plant."

"The plant secretes sweet nectar that the ants thrive on. The ants, in turn, prune the Acala vines, keeping them free from other insects and diseases. The ants use an acid-like substance in their saliva to do this. That same acid is emitted through the outer shell of their bodies, and it keeps the plant from attacking them. We have experimented with the acid produced by the Kittans, and it likewise repels the plant."

Treena was the first to realize what that meant. "That means that the Kittans are immune to attack from the Acala plant."

"Exactly," Winyee said. "They will not be affected by the growth of the plant. We, on the other hand, must take refuge in our fort to protect ourselves from attack. With our enhanced growth program, the plant will grow across the entire planet in thirty days."

"The ships must leave before the cloud covers the planet," Guanton said.

"There are two more things that should be stated," Winyee said. "First, I am working on a simulated lotion that will imitate the acid of the ant. When placed on our clothing, it will allow us to walk under the protection of the Acala bark without being attacked."

"What is the second matter?" Quill asked.

"I believe the lack of sunlight will eventually kill the Acala vines."

~~~~~~~~~~

Quanyo and Ascon were summoned before the Council. It was the first time they were close enough to talk in one section. They stood outside the Council chamber waiting to be called.

Quanyo was the first to speak. "How are you, Ascon?"

"I am well, Quanyo."

"I have heard of your exploits against the Kagan pirates. You have become a great warrior and leader of our people."

"Guanton taught me well," Ascon said coldly. Quanyo took the hint and remained silent.

"Are you happy with Arika?"

The question surprised Quanyo. "Yes, I am very happy. I love her. "What about you? I heard you took Colette as a mate."

"Yes, I love her very much."

"Ascon, I would like to…"

The doors to the Council room slid open, and they were welcomed in.

"We hope the two of you have put your past disagreements behind you. You will need to work closely together," Quill said.

"No problems exist between us, my lord," Ascon said.

"Good. We have urgent assignments for both of you. The two new battle cruisers are ready for launch. Each of you has been given one to command."

"Ascon, you will take your force and eliminate the pirate threat on Latbee. We will need a steady supply of crystals from Gabet. Establish an outpost there so that the Kagans never pose a threat again."

"Yes, my lord," Ascon said.

"Quanyo, you will go ahead of *Ringnon One* as she heads to establish a new colony on Earth. Guanton has told us of an area on Earth called Antarctica essentially uninhabited. You will claim that area for Ringnon."

"Sir, what will happen to the Kittans? Antarctica is much too cold for them to live."

"Guanton has suggested some of the vast swampland on Earth as a possibility. He mentioned the Amazon, for instance. You may present that idea to your friend, Gribec. We will allow a contingent of five thousand Kittans to leave on *Ringnon One*. But their decision must be made quickly. We must launch in thirty days before the cloud surrounds the planet."

"What of the rest of the Kittans?" Quanyo asked.

"That is the best we can do," Torlack said in disgust. "They are already taking the place of five thousand Ringnonians."

"*Ringnon One* can only hold fifty thousand, Quanyo," Quill said. "That means that five thousand Ringnonians remain here, hoping we can somehow kill this plague. We don't wish to be hard, but we must look out for our people. I hope you understand."

"I understand, my lord. I will do my best. Thank you for the honor."

They both bowed as they left.

"I hope you meant what you said, Ascon," Quanyo said, extending his hand.

"I did," Ascon said, grabbing the hand of the older Ringnonian.

The two large battle cruisers were constructed during the peaceful period. A third was under construction and six months from being operational.

The first ship, the *Gorlon*, was named after the Ringnonian warrior and former commander of *Ringnon Two*. It was Quanyo's command. As he walked its decks, pride swelled in his heart. Kotkye was assigned as his second in command and chief engineer.

The second ship was named the *Quikat*. That name would remind the Ringnonians of the last city to fall victim to the plague on Ringnon. Ascon sat on the bridge of his new command, marveling at its craftsmanship. It was fifty times larger than the *Winyee* and loaded with the newest Ringnonian technology. Revel was assigned as his second-in-command, and the remaining Ring-Men were assigned to his crew.

Both ships were equipped with Gitan-Rays and multiple weapon systems, making them floating fortresses. Each could carry one thousand crew members, including fifty Kittan warriors. Gribec volunteered to go with his friend Quanyo as the lead Kittan representative on the *Gorlon*.

"I will miss you, my love," Quanyo said as he embraced Arika.

"Take care of your mother, Ascon." He kissed the boy on the forehead, turned quickly, and left for his ship.

The *Gorlon* left two weeks before the other vessels.

~~~~~~~~~~~~~~~

Ascon held Colette in his arms. "I have never been as happy as I have been with you."

Colette said nothing but wept quietly in his arms and held him tightly.

"I don't want to remember you crying, my love. We will be together very shortly. Now dry your eyes and give me the smile that warms my heart."

She obliged, and they kissed.

The *Ringnon One* was also refitted and supplied for the long journey to Earth. The Council and most of the Ringnonians prepared to leave Kittan. Quill was in command, with Torlack as second. Gribec and his people agreed to send five thousand Kittans to establish a colony on Earth.

Of the five thousand Ringnonians remaining on Kittan, four thousand were elderly and volunteered to stay behind. The others were scientists, engineers, and warriors. Guanton would remain behind in command of that group. Wotkye insisted on staying with Guanton and was assigned as his second-in-command.

"You don't have to do this. You know the Council wanted you to come with us," Quill said to his brother.

"Winyee and I must stay," Guanton said. "Killing this disease would avenge the death of our son. Besides, there are all these to protect." He pointed to the massed group assembled to see the *Ringnon One* leave.

"I am sorry there was not enough time to get everyone off Kittan," Quill said.

Guanton assured him, "Don't worry, my brother. We will find a way to save them. I have loaded the codes for the Earth satellites into the computers of the *Gorlon* and *Ringnon One*."

"We must leave, sir," said a captain walking toward Quill. "The window is closing quickly."

Quill embraced his brother and whispered, "If the third cruiser is not ready in time, take the *Winyee* and try to get out of here. Promise me."

"I promise not to ever dishonor you, my dear brother," Guanton said.

Quill released him and hugged Winyee, who was standing next to Guanton.

"Take care of him," he said as he released her.

Tears were in his eyes as he turned and walked toward the *Ringnon One*. A half-hour later, the two vessels were launched as the remnant on Kittan waved farewell.

As the ships cleared the western sky, the clouds encompassed the planet. Kittan was surrounded and in the dark.

Ringnon Pronunciation	
Ankwot-(Ank-What)	Quanyo-(Kwan-Yo)
Ascon-(As-Con)	Quikat-(Qwi-Cat)
Claban-(Clay-Ban)	Quill-(Kwill)
Colette-(Coal-Let)	Revel-(Rev-L)
Cooloo-(Coo-Lou)	Slawoo-(Slaw-Woo)
Dunwol-(Done-Wall)	Tooloon-(Too-Loon)
Flotoon-(Flow-Toon)	Torlack-(Tor-Lack)
Gribec-(Grib-Beck)	Twonay-(Twah-Nay)
Guanton-(Gwan-Ton)	Wajee-(Wat-Gee)
Gutlap-(Gut-Lap)	Winyee- (Win-Yee)
Kitaw-(Kit-Ah)	Wotkye-(What-Keye)
Kotkye-(Kot-Keye)	

The Ringnonian

Saga

Book Three

Return to Earth

Chapter One

Earth

Quanyo looked at Earth from the bridge of the *Gorlon* as it closed in on the planet. It looked beautiful from his vantage.

"Is that Earth?" Gribec squeaked.

"Yes, that's it. It looks peaceful enough, but the inhabitants are always at odds," Quanyo said.

"Then they should be easy to conquer," Gribec quipped.

"The council wants to use diplomacy first to see if we can coexist," Quanyo said as he turned to face Gribec.

Gribec looked puzzled. "We will be taking over sections of the planet, correct?"

"Yes, but the area that we will inhabit is sparsely populated and unwanted due to the extreme cold," Quanyo said.

"That will not suffice for my people," Gribec said, growing angry.

"Relax, my friend," Quanyo stated. Quanyo had gotten to know his friend very well during their time together. Gribec could quickly become angry, but Quanyo knew how to calm him; they trusted each other.

"The council has promised you an area suitable for your people. The Amazon will be yours; I promise you," said Quanyo.

Gribec grunted in agreement.

"Head for the southernmost point," Quanyo ordered. "The humans call it Antarctica."

~~~~~~~~~

President Bill Welch leaned forward and lifted the sealed report from his desk. *What a mess*, he thought. "How bad is it, General?"

General Weaver ran his hand through his partially greying hair and picked up his report copy.

"They are very close to the Canadian border, Mr. President. The combined Russian and North Korean armies now control much of North Alaska. They have landed troops on both Diomedes and are partially complete with the bridge connecting Beringia."

"What is the navy doing?" asked the president.

"As you know, Russian satellite control extends two hundred miles from their border. That includes the Bering Straits, and that prevents us from attacking from the air. Our aircraft carriers are useless. Our subs can't launch missiles since they'll be knocked from the sky."

"That means it's a naval battle with cruisers and destroyers firing on land-based troops," the president said, summing up what he already knew.

"What do you think, Dan?" The president asked without turning to face his friend and confidant seated on a couch.

"Mr. President. this is going to be a land battle. If they get their heavy equipment across that bridge, we better have all our armor ready to repel them," Watson said. " If they enter Canada, our entire northern border will be exposed."

"And the Ring-Men?" the president asked.

"So far, they have only attacked in two sections." Weaver tapped his iPad, and images appeared on the wall screen.

"As you can see, they are not as large as the original Ring-Men or Ringnonians. They average about seven and a half to eight feet tall. But they are stockier and very muscular."

"These are mutants, then?" Watson asked.

"Yes!" Weaver said. "We had reports of them experimenting on Quanyo ten years ago. But when we heard about his escape, we assumed that the North Koreans were unsuccessful with their experiments. We were wrong! The last report indicates that there are over ten thousand of the brutes, and more are being produced in their labs daily."

"Is there any good news?" Watson asked.

"Well, the enemy advance has halted at the area where their satellite coverage ends. But if they complete that bridge…"

"Thank you, General Weaver; we'll see what we can come up with at the Joint Chiefs meeting this afternoon."

Weaver gathered his belongings and left the Oval Office.

Watson remained seated as the president got up and poured scotch for them both.

"Well?" the president prompted.

"The Nanos?" Watson asked.

"We have four left. Our best scientists have not been able to replicate the process. The last time they tried, it was a disaster."

"Yes, I know, it wiped out a whole town, as I recall," Watson remembered.

"We will save them as a last resort," the president said, "I want you at the meeting this afternoon, Dan."

Watson left the Oval Office thinking about his grandson. *I should have stayed retired.*

Chapter Two

Darkness

"It's not dead; it is going dormant," Winyee observed as she held a cutting of Acala bark. "We are in the dark, and the plants won't grow without sunlight."

"How long can we sustain the burning and release of vapor into the atmosphere?" Guanton asked.

"At the rate of burnoff, we have about two months before we are out of burnable material," said Winyee. But with no new shoots or branches, we will be burning the live plants soon."

"The battlecruiser is two weeks from completion," Wotkye said. "Just a few minor details, and we can launch. But it can only hold a thousand individuals. The *Winyee* can carry another hundred in a pinch."

"That still leaves almost four thousand Ringnonians, and who knows how many Kittans?" Guanton hypothesized somberly.

Winyee grabbed his hand. "We all knew what to expect, my dear."

"There is another problem we must face," Gortook said.

"We are running out of food, and so are the Kittans."

"What about the stored provisions?" Guanton asked.

"The Kittans won't eat anything that is not fresh. Anything frozen or preserved is rejected. Honey was acceptable, but production from the bees has ceased, as you know. Nothing is growing, so there is no pollen," Gortook said.

⌇⌇⌇⌇⌇⌇⌇⌇⌇

"Can we spare any honey from our stores?" Guanton asked.

"Guanton, they want meat, and with almost all the swine dead, that leaves us! There was an attack on two Ringnonians yesterday. Their carcasses were found this morning stripped of all flesh. There is no doubt that the attackers were Kittan."

"Order all Ringnonians inside the fortress until further notice. I will try to talk with the elder Kittan to see if we can resolve this," Guanton said.

"It may be too late for that. He was killed and eaten last week, according to my source," said Gortook. "They have a new leader named Weetec, and he is not a Ringnonian friend."

⌇⌇⌇⌇⌇⌇⌇⌇⌇

Guanton, Gortook, and an escort led by Wotkye and twenty well-armed Ringnonians met with Weetec and thirty Kittans in a clearing below Post One.

"Weetec, I understand that you are the new leader of the Kittans," Guanton said.

Weetec was enormous, over ten feet tall, and extremely broad at the shoulders. He did not answer Guanton. Instead, he pointed to the large red quartz stone hanging around his thick neck.

"We must continue to work together, Weetec, if we are going to survive the threat of the plague," Guanton reasoned.

"You mean the plague that you brought to my planet. The plague that has killed all our food and ruined our land," Weetec squeaked.

Guanton looked at Wotkye and gave him non-verbal instructions. Wotkye alerted the bodyguard, and they quietly unlatched their gun safeties.

"Weetec, we did not bring the plague; it was headed to this planet and every planet in this system. We are trying to find a way to kill it, but—"

"Enough of your lies!" Weetec screamed. "We want food!"

"We are willing to share our stored provisions with you, Weetec," Guanton said.

"No," he shouted. "We want you to give us some of your people. The older ones if you must. But we want them now. We eat our older ones when food is scarce. We must provide for the younger and stronger. That is how I became leader!"

"That is not our way, Weetec," Guanton said firmly. "Gribec was a great leader and our friend and ally, and I am…."

"I don't wish to hear about that traitor to our people," Weetec shouted. He pointed to Gortook. "That one there, he is old. We will take him!"

Guanton and Gortook looked at each other in amazement. "No, I am afraid you can't have him or any other Ringnonian."

"Then we will come and take all we want, and none of you will survive," Weetec threatened.

"If you come, Weetec, many of you will die," Guanton said calmly. "Then they will become the food we need," Weetec countered.

Wotkye and his team covered as Guanton and Gortook returned to Post One.

"I thought you were going to give me to them," Gortook joked.

Guanton looked down at the smaller Ringnonian. "No, they would not be satisfied with you. You are too tough to consume. But we must prepare for an all-out attack and finish the battlecruiser."

Chapter Three

Hyun

Hanuel studied his work, Hyun. He was as proud of the creation as much as his offspring.

"Hyun, my son," he said.

"Yes, Ahbojee," Hyun bellowed as he walked toward Hanuel.

"Time for your tonic, my son," Hanuel said, handing him a mug of a brew specially concocted for the giant.

Hanuel was the foremost hematologist and embryologist in North Korea. Using Quanyo's blood, he isolated the DNA components and tried mixing them with human DNA. After hundreds of failed attempts, he began mixing the Ringnonians' molecules with the DNA of animals. Still, there was no success.

Finally, he tried the bird kingdom. He blended Ringnonian DNA with that of the Eurasian Eagle Owl and successfully produced his first cloned Ring-Man.

Hyun was eight feet tall with broad shoulders and a chiseled body. His extremely large head framed large eyes with owl-like tufts that pushed back to the center of his scalp. He was incredibly strong, and his eyesight was extraordinary, especially at night.

In Hanuel's view, none could compare to what he considered his firstborn. There were weaknesses, though. For instance, the uncontrollable temper he displayed at times. But a tonic made from opioids relaxed Hyun to sleep.

Under pressure from the government, Hanuel cloned over ten thousand like Hyun. They were known in North Korea as Geodaehan (Ho-Day-On), which means giant.

Hanuel smiled as he watched Hyun gulp down the mixture he depended on. "How are things going?" he asked.

"Very well, so far. The engineers tell me that the bridge should be complete in a month."

"Then we can move further south?" Hanuel asked.

"Yes, but the American air force concerns me. Once we leave our satellite coverage, we will have no protection."

"What will you do?"

"When the bridge is complete, we will bring up the armor, the regular army, and the Russians. We will then attack to soften them and bring up the Ho-Day-On."

"Yes, but we will also need good weather, my son," Hanuel added.

~~~~~~~~~~

"Hello, my dearest, or should I say, President Dearest," Eileen Welch said into the receiver. "Do you feel like Chinese tonight?"

"Whatever you want, my sweet," replied the voice on the other end.

"Great, I will have my secretary reserve a table for two and a big table for the twenty agents coming along. Lao Chungs, say eight?"

"That will work, my sweet. I will meet you there." Bill Welch hung up and thought about his lovely wife. The press made a big deal about their age difference. *Twenty years is not that much.*

He loved Eileen and her son Dexter. Their first anniversary was coming, and he wanted to take her somewhere beside Camp David. *But where? The press will eat me alive if I'm traveling during this crisis.*

Eileen leaned back in her limo and thought about her first husband, Dexter. *Ten years, and I still dream of seeing him mangled.* She fought back a tear and wiped her eyes.

~~~~~~~~

The *Gorlon* slid quietly to a stop above a huge ice glacier. Quanyo ordered the weapons officer to use the Gitan ray to cut into the glacier. The *Gorlon* eased into the ice undiscovered.

"Monitor all news and radio communication. Let's see what's been happening here on Earth," Quanyo ordered.

The crew of the *Gorlon* shifted into activity. Pipes were burrowed into the almost three miles of ice beneath the ship. Once they reached sea level, pumps would suck up the seawater into the desalinization tanks that could then supply fresh water to the ship. The rapid growth system would grow enough food for the entire crew with fresh water available.

Underwater fish-capturing vessels were also released to draw on the bounty of sea life in the Antarctic Ocean.

"They are at war again," reported the communication officer, Critee.

"Which nations are warring now?" Quanyo asked.

"America and Canada are fighting Russia and North Korea."

Quanyo thought back to the cruelty of the North Koreans.

"There is something else that you should know," Critee said. "There are reports that the North Koreans are using what appear to be Ring-Men in their army."

Chapter Four

Latbee

The *Quikat* hovered above the castle as the gunners looked for any threat to the approaching attack force. The castle guns were silent, but Ascon knew the real danger lay inside the walls.

Ascon led the first group of twenty soldiers through the blasted fortress doors. Revel led a second group of thirty in support.

"It's quiet, but I know they are in there, and we need to root them out," Ascon radioed.

Ascon signaled a trooper to come forward. He placed a charge on the fortress's inner door. Ten seconds later, a blast from the charge left a twenty-foot gaping hole. There was still no sound. Ascon sent in the first five Ringnonians. He followed with the rest of the squad.

As the lead scout turned to signal further advance, he was decapitated by a blast from a Kagan laser.

The Kagans uncovered from hidden trap doors and mixed with the Ringnonians hand-to-hand.

A large Kagan swung a curved axe at Ascon's head. He ducked and spun beneath the Kagan, slashing through his belly with his knife.

Another Kagan came from behind and fired at Ascon's head. The shot barely missed. Ascon returned fire from his blaster, striking the Kagan in the neck.

Two Ringnonians were set ablaze by a Kagan firing a flamethrower. Revel entered with his platoon. The big Ring-Man threw his knife, and it lodged in the neck of the Kagan.

"Pinwheel!" Ascon ordered. The soldiers formed quickly and began firing in all directions. The firepower from the forty remaining soldiers lit the darkened sky and massacred the charging Kagans.

Three minutes was all it took to wipe out all Kagan resistance. "That was close," Revel said, slapping Ascon on the shoulder.

"Yes, it was my friend. Send squads through the fort and wipe out any hiding Kagans. Also, order Cooloo and the Clabans to come forward to share in the victory."

~~~~~~~~~~

"Sir, you need to see this!" said the messenger as he excitedly ushered Ascon and Revel down to a lower level.

The bottom level opened up into a large warehouse full of Kagan booty. Captured Kagan treasure was spread out across the entire floor.

"Look at what we found hiding." The Ring-Man Dunwol pushed a Kleeten from his hiding place.

"Who are you?" Revel asked.

"That is Yelda," said Cooloo as he joined the group. "He is Krilla's younger brother. He is also just as dishonest. You should let me kill and eat him like we did his brother."

"No, please, I can be of great help to you. I know a lot of secrets about the Kagans," the Kittan pleaded.

"What secrets?" Ascon asked.

"What I know is going to be quite valuable to you," Yelda said.

"I don't think you have anything of value we need, but we are hungry. Cooloo has told me that Kleetens are delicious. Ascon pulled his knife, grabbed Yelda, and lifted him off the ground as he looked at Cooloo. How do we skin the fur from this Kleeten?"

"I know quite a bit," Yelda protested, attempting to squirm loose.

"Like what?" Revel asked.

"I know someone who can kill the plague attacking all the planets." Ascon released the Kleeten.

~~~~~~~~~

The warehouse was full of valuables, the spoils from years of Kagan pirating. The Kagans pillaged from every known society, Dalmatian, Ringnonian, even Wannee.

They also kept hostages, some of which they ransomed and others that were left to rot in the dungeons beneath the castle.

Yelda led the group through a maze of tunnels ending at a door disguised as a wall. He removed a pin from his apron and stuck it in a corresponding hole; the wall slowly opened to a row of cells. The stench hit the group in the face.

"It smells like a hundred Kagans. What a stink!" Cooloo exclaimed.

Twenty dimly lit small cells lay before them. A few of the jailed inmates stirred and began begging for help.

"Get help down here," Ascon said to a soldier. "Water and food also."

"Are you the cell keeper responsible for these prisoners?" Revel asked.

"No!" Yelda answered, "I just give them their food. They had a Kagan guard."

"From the look of them, you have not been doing a very good job," Ascon said, glaring at the Kleeten. "Where is this person you spoke about?"

Yelda moved to the last cell, ignoring the begging prisoners. "Here!" Yelda said, pointing to the cell.

Crumpled on the floor of that cell was an extremely emaciated Ringonian.

"It's Houvor," said a Ringnonian captain in the group. He was in command of the Quillow."

"Get him out of there and to sickbay immediately," Ascon ordered.

Chapter 5

Houvor

Ascon entered sickbay and saw the horrors of Kagan imprisonment.

He met the doctor attending to the patient.

"Eight of the prisoners have been starved to death. Three others won't last the night," Korlee said, shaking his head in disgust.

"What about Houvor?" Ascon asked.

"I am not sure; he is very weak. We have given him Acala bark and Acala brew, but he could go either way."

"Can I talk to him?"

"Yes, but only for a few minutes."

"Houvor?" Ascon whispered.

The Ringnonian's eyes opened.

"Greetings, Houvor. I am Ascon, Commander of the *Quikat*."

"Yes…I know you, Ascon."

He was mistaking Ascon for his father, but Ascon ignored the error. "Can you tell me what happened to your ship and crew?"

"My log chip…in cell…buried at corner of wall…back right side…."
He fell back asleep.

"That's all, Commander, please let him rest," the doctor said.

~~~~~~

The log chip revealed the story of the *Quillow* and, surprisingly, the *Ringnon Two*.

"The log chip is badly damaged, but we can get a partial picture of what happened," Cravarn explained.

Cravarn inserted the chip into the computer.

"Entry 44 One Wannee tribe has allowed a Ringnon landing on Twuonay. A lease agreement for two sections has been agreed upon.

"Entry 52 Trouble reported on *Ringnon Two*. The *Quillow* is headed to help.

"Entry 60 Arrived at *Ringnon Two*, and the ship is deserted. Power crystal deterioration. Log shows all two hundred escape pods used. Evidence of Kagan presence on *Ringnon Two*.

"Entry 61 Kagan pirate attack, over thirty vessels. The *Quillow* is damaged and headed back to Twuonay.

"Entry 70 Wannee treachery upon landing. Wannee are working with Kagans."

"That is the last entry we can salvage, Commander, Cravarn said.
"Bring the Kleeten to my quarters, Ascon ordered.

~~~~~~

Ascon sat back in his chair and drank molaka from a mug. *Kotkye's was better.* He thought about Colette and, surprisingly, about Arika, too. *Why am I thinking about her?*

But he could not help himself. He still loved her. His thoughts were interrupted by a knock on the door.

"Come in!"

Yelda smiled as he entered the commander's chamber.

"Good morning," he greeted, saluting with his right paw.

"Have a seat, Yelda, we need to talk."

"My information was helpful, was it not?"

"Yes, it was helpful, but I need more information."

"I thought you might. May I?" Yelda pointed to the pitcher of molaka and the mug.

He poured and gulped down some brew. "Molaka? Delicious! It's been quite a while since I've had any."

"The Kagans made a deal with the Wannee to betray my people," Ascon stated.

"Yes, the Wannee truly hate Ringnonians, but so do the Kagans."

"I do know that Kagans can't be trusted."

"Commander, my family have always been merchants and traders. If I may, I'd like to suggest a trade that will allow me to speak freely and divulge everything that I know."

Ascon knew it was coming. "What is it that you want, Yelda?"

"I want control of all of the trading on Latbee. It was mine before the Kagans took it. Give me Latbee, and I will tell you everything you want."

"I could also have you skinned and thrown into a pot!"

"I realize that, Commander. But what I know can satisfy your curiosity and save your people."

Ascon leaned forward in his chair. "If that is true, you have a deal."

"There is a device that can kill the plague. Ask Houvor; he knows how it works."

~~~~~~~~~~

Chapter 6

Ringnon One

Arika sat at her vanity and looked at herself in the mirror. She was forty-three, but she looked like she was twenty-three. She lifted a mug and took a sip. Winyee showed her how to make the honey-brew tea. She had also encouraged Arika to add just a pinch of crushed Acala to the mixture.

This tea is the fountain of youth!

Her buzzer rang. "Come in."

Colette came through the entry. "Aren't you ready yet? If we don't get there soon, all the muffins will be gone," she protested.

"I'm almost ready. Here, help me with this necklace." Colette came behind her and latched the clasp.

"Come, let's go," she said, pulling Arika to her feet. They left Arika's quarters and walked the hallway that led to a giant atrium.

Thousands of Ringnonians were milling about the large, open space. The Central atrium was an auditorium, dining room, and community center. Some were eating; others were enjoying the morning exercise sessions.

The *Ringnon One* was enormous. The floating planet contained a spacious greenhouse, kitchens, classrooms, and recreation areas. Forty-five thousand Ringnonians called the vessel home for the two-year journey to Earth. Twenty months were spent in hibernation sleep modules. The final four months were devoted to exercise, food growth, and training for life in the new colony.

Arika and Colette stood in line, waiting to be served breakfast.

"Look," Arika said, pointing to Quill and Treena walking together.

Most were aware of the couples' mating. Their walking in public together confirmed that. As they walked, well-wishers greeted them and bowed or saluted to congratulate the couple.

As they passed Arika and Colette, they both bowed.

Treena stopped and embraced them. The larger woman easily engulfed the smaller females. "Now I have joined you two as mated," she said joyfully.

"Yes, may you have great happiness," Arika said. She removed a small white flower from her hair and placed it in Treena's hair. "This flower signals the devotion you will always have for your mate."

"I have also been mated," Quill said as he interrupted the tender moment. "What do I get?"

"To you, my Lord, may I say that you could not have made a better choice," Colette said as she bowed again.

Quill laughed. "Come, my dear, we must continue our parade around the promenade."

~~~~~~~~~

"Treecec and five Kittan leaders want to speak to you, Commander," said the officer of the day.

Quill turned from his chair and faced Torlack. "Direct them to the conference room."

"I knew we should not have brought Kittans aboard," Torlack complained. "We cannot control their breeding. They won't sleep, so they have nothing to do but fight and mate. The lower level is a mess."

The Kittans did not respond well to the hibernation chambers. Four females had died. What made it worse was that they were carrying eggs.

There were problems with carrying five thousand Kittans on a ship designed for Ringnonians. The main one was that Kittans bred so fast.

"It is too late to complain about what we should have done," Quill said. "The question is, what are we going to do now? We still have a month to go before we reach Earth."

Ten thousand Kittans now occupied the lower levels of *Ringnon One*.

———

Treecec and the other Kittans refused to sit, indicating they were highly disturbed.

"Have you brought us here to die?" he squeaked. The others slammed their tails in agreement.

Quill, ever the diplomat, raised his hand to calm the representatives.

"Our ships are designed for sleep during long space travel. Unfortunately, your people are not sleeping, Treecec. Thus, we are now presented with the overcrowding on your levels."

"You have a lot of room, and we need more space," Treecec responded.

Let's kill them all and be done with this, Torlack spoke silently.

Quill ignored the unspoken thought.

"Please allow me to discuss this with the council, and we will get back to you."

"If not, I assure you we will take the space we need," Treecec threatened.

———

Treena, Quintan, Torlack, and Quill were the council on board *Ringnon One*. Gortook remained with Guanton on Kittan.

"I say we cut off their oxygen and jettison their remains into space," Torlack urged.

"We cannot do that!" Treena protested.

"That would not be just, Torlack," Quintan said calmly.

We are not talking about justice; we are talking about survival. Remember that every Kittan is a warrior, including the young. If they reach the upper levels, there will be many dead Ringnonians. Besides, they are not toilet trained."

"Triple the guards on the doors leading from the lower levels," Quill ordered.

Chapter 7

Siege

The sentry at Post One spoke silently to the Post Two sentry. *All clear at Post One.*

He did not have a chance to receive a reply because an arrow pierced him through his neck. A moment later, the alarm sounded as Kittans swarmed into the opening beneath Post One. Thousands of others began climbing the incline to attack Post Two on the mountain's west side.

"Gortook! Take half of the reserves and defend Post One. I will take the other half and support Post Two. Wotkye, get the *Winyee* and the two gunships airborne. Concentrate your attack on Post One; that's the most vulnerable area."

Of the five thousand Ringnonians, only one thousand were soldiers; the rest were elderly civilians. But on this day, desperation would call for all to become soldiers.

Winyee, armed with a laser shotgun, bravely followed her husband up the ramp toward the defensive position.

The Kittans attacked with a zeal driven by their hunger.

"Thousands are attacking Guanton. Where are the gunships? Gortook asked.

"Right here!" Wotkye answered.

The *Winyee* opened up with the firepower from the Gitan Ray. The Gitan took out whole sections of charging Kittans. The *Winyee's* other guns also mowed down Kittan after Kittan.

The two gunships closed in behind the Winyee, and the three ships formed a wall of suppressing fire that drove the Kittans back into the forest. As the Kittans retreated, they dragged their dead comrades with them.

The Kittans were more successful with the attack on Post Two. The rocks provided natural cover, and the inexperienced soldiers were no match for the climbing experienced Kittan warriors. Climbing over each other, they neared the top.

As the Kittans neared the parapet, they sprang high into the air and over the wall. Some were shot in mid-air by the accurate fire from the mounted machine gun lasers. But others were able to land directly on top of the defenders. The Kittans threw the dead and wounded Ringnonians over the wall.

Guanton arrived with reinforcements just in time to prevent the position from being overrun.

His group contained some of the more experienced soldiers. He divided them into four squads of fifty each. The teams spread out forty feet from each other. Guanton looked to his left and saw Winyee directly behind him. He smiled at her as he ordered, "Pinwheel!"

The surviving soldiers at the wall heard the command and fell to the ground flat against their stomachs as enormous firepower whizzed above their heads. The Kittans atop the wall were decimated.

Hundreds of dead bodies lay mangled in heaps along the top of the wall. Guanton looked over the wall to the valley below and observed the Kittans drag the bodies of the Ringonians and Kittans into the forest below.

"Throw all the bodies over the wall," Guanton ordered. "Ours, too?" A captain asked.

"Yes, all of them! The captain looked puzzled but ordered his soldiers to do as told.

Winyee walked beside Guanton and held his hand. "You are so wise, my dear."

~~~~~~~~~~

"We lost over two thousand today," Gortook said. "But we estimate that we killed over eight thousand Kittans."

"Hopefully, that will be enough food to keep the Kittans from attacking before we leave."

"That needs to be very soon," Winyee said, "Some areas in the atmosphere are beginning to lighten. We can't resupply the towers with Acala bark because of this siege. That means that the vapor mist is less dense. The plague is beginning to drift to a lower altitude with the barrier weakening."

"How long?" Guanton asked.

"I estimate that the plague will begin to attack life on the ground in about a week."

~~~~~~~~~~

"Commander, medical attendant Korlee would like to see you in sickbay."

Ascon and Revel entered sickbay to see Houvor seated upright and drinking Acala brew.

"He is a little better but still slightly confused, and there is some memory loss. He shows signs of severe torture. Please keep your visit short, Commander," Korlee said.

"Ascon, is that you?"

"Yes, my name is Ascon, but you confuse me with my father, Ascon."

"Amazing resemblance," Houvor said.

You asked to see me?"

"Yes, I did…about the plague."

"What about the plague?"

"We need to kill the plague…" His voice trailed off, and he stared straight ahead.

"Korlee!" Ascon called.

"He is suppressing some bad memories," Korlee said.

"We need to find out what he knows. Bring Yelda here," Ascon ordered.

Yelda arrived at the sickbay but avoided eye contact with Houvor.

"What happened to Houvor on Latbee, Yelda?"

"I have no idea what you mean, Commander," Yelda said. Yelda's voice brought Houvor out of his trance.

"You murderer!" he shouted.

Yelda tried to hide behind Ascon. Ascon grabbed him by the collar and redirected him into Houvor's view.

"You killed my crew! You watched as the Kagans tortured them to death one by one, and you laughed at their pain. You watched them as they…."

Houvor became motionless. He was dead.

Ascon turned to Yelda and lifted him from the ground. "You have one chance to tell me the truth. If you don't tell me what you know right now, I will turn you over to Cooloo."

"I will tell you if you allow me to live," Yelda begged. "The Kagans captured an atomizer invented by the science officer on the Trevion. But he would not show the Kagans how it worked. Finally, we got Houvor to tell us how the machine works. It crystalizes Acala bark and kills the plague. But I don't know where it is."

"You took part in the torture?"

"No, not really, I was just there."

"I don't believe you, Yelda. Sentry, take this Kleeten and give him to the Clabans."

"No, please, I know where the machine is! It's hidden in the ware-house on Latbee!"

"Take him to the holding cell. If you are lying to me, you will be supper for the Clabans." Yelda was taken away.

Ascon looked at the Houvor slumped in death. "We will bury him with full honors."

Chapter 8

Amazon

Treena came up with the solution to the Kittan problem. The temperature on the lower levels was gradually decreased until it reached forty-five degrees. Activity in the lower region slowed and eventually stopped completely.

"That won't kill them, but it will put them in cold shock," Treena explained. "However, we need to hurry to our destination. More than twenty days of the cold may be fatal for the young ones."

Quill had planned to land and establish the colony in Antarctica and then drop the Kittans. This new development meant he would need to dispatch the Kittans first to their new home, the Amazon. It also meant disabling the satellite systems of all the countries on Earth sooner than planned.

"Guanton gave us the codes to all twenty-one of the satellite systems. But once the system is shut down, it will take thirty days to reboot," Quill said.

"Shutting down the system is the only way to get the *Ringnon One* over the Amazon without being detected by the world," said Orlon, the lead scientist on *Ringnon One*. "Even then, we may still be detected by observers from the ground."

"We have no choice. Input the codes for the shutdown of the satellites. Plot a course toward the Amazon. Check atmospherics and see if we can find a rainy night in the Amazon to release our Kittan friends."

Timing was another factor to consider. It was mid-December, and the Ringnonian sleep period was fast approaching. The drop-off and establishment of the colony would have to take place within a fifteen-day window.

It will be tight, Quill thought.

~~~~~~~~~

"Commander, this report is urgent," said the soldier delivering the communique. He was frightened. If the news was bad, Hyun could lose his temper and kill him as he had other messengers.

The messenger was relieved when Hyun smiled and handed the message to Hanuel. "Our satellite system is inoperative, and so is the system of every country in the world."

~~~~~~~~~

"You've gotta be kidding me, Dan!" President Welch said in amazement.

No, sir, all of them are down," Watson said. "We can expect an attack anytime now."

~~~~~~~~~

On a rainy night in December of 2083, *Ringnon One* eased to the center of the Amazon rainforest. The temperature of the lower level was raised gradually to ninety degrees Fahrenheit.

"The Kittans are stirring," Treena advised.

"Open the lower-level doors," Quill ordered. The race to the entryway started as a trickle but became a stampede as Kittans rushed to escape *Ringnon One*.

"Good riddance," said Torlack as he watched the screen.

"Oh my, look at the little ones; they are afraid to jump," Treena said, smiling.

But larger adults pushed the young out the door. Treecec and the five leaders were the last to leave. He raised his gonyo to the camera in what appeared to be a salute and jumped to the ground, followed by the others.

"Now, we must clean those levels thoroughly!" Torlack said. Treena looked at Torlack and thought. *You are such a grumpy old Ringnonian!*

"I heard that," Torlack said.

"I meant you, too," she replied.

"Head to the Antarctic right away. I want the *Ringnon One* dug in before our sleep period begins.

~~~~~~~~~~

"We have no choice; we need to nuke them while we have the chance," said Aubrey Taylor of the Army, pointing to the screen showing a map of the occupied region in the north.

"That is not an option, general," the president said. "I am not nuking Alaska, the Bering Sea, or North Korea, for that matter."

"We can pull the B-3s out of mothballs, level the armies in Alaska, and take out that bridge simultaneously," said Wilbur Scott of the Air Force.

"What is the naval perspective?" President Welch asked, turning to Chester Whim.

"Two battle groups are ready to take action immediately. The Abraham Lincoln group is in Japanese waters, and the Ronald Reagan group is heading north from San Diego. Those air groups and their missile cruisers should have enough firepower to neutralize the threat."

"Have we got any information about the labs producing those—? What did you call them?" Flint Asbury asked, turning to his aide.

"Ho-Day-On, general, it means giant," said Colonel Peters.

"Peters, show them what we are up against if we have to take them on."

"Sirs, if I may?" Peters typed into his keypad, and a picture of a giant North Korean soldier appeared on the screen. He used a laser to point out details.

"Ho-Day-On are not as tall as the Ring-Men. They average between seven and a half to eight feet tall. Their eyesight is excellent, and they are very powerful. Notice the hands, sirs. They are unusually large. They have been cloned."

"Cloned? From who?" asked Barry Skinner.

Peters punched in a second photo that showed another giant and a smaller man.

"That is the leader of the Ho-Day-On. He is also the General of the armies we are fighting. His name is Hyun, and he is the original clone source. The man next to him is his creator, Hanuel. The two have a father-son relationship."

"What numbers are we up against?" asked Dan Watson, who had been quietly observing.

"We estimate that two hundred thousand North Koreans have crossed into Alaska along with one hundred thousand Russians.

Another five hundred thousand troops are massed in the Chukchi Peninsula waiting to cross."

"What about the Ho-Day-On?" Watson asked.

"We estimate there are ten thousand and twice that many in production."

"Finding and destroying that lab is priority one, gentlemen," said the president.

Chapter 9

Atomizer

"I hid it from the Kagans to protect against them destroying it," Yelda said.

"You lie," Cooloo said. "If you hid it, you were doing it so that you could benefit from selling it."

Yelda ignored the slight. "It is useless without a great deal of Acala bark."

"How would you know that, Yelda?" Revel pressed.

"The Kagan that questioned Houvor told me. He said that Houvor confessed that the machine was worthless without great quantities of Acala. That is why they lost interest in the machine and why I was able to hide it," Yelda said, trying to convince everyone of his innocence.

"It is more likely that you were the one torturing Houvor to extract the information. Guard, take him back to holding." The sentry grabbed Yelda by the collar and carted him away.

Orcutt, the science officer of the *Quikat*, was summoned to examine the machine.

"Yes, I can get it to work. But what the Kleeten said is correct; we will need a lot of Acala to destroy the plague on Kittan."

"How much are we talking about?" Revel asked.

"Perhaps as much as a ton," Orcutt answered.

"We have about two hundred pounds of Acala," Revel said.

"Then we must obtain more," Ascon explained.

"The only two places to get that much Acala are Nebula or Kittan. I hope never to see Nebula again, and to get to Kittan, we must go through that plague cloud," Revel said.

"Orcutt, calculate how long two hundred pounds of Acala will last if we used it to punch a hole in the cloud to get to the fort on Kittan?" Ascon asked.

Orcutt spoke aloud as he calculated in his mind. "Well... it will depend on how thick the area of cloud is... also how fast the machine pumped and then... how fast the ship was moving. We will have about ten minutes to break through to the ground."

"Get the engineers to modify the atomizer to fire from the *Quikat*."

───────

"The battlecruiser is ready, Guanton," reported Froslee, the lead engineer. "But—at most—it can only hold fifteen hundred safely."

"That still leaves over fifteen hundred to wait on the Kittans to get hungry again," Gortook calculated.

"Kittan hunger is not the main issue. It's the plague. It has been reported close to the ground. About a mile separates it from the jungle," Winyee said as she walked to join Guanton and the others. "In a week, it will be on the ground and begin killing again."

───────

"We have installed the atomizer, Commander," Orcutt said. "I think we can use the Gitan Ray to our advantage. I have connected the atomizer to the Gitan. The power from the blast of the Gitan will shoot crystalized Acala particles and increase the spread range. We will have a wider channel for the ship to cruise through. Unfortunately, using the Gitan requires more Acala. So, we have five blasts before our Acala is exhausted."

"We will leave here with a skeleton crew. Just one hundred crew-members. We will take all the Kittan warriors. They can't last on this rock. If we get stuck on Kittan, I don't want to kill the entire crew. Have the remainder of the crew work with the Clabans, fortifying Latbee in case the Kagans return. Our mission to Kittan will be very dangerous, so ask for volunteers," Ascon said.

"I volunteer!" Revel offered immediately.

"Thank you, my loyal and trusted friend, but I need you here to take command."

~~~~~~~~~~~~~

"There are thousands of Kittans heading in this direction, Commander! I think they are attacking."

"No…. it looks like they are running from something," Guanton said, looking at a screen showing live images from drone observers. The small monitors were sent airborne each morning to scan Kittan activity.

"Winyee, what is the position of the plague cloud?"

Winyee clicked from one screen to the next, checking all the drone camera angles. She stopped at one image and maximized the screen. "There…look there…the plague is on the ground."

Guanton came over to her station. "How far is that from here?"

"About sixty kilometers," Winyee calculated, looking at the screen. "Look there! Another funnel about twenty kilometers from the first one."

"Wotkye, get the *Winyee* airborne; we may have to set the Acala grove ablaze. Gortook, prepare the ship for takeoff. Start the loading procedure. Everyone but the warriors. They will stay with me."

"I will stay here with you, my dear," Winyee said as she wrapped her arms around his waist.

"You will not, my love," he replied, lifting her tear-stained face. I need you to help Gortook lead the survivors. They will need your expertise, my love."

She sobbed into his chest, and he squeezed her tight. "Now go, my love."

She left crying.

~~~~~~~~

"There she is," Cravarn said as he looked at Kittan from the bridge. "It looks different surrounded by that green cloud."

"Hopefully we can bring her back to her former beauty," Ascon said.

~~~~~~~~

Chapter 10

Landing

"Thousands of Kittans are moving toward Post One, Commander. They are not charging; in fact, they have their young walking with them. Should we fire?"

"No, not yet," Guanton said. "They are not attacking. But they want something."

"Should I get the *Winyee* airborne?" Wotkye asked.

"No, I don't want to provoke them, especially with their young so close. Let's see what they want."

"Commander, Weetec, the Kittan leader, requests to speak to you."

"Go get Gortook and Winyee and have them meet me at Post One."

~~~~~~~

"Fire up the Gitan," Ascon ordered.

The *Quikat* had been carefully prepared for the dangerous mission. The available Acala bark was crushed and dissolved into a five-thousand-gallon mixture of plague-killing liquid. With the power from the

Gitan ray, the spray could fire one hundred feet in front of the ship as it moved. The atomizer was also adapted to have four arms that extended twenty feet outward to fire in all directions.

"Well, here we go," Ascon said, looking at Cravarn, "quarter speed."

Cravarn pushed the throttle forward and aimed for an area in the cloud brighter than the rest of the dark mass.

The weapons officer, Tanley, prepared to fire the Gitan. Another Ringonian named Kwalla was in control of the hose arms.

The *Quikat* began to speed up. "Ten seconds," said Cravarn as he watched the gauges. "There is no way to tell how thick this thing is."

"Five seconds."

"Fire the Gitan," Ascon ordered.

The ship rocked as the Gitan fired a blast into the dark mass. The mixture shot forward, followed by the speeding ship. The cloud vaporized on contact with the spray.

"Fire again," Ascon ordered.

Everywhere the mist moved, the cloud disappeared. It appeared that the cloud retreated in all directions as the ship moved through the cloud.

"Extend the hoses and fire," Ascon ordered.

The cloud to the side and behind the ship absorbed the mist and disappeared.

"Slow the ship, Cravarn," Ascon said.

As the *Quikat* moved slowly forward, the cloud receded. "Fire the Gitan again."

The ship rocked as the mist shot from the Gitan. The cloud retreated on all sides, creating a huge pathway to the planet.

"I believe it is afraid of us."

"Perhaps that is because it does not know that we have enough for two more blasts," Cravarn said.

~~~~~~~~~~

Weetec and five Kittans met with Guanton and Gortook at the Post One clearing.

Weetec lowered his gonyo, indicating submission. "The sky has come down and is killing my people," he said. "I ask you to take in the young so our people will not all die off."

Before Guanton could reply, a bright burst of light shone through the dark sky.

They all looked skyward and watched the *Quikat* hurtle toward the fort.

The ship landed a hundred feet from Post One. Ascon debarked, and as he walked toward the assembled group, the ship lifted back into the air and hovered high above the clearing.

Guanton smiled with pride as he watched Ascon walk toward him.

"Hello, my Qualla," Ascon said, smiling, "would you happen to know where I can get some acala bark?"

~~~~~~~~~~~~~

The plague cloud closed the opening soon after the descent of the *Quikat*. But the clouds did not descend because the ship acted as a guard dog. If the clouds dropped too low, the *Quikat* moved toward the area, and the cloud would retreat. The cat-and-mouse game between ship and cloud became a humorous entertainment outlet for the observers below.

First on the agenda was the maintenance of the mist towers. After undergoing repairs and receiving a resupply of acala, they were again operational. The cloud was pushed back into the upper atmosphere.

Since the Kittans were naturally protected from attack from the acala vines, they became the gatherers of the needed branches. Once collected, the Ringnonians cut the limbs into smaller pieces. The pieces were then shredded and prepared for the atomizer.

Korlee worked with Winyee and prepared a smaller atomizer to be fitted for the *Winyee*. They also began working on a larger unit for the new battle cruiser named the *Kittan*.

When the mixture was ready, the *Quikat* and the *Winyee* were loaded with spray and catapulted into the air to begin the fumigation assignment.

Wotkye, on the bridge of the *Winyee*, watched the weapons officer for that mission as she fired blast after blast of the mixture into the plague that had killed her son. "This is for Guilton!" she shouted as the cloud evaporated.

Two days of cloud spraying eliminated the plague from Kittan. What was left retreated into space.

The sun shined on Kittan for the first time in two years.

Chapter 11

Antarctica

"Oka-san," Ascon said as he ran to his mother, Arika. You should have seen me today at training. I won the wetka training today, didn't I, my Qualla."

Arika had taught Ascon about his Japanese background. She wanted him to be as proud of his Japanese heritage as he was of his Ringnonian. She insisted on him calling her by the Japanese word that meant mother.

Torlack, close behind the Ring-Man, almost smiled but caught himself before showing that emotion. "You still have much work to do, but you did well. Now go and prepare for the evening meal."

Arika bowed to Torlack, and he nodded to her. "How are you, little one?"

"I am well my Qualla," Arika said. You have been so kind to Ascon and me. Thank you so much for being a father to us." Arika embraced the older Ringnonian.

Torlack felt a tear well in his eye and returned the hug. Arika had become the daughter he never had, and Ascon was like the son who died in battle years earlier.

Young Ascon had felt the prejudice of being the only Ring-Man aboard *Ringnon One*. While Arika had been accepted, particularly after her exploits in the swamp, young Ascon was not at first.

Childbearing had been discouraged in light of the crisis on Kittan. Nonetheless, there were about one hundred children aboard. Seventy-five were boys. Ringnonian children grew to full stature at seven but were not considered adults until they were twenty. The years of adolescence were spent being educated and in physical training.

At about ten years of age, they began looking at the opposite sex. Ascon was very handsome. His oriental features and long jet-black hair made him a favorite of the young female children, but, of course, led to competition and bullying from the Ringonion male children.

One Ringonian boy named Wilkee was especially cruel to Ascon. He was a large brute and very strong.

Ascon began looking forward to the hibernation sleep so that he would be freed from the constant bullying. He hid the treatment from his mother, claiming that the many bloody noses were a result of rough play.

But Torlack noticed. As Master Instructor, he could not interfere, but he approached Arika one afternoon.

"Young Ascon, is he doing well?" he asked.

"Yes, Master Torlack, but his training seems very physical. He has been bloodied several times. I am not complaining, my lord, but is this normal?"

Torlack looked directly into Arika's eyes. "He is a wonderful student. He is courageous and strong like his father. But when one is outnumbered, the results can only be defeat." He walked away as Arika pondered his riddle.

Arika began to watch Ascon covertly as he left training. Then, one afternoon, she saw Wilkee and four young Ringnonians assault her son. Her motherly instincts took over, and she stepped forward to defend her son.

"That would ruin his life," said Torlack, who had been standing behind her unnoticed.

"I have been told that you took down a Kittan with one kick, Torlack said. "Such a skill is wasted if not passed on to the next generation."

Arika began training her son in karate, and Ascon was both a willing student and quite gifted in the art.

A week later, Arika watched from her secret alcove as Ascon leveled Wilkee and two others. He stood over them, laughing as they lay with bloodied faces.

"He is truly his father's son," Torlack said proudly. "Now, if you allow, I will name him my Kitaw. Both of you will eat at my table starting this evening." Torlack walked away without waiting for a reply.

Ascon was never bullied again.

~~~~~~~~~

Ringnon One lay buried deep in the Antarctic ice. But her arrival had not gone unnoticed.

"There is no doubt, Mr. President," General Weaver said. "Our Amundsen-Scott Station and the German Neumayer station reported the sighting of the craft."

"Am I reading this right?"

"Yes, Mr. President, the ship is enormous; it displaced at least two miles of ice according to our measurements."

"Then there is no doubt that the Ringnonians are back," Watson said.

"No doubt at all. Ringnonians were seen outside the ship using what appeared to be ice mobiles," Weaver said. "I have ordered all available subs to the area. This might be the best chance to attack them with all the satellite systems offline."

"No, let's see if we can establish communication first," the president said.

<hr>

The *Ringnon One* became an underground city buried in the ice. The battlecruiser *Gorlon* was connected by a tunnel. Outside the door connecting the two ships were Arika and their son Ascon. Arika, dressed in a floral kimono with a yellow sash, waited patiently for the door to open.

Quanyo was the first Ringnonian off the ship as the door to the tunnel opened. He saw Arika, and his heart leaped. She ran into his arms. As he lifted her, he smelled her hair and kissed her passionately. Then he saw Ascon, and his heart swelled with pride. He was dressed in a blue battle tunic, and his hair was dressed in a traditional Ringnonian topknot. "Come, my son, greet your father."

Ascon ran to his father, and they embraced.

<hr>

"I must join my people in the Amazon," Gribec squeaked.

Gribec and the fifty Kittans were anxious to be with their families. But Gribec was also concerned about his position as the leader of the Kittans. He had fought hard to win the position of war leader. He wondered if he would have to fight the leader to keep that position. He was hoping that it was not Treecec.

The top level of the *Ringnon One* became the hangar. The large bay doors were camouflaged to look like the surrounding ice. The guns and the Gitan ray were moved and repositioned, making an attack from the air almost impossible. Also housed there was a fleet of smaller support vehicles and attack craft.

"Quill has permitted us to shuttle you and your warriors to the Amazon. I will miss you, my friend," Quanyo said.

"And I, you," replied Gribec.

Quanyo embraced his lizard friend.

The Kittans boarded the large shuttle that evening. Snow blew through the bay doors as the ship lifted off. It disappeared into the blizzard, headed to the Amazon.

Chapter 12

The Labs

"Thank you for appearing on our show, Mr. President," said Dr. Walter Kean.

"It is my pleasure, Dr. Kean," said former President Wilton Wiley.

"Let's get right down to it if you don't mind, Mr. President," said Kean. "You advocated for destroying these freaks when you were in office. How do you feel about the way this administration is coddling the invaders?"

"I think that it's a mistake, Dr. Kean. The Ringnonians showed us their intent when we let them leave before. As you recall, my administration used the aliens to wage war on our enemies in China. We agreed to allow them to leave, and they repaid us by destroying two of our satellites. There is no doubt in my mind that they can't be trusted."

"Isn't it also true that the First Lady's first husband was beheaded by one of those savages?" asked Kean.

"Yes, that is true." Wiley said, "But he was guilty of war crimes far worse. He was confined in a North Korean prison awaiting trial for his many criminal acts. Aided by his alien cohorts, that villain escaped custody."

"If you ask me, Mr. President, I would say they are all criminals," Kean said.

"You are not alone in that assessment, Dr. Kean. Our President is now negotiating with those same criminals. Can you imagine that?"

"It is shocking," Kean said. "After our break, we will talk more about this crisis."

Ten-year-old Dexter Orwell ran to his mother and embraced her. "Is he talking about the alien that killed my daddy?"

"Yes, baby. That evil alien was named Quanyo, and we will make him pay for that one day." Late that night, while Dexter was sleeping, Eileen made a call on her cell.

"John, I know you still love me, and I need your help with something."

~~~~~~~~~~

"There are three labs in the complex that are producing the hybrids," said Colonel John Robinson to the officers commanding the battalions in his regiment.

Many of the experienced soldiers in that group were original members of the Ring-Man division. They now formed the elite special combat unit known as Special Operation X1. The five thousand soldiers of that unit were the best-trained and best-armed group of soldiers in the world. Their formation and existence were also the most closely guarded secret in the nation.

The military unit combined CIA, NSA, and special forces units. Their missions included government overthrow, assassinations, and, at times, flat-out murder. If Special Ops X1 was called in, it meant death to the opponent.

The Ringnonian knife was still carried and worn with pride by every team member. An image of the knife was still etched in the regiment's battle flag.

"Second battalion will lead the assault. That's you, Bob," Robinson said, pointing to Captain Bob Whitaker. "Your boys up for it?"

"Yes, sir, we are ready!"

"Lindsay, the first battalion will come in on the second wave. Your group, Wallace, will be in support."

The first battalion commander, Joshua Lindsay, answered excitedly, "Yes, sir."

Ben Wallace, third battalion commander, simply said, "Hooah!"

"Once the lab is secured, our intelligence squad will come in. That's you, Quenton," Robinson said, pointing to Captain Quenton Charles.

"That's affirmative, sir," Charles said.

"Now remember, the information we obtain is as important as killing as many of the freaks as we can. The demolition unit will then set ordinance and blow the place to bits, leaving no trace of anything ever being there. Our Anti-Gravity tanks and assault vehicles will take us in low. The heli-jets will fly in above us as support. We have to be in and out in three hours."

When do we jump off, Colonel? Whitaker asked.

"Two days. The satellite system will reboot in a week, so we must complete our mission before they can strike with what is left of their air force. Any other questions? Good, you are dismissed." Colonel Will Johnson remained behind.

"You have never seen anything like those nano bombs, John," said Johnson. My command dropped the first nanos on the Ring-Men ten years ago. It took out everything, and I mean everything, around them."

"Good, I just wish we had more. I would love to drop the nanos on all those freaks and be done with them forever. Unfortunately, after we use the three we have now, we will only have one nano remaining."

"Still not able to reproduce them?"

"No, that Guanton was some smart fellow. He produced those nano bombs and the napalm mines but never gave us the formula for either. We tried to reproduce the nanos and wiped out a whole town."

"Really? Where?"

"Remember that so-called "mining accident" outside Denver? A little town called Slidell. Well, it isn't there anymore, thanks to Mr. Nano. I want you in there with the demolition squad when they go in. I don't want any mistakes."

"Hooah!"

~~~~~~~~~~

"The attack on the labs went exactly as planned," Colonel Johnson reported.

"What about the labs themselves?

"In about thirty seconds, there will be no labs."

"By the way, we are bringing back a bonus—live embryos."

~~~~~~~~~~

"The enemy is in full retreat, Mr. President," General Weaver said. "The aerial photos show some of the damage inflicted on the invaders."

Weaver showed slide after slide of the destroyed North Korean and Russian armies. "With the Russian defensive satellites inoperative, the Air Force had a field day attacking the defensive positions of both armies."

"Your decision not to bomb the bridge was merciful, Mr. President," said General Wilbur Scott, "but it has allowed thousands to escape."

"I don't want a massacre, General. I just want them out of North America and back in Russia," said the president. "Besides holding and caring for that many prisoners…how many so far, General Weaver?"

Weaver looked at his stats. "So far, over fifty thousand Russians and thirty-five thousand North Koreans have been taken prisoner."

"Do you know how much it would cost to feed eighty-five thousand men?" the president asked. "Keep that bridge open and have the military escort them back home. When they have all crossed back to Russia, blow that bridge to pieces."

"Is there any word about their leader, Hyun, and the Ho-Day-On?" Watson asked.

"No word about them," said Weaver. We are assuming that they escaped back to Russia. Until we get satellite coverage, we can't monitor the situation, either."

~~~~~~~~~~~~

Hyun and his ten thousand Ho-Day-On were not in Russia. They were hidden in the limestone caves of White Mountain, Alaska.

Hanuel looked at the messenger killed by Hyun after he had given him a negative report. He crossed the crushed soldier's body and sidled close to Hyun.

"Perhaps we should go back across the bridge while it is still intact."

"Go back to what? Have you looked at the report? They have bombed the labs and destroyed our army. All we have left are them," pointing to the Ho-Day-On.

Calm down, my son. Here, drink this," Hanuel said, handing him a mug of tonic. "Get some rest now. We will figure out our next move together."

Chapter 13

The Showdown

"You are no longer the leader here—I am," squeaked Treecec. Five Kittans standing behind him banged their tails on the ground in agreement.

"I still hold the red quartz of leadership," Gribec replied.

"It is just a piece of stone now," Treecec countered. Thousands have been born under my leadership. They belong to me. Who is with me?"

Hundreds of adult Kittans stepped forward.

Gribec looked behind him and saw the fifty that landed with him. His group was outnumbered ten to one.

"We will settle this in the old way. Combat between you and I," he stated.

Treecec, knowing Gribec's amazing fighting skills, would not be goaded into the one-on-one challenge. "We are in a new place with new ways of doing things. I have the numbers. Let us see then who will be the victor."

"Who is with me?" Gribec asked.

There was stirring behind Gribec as his three mates pushed through the crowd along with forty of his offspring. They took their station behind him. The Kittan females were armed with bows and quivers. Female Kittans were excellent archers and hunters. They had to be since they were the primary providers in their families. They hunted in packs and used various formations to bring down birds, wild boar, and larger prey. They were also tenacious protectors of their mates. The mates of Gribec's fifty companions and their offspring also joined the smaller group.

Treecec surveyed the group. "Well, I would say about three hundred...we still outnumber you. I will allow you all to live if you hand over the stone and submit to me. If not, you will all die."

"I can see that we cannot live together. We will move south, away from you," Gribec squeaked.

"And allow you to grow strong and then attack us? I don't think so. A better solution is to kill you now."

One of the elder Kittans stepped forward. "We do not need to fight like this. We are in a new land and do not know the dangers we will face. We need...."

"Shut up, you old Kittan," Treecec snapped. "The old ways are over."

Kittans squeaked loudly. Some protested the treatment of an elder, and others agreed with Treecec.

More Kittans moved in behind Gribec. Before long, about a thousand Kittans sided with Gribec and two thousand with Treecec. The rest backed away as neutrals, ready to side with the victor, whoever that may be.

Treecec began the battle by throwing his gonyo at Gribec. Gribec ducked, and it missed by inches.

Kittans raced in from all sides. Three Kittans came at Gribec. The first Kittan swung his gonyo and slashed Gribec's right arm. He parried with his gonyo and stabbed the Kittan in the throat.

315

The second Kittan came forward, but he was stopped by Gribec's accurate gonyo throw that struck the Kittan in the neck. He fell to the ground dead.

The third Kittan came from behind Gribec and prepared to strike, but he was dispatched by an arrow shot by Gribec's mate Kikee.

"Gather, now!" ordered Gribec's second mate, Tweekee.

The females quickly formed into archery formation of two levels, one standing, and the other kneeling. Each level fired in succession of the other. The firepower from the females drove the attacking Kittans back.

"We will hunt you down and kill you," Treecec threatened.

With the females supporting the withdrawal, Gribec's Kittans retreated into the swamp.

～～～～～～～

"The Acala is growing again," Winyee said. "So is the wheat. Now we can release the boars in the stockade, and soon, they will restock the planet."

Winyee was joyous. The Ringnonians and Kittans were at peace again. Winyee had cleverly saved six queen bee larvae in an area of the fort's greenhouse. Other bees, including drones, also buzzed in the restricted area. Now mature, the queens were carefully released from their confinement. They were followed by drones that would fertilize them as they started new hives. Soon honey would be available for all on Kittan to enjoy.

"You are very happy today, my love," Guanton said as he watched Winyee observing the bee's release.

"I'm almost sorry we must leave. It is such a beautiful place," she said, holding his hand.

"I know, my dear, but I feel I will be needed on Earth, and I am not leaving you behind ever again," he vowed, looking down at her."

She wrapped her arms around him and squeezed tightly.

～～～～～～～

"Well, my old friend, will you be alright here without me?" Guanton asked.

"Yes, as long as the Kittans don't decide to come back and eat me," he replied.

"Well, just in case, I am leaving five hundred soldiers behind as police. I will send reinforcements as soon as I can. Ascon is on his way back to Latbee to check on things there. With the Acala bark available here and the steady supply of crystals from Gabet, Kittan becomes the perfect supply depot."

Wotkye approached and acknowledged both commanders.

"Wotkye, you will remain here with Gortook as his second. The *Winyee* is your command. She has served us well, has she not?"

"Yes, she has, my Qualla."

"And so have you, my Wonta." Guanton embraced the taller Ringnonian, then walked up the ramp to the battlecruiser Kittan.

Chapter 14

Negotiation

Three parka-clad humans signaled outside the large Antarctic glacier. The large front bay doors opened, and the three envoys stepped inside.

Dan Watson removed his goggles and parka hood. Jonathan King and Colonel John Robinson did the same.

They walked down a hallway to a large open foyer. Two Ringnonian sentries met the diplomatic mission and led them to a glass-enclosed pod. One sentry motioned them to three seats that were set up for them. Robinson instead walked in front of the glass, peering through to scout for any weakness.

"What now?" Robinson asked.

"Now, we wait," said Watson. He was not at all happy with Robinson's presence. Watson knew how Robinson felt about the aliens. He also remembered Robinson's treachery ten years ago. But he was the commander of Special Ops X1, and the president wanted his assessment in case the negotiations were unsuccessful and other measures became necessary.

King took off his parka and sat down. He pulled a folder from his inner pocket.

"Gentlemen, allow me to do the negotiating, please."

The two sentries pushed open a sliding panel from both sides, and three Ringnonians entered. Quanyo was dressed in a red tunic and black trousers. He moved toward three large chairs at the corner of the room and stood behind the last. Next in the room came Torlack. He wore a blue tunic and a traditional black Gi. He took the first position and remained standing. Quill was the last to enter. He wore a white tunic and blue pants with a red stripe down the side. Quill took the center seat, and both Quanyo and Torlack sat down.

"I am Quill, lead council of the Ringnonian people. Who are you, and what do you want?"

"I am Jonathan King, your honor. I am Secretary of State for the United States of America."

"And what does that mean to us?" Torlack asked.

"Well, sirs, we come with questions about your purpose in coming to Earth."

"We come to claim this portion of Earth as our own," Quill said.

"So, is it your intent to claim all of Antarctica as Ringnonian property?" Robinson asked.

King looked at Robinson, annoyed at his breach of protocol, and tried to correct his statement. "What he means, sirs, is—"

"I realize exactly what he is asking. Does this area of Earth belong to the United States? Quill asked, directing his comments to Robinson.

*These puny humans. We could squash them like a Kittan roach,*thought Torlack to the others.

Quanyo laughed.

"No, it has been determined that this portion of the world belongs to no one. It is open to all nations," said King.

"Oh really, determined by whom?"

"Well, the United Nations," King answered.

"United Nations, from what I have been told, there are about two hundred nations. I don't see anything united about any of them."

"Well, the United Nations tries to keep the world at peace," King said.

"From what I have seen, it is failing at its mission," Quill said.

"Is not the United States involved in war right now?" Torlack asked.

"Yes, it is," King answered, but North Korea and Russia are the aggressors.

"Aggressors? Do you mean like the aggressors that killed Ringnonians after they peacefully came here years ago? Like the aggressors that wiped out the offspring of those Ringnonians, the Ring-Men? Like the aggressors that turned on the very soldiers that helped them win the last war against the Chinese?"

King was speechless.

"Our nation has made some mistakes," said Watson as he stood to address the panel. "What you speak of is one of our worst moments. But there are far worse things done by the United States. I assure you that our history is full of mistakes."

"Who are you?" Quill asked.

"I am Dan Watson, sir. I was a General, but now I am a consultant."

"Watson…my brother told me about you. He said you were a great warrior and one of the few humans he knew who could be trusted."

"Your brother…" Watson said.

"Yes, Guanton is my brother. You may speak, General Watson."

~~~~~~~~~~

"They have agreed to help us," Watson said.

"That's great, but what is the cost?" the president asked.

"A section of Alaska northeast of Fairbanks and extending into the Yukon territory. It is sparsely populated, and the Canadians have agreed," King added.

"That's all?"

"Also, a promise of no treachery," Watson said, looking directly at John Robinson seated opposite him on the chopper headed to the base station.

But Colonel John Robinson was already planning just that.

Chapter 15

Battle in Space

"Leaving hyperdrive in three…two…one," counted Cravarn at the controls of the *Quikat*. The ship slowed to impulse speed, and Latbee was visible from the bridge.

"There is a firefight on Latbee, Commander."

An explosion rocked the ship. "Condition red, shields up," Ascon ordered. Dozens of Kagan ships raced to intercept the *Quikat* as the ship moved toward Latbee.

"Tanley, open up with everything we have."

Gun ports opened, and seventy-five guns of all varieties discharged their deadly barrages on the incoming vessels.

The *Quikat* was struck again. "Check for damage," Ascon ordered. Ready torpedoes and fire when ready. The ship jerked as ten torpedoes were dispatched in rapid succession. The fast-moving projectiles found their marks, and ten Kagan vessels were blown from space.

The largest Kagan vessel moved in to take on the *Quikat*. It fired a red laser directed at the bridge. Cravarn saw the discharge and throttled left to avoid a direct hit. But the blast struck the starboard wing, and the *Quikat* lurched right.

"Fire torpedoes," Ascon said. Five torpedoes found their target, and the Kagan vessel was blown open. The remaining Kagan vessels retreated.

"Damage report, Kwalla," Ascon said, looking at the officer as he examined his monitor.

"Damage to the interlock on the starboard side. Also, the weapons station on that side has a twelve-foot gash. But the airlock has been sealed. We need to land to make repairs, Commander. There is still a lot of fighting around the fort, Commander," Kwalla added.

"Contact the fort. Tell them that we are on our way."

Revel described the dire situation.

"You are here just in time, Ascon. The Kagans have breached the walls. We're holding an inner position, but I don't know for how long."

"Where are the Clabans?" Ascon asked.

"They are stuck on Gabet. There were too many Kagan ships to risk them coming to support us," Revel explained.

"We destroyed several Kagan ships, and they retreated," Ascon reported.

"I will try to contact them to see if they will come to our aid," Revel said.

"We are coming in from the west. Hold on, Revel, relief is on the way."

The *Quikat* used the Gitan to cut into the soil, and it landed two kilometers from the fort. The top guns were aimed at the approaches to the ship.

Ascon divided nine hundred soldiers into three sections. The Ring-Man Witawn led the right wing, and the Ringnonian Kwalla the left.

"My group will take the center," Ascon said. "Keep in contact visually so we can communicate. Wait for me to signal your units forward."

Ascon left Cravarn in command of the *Quikat* and the Ring-Man Slawoo in charge of a rear company of dug-in soldiers. They would protect the ship and give cover if retreat became necessary. The guns from the *Quikat* would also be available for that task.

Ascon and his troopers moved forward slowly. The ground was level and open with very little cover, except for a large rock formation two hundred feet from the fort.

The noise from the fighting inside the walls was muffled, and there appeared to be very little activity at the walls.

As the unit moved forward, the Kagans opened fire. Lasers fired from openings along the fort wall lit the night sky. One of the Kagans' primary weapons was the pulse flamethrower. It fired round after round of six-inch balls of fire that exploded on contact and engulfed its victim.

Five Ringnonians to Ascon's left were hit in succession and set ablaze. Two others to his right were cut in half by the machine gun lasers.

"Head for those rocks," Ascon commanded as soldiers dropped around him. The team ran a hundred yards to the formation and hid below its protection.

Of the three hundred in his group, half lay dead or wounded in the open field.

Witawn moved to the right with his troopers laying down suppressing fire for Ascon's team. But they too soon began to take heavy fire from the dug-in Kagans on the wall.

"Fall back, Witawn. You too, Kwalla," Ascon ordered, "Get the ship into the air, Cravarn. Head toward my position and take out those guns on the wall."

The *Quikat* fired its engines and left its submerged position headed toward Ascon's.

"The Clabans are trying to leave, but some pirate ships are still hindering their departure," Revel said.

Cravarn, blast this front wall, get to Gabet, and escort the Clabans.

"How are you doing, Revel?" Ascon asked.

"We are holding on. The Kagans are not moving forward; they appear to be trying to get their treasure out from the lower levels. I don't know how they got inside."

"Wanna bet that Yelda is involved?" Ascon sneered.

The *Quikat* appeared above Ascon's position and began concentrating fire on the gun ports. Fireballs from the fort hit the vessel's stern but did little damage. On the other hand, the gunports at the fort were disintegrated by the power of the *Quikat's* guns.

"I am headed to Gabet, Commander," Cravarn reported.

With the guns silenced at the fort's entrance, Ascon ordered Witawn and Kwalla forward. The wounded in his group were given Acala and triaged by medical teams.

"We need to get some of these to sickbay immediately," Korlee warned.

"As soon as we take the fort and kill these Kagans," Ascon countered.

But the Kagans were gone.

Revel met Ascon on the lower level.

"The treasure room is empty, and Yelda's guards are dead," Dunwol explained.

"And let me guess…Yelda is gone, too," Ascon assumed.

~~~~~~

A torpedo from *Quikat* made quick work of the one remaining pirate ship holding up the transport of the Clabans. Five shuttles lifted off Gabet with over a thousand miners armed and ready for action.

When Cooloo arrived, he assessed the situation immediately. "The Kagans have escaped, haven't they? But they are not far away."

"What do you mean?" Revel asked.

"They have used the escape tunnel."

"What tunnel?"

"The tunnel that we Clabans dug years ago. Yelda knew of it. It comes out ten Kilometers from the fort. They cannot be moving very fast with all of the loot they are carrying. If we hurry, we can catch them as they leave."

~~~~~~~~~~

Cooloo guided the *Quikat* to where the tunnel exited. They found four pirate vessels on the ground waiting for the escaping Kagans. The Ringnonian vessel blew the ships to bits before they could make a getaway.

The Ringnonians and Clabans waited in ambush for the unsuspecting Kagans.

Ten minutes later, the Kagans pushed through the exit opening of the tunnel. They immediately saw the smoldering vessels. Then, a deadly crossfire overwhelmed them. The first salvo killed more than a hundred.

The camouflaged door leading from the fort into the tunnel was also discovered.

Orcutt rigged a special surprise for any Kagans trying to escape back that way. He found two working pulse flamethrowers and joined them together. He placed the flame guns in the entryway of the escape tunnel and waited.

The Kagans began heading back to the fort through the tunnel. Revel waited until he saw the first Kagan running toward the opening, and then he ordered, "Fire!"

The pulsating flame cannons sent fireball after fireball toward the panicked Kagans. Hundreds burned alive in the tunnel. Again, they headed back toward the exit escape opening. As they came out, they were mowed down by Ringnonian and Claban firepower.

A few Kagans raised their claws to surrender.

"Kill them," Ascon ordered. Not one Kagan survived.

The last to leave the exit was Yelda, who quietly slipped out the door and tried to plead his case.

"Thank you, my friends. I don't know how I would have escaped their clutches without you," he uttered.

Ascon looked at Cooloo. "Enjoy your supper, my friend." Cooloo licked his lips and smiled as he looked at Yelda.

Chapter 16

Division in the Amazon

"As we head to the waterfall named Presidente Figueiredo, we will see some amazing sights," said Maria Fontes. The passengers were an American family of four with a twelve-year-old girl and an eight-year-old boy. Maria started to refuse the assignment, but the pilot told her the client was paying double. So, she agreed to guide her second four-hour tour of the day.

"I feel sick, Daddy," the young boy said to his father.

"Here, please use this," she said, handing the boy a barf bag. Maria still felt queasy from the clean-up from the previous group. *Why do they bring children on these tours?* thought Maria. "Please lay your head back. More air, DD."

Darryl Denton was an ex-military pilot now employed by the Nakita Tour company. "You got it, Maria."

The pilot flew the chopper just two hundred feet above the dense tree cover to avoid the higher clouds on that drizzly afternoon.

"If you look below, you can see part of the amazing Amazon rainforest. The rainforest is over two million square miles. That means that it is half the size of your home, the United States. We are headed for...."

"What is that?" asked the young daughter, looking out the window.

Maria looked out the window to the clearing below. Green, upright lizard-like creatures were fording a river. "Meu Deus," she exclaimed, looking at the strange beasts. "I have never seen anything like those. DD, do you see this?"

"Yes, I'm swinging around to get a better look."

Many Kittans reacted to the helicopter by lifting their gonyos and motioning as if to throw the weapons. Others hurried to cross the channel to the other side.

"They look like large lizards. There are hundreds of them. I have to report this right away."

~~~~~~~~~

Gribec watched the Kittans as they hurriedly crossed the river. He needed to separate from the numerically stronger group led by Treecec.

Kittans were a clan society. The leaders were normally selected from one of five major clans. Non-clan, or outcasts as they were called, tried to gain acceptance into a clan by mating with a clan member. If accepted, either male or female could claim lineage into that clan.

Of the five thousand Kittans chosen to leave the home planet, three thousand were clan members. The rest were outsiders, and more than half were females.

Treecec was an outsider. He was also the largest and fiercest Kittan aboard the *Ringnon One*. Treecec took control soon after takeoff by challenging and killing the five clan leaders and becoming the herd chieftain.

It did not matter to Treecec that he was not clan-related because he planned to start his clan. He began mating with as many of the females as possible. He also encouraged breeding among the outcasts. Many of the eggs produced by clan females were mysteriously damaged.

Thus, at the journey's end, the outcast brood outnumbered clan progeny three to one. Of the ten thousand Kittans that jumped into the Amazon, only three thousand claimed clan affiliation.

"We must get far away from Treecec," Gribec said to one of his many sons. "When we are settled, we will breed and then have the numbers to deal with him."

~~~~~~~~~~

"Here is the report on those raids outside Manaus, Madame Governor," said Carlos Fuentes. "I have downloaded the photos to your computer."

Governor Ana Rocha looked tired from the strain of many problems. She sat back in her chair and punched at the keypad.

"What is the world?" she said. "Those lizards are walking upright."

"Keep scrolling, Governor," Fuentes said.

"That thing is enormous," she said.

"Yes, that one measured about nine feet tall."

"That looks like a spear in his hand."

"And they know how to use it, too. That one was killed after taking down three State police officers. One officer was bitten and died two minutes later. Another was beheaded by that weapon. The third was sprayed with a nasty acid that practically melted his head."

"The Governor scrolled through the images in disbelief. We need to find out how many of these things are out there and what in the world they are."

"I have called in an American herpetologist to examine the carcass."

"Get me a call to the president as quickly as possible. This may be a danger to our neighboring states. We may need to call in the Federal Army," she said as she looked at the photos.

~~~~~~~~~~

"Is this serious?" Watson asked.

"King got the information from his source in Brazil who examined the thing," the president said.

"A ten-foot lizard with a spear?"

"I believe it is called a Triton, and yes, quite skilled at using it, too."

"You know somebody in the military down there, don't you?"

"Yes, Eduardo Garcia and I worked on that military exercise in Panama a few years ago."

"Do you want me to feel him out and see what he knows?"

"Yes, and I can't help but think that the Ringnonians are involved somehow. You and King meet with them next week. Try to see if they know anything about the lizards."

~~~~~~~

"They are called Kittans, and yes, we released them in the Amazon. Their planet is possibly destroyed, and they need a home," Quill stated unashamedly.

"They are creating havoc among the population and possibly destroying the delicate ecosystem there," King said to the panel consisting of Torlack, Treena, and Quill.

"Creating havoc in the ecosystem. Really?" Treena stated. "You people here on Earth are the ones destroying the ecosystem worldwide. You are the threat that is destroying the Amazon. The rainforests of this planet absorb more than twenty percent of the carbon dioxide in the atmosphere. They also contain half the world's wildlife and two-thirds of the plant life. Yet under your guardianship, you have allowed twenty percent of it to be destroyed, and you have done nothing."

"Madam, I assure you that organizations are trying to save the Amazon," King said.

"Organizations? You are joking! Well, I assure you of this. The Kittans will no doubt be a threat to humans, but they will only kill the animals they need to eat. They will not destroy entire species of animals and plants and trees as you humans have done."

Quill looked at his mate and thought at her. *Go easy, my dear, sweet, scientist mate. You may upset my son you are carrying.*

Treena shot him a furtive glance and rubbed the bulge that was becoming noticeable.

"We will send a representative to speak to the leader of the Kittans," Quill said.

"They have a leader?" Watson asked.

"Yes, they are also quite intelligent, warlike, and dangerous when provoked. Order your armies to stand down until we can help remedy the situation."

"I am afraid that it is too late for that. A battalion of Brazilian soldiers were slaughtered last week by the Kittans," King said.

~~~~~~~~~~

Chapter 17

Battle of the Amazon

John Robinson watched the sleek ship hover above a clearing close to where over one thousand Brazilian soldiers were massacred. Their bodies were removed, but blood still stained the ground. Forensic teams combed the battlefield, looking for clues as to how they died.

"Is that a gunship?" Sergeant Garnett asked.

"Their technology is superior to ours," Robinson observed.

The transport battle cruiser set down in the clearing. The service door opened, and a Ringnonian proceeded down the ramp.

"That's Quanyo," Robinson stated. "The Chinese leader, Quanyo?"

"Yep, that's him."

Quanyo left two days after the summit with King. A team of fourteen Ringnonian warriors accompanied Quanyo on the mission.

"Contact Gribec. See if he and his Kittans will go deeper into the Amazon, further away from the population. Also, find a suitable location so that we can begin the growth of the Acala," Quill ordered.

Quanyo surveyed the scene as hundreds of observers looked at him in amazement.

"Senior Quanyo, I am Colonel Jose Santiago. Welcome to Brazil! This is Colonel John Robinson of the American Army," he introduced.

Robinson and Garnett saluted.

Quanyo ignored the military gesture. "Robinson…I have heard that name before."

"Yes, I worked closely with Guanton and the Ring-Men some years ago."

"You were also responsible for trying to kill them. Were you not?"

"No, that was not me. Ascon and the Ring-Men were my brothers in arms."

Quanyo eyed Robinson suspiciously. "We shall see."

~~~~~~~~~~

Robinson, Garnett, and ten members of Special Ops X1 sat opposite the Ringnonians. Robinson selected his unit's tallest and broadest members, but they looked like children compared to the larger soldiers.

Banter Guinn was the smallest human aboard. The herpetologist was a brilliant scientist and also a CIA operative. "He's a bit frightening," he whispered to Garnett.

"He has done some frightening things, also," Garnett admitted.

"That lizard I examined was scary, too. Ten feet tall, and its glands contained an acid so powerful that one drop melted the specimen spoon. What a weapon that would make!"

"We have contact, Commander," explained the copilot.

Ten drones the size of eyeballs had been sent out from the ship to reconnoiter. Searching for any sign of Kittan activity, the drones scouted above and beneath the thick forest canopy.

"There look, stragglers! They look wounded."

"Guide all eyes to this position."

All the electronic observers were directed to the area. Quanyo could now see the entire perimeter and disposition of the Kittans.

"How many do you estimate?" Quanyo wondered.

"The computer counts over seven thousand," said the engineer.

"That's not enough! Robinson, how many Kittans were killed by the Brazilians?"

"Eleven carcasses were found. We assumed that they carried off their dead."

"Kittans aren't that sentimental. They only carry off their dead if they're hungry. No, the group has split. This is probably Treecec's herd."

The herd looked at rest by a lake. Quanyo ordered the ship to the north so that his unit could come in behind them.

"We must approach them cautiously. I will attempt to talk to the leader. Follow the lead of my Ringnonians. If we move, you move, understood?"

Robinson looked at his men, and they chanted, "Hooah!"

"Quanyo drew a circle on a board. I am going to show you a defensive formation called the pinwheel. Think of the formation as a clock. The Ringnonians will be at five, ten, fifteen, and so on.

Robinson, you and your men will be the minutes on the clock."

Robinson and his men examined the drawing. "So, we will have interlocking fire?" he questioned.

"Correct, and if there are casualties, the circle will shrink and still maintain firepower. Now, remember, we want to try a peaceful solution first. The Kittans are fierce; if they come at us, it will be in waves."

"Where should I be?" asked Guinn.

"Stay close to Robinson and retreat to the center if trouble arises. Three of my troopers will stay with the ship. Drop us and then stay airborne, understood."

"Yes, Commander!" they responded.

"You have fought them before, Commander"? asked Garnett with a measure of respect.

"Yes, too many times."

~~~~~~~~~~

The ship dropped the team one kilometer from the lake.

"Stay close, no more than five feet apart," Quanyo whispered into the radio. Though he did not need a radio to keep in contact with the Ringnonians, he did need one to communicate with the humans and the ship.

He was careful about the time he selected for the parlay. If there was trouble, the cover of night might help the team escape. The team walked carefully as they approached a stand of trees.

Quanyo heard a whistling chirp. The team knelt in the tall grass. Quanyo tweaked what sounded like bird whistles.

A Ringnonian named Bunwal translated for Robinson and Guinn. "I am Ringnonian, my name is Quanyo."

"What do you want, Ringnonian?"

"I want to talk to your leader. Who is he?"

"Treecec leads us," was the answer.

"Treecec? I have heard of Treecec. He is a great warrior. Ask him if he would allow me the honor of talking to the greatest Kittan leader."

There was a pause. Five minutes later, an answer. "You can come—alone."

"I am a chief," Quanyo replied, "A chief must bring a bodyguard." Another pause.

"You may bring them. But we will watch carefully, Quanyo."

"Bring the ship in close, Quanyo radioed. Be ready to pick us up and cover a retreat. He stood up. "Let's go."

Chapter 18

Parlay

"The Russians and North Koreans are suing for peace," King said excitedly.

"I thought they would, once the Air Force and Navy blew the heck out of them," Watson said.

"They have also guaranteed not to use their satellite coverage over Alaska so we can blast the rest of those pests with impunity," King said.

"Are you forgetting about the hostages they are holding? It won't look very good if we kill that many voters," the president quipped.

"The army has lost thousands fighting the Ho-Day-On. I'm afraid our ground troops are no match for them," King said. "They have an unbelievable ability to attack at night. Small raiding parties have shown up like roaches in the night and spooked even our most seasoned troops."

"Well, Mr. President," Watson said, "the area they are holding has been ceded to the Ringnonians. If you have an infestation, you'd best call in an expert."

"You read my mind, Dan Watson," the president said. "Contact our Ringnonian friends to see if they can help us with our pest problem."

~~~~~~~~~~

"The Americans want us to clear the Alaskan area of the North Korean giants," Quill said.

"Why don't they do it themselves?" Torlack suggested. "Didn't the Russians and North Koreans agree not to use the satellites against their aircraft? Why don't they just use air power and blast their remaining enemies?"

"The Ho-Day-On, as they are called, hold over one hundred thousand hostages. They have been sending small raiding parties into the United States and Canada and capturing humans. They are using them as human shields to prevent mass bombings of their troops," Quill said.

"Why should we get involved?" Torlack asked.

"For two reasons, my friend. First, the land they hold is the area given to our people. And secondly, those soldiers pose a threat to our security. They must be removed to an area far away from us or destroyed."

"I don't think the lives of one hundred thousand humans are worth the life of one Ringnonian," Torlack said.

"Interesting that you should feel that way. Is not Ascon, your Kitaw, half-human?"

Torlack was silent as he thought about his ward.

"We will attempt to meet with the Ho-Day-On to see if they can be persuaded to return home. Even though all reports indicate they are not wanted in North Korea, either."

~~~~~~~~~~

Quanyo and his company walked through a gap in the trees into a large open jungle clearing. Hundreds of green eyes appeared, watching the team as they neared a group of twenty Kittans. One Kittan stood a foot taller than the others. Quanyo assumed correctly that it was Treecec.

"What do you want, Ringnonian?" he asked.

"Greetings, you must be Treecec," Quanyo said.

"I am Treecec, and I ask again, what do you want?"

"I wish to talk to the leader of the Kittans. The Kittans agreed that they would settle quietly in the area known as the Amazon."

"I made no such agreement. Our first battle with the inhabitants of this place shows me that they are weak. If what they showed me was the extent of their abilities, we will easily rule the Amazon in a short while."

The other Kittans banged their tails in agreement.

"I assure you that they are worthy opponents. Besides, an agreement was made with Gribec, and it is binding on all Kittans. By the way, where is Gribec?" Quanyo said as he passed an unspoken message to his troopers.

Bunwal nudged Robinson, who took the hint and unlocked the safety on his blaster. His men did the same, and Guinn took a step back.

"Gribec is no longer the leader here. He will be dead when we find him. I will not allow you to leave here and join that traitor," he said, raising his gonyo.

Hundreds of Kittans charged in from the tree line.

"Pinwheel," Quanyo ordered.

The formation formed quickly, and Kittans began to fall as the power from the guns laced into the charging horde.

Gonyos hurled at the ring of warriors, fell unsuccessfully, or bounced off the soldiers' body armor. Quanyo aimed at Treecec, but a Kittan shielded the leader and took the discharge. He fell dead. Treecec retreated behind a wall of attacking Kittans.

Bodies of Kittans began to pile, blocking the soldiers' retreat through the entryway.

"Rootaw, bring in the ship. We are cut off."

Cannon fire erupted as the ship hovered above the tree line. A blast centered at the massed dead bodies sent Kittan body parts hurtling into the air. The blast also cleared a path out of the trap.

The team broke formation and slowly retreated, firing as they backed toward the opening. A gonyo struck and lodged in the leg of Sergeant

Garnett. He crumpled to the ground. Bunwal lifted and draped the American across his shoulders, and Garnett continued firing from that position.

The ship continued to cover the retreat as the team reached the clearing. Once there, Quanyo yelled, "Pinwheel!" The team formed again. Garnett was thrown to the center and lay there as Guinn assisted him. Affected by the poison from the gonyo, he began foaming at the mouth. Quanyo pushed a piece of Acala bark into his jaws and returned to firing from the center position.

The ship retreated from the exit opening, landed behind the group, and opened fire.

Kittans continued to charge from all directions.

"Get your men inside, Robinson," Quanyo ordered.

The Americans retreated to the safety of the ship. Garnett was remarkably better and able to retreat with Guinn's help.

"Ringnonians, into the ship." The team kept up the constant barrage as they retreated one by one into the vessel. Quanyo was the last to board. The ship took off amid a hail of thrown gonyos.

~~~~~~~~~

"My name is Quill. You must be Hyun?"

"Yes, I am Hyun, general of the Ho-Day-On."

The meeting had been set up near Fairbanks, Alaska, in a clearing along a river overflowing from the spring thaw. Quill arrived there on the large battle cruiser, the *Gorlon*. A thousand Ringnonian warriors accompanied him.

The invitation sent to the Ho-Day-On was well received. Hanuel was particularly eager to find a solution to the stalemate. The army was tired and cold, and some Ho-Day-On had died for unknown reasons. Hanuel was concerned that it might be due to some genetic defect. He realized he needed to return to his labs to test and find a remedy.

Hyun, too, was ready to return home, but for a different reason. Provisions were not an issue. American airlifts supplied enough food to feed his army and the hostages he held. But there was a shortage of opium.

"There is no more, my son," Hanuel told Hyun.

Without his special tonic, Hyun's mood swings became more violent and deadly.

"He has killed two of his aides," said one soldier to another as Hanuel passed within earshot.

Hanuel advised Hyun to accept the meeting.

"What do you want?" he said, wincing in pain from a migraine.

"Are you well?" Quill asked.

"My head hurts, but it is not your concern."

"Here, chew this," Quill said, handing him a piece of Acala.

"What is it, poison?"

"Not at all. Look, I will have some also."

Hyun took the morsel and slowly placed it in his mouth. His headache disappeared. "What drug is this?

"It is not a drug; it just relieves pain. You looked like you needed some relief."

"Thank you," Hyun said.

"You also look like you need relief from your situation."

"We have the stronger position. We have many of their people. They will not attack."

"Eventually, they will tire of waiting and destroy you."

"Let them try."

"Wouldn't you rather go home with your army intact?"

"Yes, but we have no way home."

"Perhaps I can make a way."

~~~~~~~~~~~~~~~~

"He's done what?" King asked as he entered the Oval Office.

"Quill has shuttled the Ho-Day-On back to Russia. Close to ten thousand giant soldiers are marching back to North Korea,"Watson said.

"What's left of the Russian and North Korean Air Forces will blast them to pieces," King said.

"No, they already tried that. Someone is overriding both countries' satellite systems and shooting jets from the sky."

President Bill Welch turned from his desk and looked out the window.

"You know what that means, gentlemen? The Ringnonians are controlling those satellites. That means that they can control ours also."

Chapter 19

Gribec

"We found them," Bunwal announced as the ship hung above an area known as the Vale do Javari region of the Amazon.

"This dense and unfriendly landscape is home to some of Earth's deadliest creatures and the most unexplored region on the planet," Guinn explained.

Quanyo had searched for Gribec and the Kittans for two days. Finally, one of the little eyes spotted the herd.

The team fast-roped from the hovering ship into the thick forest below. The twelve-man team comprised Quanyo, Robinson, six Ringnonians, and four Americans.

"Stay in radio contact and track our location in case we need you," Quanyo instructed.

"What did you give Sargent Garnett?" Robinson asked as they trudged through the jungle.

"A little something from a faraway planet. It's called Acala bark—a curative."

"Well, it saved his life. Thank you, he's been with me a long time."

"We intended to grow it here in the Amazon. But Gribec needs to control his Kittans, who, in turn, can control the Acala vines as they grow. If left uncontrolled, the Acala can be as deadly as it can be helpful."

Quanyo stopped, and the team followed suit. The jungle was eerily silent.

"Hello," he tweaked loudly. "I am Quanyo, and I am looking for my friend, the great war chieftain Gribec."

Minutes passed without a reply.

Finally, a Kittan broke through the deep brush, gonyo in hand. It was Gribec.

~~~~~~~~~

The team was escorted to an area where vines and limbs intertwined into a thatched jungle covering. A few thousand Kittans went about daily activities in an encampment with two fast-flowing streams.

"This is a wonderful place," Gribec squeaked.

"I am glad you are pleased with your new home. But we met the other leader of the Kittans. We had a run-in with Treecec a little distance from here."

"That disrespectful Kittan. When we have grown in strength, I will deal with him."

"Why wait? I have seen you both in battle, and you have superior skills."

"He would never face me in combat. He knows that it would mean his death. Unless…"

"Unless what?"

"Unless I were to shame him in front of his clan. I would have to call for Tookee."

"What is Tookee?"

"It is a faceoff between two leaders and their seconds. Three opponents on each side fight to the death."

"He has two powerful sons, and I have one to match. But you could serve as the other second Quanyo, if you agree."

"I agree, my friend."

~~~~~~~~~~~~~

The battlecruiser floated above Treecec's encampment. Kittans lifted their gonyos and motioned as if to throw at the out-of-range ship.

Gribec squeaked into the microphone, and his message was amplified to the Kittans below.

"Treecec, you are not the true leader of Kittans. You are a coward. I call for Tookee. Face me, you gutless Kittan."

Kittans lowered their gonyos as they soaked in the message. Many Kittans began banging the butts of their gonyos on the ground. Others thumped their tails against the earth. The noise of almost seven thousand Kittans became a continuous unified thudding.

"They are making Treecec answer my challenge," Gribec explained. "He will look very weak if he refuses."

Treecec moved into the crowd's center as the Kittans returned to give him space. He raised his gonyo skyward and then threw the spear into the ground.

"He has accepted," Gribec smirked.

~~~~~~~~~~~~~

The ship landed amid the encircled Kittans. The entire tribe had assembled for the deadly contest.

"Leave your weapons," Gribec told Quanyo. You may bring your knife. You will be given a gonyo. I hope you still remember how to use it."

"Three of you will man the ship's guns. Be prepared in case of treachery. The rest of you must stay close to the ship and observe from outside. Bunwal, you will be in command if something happens to me."

"Yes, Commander," answered the entire crew, including the Americans.

Gribec marched down the exit ramp, followed by his son. Quanyo moved down next, followed by the rest of the crew.

Gribec wore his red quartz leadership emblem.

He stepped into an open area set up for the competition. The large circle was rimmed by downward-pointing gonyos planted in the ground.

Six gonyos were placed opposite each other in the center of the circle. Kittan knives were also placed similarly.

Gribec stationed himself in front of the center gonyo. His son moved to his right. Gribec motioned Quanyo to take the position on his left.

Treecec entered the circle wearing a yellow quartz stone around his large neck. He took his position opposite Gribec, and they glared eye to eye. His seconds took their places to the right and left.

Treecec stood at least a foot taller than Gribec. His sons, though shorter, were both taller than their two opponents. An entourage of three older Kittans moved in as officials of the ceremony. They carried gonyos and bows.

"Tookee has been called for," tweaked the older Kittan. "The winner will be declared the leader of the Kittans."

"A Ringnonian cannot lead the Kittans," Treecec stated.

"If I am the victor, I will leave you to select a new leader. But that will not be the case. You are going to die today, Treecec," Quanyo tweaked.

"Brave words for someone who needs blasters to fight with," Treecec goaded.

"Enough," snapped the elder Kittan. "Have some respect for tradition, Treecec."

Treecec glared threateningly at the Kittan.

But the Kittan did not back down, and the crowd of Kittans showed their support of the elder by banging tails and gonyos.

Treecec seethed as he looked Gribec in the eyes. "Begin Tookee," he said.

"Remove your gonyos."

The contestants removed the weapons.

"Remove knives."

They all removed them, except for Quanyo, who threw the Kittan knife to the side as he pulled his Ringnonian blade.

The three older Kittans walked back to the perimeter. "Begin Tookee!"

Each adversary squared off.

Treecec came straight at Gribec. He lunged forward with his gonyo, and Gribec parried and moved left.

Quanyo's opponent broke from his match and swung his weapon at Gribec's neck. Gribec avoided the gonyo and rolled away.

"What was that?" Quanyo asked Gribec.

"There are no rules, my friend. Except that you are not allowed to throw your weapons," Gribec tweaked.

"Is there anything else I shouldn't do?"

"Don't get killed," Gribec said.

Treecec and Quanyo's opponents approached.

Treecec's lunged and swung his gonyo at Gribec again. He also slashed with his blade, striking Gribec in the shoulder.

In the meantime, Gribec's son had been wounded and was badly overmatched by his larger opponent. He asked for help.

"Is that the son I saved on Kittan?" Quanyo asked.

"Yes," Gribec said as he backed away from Treecec.

Quanyo left his opponent and went to the aid of Gribec's son. Running with his gonyo pointed straight at the Kittan, he lunged, and the Kittan parried. Quanyo rolled beneath the Kittan and stuck his blade deep into its belly. The Kittan screamed as he fell to the ground dead.

Gribec's son, badly wounded, fell to the ground. The contest was two against two.

Gribec went on the offensive and attacked Treecec. Swinging his gonyo left and right, Gribec drove Treecec backward. The crowd banged tail and gonyo in approval as the tide turned.

Quanyo went to work on the other Kittan. The Kittan swung its large tail in an attempt to trip Quanyo. Quanyo bounced above the swipe, and as he jumped, he stuck his gonyo into the Kittan's throat.

"Now you will die, Treecec," Gribec said.

Treecec, tired and losing momentum, pulled back and threw his gonyo. He missed.

Three Kittan arrows struck him in his abdomen. He fell to his knees as green ooze exited his mouth.

The three older Kittans had fired the arrows that ended the contest.

"Gribec is the winner of Tookee. He is our leader." The noise from the banging tails and gonyos indicated the approval of the Kittan spectators.

The elder moved toward the dead Kittan and pulled the quartz stone from Treecec's neck.

"You dishonored yourself by throwing your weapon," he chided the corpse.

He walked to Gribec and handed him the stone.

Gribec raised the quartz and also raised his gonyo. The surrounding Kittans lowered their gonyos in submission.

Gribec was the leader of all the Kittans in the Amazon.

Chapter 20

Aftereffects

"Our show is sponsored by Acala Tea, the remarkable healing tonic. If you want a drink from the fountain of youth, drink Acala Tea, and that's the truth. Now, back to our host, the Reverend Dr. Walter Kean."

"Welcome back to our show. We have a wonderful panel of esteemed guests on board today. First, we have the famed naturalist and conservationist Dr. Sheila Weber."

Weber, a fifty-two-year-old Harvard graduate, was known as a hardliner for her stance on forest preservation. Kean waited until the applause died down.

"Also, someone who needs no introduction, former President Wilton Wiley, is with us." Light applause followed his introduction. Wiley noted the response and faked a smile but seethed inside.

"To fill out our panel is retired General of Special Forces General John Robinson." A standing ovation interrupted Kean. Robinson stood and acknowledged the welcome.

"Wow, General, the audience knows a hero when they see one," Kean said. "I might add that the General is CEO of one of the foremost security firms in the world, SPOP Security. Let's start with this question. What do you think of the alien takeover of a large portion of the Amazon? Let's start with you, Dr. Weber."

"From the viewpoint of saving the rainforest, I think the alien occupation is a good thing. But my concern is that the area known as Vale Do Javari has been taken over and is now off-limits to humans. I worry about the indigenous people who live there."

"You fought against the Kittans' General. What is your assessment? Are they dangerous to humans?" Kean asked.

"As enemies, they are a formidable opponent. But their leader, Gribec, is on friendly terms with humans. He is also a close friend of the Ringnonian Quanyo. As such, he is controlled and poses no threat as far as I know."

"Quanyo. Isn't he the Ringnonian who escaped judgment for war crimes?" Wiley asked.

"I can't speak to that, Mr. President. All I know is that he is a valiant warrior."

"What about the Ringnonian presence in the Amazon?" Kean asked.

"Well, the Ringnonians are policing the Amazon and protecting the world's Acala bark supply. As you recall, before they became protectorates of the Amazon, poachers were going in but not coming out. Now, some might say they got what they deserve, but it is still human life. So, in essence, the Ringnonians are protecting people from themselves."

"Well, what about the fact that they have taken over the great state of Alaska?" Wiley asked.

"Actually, they control about two thousand square miles of Alaskan and Canadian territory. Alaska has over six hundred thousand square miles of land. So, I would hardly call their inhabitation a takeover," Weber said. "Besides, President Welch, may he rest in peace, ceded that area to the Ringnonians ten years ago for one hundred years. I say it is a small price to pay for all the Ringnonians have given us," Robinson said.

The audience stood and applauded again.

~~~~~~~

Quill surveyed the exercise yard from the balcony of his living quarters. He watched Houvor as he engaged in wetka practice with other Ringnonian children. Quill smiled as he saw his son parry and thrust the wooden sword.

He also saw Torlack watching his Kitaw Ascon, leading the class. "You are the proud father of a warrior who is ten years old today," Treena said as she wrapped her arms around her mate.

"Yes, I know, and yes, I have something special for him," he said, knowing her next question. Look there."

"What is it?"

"Open the box," he said.

She opened a wooden box that revealed a shiny new Ringnonian knife. The handle was golden and engraved with Quill's family crest.

"He will love this. Oh my, look at the workmanship!"

"Head Council, your hovercraft is waiting. The council meeting begins in thirty minutes," the intercom messaged.

"We need to go, my dear," he said.

~~~~~~~

The five-member council was whole again. Gortook on Kittan was replaced by Quanyo. Guanton had been offered the position but refused, telling Quill, "I have no time for politics, my brother. There is still a great deal to do on this planet if we are to secure its future."

Torlack, Quintan, and Treena remained on the council, with Quill as the head.

"We have several things to discuss before inviting the human delegation in. First, Torlack. Please report on Kittan."

"The planet has been reinforced with two thousand volunteers, and two thousand more are in route. The Kittans have been peaceful, and there is no report of the plague reappearing. Also, the mist dispensing towers have been modified with Gitan guns attached to atomizers just in case."

"What about Gabet?"

"Still a problem, I'm afraid. The pirate attacks are less frequent, but the Kagans are still active. As you know, we have sent the battlecruisers *Quikat* and *Gorlon* under Ascon and Kotkye to reinforce Kittan and deal with the pirates."

"What about the new battlecruiser?" Quill asked.

"The new ship will be ready in a month or so. She will be larger, faster, and more powerful than the other two ships combined. She will join the other ships when complete. Eventually, we will need to attack Kagan itself to permanently end the threat."

"That is something I am afraid will need to happen," Quill said. "Anything else?"

"Yes, one more thing. We are receiving a steady supply of crystals and have stored a five-year stockpile in the fort on Kittan. But many of the Claban miners are requesting to retire and settle somewhere."

"Not here on Earth?" Quintan asked.

"No, I am afraid that two alien species are enough on Earth at present. See if we can negotiate for a small settlement on Kittan. And you, my dear? What have you to report?"

"Guanton has informed me that the hyperdrive communication system will be online very soon," Treena said. "It will cut down communication delay to two days from Kittan and three days from Gabet."

"That is great news," Quill said.

"One more thing, Quill," Treena added. "Several countries are requesting help in designing city domes like the one here on Ringnonia."

"Quitan, do you see any issue with helping Earth's cities design domes?"

"Let me examine the specks. Some aspects of the dome system are based on Gitan technology; we don't want humans with that knowledge. Let's ask Guanton and Winyee if that is a wise idea."

All agreed.

"What about the Amazon Quanyo?"

"Gribec has restricted his people to that one area, Vale Do Javari. The Acala growth has also been restricted to a small area in the forest. Gribec also told me that his people have gotten along quite well with the indigenous population in that area. They share various hunting techniques. But poachers continue to be a problem. As Acala has become more valuable to humans, many are trying to find ways to get their hands on it."

"Double the force protecting the Amazon. We don't want humans getting their hands on Acala shoots," Quill said.

"That is all I had on our agenda. Are we ready for the human delegation?"

"I guess so," said Torlack. "Let's see what they want from us now."

~~~~~~~~~~

"So, he is a valiant warrior! He's not a war criminal!" Eileen Welch shouted sarcastically.

"Eileen, calm down," Robinson said.

"Don't tell me to calm down. I have been widowed twice. That murderer killed my husband and your friend. Why is he still alive? You should have killed him in the Amazon like you promised."

"Please be patient, Eileen."

"I am through being patient. John, recall that it was my money that helped you start that security company. Remember, too, that I am the major stockholder. I want Quanyo dead. If you can't do it, I will find someone who can." She hung up.

Robinson thought about Quanyo. He remembered his bravery in the Amazon.

I betrayed them once. I can't do it again.

Chapter 21

Assassins

Ascon looked at Colette as she slept.

Beautiful as ever; I do love you. But why am I still thinking about Arika?

Jealousy and anger crept into his heart whenever he saw Arika with Quanyo. He decided he needed to leave Earth and Arika behind, so he accepted his current assignment, hoping to forget her finally.

"Good morning, my love," Colette interrupted. "You appear to be in deep thought."

"Just thinking of a beautiful green-eyed Ringnonian that I know."

"Well, there are just a few Ringnonian females aboard the ship, so,I hope it is me."

"Yes, my love, it is you. Go back to sleep. It is early yet. I need to attend to my duties on the bridge. I will meet you for breakfast later."

I will stop thinking about Arika, and I will settle on Kittan, and we will live there happily together.

Arika, thrilled to be back in Japan, checked in on her father when she arrived in the Antarctic, only to find out that he had died three years earlier. She also contacted her brother Haruki, who was ecstatic that she was alive. Her brother owned numerous properties in Tokyo and two farms. One was located outside Tokyo, and the larger family estate on the northern island of Hokkaido where they were headed. She was proud of her older brothers' success.

She was also very proud to display her son Ascon and her husband Quanyo. They would be officially introduced to the family.

"I should be back in Ringnonia," Quanyo said. "I have never been good at introductions and diplomacy."

"I want to show you off to all my family. They will be so jealous of me."

The family traveled on a small battle transport accompanied by twenty well-armed Ringnonian soldiers. Council members were always guarded when they left the confines of their home territory.

Quanyo did not feel that he needed protection.

"Who even knows that I am going to Japan?" He asked Torlack. "I have no enemies there."

"You don't know where enemies lurk. We have alerted the Japanese government that you are traveling with your family. Besides, you are now a council member and will travel with an escort."

The ship hovered above an open field outside a large walled estate. Beneath were about a hundred people waving and beckoning the vehicle to land.

"Is that your family, Oka-san?" Ascon asked.

"Yes, some are. The others are servants but treated as family," Arika said, smiling. Arika held Quanyo's arm and looked up at him with adoration. "Come, my love, I must show you my country."

He smiled and tightened his grip on her petite arm. "Whatever makes you happy, my love." They left the ship, and Ascon and the warriors followed. They were all soon surrounded and embraced by family.

~~~~~~~~~~

"We need the donor's blood," Hanuel explained.

"There is no way we can get blood from Quanyo," Robinson said. "Perhaps another Ringnonian will suffice?"

"That will not work. It would mean a total restart of my research," Hanuel countered.

"He will not be easy to take alive," Robinson lamented.

"I would prefer alive, but, at this point, he is also useful to me dead."

"Killing him will be difficult also. He is traveling with his family, and he will have protection."

"Family? What Family?"

"His wife and son."

"He has a son? The genetic material from his son will work, but only if we can take him alive. With his DNA, I can guarantee that my work will proceed and that I will save the remainder of the Ho-Day-On. Less than a thousand of them are still alive, and half are sick."

"How is Hyun?" Robinson asked.

"As long as he is given his tonic, he is okay. But eventually, he will become sick like the others. I need Quanyo's DNA to build on my research."

"I will need some of the Ho-Day-On if we are going to pull this off. How many can I count on as support?"

"Hyun and perhaps one hundred are at your disposal."

Robinson hung up. The vial he stole was useless to the technicians and scientists at his firm. His researchers contacted Hanuel to see if they could collaborate on a solution.

Killing Quanyo will satisfy Eileen and give Hanuel what he needs at the same time.

"Ms. Wilson," he spoke through an intercom, "get Garnett for me, please."

"It's been ten years since they took control of the satellite systems. Are you telling me that they are still unwilling to negotiate on the issue of satellite control?" the president asked. She looked around at the members of the cabinet in disbelief.

"No, Madam President, they won't discuss the issue," replied Secretary of State John Gouch.

"This is ridiculous. Why did President Welch give them such a sweetheart deal in Alaska without negotiating on that issue?" President Ashley Whitaker barked.

"They called themselves guardians of the system," Gouch said.

"How did the rest of the delegation react to that news?"

"Well, most of the European countries were fine with it. Russia and North Korea reacted much like we did," recapped Secretary of the Interior Jasmine Curtz.

"I can see why. This benefits the smaller nations and takes power away from us. Did they at least say that they will discuss the matter at another time?"

"No, they stated that their decision is final," Gouch recalled.

"I find that position absurd. They're treating our sovereign nation as if we are children."

"I am afraid there is more, Madam President. They are demanding the shutdown of all nuclear facilities worldwide," Curtz added.

"You're kidding!" the president snapped.

"No, I'm afraid not. They suggest that they have a safer power source. They mentioned the accident in Chernobyl and the one last year in Seattle as reasons why nuclear reactors will no longer be permitted."

"Chernobyl was a hundred years ago!"

"That's true, but the area around Chernobyl is still toxic. They say that they will not risk Earth's future by allowing nuclear fission as a power source," Curtz explained.

"What is our position, militarily, if they try to enforce that ridiculous request?" the president asked of Gouch.

"Madam President, it was not a request. It was a demand that they were ready to enforce. With the Ringnonians in control of the satellite system, we cannot launch any air defense. They have superior air power. We can't match them on the ground either. I am afraid that militarily, we must submit."

"Madame President, is that demand something that we can live with? They have given us cures for all sorts of diseases. With the rapid food growth program, hunger has been practically eliminated world-wide. The Acala bark, though costly, extends life. Perhaps we should count our blessings," Curtz suggested.

"Wilma Curtz, I became president of the most powerful country in the world. I am not giving that power up to aliens or anybody else. We are working on some technology ourselves. Maybe we can grow some giants of our own like the North Koreans and Chinese did. I assure you—we are going to fight back."

~~~~~~~~~~

After an introductory ceremony and banquet, Quanyo walked with Haruki on the parapet around the walls of the estate.

"This land has been in my family for five hundred years. It is called a Buke-Zukuri. It was a military outpost, and my ancestors were warriors for the lord of this island. This estate was his reward for loyalty. Of course, I have made many improvements."

"It is a fine fortification," Quanyo complimented.

"Yes, it is. The walls are fifteen feet high and two hundred feet long on each side."

A servant ran up to the two with a large flat box. He bowed low and presented the box to Haruki.

"Arika tells me you are a great warrior and quite a swordsman."

Haruki removed the cloth covering the box and lifted the lid. "These have been in my family for two hundred years."

Haruki presented the swords to Quanyo.

"They are exquisite," Quanyo observed.

"The long battle sword is called a Katana. The second shorter battle sword is called Wakizashi. The last is called a Tanto. A good samurai always carries the two longer swords into battle. You are a samurai."

"I am honored." He looked at Critee and spoke silently. *Bring my Ringnonian knife to me.* Critee hurried to the ship and returned a moment later, bounding up the stairs to Quanyo.

"I have a present for you. This blade is called a Ringnonian knife. It has been in my family for hundreds of years, like your swords. I present it to you, my brother."

Haruki was visibly touched. "I, too, am honored. Remember, my brother, life is limited, but name and honor can last forever."

~~~~~~~~~~

Arika joined Quanyo on the wall overlooking the small islands on the interior walls. The three small islands were connected by bridges and decorated with flowers from the gardens. A center bridge spanned the large pond, connected the others, and led directly to the house. Beneath the bridge was an area set aside as a playground for children.

Quanyo and Arika laughed as they watched Ascon being tackled by twenty smaller children.

"He is enjoying his cousins," Arika beamed.

The sun was beginning to set on the warm afternoon.

"How do you like my family?" Arika asked.

"They are fine humans. I can see how you became so sweet," he said, stroking her hair. "Your brother is an honorable head of your family."

"Yes, he has done quite a bit for my family. My father squandered much of what my family had. He was very much in debt and abused alcohol. Haruki has used Yakuza to his advantage. All the men who work for him are very loyal, similar to the loyalty shown by Ringnonians."

"I can see that he is well respected. I feel…" Quanyo went silent.

"What's wrong?" Arika asked.

"Helicopters," he said as he stood attempting to locate direction.

"We have many private helicopters passing in this area. It's so isolated."

"These are military craft. Look there," he said, pointing to the western horizon.

Three large transport helicopters flanked by two attack craft headed in their direction.

The transports landed a half mile from the walls and began unloading soldiers. Quanyo could see that they were no ordinary soldiers. They looked like Ring-Men.

"Get the children to safety."

He looked for Bunwal and saw him sitting in the grass. "Bunwal, get the ship fired up and in the air. We have hostiles approaching. Critee, summon help from Ringnonia."

Bunwal and the other Ringnonians were taking advantage of the relaxing afternoon. They drank the plentiful ale and enjoyed the company of the twenty or more Japanese women on hand.

"Say again, Commander?" he queried.

"Explosions interrupted their fun as the gunships opened up on the perched vessel."

"Get to your weapons!" Quanyo ordered.

Bunwal was armed with a pulse-shotgun-grenade launcher, while Critee was equipped with a pulse machine gun. The rest of the Ringnonians were armed with pulse rifles and handguns. Quanyo ran toward the stacked arms and grabbed a laser shotgun and his samurai Katana.

The gunships opened up with Gatling guns on the walls of the fort. Two Ringnonians were cut down by the first salvo. The troopers spread out and began firing back with their weapons.

Bunwal fired his grenade launcher and hit the cockpit of one of the choppers. It burst into flames and crashed to the ground.

The other chopper pulled away out of range.

Haruki ran up the stairs to Quanyo. "Who are they?"

"I'm not sure. But the soldiers looked like the Korean Ho-Day-On."

"I have a small arsenal below, and my men are well-experienced in combat. You lead, and they will follow."

"I got off a call to Ringnonia before the ship was blasted. I think it got through," Crittee said.

"I hope so, but either way, it will take more than an hour for help to arrive. What about your police?" Quanyo wondered.

"I am afraid I am not on the best of terms with the police or the government either, for that matter. We are on our own," Haruki admitted.

"We cannot hope to protect the entire wall. It will be dark soon, and I think they will attack then. Split your men into two sections to cover the north and east walls. I will send two Ringnonians with each group. The rest of my troopers will cover the south and west walls. If any area is overrun, fall back across the bridge to the house, and we will defend from there."

"Very well," Haruki responded, leading his group to their station. One of his lieutenants led the other team to the assigned spot. The four Ringnonians followed.

Ascon had trailed behind his uncle and looked to his father for an assignment.

"Go back to the house, Ascon."

"Davar, I wish to fight with you."

"I know you do, my son. But right now, I need you to protect your mother. Would you do that for me?"

"Yes, Davar," he said.

Bunwal crossed over to Quanyo. "How many did you see?"

"At least a hundred, and I think they are Ring-Men, probably Ho-Day-On."

"What are they waiting for?" Bunwal asked.

"They are waiting for darkness."

Chapter 22

Treachery

"Order two hundred troopers to arm and meet me at the jetport," Torlack ordered.

"Who is attacking Quanyo?" Quill asked.

"The radio went dead after the first call for help," Torlack said.

"What do the satellites show?"

"They have identified at least forty attackers. Quanyo's transport has been destroyed."

"It is useless to send fighters. Even at maximum speed, it will take sixty minutes for them to get there, and in the dark, the enemy will be impossible to target," Torlack said. "So, we will send in ground support."

"Perhaps I should lead," Quill suggested.

"I am still war council chief, and my Kitaw is in danger. I will lead," Torlack said.

Quill watched as the older Ringnonian limped up the ramp toward the transport.

"You could order him not to go," Treena said as she came behind Quill.

"I know, my dear, but Torlack is determined to go, and I would dishonor him by not allowing it."

~~~~~~

The autumn night was moonless, and the area surrounding the fortification was pitch black. Quanyo and the defenders waited.

"I wish we had flares," Bunwal said.

The quiet was disturbed by a rocket striking the west wall. The explosion had little effect on the steel reinforced walls, but the flames revealed more than thirty Ho-Day-On closing in, some carrying grappling hooks.

"Open up," Quanyo ordered.

Tracers from machine guns lit the night sky. The first salvo dropped seven North Koreans.

Four mortar shells dropped over the wall into the center of the compound. The explosions rocked the soldiers on the wall.

"Critee, can you track the trajectory of those shells?" Quanyo asked as four more bombs hit the fort. One struck the wall, killing two of Haruki's men.

Critee pulled a handheld and did a quick assessment. "A half mile east of here. I have the coordinates."

"Feed them to Bunwal."

"Got them," Bunwal said as he elevated his shotgun grenade launcher. A second later, eight grenades were lifted from his gun.

Seven seconds later, eight explosions were seen far beyond the east wall.

The detonations took out the four mortar positions and killed twenty men from Special Ops Security. The last blast came within thirty feet of Arthur Garnett, and the concussion blew him from his feet.

~~~~~~

"The satellite imagery shows about one hundred attacking but another two hundred positioned east of the fort," said the communication officer.

"How far away, Pilot?" Torlack asked.

"Thirty minutes, Commander."

"They don't have thirty minutes. Move this ship!"

~~~~~~~~

"Darcey, move your team south and wait for my signal," Garnett said.

"I thought the boss said that we were not to engage unless we were attacked."

"Well, what do you think that was? You just take your company and get ready. If I order you in, attack, and not one of them comes out alive, and I mean no one."

~~~~~~~~

"They are over the north wall," Rootaw reported.

"Everyone, get across the bridge to the house entrance," Quanyo ordered.

The men and Ringnonians jumped from the wall and retreated across the bridge.

"How many ways into the house?" Quanyo asked Haruki.

"This entrance and one to the rear," he answered.

"Critee, you and Haruki take half the troops and defend the back entryway."

"Come this way," Haruki said as he led four Ringnonians and seven men down a hallway.

A lull in the fighting allowed Quanyo to do a quick assessment. Bunwal was wounded but still able to man his powerful weapon. The rest of the team covering the front position consisted of three Ringnonians and six men.

If they don't get here soon, we are in a lot of trouble.

~~~~~~~~~~~~~~~

"Where is the support we were promised? Hyun radioed. "Half of the Ho-Day-On are dead. We are on the west wall but don't have the strength to take them with a frontal assault."

"We are hitting them from the rear. Attack when you hear the explosions," Garnett said. "Darcey, detonate when you are ready."

"Ten-four," Darcey said.

"Alright men when those walls go down, we go in," Garnett said.

Ten seconds later, the rear wall was blown open by high explosives. The cavity produced by the blast measured fifty feet.

Haruki and his team, running the hallway to the back, were knocked from their feet by the explosion. The team reached the back entry in time to see tactical gun lights piercing through the smoke from the blast. The defenders spread out and took cover on the twenty-foot patio parallel to the entry door.

"I count about fifty attackers moving toward the back entry," Critee radioed.

When the soldiers cleared the smog, the team opened up.

When Hyun heard the explosions, his Ho-Day-On charged the bridge.

~~~~~~~~~~~~~~~

Arika and sixty women and children were hidden in the center room of the complex.

"Don't worry, Oka-san, I will protect you," Ascon told his mother.

She smiled as she watched her son guard the door to the chamber. Ascon held his Ringnonian knife in one hand and a hand blaster in the other.

But she was very worried as the sounds of battle seemed to be getting closer to their position.

"Have any of you ever fired a gun before?" she asked the huddling group.

"I have," said one woman. "Me too," said another.

Arika went to a gun cabinet and pulled three pistols from the shelves. She handed two of them to the volunteers and kept one herself.

"We will shoot anything that comes through those doors unless it is one of our own."

~~~~~~~~

The firefight at the back entry was intense, but the rear team was outnumbered and outgunned. A rocket grenade ended the battle as it blew the patio to pieces and took out the remaining soldiers. Haruki, wounded and bleeding, watched as Garnett stood above him. Garnett pulled open the shield of his helmet.

"Your government has wanted you dead for some time now," Garnett said. "I am counting my bonus money right now."

Haruki spit blood. "Too bad you won't live to spend it," he said.

Garnett smiled and shot him in the chest.

"The enemy has breached the rear entry," Critee said as he retreated down the hallway. But there was no reply from Quanyo. Critee was wounded in the right leg and bleeding badly. He was the lone survivor of the rear team. He set up at the end of the hallway where the corridor turned left and waited in ambush.

~~~~~~~~

Two Ho-Day-On tried to cross the bridge only to be mowed down by Quanyo, who was armed with a machine gun. The fighting had slowed as the dead on both sides reduced the number of contestants.

"How are you doing, Bunwal?" Quanyo asked.

Bunwal, Tatwee, and Quanyo were all that were left of the front force. The three Ringnonians had repelled four waves and killed a number of the Ho-Day-On in the process.

"I'm hit in the leg, but it is wrapped. I can still defend," Bunwal answered.

"Do you think they will come again?" Tatwee asked.

"I'm certain of it. But it is going to cost them. I count at least thirty in the clearing and beneath the bridge," Quanyo said as he looked through a small pair of night-vision glasses.

~~~~~~~~~~

"What are we waiting for?" Darcey asked. "Only one of them is left, and he is wounded."

"We are waiting for the Ho-Day-On to take the front entry or die trying," Garnett said.

"If we attack from the rear, we can help them take the position."

"We have orders to let the giants kill each other, then eliminate the survivors."

"You're kidding, right?"

"I kid you not. The government wants Quanyo dead and Hyun, too."

"Why not just blast them all?"

"They want the kid taken alive."

"What about Hanuel?

"We are taking him with us. But if he resists, we are to kill him, too."

~~~~~~~~~~

"Garnett, have you taken the rear yet?" Hyun radioed. There was no answer. "Here, you try." Hyun handed the radio to Hanuel.

"Garnett, come in. Garnett, do you copy? I don't know what's happening. Do you think they are all dead?" Hanuel asked.

"Well, I don't know about their dead, but I know how many dead we have. There are just seven of us left," Hyun said. "We are going to try one more time."

~~~~~~~~~~

"Here they come again," Quanyo said as he lifted his gun to fire. Bunwal tried to lift himself but slipped back to a seated position.

Two grenades bounced against the wall next to his position.

"Grenades!" he yelled. He threw one back across the patio, and the explosion killed the thrower. He could not reach the second grenade.

The blast killed Bunwal instantly and wounded Tatwee. Two Ho-Day-On appeared through the smoke. Tatwee turned and shot the first in the neck. The second attacker opened up with his machine gun and shot Tatwee in the chest and stomach and he slumped against the wall, dead.

Quanyo opened up with his gun and blew the soldier backward. Two quick blasts caught Quanyo in his left shoulder, but his armor absorbed most of the blast. Quanyo turned in time to shoot the gunman and the two soldiers climbing the patio behind him.

Quanyo slumped back against the wall. He pulled a piece of Acala bark and popped it into his mouth.

"It is just you and I left, Quanyo."

"Who are you?" Quanyo asked.

"I am Hyun. My father tells me that I exist because of you."

"What do you mean by that? And who is your father?"

"He is my creator, and he used parts of you to create me. But now, I am better than you. I would like to meet you before I kill you. That is, of course, if you are up to the challenge."

"Come ahead," Quanyo said.

~~~~~~~~

"We have lost three men trying to take that hallway," Darcey said.

"If we throw grenades, it will take out the surrounding rooms, and we don't know where the kid is."

"No explosives," Garnett said. "The scanners indicate that the next room contains warm bodies. The kid is probably in there with his mother. Let me see if I can work my way behind him."

"How far?" Torlack asked.

"Two minutes, Commander."

"What do the satellites show?"

"We have three images in the front and sixteen in the rear. Also, about sixty or more in one of the rooms inside."

"Set down in that clearing near the west wall," Torlack ordered.

"So, we meet at last, Quanyo," Hyun said, standing ten feet from the Ringnonian.

"You mentioned your father. Who is that?"

"Here I am, Quanyo," Hanuel said, revealing himself.

"Yes, I remember you. But you are no father or creator either, for that matter."

"I needed to experiment on you so that I could bring forth the perfection that you see before you."

"Experiment—is that what you called it? You are a torturer, and after I kill your creation, I am going to kill you."

Hyun reached behind his back and pulled a four-foot battle axe. "I am sorry to have to do this. After all, technically, we are of the same blood."

Quanyo pulled his Katan and took a frontal stance.

Garnett and three men maneuvered through two rooms to come behind Critee, but he was barricaded behind a large desk that protected his rear.

"I am behind him. When I give you the word, attack down the hallway, and we will attack from behind at the same time," Garnett said. "In three...two...one...go!"

Three soldiers barreled down the hallway facing the Ringnonian. At the same time, Garnett and three others charged from the rear.

Critee opened up on the front team and struck a soldier in the torso. But Critee was exposed to the fire from Garnett's team. They fired, striking Critee in the back. The Ringnonian turned and got off two blasts from a shotgun before he fell dead. It took out two of Garnett's men.

~~~~~~~~~~~~~

Hyun swung his axe and missed Quanyo's head by inches. Quanyo moved left and slashed downward. Hyun was quick, and he parried the thrust. Quanyo reversed right, swung his blade upward, and caught Hyun in his left shoulder.

Hyun screamed in pain. He swung his axe hard in an attempt to hit Quanyo in the midsection but was off balance and slipped to the ground. Quanyo was on top of him before he could right himself. Hyun felt the cold steel of the samurai sword around his throat.

"Please, don't! He is your brother!" Hanuel cried.

"He is not my brother," Quanyo countered.

Hanuel pulled a blaster from behind his back and shot Quanyo in the chest.

Quanyo dropped the sword and stumbled backward.

Three shots hit Hanuel in the chest. He looked down at the holes in disbelief and then fell back, dead.

Torlack and six Ringnonians came across the bridge as Quanyo crumpled. They surrounded Hyun, who was too weak to get up.

Torlack gave Quanyo a big piece of Acala. "Where are the others?"

Quanyo could only point to the house. "Get him to the ship. The rest of you come with me."

~~~~~~~~~~~~~

Three soldiers crashed through the door, but two were shot by waiting defenders. The three women who fired were shot by the third soldier. One of the women was Arika.

She fell to the ground, severely wounded.

Ascon ran to his mother and cradled her in his arms. Grief soon turned to rage, and he reached for his knife and attempted to kill the soldier. He was knocked unconscious by Garnett, who had stepped through the door.

"So, this must be the boy we are looking for," Garnett said. "Darcey, get the men back to the ships. We are on our way with the boy."

There was no answer.

"Darcey, do you copy?"

"I am afraid he cannot answer you. That is because Ringnonians have wiped out your entire force. All of you need to surrender and come out now."

"I have all these people, and this Ring-Man, and I will kill them all unless you allow us to leave."

"Of course, we will allow you to leave. Drop your weapons, and we will escort you to your ships."

Garnett looked at the four men remaining in the room.

"Well, boys, it's either fight it out or trust them to let us go. What do you think?" he asked.

"I say we fight it out," said one soldier.

"That's because you have never seen them fight," Garnett said. He picked up the radio again. "Some of these people were wounded accidentally in the firefight."

"I am coming in. If I am fired upon, you will all die very painfully."

Torlack came through the door and rushed toward Ascon, who was holding his mother. He pulled Acala from his vest and attempted to put it in her mouth. But it was too late.

~~~~~~~~~~

The five remaining soldiers and Hyun were taken back to Ringnonia to await justice.

Two days in the infirmary was all that Quanyo needed to recover fully. When he learned of Arikas' death, he was both inconsolable and full of vengeance.

The two guards at the lockup did not try to stop Quanyo. They were ordered to step aside as Quanyo entered with two swords.

The screams of the five men were heard for quite a distance.

~~~~~~~~~~

"Mr. Quintan," said Dr. Kean. You are versed in law, and you represent the Ringnonians when it comes to justice. My viewers wish to know if it is justice to allow the execution of those five brave Americans without due process."

"Just call me Quintan, Mr. Kean. I will answer you this way. They were guilty of killing the mother of one of our people. They also killed two other women. I don't know how brave it was to kill women, anyway. We are not bound by your silly rules here on Earth. If someone takes an innocent life, then their life is forfeit."

"But without trial?" Kean asked.

"More than sixty witnesses watched one of them kill those women. They were all responsible for that unprovoked attack. They were all guilty, and thus, they were all executed by one of the avengers of the victims. We will investigate and also punish those who sent the killers."

"But we believe in humane execution."

"That is another foolish concept of your justice system. Painful execution is a deterrent to the crimes perpetrated by violent people. We will not apologize for making those who hurt others feel that pain themselves."

"This is a change in our humane philosophy."

"I assure you, Mr. Kean, that is one of many new changes."

~~~~~~~~~~

"How is Hyun working out in his training with Torlack? Quill asked.

"He is an eager student, and we have cured him of all of his defects, Guanton said.

"How is Quanyo?"

"Three years, and he is still mourning Arika. But giving him the command of the new battlecruiser and his mission to conquer Kagan will occupy his mind and heart. Assigning his son to his command will also help."

"You don't wish to go back to Kittan? You know the council suggested you as the governor," Quill said.

"No, my brother, I am tired of space travel. There is still a lot to be done to straighten out Earth. Winyee and I will stay here."

"As you wish," Quill said. "It was her idea to name the battlecruiser after Arika, wasn't it?"

"Yes, it was. It is the first Ringnonian ship named after a human. Perhaps there will be others in the future that are as worthy as that fine woman."

Epilogue

"Grandpa, what a great story!" said Ashley, the thirteen-year-old.

"But, Grandpa, what happens to Quanyo?" asked Jonathan.

"I want to know what happens to Ascon and Colette!" the oldest, Jasmine, chimed in.

"Do they ever get the people who planned the attack on Quanyo?" asked Aaron.

"And what about the Kittans?" Brian wondered.

"Do the Ringnonians take over the world?" Michael asked.

"Oh, I forgot to tell you about those things, didn't I? Well, those will be stories for another day."

~~~~~~~~~~~~

Milton Keynes UK
Ingram Content Group UK Ltd.
UKHW010635270324
440147UK00002B/25